Wilkie Collins

Collection of british authors: The Woman in White

Volume I.

Wilkie Collins

Wilkie Collins

Collection of british authors: The Woman in White
Volume I.

ISBN/EAN: 9783742837080

Manufactured in Europe, USA, Canada, Australia, Japa

Cover: Foto ©Andreas Hilbeck / pixelio.de

Manufactured and distributed by brebook publishing software
(www.brebook.com)

Wilkie Collins

Collection of british authors: The Woman in White

EACH VOLUME SOLD SEPARATELY.

COLLECTION

OF

BRITISH AUTHORS

TAUCHNITZ EDITION.

VOL. 525.

THE WOMAN IN WHITE BY WILKIE COLLINS

IN TWO VOLUMES.

VOL. 1.

LEIPZIG: BERNHARD TAUCHNITZ.

PARIS: C. REINWALD & Ciᵉ, 15, RUE DES SAINTS PÈRES.

COLLECTION

OF

BRITISH AUTHORS.

VOL. 525.

THE WOMAN IN WHITE BY WILKIE COLLINS.

IN TWO VOLUMES.

VOL. I.

THE
WOMAN IN WHITE.

BY

WILKIE COLLINS,

AUTHOR OF "THE DEAD SECRET," "AFTER DARK," ETC.

IN TWO VOLUMES.

VOL. I.

LEIPZIG

BERNHARD TAUCHNITZ

1860.

PREFACE.

An experiment is attempted in this novel, which has not (so far as I know) been hitherto tried in fiction. The story of the book is told throughout by the characters of the book. They are all placed in different positions along the chain of events; and they all take the chain up in turn, and carry it on to the end.

If the execution of this idea had led to nothing more than the attainment of mere novelty of form, I should not have claimed a moment's attention for it in this place. But the substance of the book, as well as the form, has profited by it. It has forced me to keep the story constantly moving forward; and it has afforded my characters a new opportunity of expressing themselves, through the medium of the written contributions which they are supposed to make to the progress of the narrative.

In writing these prefatory lines, I cannot prevail on myself to pass over in silence the warm welcome which my story has met with, in its periodical form, among English and American readers. In the first place, that welcome has, I hope, justified me for having accepted the serious literary responsibility of appearing in the columns of "All The Year Round," immediately after Mr. Charles Dickens had occupied them with the most perfect work of constructive art that has ever proceeded from his pen. In the second place, by frankly acknowledging the recognition that I have obtained thus far, I provide for myself an opportunity of thanking many correspondents (to whom I am personally unknown) for the hearty encouragement I received from them while my work was in progress. Now, while the visionary men and women, among whom I have been living so long, are all leaving me, I remember very gratefully that "Marian" and "Laura" made such warm friends in many quarters, that I was peremptorily cautioned at a serious crisis in the story, to be careful how I treated them — that Mr. Fairlie found sympathetic fellow-sufferers, who remonstrated with me for not making Christian allowance for the state of his nerves — that Sir Percival's "secret" became sufficiently exasperating, in course of time, to be made the subject of bets (all of which I hereby declare to be "off") — and that Count Fosco suggested metaphysical considerations to the learned in such matters (which I don't quite understand to this day), besides provoking numerous inquiries as to the living model, from which he had been really taken. I can only answer these last by confessing that many models, some living, and some dead, have "sat" for him; and by hinting that the Count would not have been as true to nature as I have tried to make him, if the range of my search for materials had not extended, in his case as well as in others, beyond the narrow human limit which is represented by one man.

In presenting my book to a new class of readers, in its complete form, I have only to say that it has been carefully revised; and that the divisions of the chapters, and other minor matters of the same sort, have been altered here and there, with a view to smoothing and consolidating the story in its course through these volumes. If the readers who have waited until it was done, only prove to be as kind an audience as the readers who followed it through its weekly progress, "The Woman in White" will be the most precious impersonal Woman on the list of my acquaintance.

Before I conclude, I am desirous of addressing one or two questions, of the most harmless and innocent kind, to the Critics.

In the event of this book being reviewed, I venture to ask whether it is possible to praise the writer, or to blame him, without opening the proceedings by telling his story at second-hand? As that story is written by me — with the inevitable suppressions which the periodical system of publication forces on the novelist — the telling it fills more than a thousand closely printed pages. No small portion of this space is occupied by hundreds of little "connecting links," of trifling value in themselves, but of the utmost importance in maintaining the smoothness, the reality, and the probability of the entire narrative. If the critic tells the story *with* these, can he do it in his allotted page, or column, as the case may be? If he tells it *without* these, is he doing a fellow-labourer in another form of Art, the justice which writers owe to one another? And lastly, if he tells it at all, in any way whatever, is he doing a service to the reader, by destroying, beforehand, two main elements in the attraction of all stories — the interest of curiosity, and the excitement of surprise?

Harley Street, London,
   August 3, 1860.

THE WOMAN IN WHITE.

THE STORY BEGUN

BY

WALTER HARTRIGHT,

OF CLEMENT'S INN, TEACHER OF DRAWING.

I.

This is the story of what a Woman's patience can endure, and of what a Man's resolution can achieve.

If the machinery of the Law could be depended on to fathom every case of suspicion, and to conduct every process of inquiry with moderate assistance only from the lubricating influences of oil of gold, the events which fill these pages might have claimed their share of the public attention in a Court of Justice.

But the Law is still, in certain inevitable cases, the pre-engaged servant of the long purse; and the story is left to be told, for the first time, in this place. As the Judge might once have heard it, so the Reader shall hear it now. No circumstance of importance, from the beginning to the end of the disclosure, shall be related on hearsay evidence. When the writer of these introductory lines (Walter Hartright, by name) happens to be more closely connected than others with the incidents to be recorded, he will describe them in his own person. When his experience fails, he will retire from the position of narrator; and his task will be continued, from the point at which he has left it off, by other persons who can speak to the circumstances under notice from their own knowledge, just as clearly and positively as he has spoken before them.

Thus, the story here presented will be told by more than one pen, as the story of an offence against the laws is told in Court by more than one witness — with the same object, in both cases, to present the truth always in its most direct and most intelligible aspect; and to trace the course of one complete series of events, by making the persons who have been most closely connected with them, at each successive stage, relate their own experience, word for word.

Let Walter Hartright, teacher of drawing, aged twenty-eight years, be heard first.

II.

It was the last day of July. The long hot summer was drawing to a close; and we, the weary pilgrims of the London pavement, were beginning to think of the cloud-shadows on the corn-fields, and the autumn breezes on the sea-shore.

For my own poor part, the fading summer left me out of health, out of spirits, and, if the truth must be told, out of money as well. During the past year, I had not managed my professional resources as carefully as usual; and my extravagance now limited me to the prospect of spending the autumn economically between my mother's cottage at Hampstead, and my own chambers in town.

The evening, I remember, was still and cloudy; the London air was at its heaviest; the distant hum of the street-traffic was at its faintest; the small pulse of the life within me and the great heart of the city around me seemed to be sinking in unison, languidly and more languidly, with the sinking sun. I roused myself from the book which I was dreaming over rather than reading, and left my chambers to meet the cool night air in the suburbs. It was one of the two evenings in every week which I was accustomed to spend with my mother and my sister. So I turned my steps northward, in the direction of Hampstead.

Events which I have yet to relate, make it necessary to mention in this place that my father had been dead some years at the period of which I am now writing; and that my sister Sarah, and I, were the sole survivors of a family of five children. My father was a drawing-master before me. His exertions had made him highly successful in his profession; and his affectionate anxiety to provide for the future of those who were dependent on his labours, had impelled him, from the time of his marriage, to devote to the insuring of his life a much larger portion of his income than most men consider it necessary to set aside for that purpose. Thanks to his admirable prudence and self-denial, my mother and sister were left, after his death, as independent of the world as they had been during his lifetime. I succeeded to his connexion, and had every reason to feel grateful for the prospect that awaited me at my starting in life.

The quiet twilight was still trembling on the topmost ridges of the heath; and the view of London below me had sunk into a black gulf in the shadow of the cloudy night, when I stood before the gate of my mother's cottage. I had hardly rung the bell, before the house-door was opened violently; my worthy Italian friend, Professor Pesca, appeared in the servant's place; and darted out joyously to receive me, with a shrill foreign parody on an English cheer.

On his own account, and, I must be allowed to add, on mine also, the Professor merits the honour of a formal introduction. Accident has made him the starting-point of the strange family story which it is the purpose of these pages to unfold.

I had first become acquainted with my Italian friend by meeting him at certain great houses, where he taught his own language and I taught drawing. All I then knew of the history of his life was, that he had once held a situation in the University of Padua; that he had left Italy for political reasons (the nature of which he uniformly declined to mention to any one); and that he had been for many years respectably established in London as a teacher of languages.

1*

Without being actually a dwarf — for he was perfectly well-proportioned from head to foot — Pesca was, I think, the smallest human being I ever saw, out of a show-room. Remarkable anywhere, by his personal appearance, he was still further distinguished among the rank and file of mankind, by the harmless eccentricity of his character. The ruling idea of his life appeared to be, that he was bound to show his gratitude to the country which had afforded him an asylum and a means of subsistence, by doing his utmost to turn himself into an Englishman. Not content with paying the nation in general the compliment of invariably carrying an umbrella, and invariably wearing gaiters and a white hat, the Professor further aspired to become an Englishman in his habits and amusements, as well as in his personal appearance. Finding us distinguished, as a nation, by our love of athletic exercises, the little man, in the innocence of his heart, devoted himself impromptu to all our English sports and pastimes, whenever he had the opportunity of joining them; firmly persuaded that he could adopt our national amusements of the field, by an effort of will, precisely as he had adopted our national gaiters and our national white hat.

I had seen him risk his limbs blindly at a fox-hunt and in a cricket-field; and, soon afterwards, I saw him risk his life, just as blindly, in the sea at Brighton.

We had met there accidentally, and were bathing together. If we had been engaged in any exercise peculiar to my own nation, I should, of course, have looked after Pesca carefully; but, as foreigners are generally quite as well able to take care of themselves in the water as Englishmen, it never occurred to me that the art of swimming might merely add one more to the list of manly exercises which the Professor believed that he could learn impromptu. Soon after we had both struck out from shore, I stopped, finding my friend did not gain on me, and turned round to look for him. To my horror and amazement, I saw nothing between me and the beach but two little white arms which struggled for an instant above the surface of the water, and then disappeared from view. When I dived for him, the poor little man was lying quietly coiled up at the bottom, in a hollow of shingle, looking by many degrees smaller than I had ever seen him look before. During the few minutes that elapsed while I was taking him in, the air revived him, and he ascended the steps of the machine with my assistance. With the partial recovery of his animation came the return of his wonderful delusion on the subject of swimming. As soon as his chattering teeth would let him speak, he smiled vacantly, and said he thought it must have been the Cramp.

When he had thoroughly recovered himself and had joined me on the beach, his warm Southern nature broke through all artificial English restraints, in a moment. He overwhelmed me with the wildest expressions of affection — exclaimed passionately, in his exaggerated Italian way, that he would hold his life, henceforth, at my disposal — and declared that he should never be happy again, until he had found an opportunity of proving his gratitude by rendering me some service which I might remember, on my side, to the end of my days.

I did my best to stop the torrent of his tears and protestations, by persisting in treating the whole adventure as a good subject for a joke; and succeeded at last, as I imagined, in lessening Pesca's overwhelming sense of obligation to me. Little did I think then — little did I think afterwards when our pleasant holiday had drawn to an end — that the opportunity of serving me for which my grateful companion so ardently longed, was soon to come; that he was eagerly to seize it on the instant; and that by so doing, he was to turn the whole current of my existence into a new channel, and to alter me myself almost past recognition.

Yet, so it was. If I had not dived for Professor Pesca, when he lay under water on his shingle bed, I should, in all human probability, never have been connected with the story which these pages will relate — I should never, perhaps, have heard even the name of the woman, who has lived in all my thoughts, who has possessed herself of all my energies, who has become the one guiding influence that now directs the purpose of my life.

———————

III.

Pesca's face and manner, on the evening when we confronted each other at my mother's gate, were more than sufficient to inform me that something extraordinary had happened. It was quite useless, however, to ask him for an immediate explanation. I could only conjecture, while he was dragging me in by both hands, that (knowing my habits) he had come to the cottage to make sure of meeting me that night, and that he had some news to tell of an unusually agreeable kind.

We both bounced into the parlour in a highly abrupt and undignified manner. My mother sat by the open window, laughing and fanning herself. Pesca was one of her especial favourites; and his wildest eccentricities were always pardonable in her eyes. Poor dear soul! from the first moment when she found out that the little Professor was deeply and gratefully attached to her son, she opened her heart to him unreservedly, and took all his puzzling foreign peculiarities for granted, without so much as attempting to understand any one of them.

My sister Sarah, with all the advantages of youth, was, strangely enough, less pliable. She did full justice to Pesca's excellent qualities of heart; but she could not accept him implicitly, as my mother accepted him, for my sake. Her insular notions of propriety rose in perpetual revolt against Pesca's constitutional contempt for appearances; and she was always more or less undisguisedly astonished at her mother's familiarity with the eccentric little foreigner. I have observed, not only in my sister's case, but in the instances of others, that we of the young generation are nothing like so hearty and so impulsive as some of our elders. I constantly see old people flushed and excited by the prospect of some anticipated pleasure which altogether fails to ruffle the tranquillity of their serene grandchildren. Are we, I wonder, quite such genuine boys and girls now as our seniors were, in their time? Has the great advance in education taken rather too long a stride; and are we, in these modern days, just the least trifle in the world too well brought up?

Without attempting to answer those questions decisively, I may at least record that I never saw my mother and my sister together in Pesca's society, without finding my mother much the younger woman of the two. On this occasion, for example, while the old lady was laughing heartily over the boyish manner in which we tumbled into the parlour, Sarah was perturbedly picking up the broken pieces of a teacup, which the Professor had knocked off the table in his precipitate advance to meet me at the door.

"I don't know what would have happened, Walter," said my mother, "if you had delayed much longer. Pesca has been half-mad with impatience; and I have been half-mad with curiosity. The Professor has brought some wonderful news with him, in which he says you are concerned; and he has cruelly refused to give us the smallest hint of it till his friend Walter appeared."

"Very provoking: it spoils the Set," murmured Sarah to herself, mournfully absorbed over the ruins of the broken cup.

While these words were being spoken, Pesca, happily and fussily unconscious of the irreparable wrong which the crockery had suffered at his hands, was dragging a large arm-chair to the opposite end of the room, so as to command us all three, in the character of a public speaker addressing an audience. Having turned the chair with its back towards us, he jumped into it on his knees, and excitably addressed his small congregation of three from an impromptu pulpit.

"Now, my good dears," began Pesca (who always said "good dears," when he meant "worthy friends"), "listen to me. The time has come — I recite my good news — I speak at last."

"Hear, hear!" said my mother, humouring the joke.

"The next thing he will break, mamma," whispered Sarah, "will be the back of the best arm-chair."

"I go back into my life, and I address myself to the noblest of created beings," continued Pesca, vehemently apostrophizing my unworthy self, over the top rail of the chair. "Who found me dead at the bottom of the sea (through Cramp); and who pulled me up to the top; and what did I say when I got into my own life and my own clothes again?"

"Much more than was at all necessary," I answered, as doggedly as possible; for the least encouragement in connexion with this subject invariably let loose the Professor's emotions in a flood of tears.

"I said," persisted Pesca, "that my life belonged to my dear friend, Walter, for the rest of my days — and so it does. I said that I should never be happy again till I had found the opportunity of doing a good Something for Walter — and I have never been contented with myself till this most blessed day. Now," cried the enthusiastic little man at the top of his voice, "the overflowing happiness bursts out of me at every pore of my skin, like a perspiration; for on my faith, and soul, and honour, the something is done at last, and the only word to say now, is — Right-all-right!"

It may be necessary to explain, here, that Pesca prided himself on being a perfect Englishman in his language, as well as in his dress, manners, and amusements. Having picked up a few of our most familiar colloquial expressions, he scattered them about over his conversation whenever they happened to occur to him, turning them, in his high relish for their sound and his general ignorance of their sense, into compound words and repetitions of his own, and always running them into each other, as if they consisted of one long syllable.

"Among the fine London houses where I teach the language of my native country," said the Professor, rushing into his long-deferred explanation without another word of preface, "there is one, mighty fine, in the big place called

Portland. You all know where that is? Yes, yes — course-of-course. The fine house, my good dears, has got inside it a fine family. A Mamma, fair and fat; three young Misses, fair and fat; two young Misters, fair and fat; and a Papa, the fairest and the fattest of all, who is a mighty merchant, up to his eyes in gold — a fine man once, but seeing that he has got a naked head and two chins, fine no longer at the present time. Now mind! I teach the sublime Dante to the young Misses, and ah! — my-soul-bless-my-soul! — it is not in human language to say how the sublime Dante puzzles the pretty heads of all three! No matter — all in good time — and the more lessons the better for me. Now mind! Imagine to yourselves that I am teaching the young Misses to-day, as usual. We are all four of us down together in the Hell of Dante. At the Seventh Circle — but no matter for that: all the Circles are alike to the three young Misses, fair and fat, — at the Seventh Circle, nevertheless, my pupils are sticking fast; and I, to set them going again, recite, explain, and blow myself up red-hot with useless enthusiasm, when — a creak of boots in the passage outside, and in comes the golden Papa, the mighty merchant with the naked head and the two chins. — Ha! my good dears, I am closer than you think for to the business, now. Have you been patient so far? or have you said to yourselves, 'Deuce-what-the-deuce! Pesca is long-winded to-night?'"

We declared that we were deeply interested. The Professor went on:

"In his hand, the golden Papa has a letter; and after he has made his excuse for disturbing us in our Infernal Region with the common mortal Business of the house, he addresses himself to the three young Misses, and begins, as you English begin everthing in this blessed world that you have to say, with a great O. 'O, my dears,' says the mighty merchant, 'I have got here a letter from my friend, Mr. ———,' (the name has slipped out of my mind; but no matter; we shall come back to that: yes, yes — right-all-right). So the Papa says, 'I have got a letter from my friend, the Mister;

and he wants a recommend from me, of a drawing-master, to go down to his house in the country.' My-soul-bless-my-soul! when I heard the golden Papa say those words, if I had been big enough to reach up to him, I should have put my arms round his neck, and pressed him to my bosom in a long and grateful hug! As it was, I only bounced upon my chair. My seat was on thorns, and my soul was on fire to speak; but I held my tongue, and let Papa go on. 'Perhaps you know,' says this good man of money, twiddling his friend's letter this way and that, in his golden fingers and thumbs, 'perhaps you know, my dears, of a drawing-master that I can recommend?' The three young Misses all look at each other, and then say (with the indispensable great O to begin) 'O, dear no, Papa! But here is Mr. Pesca——' At the mention of myself I can hold no longer — the thought of you, my good dears, mounts like blood to my head — I start from my seat, as if a spike had grown up from the ground through the bottom of my chair — I address myself to the mighty merchant, and I say (English phrase), 'Dear sir, I have the man! The first and foremost drawing-master of the world! Recommend him by the post to-night, and send him off, bag and baggage (English phrase again — ha?), send him off, bag and baggage, by the train to-morrow!' 'Stop, stop,' says Papa, 'is he a foreigner, or an Englishman?' 'English to the bone of his back,' I answer. 'Respectable?' says Papa. 'Sir,' I say, (for this last question of his outrages me, and I have done being familiar with him), 'Sir! the immortal fire of genius burns in this Englishman's bosom, and, what is more, his father had it before him!' 'Never mind,' says the golden barbarian of a Papa, 'never mind about his genius, Mr. Pesca. We don't want genius in this country, unless it is accompanied by respectability — and then we are very glad to have it, very glad indeed. Can your friend produce testimonials — letters that speak to his character?' I wave my hand negligently. 'Letters?' I say. 'Ha! my-soul-bless-my-soul! I should think so, indeed! Volumes of letters and portfolios of testimonials, if you like?' 'One or two will do,' says this man of phlegm and money. 'Let him send them to me, with his name and address. And — stop, stop, Mr. Pesca — before you go to your friend, you had better take a note.' 'Bank-note!' I say, indignantly. 'No bank-note, if you please, till my brave Englishman has earned it first.' 'Bank-note!' says Papa, in a great surprise, 'who talked of bank-note? I mean a note of the terms — a memorandum of what he is expected to do. Go on with your lesson, Mr. Pesca, and I will give you the necessary extract from my friend's letter.' Down sits the man of merchandise and money to his pen, ink, and paper; and down I go once again into the Hell of Dante, with my three young Misses after me. In ten minutes' time the note is written, and the boots of Papa are creaking themselves away in the passage outside. From that moment, on my faith, and soul, and honour, I know nothing more! The glorious thought that I have caught my opportunity at last, and that my grateful service for my dearest friend in the world is as good as done already, flies up into my head and makes me drunk. How I pull my young Misses and myself out of our Infernal Region again, how my other business is done afterwards, how my little bit of dinner slides itself down my throat, I know no more than a man in the moon. Enough for me, that here I am, with the mighty merchant's note in my hand, as large as life, as hot as fire, and as happy as a king! Ha! ha! ha! right-right-right-all-right!" Here the Professor waved the memorandum of terms over his head, and ended his long and voluble narrative with his shrill Italian parody on an English cheer.

My mother rose the moment he had done, with flushed cheeks and brightened eyes. She caught the little man warmly by both hands.

"My dear, good Pesca," she said, "I never doubted your true affection for Walter—but I am more than ever persuaded of it now!"

"I am sure we are very much obliged to Professor Pesca, for Walter's sake," added Sarah. She half rose, while she spoke, as if to approach the arm-chair, in her turn; but, observing that Pesca was rapturously kissing my mother's hands, looked serious, and resumed her seat. "If the familiar little man treats my mother that way, how will he treat *me?*" Faces sometimes tell truth; and that was unquestionably the thought in Sarah's mind, as she sat down again.

Although I myself was gratefully sensible of the kindness of Pesca's motives, my spirits were hardly so much elevated as they ought to have been by the prospect of future employment now placed before me. When the Professor had quite done with my mother's hand, and when I had warmly thanked him for his interference on my behalf, I asked to be allowed to look at the note of terms which his respectable patron had drawn up for my inspection.

Pesca handed me the paper, with a triumphant flourish of the hand.

"Read!" said the little man, majestically. "I promise you, my friend, the writing of the golden Papa speaks with a tongue of trumpets for itself."

The note of terms was plain, straightforward, and comprehensive, at any rate. It informed me,

First, That Frederick Fairlie, Esquire, of Limmeridge House, Cumberland, wanted to engage the services of a thoroughly competent drawing-master, for a period of four months certain.

Secondly, That the duties which the master was expected to perform would be of a twofold kind. He was to superintend the instruction of two young ladies in the art of painting in water-colours; and he was to devote his leisure time, afterwards, to the business of repairing and mounting a valuable collection of drawings, which had been suffered to fall into a condition of total neglect.

Thirdly, That the terms offered to the person who should undertake and properly perform these duties, were four guineas a week; that he was to reside at Limmeridge House; and that he was to be treated there on the footing of a gentleman.

Fourthly, and lastly, That no person need think of applying for this situation, unless he could furnish the most unexceptionable references to character and abilities. The references were to be sent to Mr. Fairlie's friend in London, who was empowered to conclude all necessary arrangements. These instructions were followed by the name and address of Pesca's employer in Portland-place — and there the note, or memorandum, ended.

The prospect which this offer of an engagement held out was certainly an attractive one. The employment was likely to be both easy and agreeable; it was proposed to me at the autumn time of the year when I was least occupied; and the terms, judging by my personal experience in my profession, were surprisingly liberal. I knew this; I knew that I ought to consider myself very fortunate if I succeeded in securing the offered employment — and yet, no sooner had I read the memorandum than I felt an inexplicable unwillingness within me to stir in the matter. I had never in the whole of my previous experience found my duty and my inclination so painfully and so unaccountably at variance as I found them now.

"O, Walter, your father never had such a chance as this!" said my mother, when she had read the note of terms and had handed it back to me.

"Such distinguished people to know," remarked Sarah, straightening herself in her chair; "and on such gratifying terms of equality, too!"

"Yes, yes; the terms, in every sense, are tempting enough," I replied, impatiently. "But before I send in my testimonials, I should like a little time to consider ——"

"Consider!" exclaimed my mother. "Why, Walter, what is the matter with you?"

"Consider!" echoed my sister. "What a very extraordinary thing to say, under the circumstances!"

"Consider!" chimed in the Professor. "What is there to consider about? Answer me this! Have you not been complaining of your health, and have you not been longing for what you call a smack of the country breeze? Well! there in your hand is the paper that offers you perpetual choking mouthfuls of country breeze, for four months' time. Is it not so?

Ha? Again — you want money. Well! Is four golden guineas a week nothing? My-soul-bless-m soul! only give it to *me* — and my boots shall creak like the golden Papa's, with a sense of the overpowering richness of the man who walks in them! Four guineas a week, and, more than that, the charming society of two young Misses; and, more than that, your bed, your breakfast, your dinner, your gorging English teas and lunches and drinks of foaming beer, all for nothing — why, Walter, my dear good friend — deuce-what-the-deuce! — for the first time in my life I have not eyes enough in my head to look, and wonder at you!"

Neither my mother's evident astonishment at my behaviour, nor Pesca's fervid enumeration of the advantages offered to me by the new employment, had any effect in shaking my unreasonable disinclination to go to Limmeridge House. After starting all the petty objections that I could think of to going to Cumberland; and after hearing them answered, one after another, to my own complete discomfiture, I tried to set up a last obstacle by asking what was to become of my pupils in London, while I was teaching Mr. Fairlie's young ladies to sketch from nature. The obvious answer to this was, that the greater part of them would be away on their autumn travels, and that the few who remained at home might be confided to the care of one of my brother drawing-masters, whose pupils I had once taken off his hands under similar circumstances. My sister reminded me that this gentleman had expressly placed his services at my disposal, during the present season, in case I wished to leave town; my mother seriously appealed to me not to let an idle caprice stand in the way of my own interests and my own health; and Pesca piteously entreated that I would not wound him to the heart, by rejecting the first grateful offer of service that he had been able to make to the friend who had saved his life.

The evident sincerity and affection which inspired these remonstrances would have influenced any man with an atom of good feeling in his composition. Though I could not conquer my own unaccountable perversity, I had at least virtue enough to be heartily ashamed of it, and to end the discussion pleasantly by giving way, and promising to do all that was wanted of me.

The rest of the evening passed merrily enough in humorous anticipations of my coming life with the two young ladies in Cumberland. Pesca, inspired by our national grog, which appeared to get into his head, in the most marvellous manner, five minutes after it had gone down his throat, asserted his claims to be considered a complete Englishman by making a series of speeches in rapid succession; proposing my mother's health, my sister's health, my health, and the healths, in mass, of Mr. Fairlie and the two young Misses; pathetically returning thanks himself, immediately afterwards, for the whole party. "A secret, Walter," said my little friend confidentially, as we walked home together. "I am flushed by the recollection of my own eloquence. My soul bursts itself with ambition. One of these days, I go into your noble Parliament. It is the dream of my whole life to be Honourable Pesca, M. P.!"

The next morning I sent my testimonials to the Professor's employer in Portland-place. Three days passed; and I concluded, with secret satisfaction, that my papers had not been found sufficiently explicit. On the fourth day, however, an answer came. It announced that Mr. Fairlie accepted my services, and requested me to start for Cumberland immediately. All the necessary instructions for my journey were carefully and clearly added in a postscript.

I made my arrangements, unwillingly enough, for leaving London early the next day. Towards evening Pesca looked in, on his way to a dinner-party, to bid me good-by.

"I shall dry my tears in your absence," said the Professor, gaily, "with this glorious thought. It is my auspicious hand that has given the first push to your fortune in the world. Go, my friend! When your sun shines in Cumberland (English proverb), in the name of heaven, make your hay. Marry one of the two young Misses; become Honour able Hartright, M. P.; and when you are on the top of the ladder, remember that Pesca, at the bottom, has done it all!"

I tried to laugh with my little friend over his parting jest, but my spirits were not to be commanded. Something jarred in me almost painfully, while he was speaking his light farewell words.

When I was left alone again, nothing remained to be done but to walk to the Hampstead Cottage and bid my mother and Sarah good-by.

IV.

The heat had been painfully oppressive all day; and it was now a close and sultry night.

My mother and sister had spoken so many last words, and had begged me to wait another five minutes so many times, that it was nearly midnight when the servant locked the garden-gate behind me. I walked forward a few paces on the shortest way back to London; then stopped and hesitated.

The moon was full and broad in the dark blue starless sky; and the broken ground of the heath looked wild enough in the mysterious light, to be hundreds of miles away from the great city that lay beneath it. The idea of descending any sooner than I could help into the heat and gloom of London repelled me. The prospect of going to bed in my airless chambers, and the prospect of gradual suffocation, seemed, in my present restless frame of mind and body, to be one and the same thing. I determined to stroll home in the purer air, by the most round-about way I could take; to follow the white winding paths across the lonely heath; and to approach London through its most open suburb by striking into the Finchley-road, and so getting back, in the cool of the new morning, by the western side of the Regent's Park.

I wound my way down slowly over the Heath, enjoying

the divine stillness of the scene, and admiring the soft alternations of light and shade as they followed each other over
the broken ground on every side of me. So long as I was proceeding through this first and prettiest part of my night-walk,
my mind remained passively open to the impressions produced by the view; and I thought but little on any subject —
indeed, so far as my own sensations were concerned, I can
hardly say that I thought at all.

But when I had left the Heath, and had turned into the
by-road, where there was less to see, the ideas naturally
engendered by the approaching change in my habits and
occupations, gradually drew more and more of my attention
exclusively to themselves. By the time I had arrived at the
end of the road, I had become completely absorbed in my
own fanciful visions of Limmeridge House, of Mr. Fairlie,
and of the two Ladies whose practice in the art of water-colour
painting I was so soon to superintend.

I had now arrived at that particular point of my walk
where four roads met — the road to Hampstead, along which
I had returned; the road to Finchley; the road to West End;
and the road back to London. I had mechanically turned in
this latter direction, and was strolling along the lonely high-
road — idly wondering, I remember, what the Cumberland
young ladies would look like — when, in one moment, every
drop of blood in my body was brought to a stop by the touch
of a hand laid lightly and suddenly on my shoulder from behind me.

I turned on the instant, with my fingers tightening round
the handle of my stick.

There, in the middle of the broad, bright high-road —
there, as if it had that moment sprung out of the earth or
dropped from the heaven — stood the figure of a solitary Woman, dressed from head to foot in white garments; her face
bent in grave inquiry on mine, her hand pointing to the dark
cloud over London, as I faced her.

I was far too seriously startled by the suddenness with
which this extraordinary apparition stood before me, in the

dead of night and in that lonely place, to ask what she wanted. The strange woman spoke first.

"Is that the road to London?" she said.

I looked attentively at her, as she put that singular question to me. It was then nearly one o'clock. All I could discern distinctly by the moonlight, was a colourless, youthful face, meagre and sharp to look at, about the cheeks and chin; large, grave, wistfully-attentive eyes; nervous, uncertain lips; and light hair of a pale, brownish-yellow hue. There was nothing wild, nothing immodest in her manner: it was quiet and self-controlled, a little melancholy and a little touched by suspicion; not exactly the manner of a lady, and, at the same time, not the manner of a woman in the humblest rank of life. The voice, little as I had yet heard of it, had something curiously still and mechanical in its tones, and the utterance was remarkably rapid. She held a small bag in her hand: and her dress — bonnet, shawl, and gown all of white — was, so far as I could guess, certainly not composed of very delicate or very expensive materials. Her figure was slight, and rather above the average height — her gait and actions free from the slightest approach to extravagance. This was all that I could observe of her, in the dim light and under the perplexingly-strange circumstances of our meeting. What sort of a woman she was, and how she came to be out alone in the high-road, an hour after midnight, I altogether failed to guess. The one thing of which I felt certain was, that the grossest of mankind could not have misconstrued her motive in speaking, even at that suspiciously late hour and in that suspiciously lonely place.

"Did you hear me?" she said, still quietly and rapidly, and without the least fretfulness or impatience. "I asked if that was the way to London."

"Yes," I replied, "that is the way: it leads to St. John's Wood and the Regent's Park. You must excuse my not answering you before. I was rather startled by your sudden appearance in the road; and I am, even now, quite unable to account for it."

"You don't suspect me of doing anything wrong, do you? I have done nothing wrong. I have met with an accident — I am very unfortunate in being here alone so late. Why do you suspect me of doing wrong?"

She spoke with unnecessary earnestness and agitation, and shrank back from me several paces. I did my best to reassure her.

"Pray don't suppose that I have any idea of suspecting you," I said, "or any other wish than to be of assistance to you, if I can. I only wondered at your appearance in the road, because it seemed to me to be empty the instant before I saw you."

She turned, and pointed back to a place at the junction of the road to London and the road to Hampstead, where there was a gap in the hedge.

"I heard you coming," she said, "and hid there to see what sort of man you were, before I risked speaking. I doubted and feared about it till you passed; and then I was obliged to steal after you, and touch you."

Steal after me, and touch me? Why not call to me? Strange, to say the least of it.

"May I trust you?" she asked. "You don't think the worse of me because I have met with an accident?" She stopped in confusion; shifted her bag from one hand to the other; and sighed bitterly.

The loneliness and helplessness of the woman touched me. The natural impulse to assist her and to spare her, got the better of the judgment, the caution, the worldly tact, which an older, wiser, and colder man might have summoned to help him in this strange emergency.

"You may trust me for any harmless purpose," I said. "If it troubles you to explain your strange situation to me, don't think of returning to the subject again. I have no right to ask you for any explanations. Tell me how I can help you; and if I can, I will."

"You are very kind, and I am very, very thankful to have met you." The first touch of womanly tenderness that I had heard from her, trembled in her voice as she said the words; but no tears glistened in those large, wistfully-attentive eyes of hers, which were still fixed on me. "I have only been in London once before," she went on; more and more rapidly; "and I know nothing about that side of it, yonder. Can I get a fly, or a carriage of any kind? Is it too late? I don't know. If you could show me where to get a fly — and if you will only promise not to interfere with me, and to let me leave you, when and how I please — I have a friend in London who will be glad to receive me — I want nothing else — will you promise?"

She looked anxiously up and down the road; shifted her bag again from one hand to the other; repeated the words, "Will you promise?" and looked hard in my face, with a pleading fear and confusion that it troubled me to see.

What could I do? Here was a stranger utterly and helplessly at my mercy — and that stranger a forlorn woman. No house was near; no one was passing whom I could consult; and no earthly right existed on my part to give me a power of control over her, even if I had known how to exercise it. I trace these lines, self-distrustfully, with the shadows of after-events darkening the very paper I write on; and still I say, what could I do?

What I did do, was to try and gain time by questioning her.

"Are you sure that your friend in London will receive you at such a late hour as this?" I said.

"Quite sure. Only say you will let me leave you when and how I please — only say you won't interfere with me. Will you promise?"

As she repeated the words for the third time, she came close to me, and laid her hand, with a sudden gentle stealthiness, on my bosom — a thin hand; a cold hand (when I removed it with mine) even on that sultry night. Remember that I was young; remember that the hand with touched me was a woman's.

"Will you promise?"

"Yes."

One word! The little familiar word that is on everybody's lips, every hour in the day. Oh me! and I tremble, now, when I write it.

We set our faces towards London, and walked on together in the first still hour of the new day — I, and this woman, whose name, whose character, whose story, whose objects in life, whose very presence by my side, at that moment, were fathomless mysteries to me. It was like a dream. Was I Walter Hartright? Was this the well-known, uneventful road, where holiday people strolled on Sundays? Had I really left, little more than an hour since, the quiet, decent, conventionally-domestic atmosphere of my mother's cottage? I was too bewildered — too conscious also of a vague sense of something like self-reproach — to speak to my strange companion for some minutes. It was her voice again that first broke the silence between us.

"I want to ask you something," she said, suddenly. "Do you know many people in London?"

"Yes, a great many."

"Many men of rank and title?" There was an unmistakable tone of suspicion in the strange question. I hesitated about answering it.

"Some," I said, after a moment's silence.

"Many" — she came to a full stop, and looked me searchingly in the face — "many men of the rank of Baronet?"

Too much astonished to reply, I questioned her in my turn.

"Why do you ask?"

"Because I hope, for my own sake, there is one Baronet that you don't know."

"Will you tell me his name?"

"I can't — I daren't — I forget myself, when I mention it." She spoke loudly and almost fiercely, raised her clenched hand in the air, and shook it passionately; then, on a sudden, controlled herself again, and added, in tones lowered to a whisper: "Tell me which of them *you* know."

I could hardly refuse to humour her in such a trifle, and I mentioned three names. Two, the names of fathers of families whose daughters I taught; one, the name of a bachelor who had once taken me a cruise in his yacht, to make sketches for him.

"Ah! you *don't* know him," she said, with a sigh of relief. "Are you a man of rank and title yourself?"

"Far from it.   I am only a drawing-master."

As the reply passed my lips — a little bitterly, perhaps — she took my arm with the abruptness which characterised all her actions.

"Not a man of rank and title," she repeated to herself. "Thank God! I may trust *him*."

I had hitherto contrived to master my curiosity out of consideration for my companion; but it got the better of me, now.

"I am afraid you have serious reason to complain of some man of rank and title?" I said. "I am afraid the baronet, whose name you are unwilling to mention to me, has done you some grievous wrong? Is he the cause of your being out here at this strange time of night?"

"Don't ask me; don't make me talk of it," she answered. "I'm not fit, now. I have been cruelly used and cruelly wronged. You will be kinder than ever, if you will walk on fast, and not speak to me. I sadly want to be silent — I sadly want to quiet myself, if I can."

We moved forward again at a quick pace; and for half an hour, at least, not a word passed on either side. From time to time, being forbidden to make any more inquiries, I stole a look at her face. It was always the same; the lips close shut, the brow frowning, the eyes looking straight forward, eagerly and yet absently. We had reached the first houses, and were close on the new Wesleyan College, before her set features relaxed, and she spoke once more.

"Do you live in London?" she said.

"Yes." As I answered, it struck me that she might have formed some intention of appealing to me for assistance or advice, and that I ought to spare her a possible disappointment by warning her of my approaching absenee from home. So I added: "But to-morrow I shall be away from London for some time. I am going into the country."

"Where?" she asked. "North, or south?"

"North — to Cumberland."

"Cumberland!" she repeated the word tenderly. "Ah! 1 wish I was going there, too. I was once happy in Cumberland."

I tried again to lift the veil that hung between this woman and me.

"Perhaps you were born," I said, "in the beautiful Lake country."

"No," she answered. "I was born in Hampshire; but 1 once went to school for a little while in Cumberland. Lakes? I don't remember any lakes. It's Limmeridge village, and Limmeridge House, I should like to see again."

It was my turn, now, to stop suddenly. In the exeited state of my euriosity, at that moment, the chance reference to Mr. Fairlie's place of residenee, on the lips of my strange companion, staggered me with astonishment.

"Lid you hear anybody calling after us?" she asked, looking up and down the road affrightedly, the instant 1 stopped.

"No, no. I was only struck by the name of Limmeridge House — I heard it mentioned by some Cumberland people a few days since."

"Ah! not *my* people. Mrs. Fairlie is dead; and her husband is dead; and their little girl may be married and gone away by this time. I can't say who lives at Limmeridge now. If any more are left there of that name, I only know I love them for Mrs. Fairlie's sake."

She seemed about to say more; but while she was speaking, we came within view of the turnpike, at the top of the

Avenue-road. Her hand tightened round my arm, and she looked anxiously at the gate before us.

"Is the turnpike man looking out?" she asked.

He was not looking out; no one else was near the place when we passed through the gate. The sight of the gas-lamps and houses seemed to agitate her, and to make her impatient.

"This is London," she said. "Do you see any carriage I can get? I am tired and frightened. I want to shut myself in, and be driven away."

I explained to her that we must walk a little further to get to a cab-stand, unless we were fortunate enough to meet with an empty vehicle; and then tried to resume the subject of Cumberland. It was useless. That idea of shutting herself in, and being driven away, had now got full possession of her mind. She could think and talk of nothing else.

We had hardly proceeded a third of the way down the Avenue-road, when I saw a cab draw up at a house a few doors below us, on the opposite side of the way. A gentleman got out and let himself in at the garden door. I hailed the cab, as the driver mounted the box again. When we crossed the road, my companion's impatience increased to such an extent that she almost forced me to run.

"It's so late," she said. "I am only in a hurry because it's so late."

"I can't take you, sir, if you're not going towards Tottenham-court-road," said the driver, civilly, when I opened the cab door. "My horse is dead beat, and I can't get him no further than the stable."

"Yes, yes. That will do for me. I'm going that way — I'm going that way." She spoke with breathless eagerness, and pressed by me into the cab.

I had assured myself that the man was sober as well as civil, before I let her enter the vehicle. And now, when she was seated inside, I entreated her to let me see her set down safely at her destination.

"No, no, no," she said, vehemently. "I'm quite safe and quite happy now. If you are a gentleman, remember your promise. Let him drive on, till I stop him. Thank you — oh! thank you, thank you!"

My hand was on the cab door. She caught it in hers, kissed it, and pushed it away. The cab drove off at the same moment — I started into the road, with some vague idea of stopping it again, I hardly knew why — hesitated from dread of frightening and distressing her — called, at last, but not loudly enough to attract the driver's attention. The sound of the wheels grew fainter in the distance — the cab melted into the black shadows on the road — the woman in white was gone.

Ten minutes, or more, had passed. I was still on the same side of the way; now mechanically walking forward a few paces; now stopping again absently. At one moment, I found myself doubting the reality of my own adventure; at another, I was perplexed and distressed by an uneasy sense of having done wrong, which yet left me confusedly ignorant of how I could have done right. I hardly knew where I was going, or what I meant to do next; I was conscious of nothing but the confusion of my own thoughts, when I was abruptly recalled to myself — awakened I might almost say — by the sound of rapidly approaching wheels close behind me.

I was on the dark side of the road, in the thick shadow of some garden trees, when I stopped to look round. On the opposite, and lighter side of the way, a short distance below me, a policeman was strolling along in the direction of the Regent's Park.

The carriage passed me — an open chaise driven by two men.

"Stop!" cried one. "There's a policeman. Let's ask him."

The horse was instantly pulled up, a few yards beyond the dark place where I stood.

"Policeman!" cried the first speaker. "Have you seen a woman pass this way?"

"What sort of woman, sir?"

"A woman in a lavender-coloured gown —"

"No, no," interposed the second man. "The clothes we gave her were found on her bed. She must have gone away in the clothes she wore when she came to us. In white, policeman. A woman in white."

"I haven't seen her, sir."

"If you, or any of your men meet with the woman, stop her, and send her in careful keeping to that address. I'll pay all expenses, and a fair reward into the bargain."

The policeman looked at the card that was handed down to him.

"Why are we to stop her, sir? What has she done?"

"Done! She has escaped from my Asylum. Don't forget: a woman in white. Drive on."

V.

"She has escaped from my Asylum."

I cannot say with truth that the terrible inference which those words suggested flashed upon me like a new revelation. Some of the strange questions put to me by the woman in white, after my ill-considered promise to leave her free to act as she pleased, had suggested the conclusion either that she was naturally flighty and unsettled, or that some recent shock of terror had disturbed the balance of her faculties. But the idea of absolute insanity which we all associate with the very name of an Asylum, had, I can honestly declare, never occurred to me, in connexion with her. I had seen nothing, in her language or her actions, to justify it at the time; and, even with the new light thrown on her by the words which the stranger had addressed to the policeman, I could see nothing to justify it now.

What had I done? Assisted the victim of the most horrible of all false imprisonments to escape; or cast loose on the wide world of London an unfortunate creature, whose actions it was my duty, and every man's duty, mercifully to control? I turned sick at heart when the question occurred to me, and when I felt self-reproachfully that it was asked too late.

In the disturbed state of my mind, it was useless to think of going to bed, when I at last got back to my chambers in Clement's Inn. Before many hours elapsed it would be necessary to start on my journey to Cumberland. I sat down and tried, first to sketch, then to read — but the woman in white got between me and my pencil, between me and my book. Had the forlorn creature come to any harm? That was my first thought, though I shrank selfishly from confronting it. Other thoughts followed, on which it was less harrowing to dwell. Where had she stopped the cab? What had become of her now? Had she been traced and captured by the men in the chaise? Or was she still capable of controlling her own actions; and were we two following our widely-parted roads towards one point in the mysterious future, at which we were to meet once more?

It was a relief when the hour came to lock my door, to bid farewell to London pursuits, London pupils, and London friends, and to be in movement again towards new interests and a new life. Even the bustle and confusion at the railway terminus, so wearisome and bewildering at other times, roused me and did me good.

My travelling instructions directed me to go to Carlisle, and then to diverge by a branch railway which ran in the direction of the coast. As a misfortune to begin with, our engine broke down between Lancaster and Carlisle. The delay occasioned by this accident caused me to be too late for the branch train, by which I was to have gone on immediately. I had to wait some hours; and when a later train finally deposited me at the nearest station to Limmeridge House, it was past ten, and the night was so dark that I could hardly see my way to the pony-chaise which Mr. Fairlie had ordered to be in waiting for me.

The driver was evidently discomposed by the lateness of my arrival. He was in that state of highly-respectful sulkiness which is peculiar to English servants. We drove away slowly through the darkness in perfect silence. The roads were bad, and the dense obscurity of the night increased the difficulty of getting over the ground quickly. It was, by my watch, nearly an hour and a half from the time of our leaving the station before I heard the sound of the sea in the distance, and the crunch of our wheels on a smooth gravel drive. We had passed one gate before entering the drive, and we passed another before we drew up at the house. I was received by a solemn man-servant out of livery, was informed that the family had retired for the night, and was then led into a large and lofty room where my supper was awaiting me, in a forlorn manner, at one extremity of a lonesome mahogany wilderness of dining-table.

I was too tired and out of spirits to eat or drink much, especially with the solemn servant waiting on me as elaborately as if a small dinner-party had arrived at the house instead of a solitary man. In a quarter of an hour I was ready to be taken up to my bed-chamber. The solemn servant conducted me into a prettily furnished room — said, "Breakfast at nine o'clock, sir" — looked all round him to see that everything was in its proper place — and noiselessly withdrew.

"What shall I see in my dreams to-night?" I thought to myself, as I put out the candle; "the woman in white? or the unknown inhabitants of this Cumberland mansion?" It was a strange sensation to be sleeping in the house, like a friend of the family, and yet not to know one of the inmates, even by sight!

VI.

When I rose the next morning and drew up my blind, the sea opened before me joyously under the broad August sunlight, and the distant coast of Scotland fringed the horizon with its lines of melting blue.

The view was such a surprise, and such a change to me, after my weary London experience of brick and mortar landscape, that I seemed to burst into a new life and a new set of thoughts the moment I looked at it. A confused sensation of having suddenly lost my familiarity with the past, without acquiring any additional clearness of idea in reference to the present or the future, took possession of my mind. Circumstances that were but a few days old, faded back in my memory, as if they had happened months and months since. Pesca's quaint announcement of the means by which he had procured me my present employment; the farewell evening I had passed with my mother and sister; even my mysterious adventure on the way home from Hampstead, had all become like events which might have occurred at some former epoch of my existence. Although the woman in white was still in my mind, the image of her seemed to have grown dull and faint already.

A little before nine o'clock, I descended to the ground-floor of the house. The solemn man-servant of the night before met me wandering among the passages, and compassionately showed me the way to the breakfast-room.

My first glance round me, as the man opened the door, disclosed a well-furnished breakfast-table, standing in the middle of a long room, with many windows in it. I looked from the table to the window farthest from me, and saw a lady standing at it, with her back turned towards me. The instant my eyes rested on her, I was struck by the rare beauty of her form, and by the unaffected grace of her attitude. Her figure was tall, yet not too tall; comely and well-developed, yet not fat; her head set on her shoulders with an easy, pliant firmness; her waist, perfection in the eyes of a man, for it occupied its natural place, it filled out is natural circle, it was visibly and delightfully undeformed by stays. She had not heard my entrance into the room; and I allowed myself the luxury of admiring her for a few moments, before I moved one of the chairs near me, as the least embarrassing means of attracting her attention. She turned towards me immediately. The easy elegance of every movement of her limbs and body as soon as she began to advance from the far end of the room, set me in a flutter of expectation to see her face clearly. She left the window — and I said to myself, The lady is dark. She moved forward a few steps — and I said to myself, The lady is young. She approached nearer — and I said to myself (with a sense of surprise which words fail me to express), The lady is ugly!

Never was the old conventional maxim, that Nature cannot err, more flatly contradicted — never was the fair promise of a lovely figure more strangely and startingly belied by the face and head that crowned it. The lady's complexion was almost swarthy, and the dark down on her upper lip was almost a moustache. She had a large, firm, masculine mouth and jaw; prominent, piercing, resolute brown eyes; and thick, coal-black hair, growing unusually low down on her forehead. Her expression — bright, frank, and intelligent — appeared, while she was silent, to be altogether wanting in those feminine attractions of gentleness and pliability, without which the beauty of the handsomest woman alive is beauty incomplete. To see such a face as this set on shoulders that a sculptor would have longed to model — to be charmed by the modest graces of action through which the symmetrical limbs betrayed their beauty when they moved, and then to be almost repelled by the masculine form and masculine look of the features in which the perfectly shaped figure ended — was to feel a sensation oddly akin to the helpless discomfort familiar to us all in sleep, when we recognise yet cannot reconcile the anomalies and contradictions of a dream.

"Mr. Hartright?" said the lady, interrogatively; her dark face lighting up with a smile, and softening and growing womanly the moment she began to speak. "We resigned all hope of you last night, and went to bed as usual. Accept my apologies for our apparent want of attention; and allow me to introduce myself as one of your pupils. Shall we shake hands? I suppose we must come to it sooner or later — and why not sooner?"

These odd words of welcome were spoken in a clear, ringing, pleasant voice. The offered hand — rather large, but beautifully formed — was given to me with the easy, unaffected self-reliance of a highly-bred woman. We sat down together at the breakfast-table in as cordial and customary a manner as if we had known each other for years, and had met at Limmeridge House to talk over old times by previous appointment.

"I hope you come here good-humouredly determined to make the best of your position," continued the lady. "You will have to begin this morning by putting up with no other company at breakfast than mine. My sister is in her own room, nursing that essentially feminine malady, a slight headache; and her old governess, Mrs. Vesey, is charitably attending on her with restorative tea. My uncle, Mr. Fairlie, never joins us at any of our meals: he is an invalid and keeps bachelor state in his own apartments. There is nobody else in the house but me. Two young ladies have been staying here, but they went away yesterday, in despair; and no wonder. All through their visit (in consequence of Mr. Fairlie's invalid condition) we produced no such convenience in the house as a flirtable, danceable, small-talkable creature of the male sex; and the consequence was, we did nothing but quarrel, especially at dinner-time. How can you expect four women to dine together alone every day, and not quarrel? We are such fools, we can't entertain each other at table. You see I don't think much of my own sex, Mr. Hartright — which will you have, tea or coffee? — no woman does think much of her own sex, although few of them confess it as freely as I do. Dear me, you look puzzled. Why? Are you wondering what you will have for breakfast? or are you surprised at my careless way of talking? In the first case, I advise you, as a friend, to have nothing to do with that cold ham at your elbow, and to wait till the omelette comes in. In the second case, I will give you some tea to compose your spirits, and do all a woman can (which is very little, by-the-by) to hold my tongue."

She handed me my cup of tea, laughing gaily. Her light flow of talk, and her lively familiarity of manner with a total stranger, were accompanied by an unaffected naturalness and an easy inborn confidence in herself and her position, which would have secured her the respect of the most audacious man breathing. While it was impossible to be formal and reserved in her company, it was more than impossible to take the faintest vestige of a liberty with her, even in thought. I felt this instinctively, even while I caught the infection of her own bright gaiety of spirits — even while I did my best to answer her in her own frank, lively way.

"Yes, yes," she said, when I had suggested the only explanation I could offer, to account for my perplexed looks, "I understand. You are such a perfect stranger in the house, that you are puzzled by my familiar references to the worthy inhabitants. Natural enough: I ought to have thought of it before. At any rate, I can set it right now. Suppose I begin with myself, so as to get done with that part of the subject as soon as possible? My name is Marian Halcombe; and I am as inaccurate, as women usually are, in calling Mr. Fairlie my uncle, and Miss Fairlie my sister. My mother was twice married: the first time to Mr. Halcombe, my father; the second time to Mr. Fairlie, my half-sister's father. Except that we are both orphans, we are in every respect as unlike each other as possible. My father was a poor man, and Miss Fairlie's father was a rich man. I have got nothing and she has a fortune. I am dark and ugly, and she is fair and pretty. Everybody thinks me crabbed and odd (with perfect justice); and everybody thinks her sweet-tempered and charming (with more justice still). In short, she is an angel; and I am — Try some of that marmalade, Mr. Hartright, and finish the sentence, in the name of female propriety, for yourself. What am I to tell you about Mr. Fairlie? Upon my honour, I hardly know. He is sure to send for you after breakfast, and you can study him for yourself. In the mean time, I may inform you, first, that he is the late Mr. Fairlie's younger brother; secondly, that he is a single man; and, thirdly, that he is Miss Fairlie's guardian. I won't live without her, and she can't live without me; and that is how I come to be at Limmeridge House. My sister and I are honestly fond of each other; which, you will say, is perfectly unaccountable, under the circumstances, and I quite agree with you — but so it is. You must please both of us, Mr. Hartright, or please neither of us: and, what is still more trying, you will be thrown entirely upon our society. Mrs. Vesey is an excellent person, who possesses all the cardinal virtues, and counts for nothing; and Mr. Fairlie is too great an invalid to be a companion for anybody. I don't know what is the matter with him, and the doctors don't know what is the matter with him, and he doesn't know himself what is the matter with him. We all say it's on the nerves, and we none of us know what we mean when we say it. However, I advise you to humour his little peculiarities, when you see him to-day. Admire his collection of coins, prints, and water-colour drawings, and you will win his heart. Upon my word, if you can be contented with a quiet country life, I don't see why you should not get on very well here. From breakfast to lunch, Mr. Fairlie's drawings will occupy you. After lunch, Miss Fairlie and I shoulder our sketch-books, and go out to misrepresent nature, under your directions. Drawing is *her* favourite whim, mind, not mine. Women can't draw — their minds are too flighty, and their eyes are too inattentive. No matter — my sister likes it; so I waste paint and spoil paper, for her sake, as composedly as any woman in England. As for the evenings, I think we can help you through them. Miss Fairlie plays delightfully. For my own poor part, I don't know one note of music from the other; but I can match you at chess, back-gammon, écarté, and (with the inevitable female drawbacks) even at billiards as well. What do you think of the programme? Can you reconcile yourself to our quiet, regular life? or do you mean to be restless, and secretly thirst for change and adventure, in the humdrum atmosphere of Limmeridge House?"

She had run on thus far, in her gracefully bantering way, with no other interruptions on my part than the unimportant replies which politeness required of me. The turn of the expression, however, in her last question, or rather the one chance word, "adventure," lightly as it fell from her lips, recalled my thoughts to my meeting with the woman in white, and urged me to discover the connexion which the stranger's own reference to Mrs. Fairlie informed me must once have existed between the nameless fugitive from the Asylum, and the former mistress of Limmeridge House.

"Even if I were the most restless of mankind," I said, "I should be in no danger of thirsting after adventures for some time to come. The very night before I arrived at this house, I met with an adventure; and the wonder and excitement of it, I can assure you, Miss Halcombe, will last me for the whole term of my stay in Cumberland, if not for a much longer period."

"You don't say so, Mr. Hartright! May I hear it?"

"You have a claim to hear it. The chief person in the adventure was a total stranger to me, and may perhaps be a total stranger to you; but she certainly mentioned the name of the late Mrs. Fairlie in terms of the sincerest gratitude and regard."

"Mentioned my mother's name! You interest me indescribably. Pray go on."

I at once related the circumstances under which I had met the woman in white, exactly as they had occurred; and I repeated what she had said to me about Mrs. Fairlie and Limmeridge House, word for word.

Miss Halcombe's bright resolute eyes looked eagerly into mine, from the beginning of the narrative to the end. Her face expressed vivid interest and astonishment, but nothing more. She was evidently as far from knowing of any clue to the mystery as I was myself.

"Are you quite sure of those words referring to my mother?" she asked.

"Quite sure," I replied. "Whoever she may be, the woman was once at school in the village of Limmeridge, was treated with especial kindness by Mrs. Fairlie, and, in grateful remembrance of that kindness, feels an affectionate interest in all surviving members of the family. She knew that Mrs.

Fairlie and her husband were both dead; and she spoke of Miss Fairlie as if they had known each other when they were children."

"You said, I think, that she denied belonging to this place?"

"Yes, she told me she came from Hampshire."

"And you entirely failed to find out her name?"

"Entirely."

"Very strange. I think you were quite justified, Mr. Hartright, in giving the poor creature her liberty, for she seems to have done nothing in your presence to show herself unfit to enjoy it. But I wish you had been a little more resolute about finding out her name. We must really clear up this mystery, in some way. You had better not speak of it yet to Mr. Fairlie, or to my sister. They are both of them, I am certain, quite as ignorant of who the woman is, and of what her past history in connexion with us can be, as I am myself. But they are also, in widely different ways, rather nervous and sensitive; and you would only fidget one and alarm the other to no purpose. As for myself, I am all aflame with curiosity, and I devote my whole energies to the business of discovery from this moment. When my mother came here, after her second marriage, she certainly established the village school just as it exists at the present time. But the old teachers are all dead, or gone elsewhere; and no enlightenment is to be hoped for from that quarter. The only other alternative I can think of —"

At this point we were interrupted by the entrance of the servant, with a message from Mr. Fairlie, intimating that he would be glad to see me, as soon as I had done breakfast.

"Wait in the hall," said Miss Halcombe, answering the servant for me, in her quick, ready way. "Mr. Hartright will come out directly. I was about to say," she went on, addressing me again, "that my sister and I have a large collection of my mother's letters, addressed to my father and to hers. In the absence of any other means of getting information, I will pass the morning in looking over my mother's correspondence with Mr. Fairlie. He was fond of London, and was constantly away from his country home; and she was accustomed, at such times, to write and report to him how things went on at Limmeridge. Her letters are full of references to the school in which she took so strong an interest; and I think it more than likely that I may have discovered something when we meet again. The luncheon hour is two, Mr. Hartright. I shall have the pleasure of introducing you to my sister by that time, and we will occupy the afternoon in driving round the neighbourhood and showing you all our pet points of view. Till two o'clock, then, farewell."

She nodded to me with the lively grace, the delightful refinement of familiarity, which characterised all that she did and all that she said; and disappeared by a door at the lower end of the room. As soon as she had left me, I turned my steps towards the hall, and followed the servant on my way, for the first time, to the presence of Mr. Fairlie.

VII.

My conductor led me up-stairs into a passage which took us back to the bedchamber in which I had slept during the past night; and opening the door next to it, begged me to look in.

"I have my master's orders to show you your own sitting-room, sir," said the man, "and to inquire if you approve of the situation and the light."

I must have been hard to please, indeed, if I had not approved of the room, and of everything about it. The bow-window looked out on the same lovely view which I had admired, in the morning, from my bedroom. The furniture was the perfection of luxury and beauty; the table in the centre was bright with gaily bound books, elegant conveniences for writing, and beautiful flowers; the second table near the window, was covered with all the necessary materials for mounting water-colour drawings, and had a little easel attached to it, which I could expand or fold up at will; the walls were hung with gaily tinted chintz; and the floor was spread with Indian matting in maize-colour and red. It was the prettiest and most luxurious little sitting-room I had ever seen; and I admired it with the warmest enthusiasm.

The solemn servant was far too highly trained to betray the slightest satisfaction. He bowed with icy deference when my terms of eulogy were all exhausted, and silently opened the door for me to go out into the passage again.

We turned a corner, and entered a long second passage, ascended a short flight of stairs at the end, crossed a small circular upper hall, and stopped in front of a door covered with dark baize. The servant opened this door, and led me on a few yards to a second; opened that also, and disclosed two curtains of pale sea-green silk hanging before us; raised one of them noiselessly; softly uttered the words, "Mr. Hartright," and left me.

I found myself in a large, lofty room, with a magnificent carved ceiling, and with a carpet over the floor, so thick and soft that it felt like piles of velvet under my feet. One side of the room was occupied by a long bookcase of some rare inlaid wood that was quite new to me. It was not more than six feet high, and the top was adorned with statuettes in marble, ranged at regular distances one from the other. On the opposite side stood two antique cabinets; and between them, and above them, hung a picture of the Virgin and Child, protected by glass, and bearing Raphael's name on the gilt tablet at the bottom of the frame. On my right hand and on my left, as I stood inside the door, were chiffoniers and little stands in buhl and marquetterie, loaded with figures in Dresden china, with rare vases, ivory ornaments, and toys and curiosities that sparkled at all points with gold, silver, and precious stones. At the lower end of the room, opposite to me, the windows were concealed and the sunlight was tempered by large blinds of the same pale sea-green colour as the curtains over the door.   The light thus produced was deliciously soft, mysterious, and subdued; it fell equally upon all the objects in the room; it helped to intensify the deep silence, and the air of profound seclusion that possessed the place; and it surrounded, with an appropriate halo of repose, the solitary figure of the master of the house, leaning back, listlessly composed, in a large easy-chair, with a reading-easel fastened on one of its arms, and a little table on the other.

If a man's personal appearance, when he is out of his dressing-room, and when he has passed forty, can be accepted as a safe guide to his time of life — which is more than doubtful — Mr. Fairlie's age, when I saw him, might have been reasonably computed at over fifty and under sixty years. His beardless face was thin, worn, and transparently pale, but not wrinkled; his nose was high and hooked; his eyes were of a dim grayish blue, large, prominent, and rather red round the rims of the eyelids; his hair was scanty, soft to look at, and of that light sandy colour which is the last·to disclose its own changes towards gray. He was dressed in a dark frock-coat, of some substance much thinner than cloth, and in waistcoat and trousers of spotless white. His feet were effeminately small, and were clad in buff-coloured silk stockings, and little womanish bronze-leather slippers. Two rings adorned his· white delicate hands, the value of which even my inexperienced observation detected to be all but priceless. Upon the whole, he had a frail, languidly-fretful, over-refined look — something singularly and unpleasantly delicate in its association with a man, and, at the same time, something which could by no possibility have looked natural and appropriate if it had been transferred to the personal appearance of a woman. My morning's experience of Miss Halcombe had predisposed me to be pleased with everybody in the house; but my sympathies shut themselves up resolutely at the first sight of Mr. Fairlie.

On approaching nearer to him, I discovered that he was not so entirely without occupation as I had at first supposed.

Placed amid the other rare and beautiful objects on a large round table near him, was a dwarf cabinet in ebony and silver, containing coins of all shapes and sizes, set out in little drawers lined with dark purple velvet. One of these drawers lay on the small table attached to his chair; and near it were some tiny jewellers' brushes, a washleather "stump," and a little bottle of liquid, all waiting to be used in various ways for the removal of any accidental impurities which might be discovered on the coins. His frail white fingers were listlessly toying with something which looked, to my uninstructed eyes, like a dirty pewter medal with ragged edges, when I advanced within a respectful distance of his chair, and stopped to make my bow.

"So glad to possess you at Limmeridge, Mr. Hartright," he said, in a querulous, croaking voice, which combined, in anything but an agrecable manner, a discordantly high tone with a drowsily languid utterance. "Pray sit down. And don't trouble yourself to move the chair, please. In the wretched state of my nerves, movement of any kind is exquisitely painful to me. Have you seen your studio? Will it do?"

"I have just come from seeing the room, Mr. Fairlie; and I assure you —"

He stopped me in the middle of the sentence, by closing his eyes, and holding up one of his white hands imploringly. I paused in astonishment; and the croaking voice honoured me with this explanation:

"Pray excuse me. But *could* you contrive to speak in a lower key? In the wretched state of my nerves, loud sound of any kind is indescribable torture to me. You will pardon an invalid? I only say to you what the lamentable state of my health obliges me to say to everybody. Yes. And you really like the room?"

"I could wish for nothing prettier and nothing more comfortable," I answered, dropping my voice, and beginning to discover already that Mr. Fairlie's selfish affectation and Mr. Fairlie's wretched nerves meant one and the same thing.

"So glad. You will find your position here, Mr. Hartright,

properly recognized. There is none of the horrid English barbarity of feeling about the social position of an artist, in this house. So much of my early life has been passed abroad, that I have quite cast my insular skin in that respect. I wish I could say the same of the gentry — detestable word, but I suppose I must use it — of the gentry in the neighbourhood. They are sad Goths in Art, Mr. Hartright. People, I do assure you, who would have opened their eyes in astonishment, if they had seen Charles the Fifth pick up Titian's brush for him. Do you mind putting this tray of coins back in the cabinet, and giving me the next one to it? In the wretched state of my nerves, exertion of any kind is unspeakably disagreeable to me. Yes. Thank you."

As a practical commentary on the liberal social theory which he had just favoured me by illustrating, Mr. Fairlie's cool request rather amused me. I put back one drawer and gave him the other, with all possible politeness. He began trifling with the new set of coins and the little brushes immediately; languidly looking at them and admiring them all the time he was speaking to me.

"A thousand thanks and a thousand excuses. Do you like coins? Yes. So glad we have another taste in common besides our taste for Art. Now, about the pecuniary arrangements between us — do tell me — are they satisfactory?"

"Most satisfactory, Mr. Fairlie."

"So glad. And — what next? Ah! I remember. Yes. In reference to the consideration which you are good enough to accept for giving me the benefit of your accomplishments in art, my steward will wait on you at the end of the first week, to ascertain your wishes. And — what next? Curious, is it not? I had a great deal more to say; and I appear to have quite forgotten it. Do you mind touching the bell? In that corner. Yes. Thank you."

I rang; and a new servant noiselessly made his appearance — a foreigner, with a set smile and perfectly brushed hair — a valet every inch of him.

"Louis," said Mr. Fairlie, dreamily dusting the tips of his

fingers with one of the tiny brushes for the coins, "I made some entries in my tablettes this morning. Find my tablettes. A thousand pardons, Mr. Hartright, I'm afraid I bore you."

As he wearily closed his eyes again, before I could answer, and as he did most assuredly bore me, I sat silent, and looked up at the Madonna and Child by Raphael. In the mean time, the valet left the room, and returned shortly with a little ivory book. Mr. Fairlie, after first relieving himself by a gentle sigh, let the book drop open with one hand, and held up the tiny brush with the other, as a sign to the servant to wait for further orders.

"Yes. Just so!" said Mr. Fairlie, consulting the tablettes. "Louis, take down that portfolio." He pointed, as he spoke, to several portfolios placed near the window, on mahogany stands. "No. Not the one with the green back — that contains my Rembrandt etchings, Mr. Hartright. Do you like etchings? Yes? So glad we have another taste in common. The portfolio with the red back, Louis. Don't drop it! You have no idea of the tortures I should suffer, Mr. Hartright, if Louis dropped that portfolio. Is it safe on the chair? Do *you* think it safe, Mr. Hartright? Yes? So glad. Will you oblige me by looking at the drawings, if you really think they are quite safe. Louis, go away. What an ass you are. Don't you see me holding the tablettes? Do you suppose I want to hold them? Then why not relieve me of the tablettes without being told? A thousand pardons, Mr. Hartright; servants are such asses, are they not? Do tell me — what do you think of the drawings? They have come from a sale in a shocking state — I thought they smelt of horrid dealers' and brokers' fingers when I looked at them last. *Can* you undertake them?"

Although my nerves were not delicate enough to detect the odour of plebeian fingers which had offended Mr. Fairlie's nostrils, my taste was sufficiently educated to enable me to appreciate the value of the drawings, while I turned them over. They were, for the most part, really fine specimens of English water-colour Art; and they had deserved much better treatment at the hands of their former possessor than they appeared to have received.

"The drawings," I answered, "require careful straining and mounting; and, in my opinion, they are well worth —"

"I beg your pardon," interposed Mr. Fairlie. "Do you mind my closing my eyes while you speak? Even this light is too much for them. Yes?"

"I was about to say that the drawings are well worth all the time and trouble —"

Mr. Fairlie suddenly opened his eyes again, and rolled them with an expression of helpless alarm in the direction of the window.

"I entreat you to excuse me, Mr. Hartright," he said, in a feeble flutter. "But surely I hear some horrid children in the garden — my private garden — below?"

"I can't say, Mr. Fairlie. I heard nothing myself."

"Oblige me — you have been so very good in humouring my poor nerves — oblige me by lifting up a corner of the blind. Don't let the sun in on me, Mr. Hartright! Have you got the blind up? Yes? Then will you be so very kind as to look into the garden and make quite sure?"

I complied with this new request. The garden was carefully walled in, all round. Not a human creature, large or small, appeared in any part of the sacred seclusion. I reported that gratifying fact to Mr. Fairlie.

"A thousand thanks. My fancy, I suppose. There are no children, thank Heaven, in the house; but the servants (persons born without nerves) will encourage the children from the village. Such brats — oh, dear me, such brats! Shall I confess it, Mr. Hartright? — I sadly want a reform in the construction of children. Nature's only idea seems to be to make them machines for the production of incessant noise. Surely our delightful Raffaello's conception is infinitely preferable?"

He pointed to the picture of the Madonna, the upper part of which represented the conventional cherubs of Italian Art, celestially provided with sitting accommodation for their chins, on balloons of buffcoloured cloud.

"Quite a model family!" said Mr. Fairlie, leering at the cherubs. "Such nice round faces, and such nice soft wings, and — nothing else. No dirty little legs to run about on, and no noisy little lungs to scream with. How immeasurably superior to the existing construction! I will close my eyes again, if you will allow me. And you really can manage the drawings? So glad. Is there anything else to settle? if there is, I think I have forgotten it. Shall we ring for Louis again?"

Being, by this time, quite as anxious, on my side, as Mr. Fairlie evidently was on his, to bring the interview to a speedy conclusion, I thought I would try to render the summoning of the servant unnecessary, by offering the requisite suggestion on my own responsibility.

"The only point, Mr. Fairlie, that remains to be discussed," I said, "refers, I think, to the instruction in sketching which I am engaged to communicate to the two young ladies."

"Ah! just so," said Mr. Fairlie. "I wish I felt strong enough to go into that part of the arrangement — but I don't. The ladies, who profit by your kind services, Mr. Hartright, must settle, and decide, and so on, for themselves. My niece is fond of your charming art. She knows just enough about it to be conscious of her own sad defects. Please take pains with her. Yes. Is there anything else? No. We quite understand each other — don't we? I have no right to detain you any longer from your delightful pursuit — have I? So pleasant to have settled everything — such a sensible relief to have done business. Do you mind ringing for Louis to carry the portfolio to your own room?"

"I will carry it there, myself, Mr. Fairlie, if you will allow me."

"Will you really? Are you strong enough? How nice to be so strong! Are you sure you won't drop it? So glad to possess you at Limmeridge, Mr. Hartright. I am such a sufferer that I hardly dare hope to enjoy much of your society. Would you mind taking great pains not to let the doors bang, and not to drop the portfolio? Thank you. Gently with the curtains, please — the slightest noise from them goes through me like a knife. Yes. *Good* morning!"

When the sea-green curtains were closed, and when the two baize doors were shut behind me, I stopped for a moment in the little circular hall beyond, and drew a long, luxurious breath of relief. It was like coming to the surface of the water, after deep diving, to find myself once more on the outside of Mr. Fairlie's room.

As soon as I was comfortably established for the morning in my pretty little studio, the first resolution at which I arrived was to turn my steps no more in the direction of the apartments occupied by the master of the house, except in the very improbable event of his honouring me with a special invitation to pay him another visit. Having settled this satisfactory plan of future conduct, in reference to Mr. Fairlie, I soon recovered the serenity of temper of which my employer's haughty familiarity and impudent politeness had, for the moment, deprived me. The remaining hours of the morning passed away pleasantly enough, in looking over the drawings, arranging them in sets, trimming their ragged edges, and accomplishing the other necessary preparations in anticipation of the business of mounting them. I ought, perhaps, to have made more progress than this; but, as the luncheon-time drew near, I grew restless and unsettled, and felt unable to fix my attention on work, even though that work was only of the humble manual kind.

At two o'clock, I descended again to the breakfast-room, a little anxiously. Expectations of some interest were connected with my approaching reappearance in that part of the house. My introduction to Miss Fairlie was now close at hand; and, if Miss Halcombe's search through her mother's letters had produced the result which she anticipated, the time had come for clearing up the mystery of the woman in white.

VIII.

When I entered the room, I found Miss Halcombe and an elderly lady seated at the luncheon-table.

The elderly lady, when I was presented to her, proved to be Miss Fairlie's former governess, Mrs. Vesey, who had been briefly described to me by my lively companion at the break-fast-table, as possessed of "all the cardinal virtues, and counting for nothing." I can do little more than offer my humble testimony to the truthfulness of Miss Halcombe's sketch of the old lady's character. Mrs. Vesey looked the personification of human composure, and female amiability. A calm enjoyment of a calm existence beamed in drowsy smiles on her plump, placid face. Some of us rush through life; and some of us saunter through life. Mrs. Vesey *sat* through life. Sat in the house, early and late; sat in the garden; sat in unexpected window-seats in passages; sat (on a camp-stool) when her friends tried to take her out walking; sat before she looked at anything, before she talked of anything, before she answered, Yes, or No, to the commonest question — always with the same serene smile on her lips, the same vacantly attentive turn of her head, the same snugly-comfortable position of her hands and arms, under every possible change of domestic circumstances. A mild, a compliant, an unutterably tranquil and harmless old lady, who never by any chance suggested the idea that she had been actually alive since the hour of her birth. Nature has so much to do in this world, and is engaged in generating such a vast variety of co-existent productions, that she must surely be now and then too flurried and confused to distinguish between the different processes that she is carrying on at the same time. Starting from this point of view, it will always remain my private persuasion that Nature was absorbed in making cabbages when Mrs. Vesey was born, and that the good lady suffered the consequences of a vegetable preoccupation in the mind of the Mother of us all.

"Now, Mrs. Vesey," said Miss Halcombe, looking brighter, sharper, and readier than ever, by contrast with the undemonstrative old lady at her side, "what will you have? A cutlet?"

Mrs. Vesey crossed her dimpled hands on the edge of the table; smiled placidly; and said, "Yes, dear."

"What is that opposite Mr. Hartright? Boiled chicken, is it not? I thought you liked boiled chicken better than cutlet, Mrs. Vesey?"

Mrs. Vesey took her dimpled hands off the edge of the table and crossed them on her lap instead; nodded contemplatively at the boiled chicken, and said, "Yes, dear."

"Well, but which will you have, to-day? Shall Mr. Hartright give you some chicken? or shall I give you some cutlet?"

Mrs. Vesey put one of her dimpled hands back again on the edge of the table; hesitated drowsily; and said, "Which you please, dear."

"Mercy on me! it's a question for your taste, my good lady, not for mine. Suppose you have a little of both? and suppose you begin with the chicken, because Mr. Hartright looks devoured by anxiety to carve for you."

Mrs. Vesey put the other dimpled hand back on the edge of the table; brightened dimly, one moment; went out again the next; bowed obediently; and said, "If you please, sir."

Surely a mild, a compliant, an unutterably tranquil and harmless old lady? But enough, perhaps, for the present, of Mrs. Vesey.

All this time, there were no signs of Miss Fairlie. We finished our luncheon; and still she never appeared. Miss Halcombe, whose quick eye nothing escaped, noticed the looks that I cast, from time to time, in the direction of the door.

"I understand you, Mr. Hartright," she said; "you are wondering what has become of your other pupil. She has been down stairs, and has got over her headache; but has not sufficiently recovered her appetite to join us at lunch. If you will put yourself under my charge, I think I can undertake to find her somewhere in the garden."

She took up a parasol, lying on a chair near her, and led the way out, by a long window at the bottom of the room, which opened on to the lawn. It is almost unnecessary to say that we left Mrs. Vesey still seated at the table, with her dimpled hands still crossed on the edge of it; apparently settled in that position for the rest of the afternoon.

As we crossed the lawn, Miss Halcombe looked at me significantly, and shook her head.

"That mysterious adventure of yours," she said, "still remains involved in its own appropriate midnight darkness. I have been all the morning looking over my mother's letters, and I have made no discoveries yet. However, don't despair, Mr. Hartright. This is a matter of curiosity; and you have got a woman for your ally. Under such conditions success is certain, sooner or later. The letters are not exhausted. I have three packets still left, and you may confidently rely on my spending the whole evening over them."

Here, then, was one of my anticipations of the morning still unfulfilled. I began to wonder, next, whether my introduction to Miss Fairlie would disappoint the expectations that I had been forming of her since breakfast-time.

"And how did you get on with Mr. Fairlie?" inquired Miss Halcombe, as we left the lawn and turned into a shrubbery. "Was he particularly nervous this morning? Never mind considering about your answer, Mr. Hartright. The mere fact of your being obliged to consider is enough for me. I see in your face that he *was* particularly nervous; and, as I am amiably unwilling to throw you into the same condition, I ask no more."

We turned off into a winding path while she was speaking, and approached a pretty summer-house, built of wood, in the form of a miniature Swiss châlet. The one room of the summer-house, as we ascended the steps at the door, was occupied by a young lady. She was standing near a rustic table, looking out at the inland view of moor and hill presented by a gap in the trees, and absently turning over the leaves of a little sketch-book that lay at her side. This was Miss Fairlie.

How can I describe her? How can I separate her from my own sensations, and from all that has happened in the later time? How can I see her again as she looked when my eyes first rested on her — as she should look, now, to the eyes that are about to see her in these pages?

The water-colour drawing that I made of Laura Fairlie, at an after period, in the place and attitude in which I first saw her, lies on my desk while I write. I look at it, and there dawns upon me brightly, from the dark greenish-brown background of the summer-house, a light, youthful figure, clothed in a simple muslin dress, the pattern of it formed by broad alternate strips of delicate blue and white. A scarf of the same material sits crisply and closely round her shoulders, and a little straw hat of the natural colour, plainly and sparingly trimmed with ribbon to match the gown, covers her head, and throws its soft pearly shadow over the upper part of her face. Her hair is of so faint and pale a brown — not flaxen, and yet almost as light; not golden, and yet almost as glossy — that it nearly melts, here and there, into the shadow of the hat. It is plainly parted and drawn back over her ears, and the line of it ripples naturally as it crosses her forehead. The eyebrows are rather darker than the hair, and the eyes are of that soft, limpid, turquoise blue, so often sung by the poets, so seldom seen in real life. Lovely eyes in colour, lovely eyes in form — large and tender and quietly thoughtful — but beautiful above all things in the clear truthfulness of look that dwells in their inmost depths, and shines through all their changes of expression with the light of a purer and a better world. The charm — most gently and yet most distinctly expressed — which they shed over the whole face, so covers and transforms its little natural human blemishes elsewhere, that it is difficult to estimate the relative merits and defects of the other features. It is hard to see that the lower part of the face is too delicately refined away towards the chin to be in full and fair proportion with the upper part; that the nose, in escaping the aquiline bend (always hard and cruel in a woman, no matter how abstractedly perfect it may be), has erred a little in the other extreme, and has missed the ideal straightness of line; and that the sweet, sensitive lips are subject to a slight nervous contraction, when she smiles, which draws them upward a little at one corner, towards the cheek. It might be possible to note these blemishes in another woman's face, but it is not easy to dwell on them in hers, so subtly are they connected with all that is individual and characteristic in her expression, and so closely does the expression depend for its full play and life, in every other feature, on the moving impulse of the eyes.

Does my poor portrait of her, my fond, patient labour of long and happy days, show me these things? Ah, how few of them are in the dim mechanical drawing, and how many in the mind with which I regard it! A fair, delicate girl, in a pretty light dress, trifling with the leaves of a sketch-book, while she looks up from it with truthful, innocent blue eyes — that is all the drawing can say; all, perhaps, that even the deeper reach of thought and pen can say in their language, either. The woman who first gives life, light, and form to our shadowy conceptions of beauty, fills a void in our spiritual nature that has remained unknown to us till she appeared. Sympathies that lie too deep for words, too deep almost for thoughts, are touched, at such times, by other charms than those which the senses feel and which the resources of expression can realise. The mystery which underlies the beauty of women is never raised above the reach of all expression until it has claimed kindred with the deeper mystery in our own souls. Then, and then only, has it passed beyond the narrow region on which light falls, in this world, from the pencil and the pen.

Think of her as you thought of the first woman who quickened the pulses within you that the rest of her sex had no art to stir. Let the kind, candid blue eyes meet yours, as they met mine, with the one matchless look which we both remember so well. Let her voice speak the music that you once loved best, attuned as sweetly to your ear as to mine. Let her footstep, as she comes and goes, in these pages, be like that other footstep to whose airy fall your own heart once beat time. Take her as the visionary nursling of your own fancy; and she will grow upon you, all the more clearly, as the living woman who dwells in mine.

Among the sensations that crowded on me, when my eyes first looked upon her — familiar sensations which we all know, which spring to life in most of our hearts, die again in so many, and renew their bright existence in so few — there was one that troubled and perplexed me; one that seemed strangely inconsistent and unaccountably out of place in Miss Fairlie's presence.

Mingling with the vivid impression produced by the charm of her fair face and head, her sweet expression, and her winning simplicity of manner, was another impression, which, in a shadowy way, suggested to me the idea of something wanting. At one time it seemed like something wanting in *her;* at another, like something wanting in myself, which hindered me from understanding her as I ought. The impression was always strongest, in the most contradictory manner, when she looked at me; or, in other words, when I was most conscious of the harmony and charm of her face, and yet, at the same time, most troubled by the sense of an incompleteness which it was impossibe to discover. Something wanting, something wanting — and where it was, and what it was, I could not say.

The effect of this curious caprice of fancy (as I thought it then) was not of a nature to set me at my ease, during a first interview with Miss Fairlie. The few kind words of welcome which she spoke found me hardly self-possessed enough to thank her in the customary phrases of reply. Observing my hesitation, and no doubt attributing it, naturally enough, to some momentary shyness on my part, Miss Halcombe took the business of talking, as easily and readily as usual, into her own hands.

"Look there, Mr. Hartright," she said, pointing to the sketch-book on the table, and to the little delicate wandering hand that was still trifling with it. "Surely you will acknowledge that your model pupil is found at last? The moment she hears that you are in the house, she seizes her inestimable sketch-book, looks universal Nature straight in the face, and longs to begin!"

Miss Fairlie laughed with a ready good-humour, which broke out as brightly as if it had been part of the sunshine above us, over her lovely face.

"I must not take credit to myself where no credit is due," she said, her clear, truthful blue eyes looking alternately at Miss Halcombe and at me. "Fond as I am of drawing, I am so conscious of my own ignorance that I am more afraid than anxious to begin. Now I know you are here, Mr. Hartright, I find myself looking over my sketches, as I used to look over my lessons when I was a little girl, and when I was sadly afraid that I should turn out not fit to be heard."

She made the confession very prettily and simply, and, with quaint, childish earnestness, drew the sketch-book away close to her own side of the table. Miss Halcombe cut the knot of the little embarrassment forthwith, in her resolute, downright way.

"Good, bad, or indifferent," she said, "the pupil's sketches must pass through the fiery ordeal of the master's judgment — and there's an end of it. Suppose we take them with us in the carriage, Laura, and let Mr. Hartright see them, for the first time, under circumstances of perpetual jolting and interruption? If we can only confuse him all through the drive, between Nature as it is, when he looks up at the view, and Nature as it is not, when he looks down again at our sketch-books, we shall drive him into the last desperate refuge of paying us compliments, and shall slip through his professional fingers with our pet feathers of vanity all unruffled."

"I hope Mr. Hartright will pay *me* no compliments," said Miss Fairlie, as we all left the summer-house.

"May I venture to inquire why you express that hope?" I asked.

"Because I shall believe all that you say to me," she answered, simply.

In those few words she unconsciously gave me the key to her whole character; to that generous trust in others which, in her nature, grew innocently out of the sense of her own truth. I only knew it intuitively then. I know it by experience now.

We merely waited to rouse good Mrs. Vesey from the place which she still occupied at the deserted luncheon-table, before we entered the open carriage for our promised drive. The old lady and Miss Halcombe occupied the back seat; and Miss Fairlie and I sat together in front, with the sketch-book open between us, fairly exhibited at last to my professional eyes. All serious criticism on the drawings, even if I had been disposed to volunteer it, was rendered impossible by Miss Halcombe's lively resolution to see nothing but the ridiculous side of the Fine Arts, as practised by herself, her sister, and ladies in general. I can remember the conversation that passed far more easily than the sketches that I mechanically looked over. That part of the talk, especially, in which Miss Fairlie took any share is still as vividly impressed on my memory as if I had heard it only a few hours ago.

Yes! let me acknowledge that, on this first day, I let the charm of her presence lure me from the recollection of myself and my position. The most trifling of the questions that she put to me, on the subject of using her pencil and mixing her colours; the slightest alterations of expression in the lovely eyes that looked into mine, with such an earnest desire to learn all that I could teach, and to discover all that I could show, attracted more of my attention than the finest view we passed through, or the grandest changes of light and shade, as they flowed into each other over the waving moorland, and the level beach. At any time, and under any circumstances of human interest, is it not strange to see how little real hold the objects of the natural world amid which we live can gain on our hearts and minds? We go to Nature for comfort in trouble, and sympathy in joy, only in books. Admiration of those beauties of the inanimate world, which modern poetry so largely and so eloquently describes, is not, even in the best of us, one of the original instincts of our nature. As children, we none of us possess it. No uninstructed man or woman possesses it. Those whose lives are most exclusively passed amid the ever-changing wonders of sea and land are also those who are most universally insensible to every aspect of Nature not directly associated with the human interest of their calling. Our capacity of appreciating the beauties of the earth we live on is, in truth, one of the civilised accomplishments which we all learn, as an Art; and, more, that very capacity is rarely practised by any of us except when our minds are most indolent and most unoccupied. How much share have the attractions of Nature ever had in the pleasurable or painful interests and emotions of ourselves or our friends? What space do they ever occupy in the thousand little narratives of personal experience which pass every day by word of mouth from one of us to the other? All that our minds can compass, all that our hearts can learn, can be accomplished with equal certainty, equal profit, and equal satisfaction to ourselves, in the poorest as in the richest prospect that the face of the earth can show. There is surely a reason for this want of inborn sympathy between the creature and the creation around it, a reason which may perhaps be found in the widely differing destinies of man and his earthly sphere. The grandest mountain prospect that the eye can range over is appointed to annihilation. The smallest human interest that the pure heart can feel is appointed to immortality.

We had been out nearly three hours, when the carriage again passed through the gates of Limmeridge House.

On our way back, I had let the ladies settle for themselves the first point of view which they were to sketch, under my instructions, on the afternoon of the next day. When they withdrew to dress for dinner, and when I was alone again in my little sitting-room, my spirits seemed to leave me on a sudden. I felt ill at ease and dissatisfied with myself, I hardly knew why. Perhaps I was now conscious, for the first time, of having enjoyed our drive too much in the character of a guest, and too little in the character of a drawing-master. Perhaps that strange sense of something wanting, either in Miss Fairlie or in myself, which had perplexed me when I was first introduced to her, haunted me still. Anyhow, it was a relief to my spirits when the dinner-hour called me out of my solitude, and took me back to the society of the ladies of the house.

I was struck, on entering the drawing-room, by the curious contrast, rather in material than in colour, of the dresses which they now wore. While Mrs. Vesey and Miss Halcombe were richly clad (each in the manner most becoming to her age), the first in silver-gray, and the second in that delicate primrose-yellow colour which matches so well with a dark complexion and black hair, Miss Fairlie was unpretendingly and almost poorly dressed in plain white muslin. It was spotlessly pure; it was beautifully put on; but still it was the sort of dress which the wife or daughter of a poor man might have worn; and it made her, so far as externals went, look less affluent in circumstances than her own governess. At a later period, when I learnt to know more of Miss Fairlie's character, I discovered that this curious contrast, on the wrong side, was due to her natural delicacy of feeling and natural intensity of aversion to the slightest personal display of her own wealth. Neither Mrs. Vesey nor Miss Halcombe could ever induce her to let the advantage in dress desert the two ladies who were poor, to lean to the side of the one lady who was rich.

When the dinner was over, we returned together to the drawing-room. Although Mr. Fairlie (emulating the magnificent condescension of the monarch who had picked up Titian's brush for him) had instructed his butler to consult my wishes in relation to the wine that I might prefer after dinner, I was resolute enough to resist the temptation of sitting in solitary grandeur among bottles of my own choosing, and sensible enough to ask the ladies' permission to leave the table with them habitually, on the civilised foreign plan, during the period of my residence at Limmeridge House.

The drawing-room, to which we had now withdrawn for the rest of the evening, was on the ground-floor, and was of the same shape and size as the breakfast-room. Large glass doors at the lower end opened on to a terrace, beautifully ornamented along its whole length with a profusion of flowers.

The soft, hazy twilight was just shading leaf and blossom alike into harmony with its own sober hues, as we entered the room; and the sweet evening scent of the flowers met us with its fragrant welcome through the open glass doors. Good Mrs. Vesey (always the first of the party to sit down) took possession of an arm-chair in a corner, and dozed off comfortably to sleep. At my request, Miss Fairlie placed herself at the piano. As I followed her to a seat near the instrument, I saw Miss Halcombe retire into a recess of one of the side windows, to proceed with the search through her mother's letters by the last quiet rays of the evening light.

How vividly that peaceful home-picture of the drawing-room comes back to me while I write! From the place where I sat I could see Miss Halcombe's graceful figure, half of it in soft light, half in mysterious shadow, bending intently over the letters in her lap; while, nearer to me, the fair profile of the player at the piano was just delicately defined against the faintly deepening background of the inner wall of the room. Outside, on the terrace, the clustering flowers and long grasses and creepers waved so gently in the light evening air, that the sound of their rustling never reached us. The sky was without a cloud; and the dawning mystery of moonlight began to tremble already in the region of the eastern heaven. The sense of peace and seclusion soothed all thought and feeling into a rapt, unearthly repose; and the balmy quiet that deepened ever with the deepening light, seemed to hover over us with a gentler influence still, when there stole upon it from the piano the heavenly tenderness of the music of Mozart. It was an evening of sights and sounds never to forget.

We all sat silent in the places we had chosen — Mrs. Vesey still sleeping, Miss Fairlie still playing, Miss Halcombe still reading — till the light failed us. By this time the moon had stolen round to the terrace, and soft, mysterious rays of light were slanting already across the lower end of the room. The change from the twilight obscurity was so beautiful, that we banished the lamps, by common consent, when the servant brought them in; and kept the large room unlighted, except by the glimmer of the two candles at the piano.

For half an hour more, the music still went on. After that, the beauty of the moonlight view on the terrace tempted Miss Fairlie out to look at it; and I followed her. When the candles at the piano had been lighted, Miss Halcombe had changed her place, so as to continue her examination of the letters by their assistance. We left her, on a low chair, at one side of the instrument, so absorbed over her reading that she did not seem to notice when we moved.

We had been out on the terrace together, just in front of the glass doors, hardly so long as five minutes, I should think; and Miss Fairlie was, by my advice, just tying her white handkerchief over her head as a precaution against the night air — when I heard Miss Halcombe's voice — low, eager, and altered from its natural lively tone — pronounce my name.

"Mr. Hartright," she said, "will you come here for a minute? I want to speak to you."

I entered the room again immediately. The piano stood about half way down along the inner wall. On the side of the instrument farthest from the terrace, Miss Halcombe was sitting with the letters scattered on her lap, and with one in her hand selected from them, and held close to the candle. On the side nearest to the terrace there stood a low ottoman, on which I took my place. In this position, I was not far from the glass doors; and I could see Miss Fairlie plainly, as she passed and repassed the opening on to the terrace; walking slowly from end to end of it in the full radiance of the moon.

"I want you to listen while I read the concluding passages in this letter," said Miss Halcombe. "Tell me if you think they throw any light upon your strange adventure on the road to London. The letter is addressed by my mother to her second husband, Mr. Fairlie; and the date refers to a period of between eleven and twelve years since. At that time, Mr. and Mrs. Fairlie, and my half-sister Laura, had been living for years in this house; and I was away from them, completing my education at a school in Paris."

She looked and spoke earnestly, and, as I thought, a little uneasily, as well.   At the moment when she raised the letter to the candle before beginning to read it, Miss Fairlie passed us on the terrace, looked in for a moment, and, seeing that we were engaged, slowly walked on.

Miss Halcombe began to read, as follows:

"'You will be tired, my dear Philip, of hearing perpetually about my schools and my scholars.   Lay the blame, pray, on the dull uniformity of life at Limmeridge, and not on me.   Besides, this time, I have something really interesting to tell you about a new scholar.

"'You know old Mrs. Kempe, at the village shop.   Well, after years of ailing, the doctor has at last given her up, and she is dying slowly, day by day.   Her only living relation, a sister, arrived last week to take care of her.   This sister comes all the way from Hampshire — her name is Mrs. Catherick. Four days ago Mrs. Catherick came here to see me, and . brought her only child with her, a sweet little girl about a year older than our darling Laura —'"

As the last sentence fell from the reader's lips, Miss Fairlie passed us on the terrace once more.   She was softly singing to herself one of the melodies which she had been playing earlier in the evening.   Miss Halcombe waited till she had passed out of sight again; and then went on with the letter:

"'Mrs. Catherick is a decent, well-behaved, respectable woman; middle aged, and with the remains of having been moderately, only moderately, nice-looking.   There is something in her manner and her appearance, however, which I can't make out.   She is reserved about herself to the point of downright secrecy; and there is a look in her face — I can't describe it — which suggests to me that she has something on her mind.   She is altogether what you would call a walking mystery.   Her errand at Limmeridge House, however, was simple enough.   When she left Hampshire to nurse her sister,

Mrs. Kempe, through her last illness, she had been obliged to
bring her daughter with her, through having no one at home
to take care of the little girl. Mrs. Kempe may die in a week's
time, or may linger on for months; and Mrs. Catherick's object was to ask me to let her daughter, Anne, have the benefit
of attending my school; subject to the condition of her being
removed from it to go home again with her mother, after Mrs.
Kempe's death. I consented at once; and when Laura and I
went out for our walk, we took the little girl (who is just eleven
years old) to the school, that very day.'"

Once more, Miss Fairlie's figure, bright and soft in its
snowy muslin dress — her face prettily framed by the white
folds of the handkerchief which she had tied under her chin—
passed by us in the moonlight. Once more, Miss Halcombe
waited till she was out of sight; and then went on:

"'I have taken a violent fancy, Philip, to my new scholar,
for a reason which I mean to keep till the last for the sake of
surprising you. Her mother having told me as little about the
child as she told me of herself, I was left to discover (which I
did on the first day when we tried her at lessons) that the poor
little thing's intellect is not developed as it ought to be at her
age. Seeing this, I had her up to the house the next day, and
privately arranged with the doctor to come and watch her and
question her, and tell me what he thought. His opinion is
that she will grow out of it. But he says her careful bringing-
up at school is a matter of great importance just now, because
her unusual slowness in acquiring ideas implies an unusual te-
nacity in keeping them, when they are once received into her
mind. Now, my love, you must not imagine, in your off-hand
way, that I have been attaching myself to an idiot. This poor
little Anne Catherick is a sweet, affectionate, grateful girl;
and says the quaintest, prettiest things (as you shall judge by
an instance), in the most oddly sudden, surprised, half-
frightened way. Although she is dressed very neatly, her
clothes show a sad want of taste in colour and pattern. So I

arranged, yesterday, that some of our darling Laura's old white frocks and white hats should be altered for Anne Catherick; explaining to her that little girls of her complexion looked neater and better all in white than in anything else. She hesitated and seemed puzzled for a minute; then flushed up, and appeared to understand. Her little hand clasped mine suddenly. She kissed it, Philip; and said (oh, so earnestly!), " "I will always wear white as long as I live. It will help me to remember you, ma'am, and to think that I am pleasing you still, when I go away and see you no more." " This is only one specimen of the quaint things she says so prettily. Poor little soul! She shall have a stock of white frocks, made with good deep tucks, to let out for her as she grows—'"

Miss Halcombe paused, and looked at me across the piano.

"Did the forlorn woman whom you met in the high road seem young?" she asked. "Young enough to be two or three-and-twenty?"

"Yes, Miss Halcombe, as young as that."

"And she was strangely dressed, from head to foot, all in white?"

"All in white."

While the answer was passing my lips, Miss Fairlie glided into view on the terrace, for the third time. Instead of proceeding on her walk, she stopped, with her back turned towards us; and, leaning on the balustrade of the terrace, looked down into the garden beyond. My eyes fixed upon the white gleam of her muslin gown and head-dress in the moonlight, and a sensation, for which I can find no name — a sensation that quickened my pulse, and raised a fluttering at my heart — began to steal over me.

"All in white?" Miss Halcombe repeated. "The most important sentences in the letter, Mr. Hartright, are those at the end, which I will read to you immediately. But I can't help dwelling a little upon the coincidence of the white costume of the woman you met, and the white frocks which produced that strange answer from my mother's little scholar. The doctor may have been wrong when he discovered the child's defects of intellect, and predicted that she would 'grow out of them.' She may never have grown out of them; and the old grateful fancy about dressing in white, which was a serious feeling to the girl, may be a serious feeling to the woman still."

I said a few words in answer — I hardly know what. All my attention was concentrated on the white gleam of Miss Fairlie's muslin dress.

"Listen to the last sentences of the letter," said Miss Halcombe. "I think they will surprise you."

As she raised the letter to the light of the candle, Miss Fairlie turned from the balustrade, looked doubtfully up and down the terrace, advanced a step towards the glass doors, and then stopped, facing us.

Meanwhile, Miss Halcombe read me the last sentences to which she had referred:

"'And now, my love, seeing that I am at the end of my paper, now for the real reason, the surprising reason, for my fondness for little Anne Catherick. My dear Philip, although she is not half so pretty, she is nevertheless, by one of those extraordinary caprices of accidental resemblance which one sometimes sees, the living likeness, in her hair, her complexion, the colour of her eyes, and the shape of her face —'"

I started up from the ottoman, before Miss Halcombe could pronounce the next words. A thrill of the same feeling which ran through me when the touch was laid upon my shoulder on the lonely high-road, chilled me again.

There stood Miss Fairlie, a white figure, alone in the moonlight; in her attitude, in the turn of her head, in her complexion, in the shape of her face, the living image, at that distance and under those circumstances, of the woman in white! The doubt which had troubled my mind for hours and hours past, flashed into conviction in an instant. That "something wanting" was my own recognition of the ominous likeness between the fugitive from the asylum and my pupil at Limmeridge House.

"You see it!" said Miss Halcombe. She dropped the useless letter, and her eyes flashed as they met mine. "You see it now, as my mother saw it eleven years since!"

"I see it — more unwillingly than I can say. To associate that forlorn, friendless, lost woman, even by an accidental likeness only, with Miss Fairlie, seems like casting a shadow on the future of the bright creature who stands looking at us now. Let me lose the impression again, as soon as possible. Call her in, out of the dreary moonlight — pray call her in!"

"Mr. Hartright, you surprise me. Whatever women may ne, I thought that men, in the nineteenth century, were above superstition."

"Pray call her in!"

"Hush, hush! She is coming of her own accord. Say nothing in her presence. Let this discovery of the likeness be kept a secret between you and me. Come in, Laura; come in, and wake Mrs. Vesey with the piano. Mr. Hartright is petitioning for some more music, and he wants it, this time, of the lightest and liveliest kind."

IX.

So ended my eventful first day at Limmeridge House.

Miss Halcombe and I kept our secret. After the discovery of the likeness no fresh light seemed destined to break over the mystery of the woman in white. At the first safe opportunity Miss Halcombe cautiously led her half-sister to speak of their mother, of old times, and of Anne Catherick. Miss Fairlie's recollections of the little scholar at Limmeridge were, however, only of the most vague and general kind. She remembered the likeness between herself and her mother's favourite pupil, as something which had been supposed to exist in past times; but she did not refer to the gift of the white dresses, or to the singular form of words in which the child had artlessly expressed her gratitude for them. She remembered that Anne had remained at Limmeridge for a few months only, and had then left it to go back to her home in Hampshire; but she could not say whether the mother and daughter had ever returned, or had ever been heard of afterwards. No further search, on Miss Halcombe's part, through the few letters of Mrs. Fairlie's writing which she had left unread, assisted in clearing up the uncertainties still left to perplex us. We had identified the unhappy woman whom I had met in the night-time, with Anne Catherick — we had made some advance, at least, towards connecting the probably defective condition of the poor creature's intellect with the peculiarity of her being dressed all in white, and with the continuance, in her maturer years, of her childish gratitude towards Mrs. Fairlie — and there, so far as we knew at that time, our discoveries had ended.

The days passed on, the weeks passed on; and the track of the golden autumn wound its bright way visibly through the green summer of the trees. Peaceful, fast-flowing, happy time! my story glides by you now, as swiftly as you once glided by me. Of all the treasures of enjoyment that you poured so freely into my heart, how much is left me that has purpose and value enough to be written on this page? Nothing but the saddest of all confessions that a man can make — the confession of his own folly.

The secret which that confession discloses should be told with little effort, for it has indirectly escaped me already. The poor weak words which have failed to describe Miss Fairlie, have succeeded in betraying the sensations she awakened in me. It is so with us all. Our words are giants when they do us an injury, and dwarfs when they do us a service.

I loved her.

Ah! how well I know all the sadness and all the mockery that is contained in those three words. I can sigh over my mournful confession with the tenderest woman who reads it and pities me. I can laugh at it as bitterly as the hardest man who tosses it from him in contempt. I loved her! Feel for me, or despise me, I confess it with the same immovable resolution to own the truth.

Was there no excuse for me? There was some excuse to be found, surely, in the conditions under which my term of hired service was passed at Limmeridge House.

My morning hours succeeded each other calmly in the quiet and seclusion of my own room. I had just work enough to do, in mounting my employer's drawings, to keep my hands and eyes pleasurably employed, while my mind was left free to enjoy the dangerous luxury of its own unbridled thoughts. A perilous solitude, for it lasted long enough to enervate, not long enough to fortify me. A perilous solitude, for it was followed by afternoons and evenings spent, day after day and week after week, alone in the society of two women, one of whom possessed all the accomplishments of grace, wit, and high-breeding, the other all the charms of beauty, gentleness, and simple truth, that can purify and subdue the heart of man. Not a day passed, in that dangerous intimacy of teacher and pupil, in which my hand was not close to Miss Fairlie's; my cheek, as we bent together over her sketch-book, almost touching hers. The more attentively she watched every movement of my brush, the more closely I was breathing the perfume of her hair, and the warm fragrance of her breath. It was part of my service, to live in the very light of her eyes — at one time to be bending over her, so close to her bosom as to tremble at the thought of touching it; at another, to feel her bending over me, bending so close to see what I was about, that her voice sank low when she spoke to me, and her ribbons brushed my cheek in the wind before she could draw them back.

The evenings which followed the sketching excursions of the afternoon, varied, rather than checked, these innocent, these inevitable familiarities. My natural fondness for the music which she played with such tender feeling, such delicate womanly taste, and her natural enjoyment of giving me back, by the practice of her art, the pleasure which I had offered to her by the practice of mine, only wove another tie which drew us closer and closer to one another. The accidents of conversation; the simple habits which regulated even such a little thing as the position of our places at table; the play of Miss Halcombe's ever-ready raillery, always directed against my anxiety, as teacher, while it sparkled over her enthusiasm as pupil; the harmless expression of poor Mrs. Vesey's drowsy approval which connected Miss Fairlie and me as two model young people who never disturbed her — every one of these trifles, and many more, combined to fold us together in the same domestic atmosphere, and to lead us both insensibly to the same hopeless end.

I should have remembered my position, and have put myself secretly on my guard. I did so; but not till it was too late. All the discretion, all the experience, which had availed me with other women, and secured me against other temptations, failed me with her. It had been my profession, for years past, to be in this close contact with young girls of all ages, and of all orders of beauty. I had accepted the position as part of my calling in life; I had trained myself to leave all the sympathies natural to my age in my employer's outer hall, as coolly as I left my umbrella there before I went up-stairs. I had long since learnt to understand, composedly and as a matter of course, that my situation in life was considered a guarantee against any of my female pupils feeling more than the most ordinary interest in me, and that I was admitted among beautiful and captivating women, much as a harmless domestic animal is admitted among them. This guardian experience I had gained early; this guardian experience had sternly and strictly guided me straight along my own poor narrow path, without once letting me stray aside, to the right hand or to the left. And now, I and my trusty talisman were parted for the first time. Yes, my hardly-earned self-control was as completely lost to me as if I had never possessed it; lost to me, as it is lost every day to other men, in other critical situations, where women are concerned, I know, now, that I should have questioned myself from the first. I should have asked why any room in the house was better than home to me when she entered it, and barren as a desert when she went out again — why I always noticed and remembered the little changes in her dress that I had noticed and remembered in no other woman's before — why I saw her, heard her, and touched her (when we shook hands at night and morning) as I had never seen, heard, and touched any other woman in my life? I should have looked into my own heart, and found this new growth springing up there, and plucked it out while it was young. Why was this easiest, simplest work of self-culture always too much for me? The explanation has been written already in the three words that were many enough, and plain enough, for my confession. I loved her.

The days passed, the weeks passed; it was approaching the third month of my stay in Cumberland. The delicious monotony of life in our calm seclusion, flowed on with me like a smooth stream with a swimmer who glides down the current. All memory of the past, all thought of the future, all sense of the falseness and hopelessness of my own position, lay hushed within me into deceitful rest. Lulled by the Syren-song that my own heart sung to me, with eyes shut to all sight, and ears closed to all sound of danger, I drifted nearer and nearer to the fatal rocks. The warning that aroused me at last, and startled me into sudden, self-accusing consciousness of my own weakness, was the plainest, the truest, the kindest of all warnings, for it came silently from *her*.

We had parted one night, as usual. No word had fallen from my lips, at that time or at any time before it, that could betray me, or startle her into sudden knowledge of the truth. But, when we met again in the morning, a change had come over her — a change that told me all.

I shrank then — I shrink still — from invading the innermost sanctuary of her heart, and laying it open to others, as I have laid open my own. Let it be enough to say that the time when she first surprised my secret, was, I firmly believe, the time when she first surprised her own, and the time, also, when she changed towards me in the interval of one night. Her nature, too truthful to deceive others, was too noble to deceive itself. When the doubt that I had hushed asleep, first laid its weary weight on her heart, the true face owned all, and said, in its own frank simple language — I am sorry for him; I am sorry for myself.

It said this, and more, which I could not then interpret. I understood but too well the change in her manner, to greater kindness and quicker readiness in interpreting all my wishes, before others — to constraint and sadness, and nervous anxiety to absorb herself in the first occupation she could seize on, whenever we happened to be left together alone. I understood why the sweet sensitive lips smiled so rarely and so restrainedly now; and why the clear blue eyes looked at me, sometimes with the pity of an angel, sometimes with the innocent perplexity of a child. But the change meant more than this. There was a coldness in her hand, there was an unnatural immobility in her face, there was in all her movements the mute expression of constant fear and clinging self-reproach. The sensations that I could trace to herself and to me, the unacknowledged sensations that we were feeling in common, were not these. There were certain elements of the change in her that were still secretly drawing us together, and others that were, as secretly, beginning to drive us apart.

In my doubt and perplexity, in my vague suspicion of something hidden which I was left to find by my own unaided efforts, I examined Miss Halcombe's looks and manner for enlightenment. Living in such intimacy as ours, no serious alteration could take place in any one of us which did not sympathetically affect the others. The change in Miss Fairlie was reflected in her half-sister. Although not a word escaped Miss Halcombe which hinted at an altered state of feeling towards myself, her penetrating eyes had contracted a new habit of always watching me. Sometimes, the look was like suppressed anger; sometimes, like suppressed dread; sometimes, like neither — like nothing, in short, which I could understand. A week elapsed, leaving us all three still in this position of secret constraint towards one another. My situation, aggravated by the sense of my own miserable weakness and forgetfulness of myself, now too late awakened in me, was becoming intolerable. I felt that I must cast off the oppression under which I was living, at once and for ever — yet how to act for the best, or what to say first, was more than I could tell.

From this position of helplessness and humiliation, I was rescued by Miss Halcombe. Her lips told me the bitter, the necessary, the unexpected truth; her hearty kindness sustained me under the shock of hearing it; her sense and courage turned to its right use an event which threatened the worst that could happen, to me and to others, in Limmeridge House.

X.

IT was on a Thursday in the week, and nearly at the end of the third month of my sojourn in Cumberland.

In the morning, when I went down into the breakfast-room, at the usual hour, Miss Halcombe, for the first time since I had known her, was absent from her customary place at the table.

Miss Fairlie was out on the lawn. She bowed to me, but did not come in. Not a word had dropped from my lips, or from hers that could unsettle either of us — and yet the same unacknowledged sense of embarrassment made us shrink alike from meeting one another alone. She waited on the lawn; and I waited in the breakfast-room, till Mrs. Vesey or Miss Halcombe came in. How quickly I should have joined her: how readily we should have shaken hands, and glided into our customary talk, only a fortnight ago!

In a few minutes, Miss Halcombe entered. She had a

5*

preoccupied look, and she made her apologies for being late, rather absently.

"I have been detained," she said, "by a consultation with Mr. Fairlie on a domestic matter which he wished to speak to me about."

Miss Fairlie came in from the garden; and the usual morning greeting passed between us. Her hand struck colder to mine than ever. She did not look at me; and she was very pale. Even Mrs. Vesey noticed it, when she entered the room a moment after.

"I suppose it is the change in the wind," said the old lady. "The winter is coming — ah, my love, the winter is coming soon!"

In her heart and in mine it had come already!

Our morning meal — once so full of pleasant good-humoured discussions of the plans for the day — was short and silent. Miss Fairlie seemed to feel the oppression of the long pauses in the conversation; and looked appealingly to her sister to fill them up. Miss Halcombe, after once or twice hesitating and checking herself, in a most uncharacteristic manner, spoke at last.

"I have seen your uncle this morning, Laura," she said. "He thinks the purple room is the one that ought to be got ready; and he confirms what I told you. Monday is the day — not Tuesday."

While these words were being spoken, Miss Fairlie looked down at the table beneath her. Her fingers moved nervously among the crumbs that were scattered on the cloth. The paleness on her cheeks spread to her lips, and the lips themselves trembled visibly. I was not the only person present who noticed this. Miss Halcombe saw it, too; and at once set us the example of rising from table.

Mrs. Vesey and Miss Fairlie left the room together. The kind sorrowful blue eyes looked at me, for a moment, with the prescient sadness of a coming and a long farewell. I felt the answering pang in my own heart — the pang that told me

I must lose her soon, and love her the more unchangeably for the loss.

I turned towards the garden, when the door had closed on her. Miss Halcombe was standing with her hat in her hand, and her shawl over her arm, by the large window that led out to the lawn, and was looking at me attentively.

"Have you any leisure time to spare," she asked, "before you begin to work in your own room?"

"Certainly, Miss Halcombe. I have always time at your service."

"I want to say a word to you in private, Mr. Hartright. Get your hat, and come out into the garden. We are not likely to be disturbed there at this hour in the morning."

As we stepped out on to the lawn, one of the under-gardeners — a mere lad — passed us on his way to the house, with a letter in his hand. Miss Halcombe stopped him.

"Is that letter for me?" she asked.

"Nay, miss; it's just said to be for Miss Fairlie," answered the lad, holding out the letter as he spoke.

Miss Halcombe took it from him, and looked at the address.

"A strange handwriting," she said to herself. "Who can Laura's correspondent be? Where did you get this?" she continued, addressing the gardener.

"Well, miss," said the lad, "I just got it from a woman."

"What woman?"

"A woman well stricken in age."

"Oh, an old woman. Any one you knew?"

"I canna' tak' it on mysel' to say that she was other than a stranger to me."

"Which way did she go?"

"That gate," said the under-gardener, turning with great deliberation towards the south, and embracing the whole of that part of England with one comprehensive sweep of his arm.

"Curious," said Miss Halcombe; "I suppose it must be

a begging-letter. There," she added, handing the letter back to the lad, "take it to the house, and give it to one of the servants. And now, Mr. Hartright, if you have no objection, let us walk this way."

She led me across the lawn, along the same path by which I had followed her on the day after my arrival at Limmeridge. At the little summer-house in which Laura Fairlie and I had first seen each other, she stopped, and broke the silence which she had steadily maintained while we were walking together.

"What I have to say to you, I can say here."

With those words, she entered the summer-house, took one of the chairs at the little round table inside, and signed to me to take the other. I suspected what was coming when she spoke to me in the breakfast-room; I felt certain of it now.

"Mr. Hartright," she said, "I am going to begin by making a frank avowal to you. I am going to say — without phrase-making, which I detest; or paying compliments, which I heartily despise — that I have come, in the course of your residence with us, to feel a strong friendly regard for you. I was predisposed in your favour when you first told me of your conduct towards that unhappy woman whom you met under such remarkable circumstances. Your management of the affair might not have been prudent; but it showed the self-control, the delicacy, and the compassion of a man who was naturally a gentleman. It made me expect good things from you; and you have not disappointed my expectations."

She paused — but held up her hand at the same time, as a sign that she awaited no answer from me before she proceeded. When I entered the summer-house, no thought was in me of the woman in white. But, now, Miss Halcombe's own words had put the memory of my adventure back in my mind. It remained there throughout the interview — remained, and not without a result.

"As your friend," she proceeded, "I am going to tell you, at once, in my own plain, blunt, downright language, that I have discovered your secret — without help, or hint, mind, from any one else. Mr. Hartright, you have thoughtlessly allowed yourself to form an attachment — a serious and devoted attachment, I am afraid — to my sister, Laura. I don't put you to the pain of confessing it, in so many words, because I see and know that you are too honest to deny it. I don't even blame you — I pity you for opening your heart to a hopeless affection. You have not attempted to take any underhand advantage — you have not spoken to my sister in secret. You are guilty of weakness and want of attention to your own best interests, but of nothing worse. If you had acted, in any single respect, less delicately and less modestly, I should have told you to leave the house, without an instant's notice, or an instant's consultation of anybody. As it is, I blame the misfortune of your years and your position — I don't blame *you*. Shake hands — I have given you pain; I am going to give you more; but there is no help for it — shake hands with your friend, Marian Halcombe, first."

The sudden kindness — the warm, high-minded, fearless sympathy which met me on such mercifully-equal terms, which appealed with such delicate and generous abruptness straight to my heart, my honour, and my courage, overcame me in an instant. I tried to look at her, when she took my hand, but my eyes were dim. I tried to thank her, but my voice failed me.

"Listen to me," she said, considerately avoiding all notice of my loss of self-control. "Listen to me, and let us get it over at once. It is a real true relief to me that I am not obliged, in what I have now to say, to enter into the question — the hard and cruel question as I think it — of social inequalities. Circumstances which will try *you* to the quick, spare *me* the ungracious necessity of paining a man who has lived in friendly intimacy under the same roof with myself by any humiliating reference to matters of rank and station. You must leave Limmeridge House, Mr. Hartright, before more harm is done. It is my duty to say that to you; and it would be equally my duty to say it, under precisely the same serious necessity, if you were the representative of the oldest and wealthiest family in England. You must leave us, not because you are a teacher of drawing ——"

She waited a moment; turned her face full on me; and, reaching across the table, laid her hand firmly on my arm.

"Not because you are a teacher of drawing," she repeated, "but because Laura Fairlie is engaged to be married."

The last word went like a bullet to my heart. My arm lost all sensation of the hand that grasped it. I never moved and never spoke. The sharp autumn breeze that scattered the dead leaves at our feet, came as cold to me, on a sudden, as if my own mad hopes were dead leaves, too, whirled away by the wind like the rest. Hopes! Betrothed, or not betrothed, she was equally far from *me*. Would other men have remembered that in my place? Not if they had loved her as I did.

The pang passed; and nothing but the dull numbing pain of it remained. I felt Miss Halcombe's hand again, tightening its hold on my arm — I raised my head, and looked at her. Her large black eyes were rooted on me, watching the white change on my face, which I felt, and which she saw.

"Crush it!" she said. "Here, where you first saw her, crush it! Don't shrink under it like a woman. Tear it out; trample it under foot like a man!"

The suppressed vehemence with which she spoke; the strength which her will — concentrated in the look she fixed on me, and in the hold on my arm that she had not yet relinquished — communicated to mine, steadied me. We both waited for a minute, in silence. At the end of that time, I had justified her generous faith in my manhood; I had, outwardly at least, recovered my self-control.

"Are you yourself again?"

"Enough myself, Miss Halcombe, to ask your pardon and hers. Enough myself, to be guided by your advice, and to prove my gratitude in that way, if I can prove it in no other."

"You have proved it already," she answered, "by those words. Mr. Hartright, concealment is at an end between us. I cannot affect to hide from *you*, what my sister has unconsciously shown to *me*. You must leave us for her sake, as well as for your own. Your presence here, your necessary intimacy with us, harmless as it has been, God knows, in all other respects, has unsteadied her and made her wretched. I, who love her better than my own life — I, who have learnt to believe in that pure, noble, innocent nature as I believe in my religion — know but too well the secret misery of self-reproach that she has been suffering, since the first shadow of a feeling disloyal to her marriage engagement entered her heart in spite of her. I don't say — it would be useless to attempt to say it, after what has happened — that her engagement has ever had a strong hold on her affections. It is an engagement of honour, not of love — her father sanctioned it on his death-bed, two years since — she herself neither welcomed it, nor shrank from it — she was content to make it. Till you came here, she was in the position of hundreds of other women, who marry men without being greatly attracted to them or greatly repelled by them, and who learn to love them (when they don't learn to hate!) after marriage, instead of before. I hope more earnestly than words can say — and you should have the self-sacrificing courage to hope too — that the new thoughts and feelings which have disturbed the old calmness and the old content, have not taken root too deeply to be ever removed. Your absence (if I had less belief in your honour, and your courage, and your sense, I should not trust to them as I am trusting now) — your absence will help my efforts; and time will help us all three. It is something to know that my first confidence in you was not all misplaced. It is something to know that you will not be less honest, less manly, less considerate towards the pupil whose relation to yourself you have had the misfortune to forget, than towards the stranger and the outcast whose appeal to you was not made in vain."

Again the chance reference to the woman in white! Was there no possibility of speaking of Miss Fairlie and of me without raising the memory of Anne Catherick, and setting her between us like a fatality that it was hopeless to avoid?

"Tell me what apology I can make to Mr. Fairlie for breaking my engagement," I said. "Tell me when to go after that apology is accepted. I promise implicit obedience to you and to your advice."

"Time is, every way, of importance," she answered. "You heard me refer this morning to Monday next, and to the necessity of setting the purple room in order. The visitor whom we expect on Monday ——"

I could not wait for her to be more explicit. Knowing what I knew now, the memory of Miss Fairlie's look and manner at the breakfast-table told me that the expected visitor at Limmeridge House was her future husband. I tried to force it back; but something rose within me at that moment stronger than my own will; and I interrupted Miss Halcombe.

"Let me go to-day," I said, bitterly. "The sooner the better."

"No; not to-day," she replied. "The only reason you can assign to Mr. Fairlie for your departure, before the end of your engagement, must be that an unforeseen necessity compels you to ask his permission to return at once to London. You must wait till to-morrow to tell him that, at the time when the post comes in, because he will then understand the sudden change in your plans, by associating it with the arrival of a letter from London. It is miserable and sickening to descend to deceit, even of the most harmless kind — but I know Mr. Fairlie, and if you once excite his suspicions that you are trifling with him, he will refuse to release you. Speak to him on Friday morning; occupy yourself afterwards (for the sake of your own interests with your employer), in leaving your unfinished work in as little confusion as possible, and quit this place on Saturday. It will be time enough, then, Mr. Hartright, for you, and for all of us."

Before I could assure her that she might depend on my acting in the strictest accordance with her wishes, we were both startled by advancing footsteps in the shrubbery. Some one was coming from the house to seek for us! I felt the blood rush into my cheeks, and then leave them again. Could the third person who was fast approaching us, at such a time and under such circumstances, be Miss Fairlie?

It was a relief — so sadly, so hopelessly was my position towards her changed already — it was absolutely a relief to me, when the person who had disturbed us appeared at the entrance of the summer-house, and proved to be only Miss Fairlie's maid.

"Could I speak to you for a moment, miss?" said the girl, in rather a flurried, unsettled manner.

Miss Halcombe descended the steps into the shrubbery, and walked aside a few paces with the maid.

Left by myself, my mind reverted, with a sense of forlorn wretchedness which it is not in any words that I can find to describe, to my approaching return to the solitude and the despair of my lonely London home. Thoughts of my kind old mother, and of my sister, who had rejoiced with her so innocently over my prospects in Cumberland — thoughts whose long banishment from my heart it was now my shame and my reproach to realise for the first time — came back to me with the loving mournfulness of old, neglected friends. My mother and my sister, what would they feel when I returned to them from my broken engagement, with the confession of my miserable secret — they who had parted from me so hopefully on that last happy night in the Hampstead cottage!

Anne Catherick again! Even the memory of the farewell evening with my mother and my sister could not return to me now, unconnected with that other memory of the moonlight walk back to London. What did it mean? Were that woman and I to meet once more? It was possible, at the least. Did she know that I lived in London? Yes; I had told her so, either before or after that strange question of hers, when she had asked me so distrustfully if I knew many men of the rank of Baronet. Either before or after — my mind was not calm enough, then, to remember which.

A few minutes elapsed before Miss Halcombe dismissed

the maid and came back to me. She, too, looked flurried and unsettled, now.

"We have arranged all that is necessary, Mr. Hartright," she said. "We have understood each other, as friends should; and we may go back at once to the house. To tell you the truth, I am uneasy about Laura. She has sent to say she wants to see me directly; and the maid reports that her mistress is apparently very much agitated by a letter that she has received this morning — the same letter, no doubt, which I sent on to the house before we came here."

We retraced our steps together hastily along the shrubbery path. Although Miss Halcombe had ended all that she thought it necessary to say, on her side, I had not ended all that I wanted to say on mine. From the moment when I had discovered that the expected visitor at Limmeridge was Miss Fairlie's future husband, I had felt a bitter curiosity, a burning envious eagerness, to know who he was. It was possible that a future opportunity of putting the question might not easily offer; so I risked asking it on our way back to the house.

"Now that you are kind enough to tell me we have understood each other, Miss Halcombe," I said; "now that you are sure of my gratitude for your forbearance and my obedience to your wishes, may I venture to ask who" — (I hesitated; I had forced myself to think of him, but it was harder still to speak of him, as her promised husband) "who the gentleman engaged to Miss Fairlie, is?"

Her mind was evidently occupied with the message she had received from her sister. She answered, in a hasty, absent way:

"A gentleman of large property, in Hampshire."

Hampshire! Anne Catherick's native place. Again, and yet again, the woman in white. There *was* a fatality in it.

"And his name?" I said, as quietly and indifferently as I could.

"Sir Percival Glyde."

Sir — Sir Percival! Anne Catherick's question — that

suspicious question about the men of the rank of Baronet whom I might happen to know — had hardly been dismissed from my mind by Miss Halcombe's return to me in the summer-house, before it was recalled again by her own answer. I stopped suddenly, and looked at her.

"Sir Percival Glyde," she repeated, imagining that I had not heard her former reply.

"Knight, or Barónet?" I asked, with an agitation that I could hide no longer.

She paused for a moment, and then answered, rather coldly:

"Baronet, of course."

XI.

Not a word more was said, on cither side, as we walked back to the house. Miss Halcombe hastened immediately to her sister's room; and I withdrew to my studio to set in order all of Mr. Fairlie's drawings that I had not yet mounted and restored before I resigned them to the care of other hands. Thoughts that I had hitherto restrained, thoughts that made my position harder than ever to endure, crowded on me now that I was alone.

She was engaged to be married; and her future husband was Sir Percival Glyde. A man of the rank of baronet, and the owner of property in Hampshire.

There were hundreds of baronets in England, and dozens of landowners in Hampshire. Judging by the ordinary rules of evidence, I had not the shadow of a reason, thus far, for connecting Sir Percival Glyde with the suspicious words of inquiry that had been spoken to me by the woman in white. And yet, I did connect him with them. Was it because he had now become associated in my mind with Miss Fairlie; Miss Fairlie being in her turn, associated with Anne Catherick, since the night when I had discovered the ominous likeness between them? Had the events of the morning so unnerved me already that I was at the mercy of any delusion which common chances and common coincidences might suggest to my imagination? Impossible to say. I could only feel that what had passed between Miss Halcombe and myself, on our way from the summer-house, had affected me very strangely. The foreboding of some undiscoverable danger lying hid from us all in the darkness of the future, was strong on me. The doubt whether I was not linked already to a chain of events which even my approaching departure from Cumberland would be powerless to snap asunder—the doubt whether we any of us saw the end as the end would really be — gathered more and more darkly over my mind. Poignant as it was, the sense of suffering caused by the miserable end of my brief, presumptuous love, seemed to be blunted and deadened by the still stronger sense of something obscurely impending, something invisibly threatening, that Time was holding over our heads.

I had been engaged with the drawings little more than half an hour, when there was a knock at the door. It opened, on my answering; and, to my surprise, Miss Halcombe entered the room.

Her manner was angry and agitated. She caught up a chair for herself, before I could give her one; and sat down in it, close at my side.

"Mr. Hartright," she said, "I had hoped that all painful subjects of conversation were exhausted between us, for to-day at least. But it is not to be so. There is some underhand villany at work to frighten my sister about her approaching marriage. You saw me send the gardener on to the house, with a letter addressed, in a strange handwriting, to Miss Fairlie?"

"Certainly."

"That letter is an anonymous letter — a vile attempt to injure Sir Percival Glyde in my sister's estimation. It has so agitated and alarmed her that I have had the greatest possible difficulty in composing her spirits sufficiently to allow me to leave her room and come here. I know this is a family matter on which I ought not to consult you, and in which you can feel no concern or interest —"

"I beg your pardon, Miss Halcombe. I feel the strongest possible concern and interest in anything that affects Miss Fairlie's happiness or yours."

"I am glad to hear you say so. You are the only person in the house, or out of it, who can advise me. Mr. Fairlie, in his state of health and with his horror of difficulties and mysteries of all kinds, is not to be thought of. The clergyman is a good, weak man, who knows nothing out of the routine of his duties; and our neighbours are just the sort of comfortable, jogtrot acquaintances whom one cannot disturb in times of trouble and danger. What I want to know is this: ought I, at once, to take such steps as I can to discover the writer of the letter? or ought I to wait, and apply to Mr. Fairlie's legal adviser to-morrow? It is a question — perhaps a very important one — of gaining or losing a day. Tell me what you think, Mr. Hartright. If necessity had not already obliged me to take you into my confidence under very delicate circumstances, even my helpless situation would, perhaps, be no excuse for me. But, as things are, I cannot surely be wrong, after all that has passed between us, in forgetting that you are a friend of only three months' standing."

She gave me the letter. It began abruptly, without any preliminary form of address, as follows:

"Do you believe in dreams? I hope, for your own sake, that you do. See what Scripture says about dreams and their fulfilment (Genesis xl. 8., xli. 25; Daniel iv. 18-25); and take the warning I send you before it is too late.

"Last night, I dreamed about you, Miss Fairlie. I dreamed that I was standing inside the communion rails of a church: I on one side of the altar-table, and the clergyman, with his surplice and his prayer-book, on the other.

"After a time, there walked towards us, down the aisle of the church, a man and a woman, coming to be married. You were the woman. You looked so pretty and innocent in your beautiful white silk dress, and your long white lace veil, that my heart felt for you and the tears came into my eyes.

"They were tears of pity, young lady, that heaven blesses; and, instead of falling from my eyes like the every-day tears that we all of us shed, they turned into two rays of light which slanted nearer and nearer to the man standing at the altar with you, till they touched his breast. The two rays sprang in arches like two rainbows, between me and him. I looked along them; and I saw down into his inmost heart.

"The outside of the man you were marrying was fair enough to see. He was neither tall, nor short — he was a little below the middle size. A light, active, high-spirited man — about five-and-forty years old, to look at. He had a pale face, and was bald over the forehead, but had dark hair on the rest of his head. His beard was shaven on his chin, but was let to grow, of a fine rich brown, on his cheeks and his upper lip. His eyes were brown too, and very bright; his nose straight and handsome and delicate enough to have done for a woman's. His hands the same. He was troubled from time to time with a dry hacking cough; and when he put up his white right hand to his mouth, he showed the red scar of an old wound across the back of it. Have I dreamt of the right man? You know best, Miss Fairlie; and you can say if I was deceived or not. Read, next, what I saw beneath the outside — I entreat you, read, and profit.

"I looked along the two rays of light; and I saw down into his inmost heart. It was black as night; and on it were written, in the red flaming letters which are the handwriting of the fallen angel: 'Without pity and without remorse. He has strewn with misery the paths of others, and he will live to strew with misery the path of this woman by his side.' I read that; and then the rays of light shifted and pointed over his shoulder; and there, behind him, stood a fiend, laughing. And the rays of light shifted once more, and pointed over your shoulder; and there, behind you, stood an angel weeping. And the rays of light shifted for the third time, and pointed straight between you and that man. They widened and widened, thrusting you both asunder, one from the other. And the clergyman looked for the marriage-service in vain: it was gone out of the book, and he shut up the leaves, and put it from him in despair. And I woke with my eyes full of tears and my heart beating — for *I* believe in dreams.

"Believe, too, Miss Fairlie — I beg of you, for your own sake, believe as I do. Joseph and Daniel, and others in Scripture, believed in dreams. Inquire into the past life of that man with the scar on his hand, before you say the words that make you his miserable wife. I don't give you this warning on my account, but on yours. I have an interest in your well-being that will live as long as I draw breath. Your mother's daughter has a tender place in my heart — for your mother was my first, my best, my only friend."

There, the extraordinary letter ended, without signature of any sort.

The handwriting afforded no prospect of a clue. It was traced on ruled lines, in the cramped, conventional, copybook character, technically termed "small hand." It was feeble and faint, and defaced by blots, but had otherwise nothing to distinguish it.

"'That is not an illiterate letter," said Miss Halcombe, "and, at the same time, it is surely too incoherent to be the letter of an educated person in the higher ranks of life. The reference to the bridal dress and veil, and other little expressions, seem to point to it as the production of some woman. What do you think, Mr. Hartright?"

"I think so too. It seems to me to be not only the letter of a woman, but of a woman whose mind must be —"

"Deranged?" suggested Miss Halcombe. "It struck me in that light, too."

I did not answer. While I was speaking, my eyes rested on the last sentence of the letter: "Your mother's daughter has a tender place in my heart — for your mother was my first, my best, my only friend." Those words and the doubt which had just escaped me as to the sanity of the writer of the letter, acting together on my mind, suggested an idea, which I was

literally afraid to express openly, or even to encourage secretly. I began to doubt whether my own faculties were not
in danger of losing their balance. It seemed almost like a
monomania to be tracing back everything strange that happened, everything unexpected that was said, always to the
same hidden source and the same sinister influence. I resolved, this time, in defence of my own courage and my own
sense, to come to no decision that plain fact did not warrant,
and to turn my back resolutely on everything that tempted me
in the shape of surmise.

"If we have any chance of tracing the person who has
written this," I said, returning the letter to Miss Halcombe,
"there can be no harm in seizing our opportunity the moment
it offers. I think we ought to speak to the gardener again
about the elderly woman who gave him the letter, and then to
continue our inquiries in the village. But first let me ask a
question. You mentioned just now the alternative of consulting Mr. Fairlie's legal adviser to-morrow. Is there no possibility of communicating with him earlier? Why not to-
day?"

"I can only explain," replied Miss Halcombe, "by entering
into certain particulars, connected with my sister's marriage
engagement, which I did not think it necessary or desirable to
mention to you this morning. One of Sir Percival Glyde's
objects in coming here, on Monday, is to fix the period of his
marriage, which has hitherto been left quite unsettled. He is
anxious that the event should take place before the end of the
year."

"Does Miss Fairlie know of that wish?" I asked, eagerly.

"She has no suspicion of it; and, after what has happened,
I shall not take the responsibility upon myself of enlightening
her. Sir Percival has only mentioned his views to Mr. Fairlie,
who has told me himself that he is ready and anxious, as
Laura's guardian, to forward them. He has written to
London, to the family solicitor, Mr. Gilmore. Mr. Gilmore
happens to be away in Glasgow on business; and he has replied by proposing to stop at Limmeridge House, on his way

back to town. He will arrive to-morrow, and will stay with us a few days, so as to allow Sir Percival time to plead his own cause. If he succeeds, Mr. Gilmore will then return to London, taking with him his instructions for my sister's marriage-settlement. You understand now, Mr. Hartright, why I speak of waiting to take legal advice until to-morrow? Mr. Gilmore is the old and tried friend of two generations of Fairlies; and we can trust him, as we could trust no one else."

The marriage-settlement! The mere hearing of those two words stung me with a jealous despair that was poison to my higher and better instincts. I began to think — it is hard to confess this, but I must suppress nothing from beginning to end of the terrible story that I now stand committed to reveal — I began to think, with a hateful eagerness of hope, of the vague charges against Sir Percival Glyde which the anonymous letter contained. What if those wild accusations rested on a foundation of truth? What if their truth could be proved before the fatal words of consent were spoken, and the marriage-settlement was drawn? I have tried to think, since, that the feeling which then animated me began and ended in pure devotion to Miss Fairlie's interests. But I have never succeeded in deceiving myself into believing it; and I must not now attempt to deceive others. The feeling began and ended in reckless, vindictive, hopeless hatred of the man who was to marry her.

"If we are to find out anything," I said, speaking under the new influence which was now directing me, "we had better not let another minute slip by us unemployed. I can only suggest, once more, the propriety of questioning the gardener a second time, and of inquiring in the village immediately afterwards."

"I think I may be of help to you in both cases," said Miss Halcombe, rising. "Let us go, Mr. Hartright, at once, and do the best we can together."

I had the door in my hand to open it for her — but I
6*

stopped, on a sudden, to ask an important question before we set forth.

"One of the paragraphs of the anonymous letter," I said, "contains some sentences of minute personal description. Sir Percival Glyde's name is not mentioned, I know — but does that description at all resemble him?"

"Accurately; even in stating his age to be forty-five —"

Forty-five; and she was not yet twenty-one! Men of his age married wives of her age every day: and experience had shown those marriages to be often the happiest ones. I knew that — and yet even the mention of his age, when I contrasted it with hers, added to my blind hatred and distrust of him.

"Accurately," Miss Halcombe continued, "even to the scar on his right hand, which is the scar of a wound that he received years since when he was travelling in Italy. There can be no doubt that every peculiarity of his personal appearance is thoroughly well known to the writer of the letter."

"Even a cough that he is troubled with is mentioned if I remember right?"

"Yes, and mentioned correctly. He treats it lightly himself, though it sometimes makes his friends anxious about him."

"I suppose no whispers have ever been heard against his character?"

"Mr. Hartright! I hope you are not unjust enough to let that infamous letter influence you?"

I felt the blood rush into my cheeks, for I knew that it *had* influenced me.

"I hope not," I answered, confusedly. "Perhaps I had no right to ask the question."

"I am not sorry you asked it," she said, "for it enables me to do justice to Sir Percival's reputation. Not a whisper, Mr. Hartright, has ever reached me, or my family, against him. He has fought successfully two contested elections; and has come out of the ordeal unscathed. A man who can do that, in England, is a man whose character is established."

I opened the door for her in silence, and followed her out. She had not convinced me. If the recording angel had come down from heaven to confirm her, and had opened his book to my mortal eyes, the recording angel would not have convinced me.

We found the gardener at work as usual. No amount of questioning could extract a single answer of any importance from the lad's impenetrable stupidity. The woman who had given him the letter was an elderly woman; she had not spoken a word to him; and she had gone away towards the south in a great hurry. That was all the gardener could tell us.

The village lay southward of the house. So to the village we went next.

XII.

Our inquiries at Limmeridge were patiently pursued in all directions, and among all sorts and conditions of people. But nothing came of them. Three of the villagers did certainly assure us that they had seen the woman; but as they were quite unable to describe her, and quite incapable of agreeing about the exact direction in which she was proceeding when they last saw her, these three bright exceptions to the general rule of total ignorance afforded no more real assistance to us than the mass of their unhelpful and unobservant neighbours.

The course of our useless investigations brought us, in time, to the end of the village, at which the schools established by Mrs. Fairlie were situated. As we passed the side of the building appropriated to the use of the boys, I suggested the propriety of making a last inquiry of the schoolmaster, whom we might presume to be, in virtue of his office, the most intelligent man in the place.

"I am afraid the schoolmaster must have been occupied with his scholars," said Miss Halcombe, "just at the time when the woman passed through the village, and returned again. However we can but try."

We entered the playground enclosure, and walked by the school room window, to get round to the door, which was situated at the back of the building. I stopped for a moment at the window and looked in.

The schoolmaster was sitting at his high desk, with his back to me, apparently haranguing the pupils, who were all gathered together in front of him, with one exception. The one exception was a sturdy white-headed boy, standing apart from all the rest on a stool in a corner—a forlorn little Crusoe, isolated in his own desert island of solitary penal disgrace.

The door, when we got round to it, was ajar; and the schoolmaster's voice reached us plainly, as we both stopped for a minute under the porch.

"Now, boys," said the voice, "mind what I tell you. If I hear another word spoken about ghosts in this school, it will be the worst for all of you. There are no such things as ghosts; and, therefore, any boy who believes in ghosts believes in what can't possibly be; and a boy who belongs to Limmeridge School, and believes in what can't possibly be, sets up his back against reason and discipline, and must be punished accordingly. You all see Jacob Postlethwaite standing up on the stool there in disgrace. He has been punished, not because he said he saw a ghost last night, but because he is too impudent and too obstinate to listen to reason; and because he persists in saying he saw the ghost after I have told him that no such thing can possibly be. If nothing else will do, I mean to cane the ghost out of Jacob Postlethwaite; and if the thing spreads among any of the rest of you, I mean to go a step farther, and cane the ghost out of the whole school."

"We seem to have chosen an awkward moment for our visit," said Miss Halcombe, pushing open the door at the end of the schoolmaster's address, and leading the way in.

Our appearance produced a strong sensation among the boys. They appeared to think that we had arrived for the express purpose of seeing Jacob Postlethwaite caned.

"Go home all of you to dinner," said the schoolmaster, "except Jacob. Jacob must stop where he is; and the ghost may bring him his dinner, if the ghost pleases."

Jacob's fortitude deserted him at the double disappearance of his schoolfellows and his prospect of dinner. He took his hands out of his pockets, looked hard at his knuckles, raised them with great deliberation to his eyes, and, when they got there, ground them round and round slowly, accompanying the action by short spasms of sniffing, which followed each other at regular intervals — the nasal minute guns of juvenile distress.

"We came here to ask you a question, Mr. Dempster," said Miss Halcombe, addressing the schoolmaster; "and we little expected to find you occupied in exorcising a ghost. What does it all mean? What has really happened?"

"That wicked boy has been frightening the whole school, Miss Halcombe, by declaring that he saw a ghost yesterday evening," answered the master. "And he still persists in his absurd story, in spite of all that I can say to him."

"Most extraordinary," said Miss Halcombe. "I should not have thought it possible that any of the boys had imagination enough to see a ghost. This is a new accession indeed to the hard labour of forming the youthful mind at Limmeridge — and I heartily wish you well through it, Mr. Dempster. In the mean time, let me explain why you see me here, and what it is I want."

She then put the same question to the schoolmaster, which we had asked already of almost every one else in the village. It was met by the same discouraging answer. Mr. Dempster had not set eyes on the stranger of whom we were in search.

"We may as well return to the house, Mr. Hartright," said Miss Halcombe; "the information we want is evidently not to be found."

She had bowed to Mr. Dempster, and was about to leave the schoolroom, when the forlorn position of Jacob Postle-thwaite, piteously sniffing on the stool of penitence, attracted her attention as she passed him, and made her stop good-humouredly to speak a word to the little prisoner before she opened the door.

"You foolish boy," she said, "why don't you beg Mr. Dempster's pardon, and hold your tongue about the ghost?"

"Eh!—but I saw t' ghaist," persisted Jacob Postlethwaite, with a stare of terror and a burst of tears.

"Stuff and nonsense! You saw nothing of the kind. Ghost indeed! What ghost—"

"I beg you pardon, Miss Halcombe," interposed the schoolmaster, a little uneasily—"but I think you had better not question the boy. The obstinate folly of his story is beyond all belief; and you might lead him into ignorantly—"

"Ignorantly, what?" inquired Miss Halcombe, sharply.

"Ignorantly shocking your feelings," said Mr. Dempster, looking very much discomposed.

"Upon my word, Mr. Dempster, you pay my feelings a great compliment in thinking them weak enough to be shocked by such an urchin as that!" She turned with an air of satirical defiance to little Jacob, and began to question him directly. "Come!" she said; "I mean to know all about this. You naughty boy, when did you see the ghost!"

"Yester e'en, at the gloaming," replied Jacob.

"Oh! you saw it yesterday evening, in the twilight? And what was it like?"

"Arl in white—as a ghaist should be," answered the ghost-seer, with a confidence beyond his years.

"And where was it?"

"Away yander, in t' kirkyard—where a ghaist ought to be."

"As a 'ghaist' should be—where a 'ghaist' ought to be—why, you little fool, you talk as if the manners and customs of ghosts had been familiar to you from your infancy! You have got your story at your fingers' end, at any rate. I suppose I shall hear next that you can actually tell me whose ghost it was?"

"Eh! but I just can," replied Jacob, nodding his head with an air of gloomy triumph.

Mr. Dempster had already tried several times to speak, while Miss Halcombe was examining his pupil; and he now interposed resolutely enough to make himself heard.

"Excuse me, Miss Halcombe," he said, "if I venture to say that you are only encouraging the boy by asking him these questions."

"I will merely ask one more, Mr. Dempster, and then I shall be quite satisfied. Well," she continued, turning to the boy, "and whose ghost was it?"

"T' ghaist of Mistress Fairlie," answered Jacob in a whisper.

The effect which this extraordinary reply produced on Miss Halcombe fully justified the anxiety which the schoolmaster had shown to prevent her from hearing it. Her face crimsoned with indignation — she turned upon little Jacob with an angry suddenness which terrified him into a fresh burst of tears — opened her lips to speak to him — then controlled herself — and addressed the master instead of the boy.

"It is useless," she said, "to hold such a child as that responsible for what he says. I have little doubt that the idea has been put into his head by others. If there are people in this village, Mr. Dempster, who have forgotten the respect and gratitude due from every soul in it to my mother's memory, I will find them out; and, if I have any influence with Mr. Fairlie, they shall suffer for it."

"I hope — indeed, I am sure, Miss Halcombe — that you are mistaken," said the schoolmaster. "The matter begins and ends with the boy's own perversity and folly. He saw, or thought he saw, a woman in white, yesterday evening, as he was passing the churchyard; and the figure, real or fancied, was standing by the marble cross, which he and every one else in Limmeridge knows to be the monument over Mrs. Fairlie's grave. These two circumstances are surely sufficient to have suggested to the boy himself the answer which has so naturally shocked you?"

Although Miss Halcombe did not seem to be convinced, she evidently felt that the schoolmaster's statement of the case was too sensible to be openly combated. She merely replied by thanking him for his attention, and by promising to see him again when her doubts were satisfied. This said, she bowed, and led the way out of the schoolroom.

Throughout the whole of this strange scene, I had stood apart, listening attentively, and drawing my own conclusions. As soon as we were alone again, Miss Halcombe asked me if I had formed any opinion on what I had heard.

"A very strong opinion," I answered; "the boy's story, as I believe, has a foundation in fact. I confess I am anxious to see the monument over Mrs. Fairlie's grave, and to examine the ground about it."

"You shall see the grave."

She paused after making that reply, and reflected a little as we walked on. "What has happened in the schoolroom," she resumed, "has so completely distracted my attention from the subject of the letter, that I feel a little bewildered when I try to return to it. Must we give up all idea of making any further inquiries, and wait to place the thing in Mr. Gilmore's hands, to-morrow?"

"By no means, Miss Halcombe. What has happened in the schoolroom encourages me to persevere in the investigation."

"Why does it encourage you?"

"Because it strengthens a suspicion I felt, when you gave me the letter to read."

"I suppose you had your reasons, Mr. Hartright, for concealing that suspicion from me till this moment?"

"I was afraid to encourage it in myself. I thought it was utterly preposterous — I distrusted it as the result of some perversity in my own imagination. But I can do so no longer. Not only the boy's own answers to your questions, but even a chance expression that dropped from the schoolmaster's lips in explaining his story, have forced the idea back into my mind. Events may yet prove that idea to be a delusion, Miss Halcombe; but the belief is strong in me, at this moment, that the fancied ghost in the churchyard, and the writer of the anonymous letter, are one and the same person."

She stopped, turned pale, and looked me eagerly in the face.

"What person?"

"The schoolmaster unconsciously told you. When he spoke of the figure that the boy saw in the churchyard, he called it 'a woman in white.'"

"Not Anne Catherick!"

"Yes, Anne Catherick."

She put her hand through my arm, and leaned on it heavily.

"I don't know why," she said, in low tones, "but there is something in this suspicion of yours that seems to startle and unnerve me. I feel——" She stopped, and tried to laugh it off. "Mr. Hartright," she went on, "I will show you the grave, and then go back at once to the house. I had better not leave Laura too long alone. I had better go back, and sit with her."

We were close to the churchyard when she spoke. The church, a dreary building of gray stone, was situated in a little valley, so as to be sheltered from the bleak winds blowing over the moorland all round it. The burial-ground advanced, from the side of the church, a little way up the slope of the hill. It was surrounded by a rough, low stone wall, and was bare and open to the sky, except at one extremity, where a brook trickled down the stony hill side, and a clump of dwarf trees threw their narrow shadows over the short, meagre grass. Just beyond the brook and the trees, and not far from one of the three stone stiles which afforded entrance, at various points, to the churchyard, rose the white marble cross that distinguished Mrs. Fairlie's grave from the humbler monuments scattered about it.

"I need go no farther with you," said Miss Halcombe,

pointing to the grave. "You will let me know if you find anything to confirm the idea you have just mentioned to me. Let us meet again at the house."

She left me. I descended at once to the churchyard, and crossed the stile which led directly to Mrs. Fairlie's grave.

The grass about it was too short, and the ground too hard, to show any marks of footsteps. Disappointed thus far, I next looked attentively at the cross, and at the square block of marble below it, on which the inscription was cut.

The natural whiteness of the cross was a little clouded, here and there, by weather-stains; and rather more than one half of the square block beneath it, on the side which bore the inscription, was in the same condition. The other half, however, attracted my attention at once by its singular freedom from stain or impurity of any kind. I looked closer, and saw that it had been cleaned — recently cleaned, in a downward direction from top to bottom. The boundary line between the part that had been cleaned and the part that had not, was traceable wherever the inscription left a blank space of marble — sharply traceable as a line that had been produced by artificial means. Who had begun the cleansing of the marble, and who had left it unfinished?

I looked about me, wondering how the question was to be solved. No sign of a habitation could be discerned from the point at which I was standing: the burial-ground was left in the lonely possession of the dead. I returned to the church, and walked round it till I came to the back of the building; then crossed the boundary wall beyond, by another of the stone stiles; and found myself at the head of a path leading down into a deserted stone quarry. Against one side of the quarry a little two room cottage was built; and just outside the door an old woman was engaged in washing.

I walked up to her, and entered into conversation about the church and burial-ground. She was ready enough to talk; and almost the first words she said informed me that her husband filled the two offices of clerk and sexton. I said a few words next in praise of Mrs. Fairlie's monument. The old woman shook her head, and told me I had not seen it at its best. It was her husband's business to look after it; but he had been so ailing and weak, for months and months past, that he had hardly been able to crawl into church on Sundays to do his duty; and the monument had been neglected in consequence. He was getting a little better now; and, in a week or ten days' time, he hoped to be strong enough to set to work and clean it.

This information — extracted from a long rambling answer, in the broadest Cumberland dialect — told me all that I most wanted to know. I gave the poor woman a trifle, and returned at once to Limmeridge House.

The partial cleansing of the monument had evidently been accomplished by a strange hand. Connecting what I had discovered, thus far, with what I had suspected after hearing the story of the ghost seen at twilight, I wanted nothing more to confirm my resolution to watch Mrs. Fairlie's grave, in secret, that evening; returning to it at sunset, and waiting within sight of it till the night fell. The work of cleansing the monument had been left unfinished; and the person by whom it had been begun might return to complete it.

On getting back to the house, I informed Miss Halcombe of what I intended to do. She looked surprised and uneasy, while I was explaining my purpose; but she made no positive objection to the execution of it. She only said, "I hope it may end well." Just as she was leaving me again, I stopped her to inquire, as calmly as I could, after Miss Fairlie's health. She was in better spirits; and Miss Halcombe hoped she might be induced to take a little walking exercise while the afternoon sun lasted.

I returned to my own room, to resume setting the drawings in order. It was necessary to do this, and doubly necessary to keep my mind employed on anything that would help to distract my attention from myself, and from the hopeless future that lay before me. From time to time, I paused in my work to look out of window and watch the sky as the sun sank nearer and nearer to the horizon. On one of those occasions

I saw a figure on the broad gravel walk under my window. It was Miss Fairlie.

I had not seen her since the morning; and I had hardly spoken to her then. Another day at Limmeridge was all that remained to me; and after that day my eyes might never look on her again. This thought was enough to hold me at the window. I had sufficient consideration for her, to arrange the blind so that she might not see me if she looked up; but I had no strength to resist the temptation of letting my eyes, at least, follow her as far as they could on her walk.

She was dressed in a brown cloak, with a plain black silk gown under it. On her head was the same simple straw hat which she had worn on the morning when we first met. A veil was attached to it now, which hid her face from me. By her side, trotted a little Italian greyhound, the pet companion of all her walks, smartly dressed in a scarlet cloth wrapper, to keep the sharp air from his delicate skin. She did not seem to notice the dog. She walked straight forward, with her head drooping a little, and her arms folded in her cloak. The dead leaves which had whirled in the wind before me, when I had heard of her marriage engagement in the morning, whirled in the wind before her, and rose and fell and scattered themselves at her feet, as she walked on in the pale waning sunlight. The dog shivered and trembled, and pressed against her dress impatiently for notice and encouragement. But she never heeded him. She walked on, farther and farther away from me, with the dead leaves whirling about her on the path — walked on, till my aching eyes could see her no more, and I was left alone again with my own heavy heart.

In another hour's time, I had done my work, and the sunset was at hand. I got my hat and coat in the hall, and slipped out of the house without meeting any one.

The clouds were wild in the western heaven, and the wind blew chill from the sea. Far as the shore was, the sound of the surf swept over the intervening moorland, and beat drearily in my ears, when I entered the churchyard. Not a living creature was in sight. The place looked lonelier than ever, as I chose my position, and waited and watched, with my eyes on the white cross that rose over Mrs. Fairlie's grave.

XIII

THE exposed situation of the churchyard had obliged me to be cautious in choosing the position that I was to occupy.

The main entrance to the church was on the side next to the burial-ground; and the door was screened by a porch walled in on either side. After some little hesitation, caused by natural reluctance to conceal myself, indispensable as that concealment was to the object in view, I had resolved on entering the porch. A loophole window was pierced in each of its side walls. Through one of these windows I could see Mrs. Fairlie's grave. The other looked towards the stone quarry in which the sexton's cottage was built. Before me, fronting the porch entrance, was a patch of bare burial-ground, a line of low stone wall, and a strip of lonely brown hill, with the sunset clouds sailing heavily over it before the strong, steady wind. No living creature was visible or audible — no bird flew by me; no dog barked from the sexton's cottage. The pauses in the dull beating of the surf, were filled up by the dreary rustling of the dwarf trees near the grave, and the cold faint bubble of the brook over its stony bed. A dreary scene and a dreary hour. My spirits sank fast as I counted out the minutes of the evening in my hiding-place under the church porch.

It was not twilight yet — the light of the setting sun still lingered in the heavens, and little more than the first half-hour of my solitary watch had elapsed — when I heard footsteps, and a voice. The footsteps were approaching from the other side of the church; and the voice was a woman's.

"Don't you fret, my dear, about the letter," said the voice. "I gave it to the lad quite safe, and the lad he took it from me without a word. He went his way and I went mine; and not a living soul followed me, afterwards — that I'll warrant."

These words strung up my attention to a pitch of expectation that was almost painful. There was a pause of silence, but the footsteps still advanced. In another moment, two persons, both women, passed within my range of view from the porch window. They were walking straight towards the grave; and therefore they had their backs turned towards me.

One of the women was dressed in a bonnet and shawl. The other wore a long travelling-cloak of a dark blue colour, with the hood drawn over her head. A few inches of her gown were visible below the cloak. My heart beat fast as I noted the colour — it was white.

After advancing about half-way between the church and the grave, they stopped; and the woman in the cloak turned her head towards her companion. But her side face, which a bonnet might now have allowed me to see, was hidden by the heavy, projecting edge of the hood.

"Mind you keep that comfortable warm cloak on," said the same voice which I had already heard — the voice of the woman in the shawl. "Mrs. Todd is right about your looking too particular, yesterday, all in white. I'll walk about a little, while you're here; churchyards being not at all in my way, whatever they may be in yours. Finish what you want to do, before I come back; and let us be sure and get home again before night."

With those words, she turned about, and retracing her steps, advanced with her face towards me. It was the face of an elderly woman, brown, rugged, and healthy, with nothing dishonest or suspicious in the look of it. Close to the church, she stopped to pull her shawl closer round her.

"Queer," she said to herself, "always queer, with her whims and her ways, ever since I can remember her. Harmless, though — as harmless, poor soul, as a little child."

She sighed; looked about the burial-ground nervously; shook her head as if the dreary prospect by no means pleased her; and disappeared round the corner of the church.

I doubted for a moment whether I ought to follow and speak to her, or not. My intense anxiety to find myself face to face with her companion helped me to decide in the negative.

I could ensure seeing the woman in the shawl by waiting near the churchyard until she came back — although it seemed more than doubtful whether she could give me the information of which I was in search. The person who had delivered the letter was of little consequence. The person who had written it was the one centre of interest, and the one source of information; and that person I now felt convinced was before me in the churchyard.

While these ideas were passing through my mind, I saw the woman in the cloak approach close to the grave, and stand looking at it for a little while. She then glanced all round her, and, taking a white linen cloth or handkerchief from under her cloak, turned aside towards the brook. The little stream ran into the churchyard under a tiny archway in the bottom of the wall, and ran out again, after a winding course of a few dozen yards, under a similar opening. She dipped the cloth in the water, and returned to the grave. I saw her kiss the white cross; then kneel down before the inscription, and apply her wet cloth to the cleansing of it.

After considering how I could show myself with the least possible chance of frightening her, I resolved to cross the wall before me, to skirt round it outside, and to enter the churchyard again by the stile near the grave, in order that she might see me as I approached. She was so absorbed over her employment that she did not hear me coming until I had stepped over the stile. Then, she looked up, started to her feet with a faint cry, and stood facing me in speechless and motionless terror.

"Don't be frightened," I said. "Surely, you remember me?"

I stopped while I spoke — then advanced a few steps gently — then stopped again — and so approached by little and little, till I was close to her. If there had been any doubt still left in my mind, it must have been now set at rest. There, speaking affrightedly for itself — there was the same face confronting me over Mrs. Fairlie's grave, which had first looked into mine on the high-road by night.

"You remember me?" I said. "We met very late, and I helped you to find the way to London. Surely you have not forgotten that?"

Her features relaxed, and she drew a heavy breath of relief. I saw the new life of recognition stirring slowly under the deathlike stillness which fear had set on her face.

"Don't attempt to speak to me, just yet," I went on. "Take time to recover yourself — take time to feel quite certain that I am a friend."

"You are very kind to me," she murmured. "As kind now, as you were then."

She stopped, and I kept silence on my side. I was not granting time for composure to her only, I was gaining time also for myself. Under the wan, wild evening light, that woman and I were met together again; a grave between us, the dead about us, the lonesome hills closing us round on every side. The time, the place, the circumstances under which we now stood face to face in the evening stillness of that dreary valley; the life-long interests which might hang suspended on the next chance words that passed between us; the sense that, for aught I knew to the contrary, the whole future of Laura Fairlie's life might be determined, for good or for evil, by my winning or losing the confidence of the forlorn creature who stood trembling by her mother's grave — all threatened to shake the steadiness and the self-control on which every inch of the progress I might yet make now depended. I tried hard, as I felt this, to possess myself of all my resources; I did my utmost to turn the few moments for reflection to the best account.

"Are you calmer, now?" I said, as soon as I thought it time to speak again. "Can you talk to me, without feeling frightened, and without forgetting that I am a friend?"

"How did you come here?" she asked, without noticing what I had just said to her.

"Don't you remember my telling you, when we last met, that I was going to Cumberland? I have been in Cumberland ever since; I have been staying all the time at Limmeridge House."

"At Limmeridge House!" Her pale face brightened as she repeated the words; her wandering eyes fixed on me with a sudden interest. "Ah, how happy you must have been!" she said, looking at me eagerly, without a shadow of its former distrust left in her expression.

I took advantage of her newly-aroused confidence in me, to observe her face, with an attention and a curiosity which I had hitherto restrained myself from showing, for caution's sake. I looked at her, with my mind full of that other lovely face which had so ominously recalled her to my memory on the terrace by moonlight. I had seen Anne Catherick's likeness in Miss Fairlie. I now saw Miss Fairlie's likeness in Anne Catherick — saw it all the more clearly because the points of dissimilarity between the two were presented to me as well as the points of resemblance. In the general outline of the countenance and general proportion of the features; in the colour of the hair and in the little nervous uncertainty about the lips; in the height and size of the figure, and the carriage of the head and body, the likeness appeared even more startling than I had ever felt it to be yét. But there the resemblance ended, and the dissimilarity in details began. The delicate beauty of Miss Fairlie's complexion, the transparent clearness of her eyes, the smooth purity of her skin, the tender bloom of colour on her lips, were all missing from the worn, weary face that was now turned towards mine. Although I hated myself even for thinking such a thing, still, while I looked at the woman before me, the idea would force itself into my mind that one sad change, in the future, was all that was wanting to make the likeness complete, which I now saw to be so imperfect in detail. If ever sorrow and suffering set their profaning marks on the youth and beauty of Miss Fairlie's face, then, and then only, Anne Catherick and she would be the twin-sisters of chance resemblance, the living reflexions of one another.

I shuddered at the thought. There was something horrible

in the blind, unreasoning distrust of the future which the mere passage of it through my mind seemed to imply. It was a welcome interruption to be roused by feeling Anne Catherick's hand laid on my shoulder. The touch was as stealthy and as sudden as that other touch, which had petrified me from head to foot on the night when we first met.

"You are looking at me; and you are thinking of something," she said, with her strange, breathless rapidity of utterance. "What is it?"

"Nothing extraordinary," I answered. "I was only wondering how you came here."

"I came with a friend who is very good to me. I have only been here two days."

"And you found your way to this place yesterday?"

"How do you know that?"

"I only guessed it."

She turned from me, and knelt down before the inscription once more.

"Where should I go, if not here?" she said. "The friend who was better than a mother to me, is the only friend I have to visit at Limmeridge. Oh, it makes my heart ache to see a stain on her tomb! It ought to be kept white as snow, for her sake. I was tempted to begin cleaning it yesterday; and I can't help coming back to go on with it to-day. Is there anything wrong in that? I hope not. Surely nothing can be wrong that I do for Mrs. Fairlie's sake?"

The old grateful sense of her benefactress's kindness was evidently the ruling idea still in the poor creature's mind — the narrow mind which had but too plainly opened to no other lasting impression since that first impression of her younger and happier days. I saw that my best chance of winning her confidence lay in encouraging her to proceed with the artless employment which she had come into the burial-ground to pursue. She resumed it at once, on my telling her she might do so; touching the hard marble as tenderly as if it had been a sentient thing, and whispering the words of the inscription to herself, over and over again, as if the lost days of her girlhood had returned and she was patiently learning her lesson once more at Mrs. Fairlie's knees.

"Should you wonder very much," I said, preparing the way as cautiously as I could for the questions that were to come, "if I owned that it is a satisfaction to me, as well as a surprise, to see you here? I felt very uneasy about you after you left me in the cab."

She looked up quickly and suspiciously.

"Uneasy," she repeated. "Why?"

"A strange thing happened, after we parted, that night. Two men overtook me in a chaise. They did not see where I was standing; but they stopped near me, and spoke to a policeman, on the other side of the way."

She instantly suspended her employment. The hand holding the damp cloth with which she had been cleaning the inscription, dropped to her side. The other hand grasped the marble cross at the head of the grave. Her face turned towards me slowly, with the blank look of terror set rigidly on it once more. I went on at all hazards; it was too late now to draw back.

"The two men spoke to the policeman," I said, "and asked him if he had seen you. He had not seen you; and then one of the men spoke again, and said you had escaped from his Asylum."

She sprang to her feet, as if my last words had set the pursuers on her track.

"Stop! and hear the end," I cried. "Stop! and you shall know how I befriended you. A word from me would have told the men which way you had gone — and I never spoke that word. I helped your escape — I made it safe and certain. Think, try to think. Try to understand what I tell you."

My manner seemed to influence her more than my words. She made an effort to grasp the new idea. Her hands shifted the damp cloth hesitatingly from one to the other, exactly as they had shifted the little travelling-bag on the night when I first saw her. Slowly the purpose of my words seemed to force its way through the confusion and agitation of her mind. Slowly, her features relaxed, and her eyes looked at me with their expression gaining in curiosity what it was fast losing in fear.

"*You* don't think I ought to be back in the Asylum, do you?" she said.

"Certainly not. I am glad you escaped from it; I am glad I helped you."

"Yes, yes; you did help me indeed; you helped me at the hard part," she went on, a little vacantly. "It was easy to escape, or I should not have got away. They never suspected me as they suspected the others. I was so quiet, and so obedient, and so easily frightened. The finding London was the hard part; and there you helped me. Did I thank you at the time? I thank you now, very kindly."

"Was the Asylum far from where you met me? Come! show that you believe me to be your friend, and tell me where it was."

She mentioned the place — a private Asylum, as its situation informed me; a private Asylum not very far from the spot where I had seen her — and then, with evident suspicion of the use to which I might put her answer, anxiously repeated her former inquiry: "*You* don't think I ought to be taken back, do you?"

"Once again, I am glad you escaped; I am glad you prospered well, after you left me," I answered. "You said you had a friend in London to go to. Did you find the friend?"

"Yes. It was very late; but there was a girl up at needlework in the house, and she helped me to rouse Mrs. Clements. Mrs. Clements is my friend. A good, kind woman, but not like Mrs. Fairlie. Ah, no, nobody is like Mrs. Fairlie!"

"Is Mrs. Clements an old friend of yours? Have you known her a long time?"

"Yes; she was a neighbour of ours once, at home, in Hampshire; and liked me, and took care of me when I was a

little girl. Years ago, when she went away from us, she wrote
down in my prayer-book for me, where she was going to live
in London, and she said, 'If you are ever in trouble, Anne,
come to me. I have no husband alive to say me nay, and no
children to look after; and I will take care of you.' Kind
words, were they not? I suppose I remember them because
they were kind. It's little enough I remember besides — little
enough, little enough !"

"Had you no father or mother to take care of you?"

"Father? I never saw him; I never heard mother speak of
him. Father? Ah, dear! he is dead I suppose."

"And your mother?"

"I don't get on well with her. We are a trouble and a fear
to each other."

A trouble and a fear to each other! At those words,
the suspicion crossed my mind for the first time, that her
mother might be the person who had placed her under
restraint.

"Don't ask me about mother," she went on. "I'd rather
talk of Mrs. Clements. Mrs. Clements is like you, she doesn't
think that I ought to be back in the Asylum; and she is as
glad as you are that I escaped from it. She cried over my
misfortune, and said it must be kept secret from everybody."

Her "misfortune." In what sense was she using that word?
In a sense which might explain her motive in writing the anonymous letter? In a sense which might show it to be the too
common and too customary motive that has led many a woman to interpose anonymous hindrances to the marriage of
the man who has ruined her? I resolved to attempt the clearing up of this doubt, before more words passed between us on
either side.

"What misfortune?" I asked.

"The misfortune of my being shut up," she answered,
with every appearance of feeling surprised at my question.
"What other misfortune could there be?"

I determined to persist, as delicately and forbearingly as

possible. It was of very great importance that I should be absolutely sure of every step in the investigation that I now gained in advance.

"There is another misfortune," I said, "to which a woman may be liable, and by which she may suffer life-long sorrow and shame."

"What is it?" she asked, eagerly.

"The misfortune of believing too innocently in her own virtue, and in the faith and honour of the man she loves," I answered.

She looked up at me, with the artless bewilderment of a child. Not the slightest confusion or change of colour; not the faintest trace of any secret consciousness of shame struggling to the surface, appeared in her face — that face which betrayed every other emotion with such transparent clearness. No words that ever were spoken could have assured me, as her look and manner now assured me, that the motive which I had assigned for her writing the letter and sending it to Miss Fairlie was plainly and distinctly the wrong one. That doubt, at any rate, was now set at rest; but the very removal of it opened a new prospect of uncertainty. The letter, as I knew from positive testimony, pointed at Sir Percival Glyde, though it did not name him. She must have had some strong motive, originating in some deep sense of injury, for secretly denouncing him to Miss Fairlie, in such terms as she had employed — and that motive was unquestionably not to be traced to the loss of her innocence and her character. Whatever wrong he might have inflicted on her was not of that nature. Of what nature could it be?

"I don't understand you," she said, after evidently trying hard, and trying in vain to discover the meaning of the words I had last said to her.

"Never mind," I answered. "Let us go on with what we were talking about. Tell me how long you stayed with Mrs. Clements in London, and how you came here."

"How long?" she repeated. "I stayed with Mrs. Clements till we both came to this place, two days ago."

"You are living in the village, then?" I said. "It is strange I should not have heard of you, though you have only been there two days."

"No, no; not in the village. Three miles away at a farm. Do you know the farm? They call it Todd's Corner."

I remembered the place perfectly; we had often passed by it in our drives. It was one of the oldest farms in the neighbourhood, situated in a solitary, sheltered spot, inland at the junction of two hills.

"They are relations of Mrs. Clements at Todd's Corner," she went on, "and they had often asked her to go and see them. She said she would go, and take me with her, for the quiet and the fresh air. It was very kind, was it not? I would have gone anywhere to be quiet, and safe, and out of the way. But when I heard that Todd's Corner was near Limmeridge — oh! I was so happy I would have walked all the way barefoot to get there, and see the schools and the village and Limmeridge House again. They are very good people at Todd's Corner. I hope I shall stay there a long time. There is only one thing I don't like about them, and don't like about Mrs. Clements —"

"What is it?"

"They will tease me about dressing all in white — they say it looks so particular. How do they know? Mrs. Fairlie knew best. Mrs. Fairlie would never have made me wear this ugly blue cloak. Ah! she was fond of white in her lifetime; and here is white stone about her grave — and I am making it whiter for her sake. She often wore white herself; and she always dressed her little daughter in white. Is Miss Fairlie well and happy? Does she wear white now, as she used when she was a girl?"

Her voice sank when she put the questions about Miss Fairlie; and she turned her head farther and farther away from me. I thought I detected, in the alteration of her manner, an uneasy consciousness of the risk she had run in sending the anonymous letter; and I instantly determined so to frame my answer as to surprise her into owning it.

"Miss Fairlie is not very well or very happy this morning," I said.

She murmured a few words; but they were spoken so confusedly, and in such a low tone, that I could not even guess at what they meant.

"Did you ask me why Miss Fairlie was neither well nor happy this morning?" I continued.

"No," she said, quickly and eagerly — "oh, no, I never asked that."

"I will tell you without your asking," I went on. "Miss Fairlie has received your letter."

She had been down on her knees for some little time past, carefully removing the last weather-stains left about the inscription while we were speaking together. The first sentence of the words I had just addressed to her made her pause in her occupation, and turn slowly without rising from her knees, so as to face me. The second sentence literally petrified her. The cloth she had been holding dropped from her hands; her lips fell apart; all the little colour that there was naturally in her face left it in an instant.

"How do you know?" she said, faintly. "Who showed it to you?" The blood rushed back into her face — rushed overwhelmingly, as the sense rushed upon her mind that her own words had betrayed her. She struck her hands together in despair, "I never wrote it," she gasped, affrightedly; "I know nothing about it!"

"Yes," I said, "you wrote it, and you know about it. It was wrong to send such a letter; it was wrong to frighten Miss Fairlie. If you had anything to say that it was right and necessary for her to hear, you should have gone yourself to Limmeridge House; you should have spoken to the young lady with your own lips."

She crouched down over the flat stone of the grave, till her face was hidden on it; and made no reply.

"Miss Fairlie will be as good and kind to you as her mother was, if you mean well," I went on. "Miss Fairlie will keep your secret, and not let you come to any harm. Will you see her to-morrow at the farm? Will you meet her in the garden at Limmeridge House?"

"Oh, if I could die, and be hidden and at rest with *you!*" Her lips murmured the words close on the grave-stone; murmured them in tones of passionate endearment, to the dead remains beneath. "*You* know how I love your child, for your sake! Oh, Mrs. Fairlie! Mrs. Fairlie! tell me how to save her. Be my darling and my mother once more, and tell me what to do for the best."

I heard her lips kissing the stone: I saw her hands beating on it passionately. The sound and the sight deeply affected me. I stooped down, and took the poor helpless hands tenderly in mine, and tried to soothe her.

It was useless. She snatched her hands from me, and never moved her face from the stone. Seeing the urgent necessity of quieting her at any hazard and by any means, I appealed to the only anxiety that she appeared to feel, in connexion with me and with my opinion of her — the anxiety to convince me of her fitness to be mistress of her own actions.

"Come, come," I said, gently. "Try to compose yourself, or you will make me alter my opinion of you. Don't let me think that the person who put you in the Asylum, might have had some excuse —"

The next words died away on my lips. The instant I risked that chance reference to the person who had put her in the Asylum, she sprang up on her knees. A most extraordinary and startling change passed over her. Her face, at all ordinary times so touching to look at, in its nervous sensitiveness, weakness, and uncertainty, became suddenly darkened by an expression of maniacally intense hatred and fear, which communicated a wild, unnatural force to every feature. Her eyes dilated in the dim evening light, like the eyes of a wild animal. She caught up the cloth that had fallen at her side, as if it had been a living creature that she could kill, and crushed it in both her hands with such convulsive strength that the few drops of moisture left in it trickled down on the stone beneath her.

"Talk of something else," she said, whispering through her teeth. "I shall lose myself if you talk of that."

Every vestige of the gentler thoughts which had filled her mind hardly a minute since seemed to be swept from it now. It was evident that the impression left by Mrs. Fairlie's kindness was not, as I had supposed, the only strong impression on her memory. With the grateful remembrance of her school-days at Limmeridge, there existed the vindictive remembrance of the wrong inflicted on her by her confinement in the Asylum. Who had done that wrong? Could it really be her mother?

It was hard to give up pursuing the inquiry to that final point; but I forced myself to abandon all idea of continuing it. Seeing her as I saw her now, it would have been cruel to think of anything but the necessity and the humanity of restoring her composure.

"I will talk of nothing to distress you," I said, soothingly.

"You want something," she answered, sharply and suspiciously. "Don't look at me like that. Speak to me; tell me what you want."

"I only want you to quiet yourself, and, when you are calmer, to think over what I have said."

"Said?" She paused; twisted the cloth in her hands, backwards and forwards; and whispered to herself, "What is it he said?" She turned again towards me, and shook her head impatiently. "Why don't you help me?" she asked, with angry suddenness.

"Yes, yes," I said; "I will help you; and you will soon remember. I asked you to see Miss Fairlie to-morrow, and to tell her the truth about the letter."

"Ah! Miss Fairlie — Fairlie — Fairlie —"

The mere utterance of the loved, familiar name seemed to quiet her. Her face softened and grew like itself again.

"You need have no fear of Miss Fairlie," I continued; "and no fear of getting into trouble through the letter. She knows so much about it already, that you will have no difficulty in telling her all. There can be little necessity for concealment where there is hardly anything left to conceal. You mention no names in the letter; but Miss Fairlie knows that the person you write of is Sir Percival Glyde —"

The instant I pronounced that name she started to her feet; and a scream burst from her that rang through the churchyard and made my heart leap in me with the terror of it. The dark deformity of the expression which had just left her face, lowered on it once more, with doubled and trebled intensity. The shriek at the name, the reiterated look of hatred and fear that instantly followed, told all. Not even a last doubt now remained. Her mother was guiltless of imprisoning her in the Asylum. A man had shut her up — and that man was Sir Percival Glyde.

The scream had reached other ears than mine. On one side, I heard the door of the sexton's cottage open; on the other, I heard the voice of her companion, the woman in the shawl, the woman whom she had spoken of as Mrs. Clements.

"I'm coming! I'm coming!" cried the voice, from behind the clump of dwarf trees.

In a moment more, Mrs. Clements hurried into view.

"Who are you?" she cried, facing me resolutely, as she set her foot on the stile. "How dare you frighten a poor helpless woman like that?"

She was at Anne Catherick's side, and had put one arm around her, before I could answer. "What is it, my dear?" she said. "What has he done to you?"

"Nothing," the poor creature answered. "Nothing. I'm only frightened."

Mrs. Clements turned on me with a fearless indignation, for which I respected her.

"I should be heartily ashamed of myself if I deserved that angry look," I said. "But I do not deserve it. I have unfortunately startled her, without intending it. This is not the first time she has seen me. Ask her yourself, and she will tell you that I am incapable of willingly harming her or any woman."

I spoke distinctly, so that Anne Catherick might hear and understand me: and I saw that the words and their meaning had reached her.

"Yes, yes," she said; "he was good to me once; he helped me —" She whispered the rest into her friend's ear.

"Strange, indeed!" said Mrs. Clements, with a look of perplexity. "It makes all the difference, though. I'm sorry I spoke so rough to you, sir; but you must own that appearances looked suspicious to a stranger. It's more my fault than yours, for humouring her whims, and letting her be alone in such a place as this. Come, my dear — come home now."

I thought the good woman looked a little uneasy at the prospect of the walk back, and I offered to go with them until they were both within sight of home. Mrs. Clements thanked me civilly, and declined. She said they were sure to meet some of the farm-labourers, as soon as they got to the moor.

"Try to forgive me," I said, when Anne Catherick took her friend's arm to go away. Innocent as I had been of any intention to terrify and agitate her, my heart smote me as I looked at the poor, pale, frightened face.

"I will try," she answered. "But you know too much; I'm afraid you'll always frighten me now."

Mrs. Clements glanced at me, and shook her head pityingly.

"Good night, sir," she said. "You couldn't help it, I know; but I wish it was me you had frightened, and not her."

They moved away a few steps. I thought they had left

me; but Anne suddenly stopped, and separated herself from her friend.

"Wait a little," she said. "I must say good-by."

She returned to the grave, rested both hands tenderly on the marble cross, and kissed it.

"I'm better now," she sighed, looking up at me quietly. "I forgive you."

She joined her companion again, and they left the burial-ground. I saw them stop near the church, and speak to the sexton's wife, who had come from the cottage, and had waited, watching us from a distance. Then they went on again up the path that led to the moor. I looked after Anne Catherick as she disappeared, till all trace of her had faded in the twilight — looked as anxiously and sorrowfully as if that was the last I was to see in this weary world of the woman in white.

XIV

Half an hour later, I was back at the house, and was informing Miss Halcombe of all that had happened.

She listened to me from beginning to end, with a steady, silent attention, which, in a woman of her temperament and disposition, was the strongest proof that could be offered of the serious manner in which my narrative affected her.

"My mind misgives me," was all she said when I had done. "My mind misgives me sadly about the future."

"The future may depend," I suggested, "on the use we make of the present. It is not improbable that Anne Catherick may speak more readily and unreservedly to a woman than she has spoken to me. If Miss Fairlie —"

"Not to be thought of for a moment," interposed Miss Halcombe, in her most decided manner.

"Let me suggest, then," I continued, "that you should see Anne Catherick yourself, and do all you can to win her confidence. For my own part, I shrink from the idea of alarming the poor creature a second time, as I have most unhappily alarmed her already. Do you see any objection to accompanying me to the farm-house to-morrow?"

"None whatever. I will go anywhere and do anything to serve Laura's interests. What did you say the place was called?"

"You must know it well. It is called Todd's Corner.'

"Certainly. Todd's Corner is one of Mr. Fairlie's farms. Our dairy-maid here is the farmer's second daughter. She goes backwards and forwards constantly, between this house and her father's farm; and she may have heard or seen something which it may be useful to us to know. Shall I ascertain, at once, if the girl is down stairs?"

She rang the bell, and sent the servant with his message. He returned, and announced that the dairy-maid was then at the farm. She had not been there for the last three days; and the housekeeper had given her leave to go home, for an hour or two, that evening.

"I can speak to her to-morrow," said Miss Halcombe, when the servant had left the room again. "In the mean time, let me thoroughly understand the object to be gained by my interview with Anne Catherick. Is there no doubt in your own mind that the person who confined her in the Asylum was Sir Percival Glyde?"

"There is not the shadow of a doubt. The only mystery that remains, is the mystery of his *motive*. Looking to the great difference between his station in life and hers, which seems to preclude all idea of the most distant relationship between them, it is of the last importance — even assuming that she really required to be placed under restraint — to know why *he* should have been the person to assume the serious responsibility of shutting her up —"

"In a private Asylum, I think you said?"

"Yes, in a private Asylum, where a sum of money which no poor person could afford to give, must have been paid for her maintenance as a patient."

"I see where the doubt lies, Mr. Hartright; and I promise

you that it shall be set at rest, whether Anne Catherick assists us to-morrow or not. Sir Percival Glyde shall not be long in this house without satisfying Mr. Gilmore, and satisfying me. My sister's future is my dearest care in life; and I have influence enough over her to give me some power, where her marriage is concerned, in the disposal of it."

We parted for the night.

After breakfast, the next morning, an obstacle, which the events of the evening before had put out of my memory, interposed to prevent our proceeding immediately to the farm. This was my last day at Limmeridge House; and it was necessary, as soon as the post came in, to follow Miss Halcombe's advice, and to ask Mr. Fairlie's permission to shorten my engagement by a month, in consideration of an unforeseen necessity for my return to London.

Fortunately for the probability of this excuse, so far as appearances were concerned, the post brought me two letters from London friends, that morning. I took them away at once to my own room; and sent the servant with a message to Mr. Fairlie, requesting to know when I could see him on a matter of business.

I awaited the man's return, free from the slightest feeling of anxiety about the manner in which his master might receive my application. With Mr. Fairlie's leave or without it, I must go. The consciousness of having now taken the first step on the dreary journey which was henceforth to separate my life from Miss Fairlie's seemed to have blunted my sensibility to every consideration connected with myself. I had done with my poor man's touchy pride; I had done with all my little artist vanities. No insolence of Mr. Fairlie's, if he chose to be insolent, could wound me now.

The servant returned with a message for which I was not unprepared. Mr. Fairlie regretted that the state of his health, on that particular morning, was such as to preclude all hope of his having the pleasure of receiving me. He begged, therefore, that I would accept his apologies, and kindly communicate what I had to say, in the form of a letter. Similar messages to this, had reached me, at various intervals, during my three months' residence in the house. Throughout the whole of that period, Mr. Fairlie had been rejoiced to "possess" me, but had never been well enough to see me for a second time. The servant took every fresh batch of drawings, that I mounted and restored, back to his master, with my "respects;" and returned empty-handed with Mr. Fairlie's "kind compliments," "best thanks," and "sincere regrets" that the state of his health still obliged him to remain a solitary prisoner in his own room. A more satisfactory arrangement to both sides could not possibly have been adopted. It would be hard to say which of us, under the circumstances, felt the most grateful sense of obligation to Mr. Fairlie's accommodating nerves.

I sat down at once to write the letter, expressing myself in it as civilly, as clearly, and as briefly as possible. Mr. Fairlie did not hurry his reply. Nearly an hour elapsed before the answer was placed in my hands. It was written with beautiful regularity and neatness of character, in violet-coloured ink, on note-paper as smooth as ivory and almost as thick as cardboard; and it addressed me in these terms:—

"Mr. Fairlie's compliments to Mr. Hartright. Mr. Fairlie is more surprised and disappointed than he can say (in the present state of his health) by Mr. Hartright's application. Mr. Fairlie is not a man of business, but he has consulted his steward, who is, and that person confirms Mr. Fairlie's opinion that Mr. Hartright's request to be allowed to break his engagement cannot be justified by any necessity whatever, excepting perhaps a case of life and death. If the highly-appreciative feeling towards Art and its professors, which it is the consolation and happiness of Mr. Fairlie's suffering existence to cultivate, could be easily shaken, Mr. Hartright's present proceeding would have shaken it. It has not done so—except in the instance of Mr. Hartright himself.

"Having stated his opinion—so far, that is to say, as acute

nervous suffering will allow him to state anything — Mr. Fairlie has nothing to add but the expression of his decision, in reference to the highly irregular application that has been made to him. Perfect repose of body and mind being to the last degree important in his case, Mr. Fairlie will not suffer Mr. Hartright to disturb that repose by remaining in the house under circumstances of an essentially irritating nature to both sides. Accordingly, Mr. Fairlie waives his right of refusal, purely with a view to the preservation of his own tranquillity — and informs Mr. Hartright that he may go."

I folded the letter up, and put it away with my other papers. The time had been when I should have resented it as an insult: I accepted it, now, as a written release from my engagement. It was off my mind, it was almost out of my memory, when I went down stairs to the breakfast-room, and informed Miss Halcombe that I was ready to walk with her to the farm.

"Has Mr. Fairlie given you a satisfactory answer?" she asked, as we left the house.

"He has allowed me to go, Miss Halcombe."

She looked up at me quickly; and then, for the first time since I had known her, took my arm of her own accord. No words could have expressed so delicately that she understood how the permission to leave my employment had been granted, and that she gave me her sympathy, not as my superior, but as my friend. I had not felt the man's insolent letter; but I felt deeply the woman's atoning kindness.

On our way to the farm we arranged that Miss Halcombe was to enter the house alone, and that I was to wait outside, within call. We adopted this mode of proceeding from an apprehension that my presence, after what had happened in the churchyard the evening before, might have the effect of renewing Anne Catherick's nervous dread, and of rendering her additionally distrustful of the advances of a lady who was a stranger to her. Miss Halcombe left me, with the intention of speaking, in the first instance, to the farmer's wife (of whose

friendly readiness to help her in any way she was well assured), while I waited for her in the near neighbourhood of
the house.

I had fully expected to be left alone, for some time. To my
surprise, however, little more than five minutes had elapsed,
before Miss Halcombe returned.

"Does Anne Catherick refuse to see you?" I asked, in
astonishment.

"Anne Catherick is gone," replied Miss Halcombe.

"Gone!"

"Gone, with Mrs. Clements. They both left the farm at
eight o'clock this morning."

I could say nothing — I could only feel that our last chance
of discovery had gone with them.

"All that Mrs. Todd knows about her guests, I know," Miss
Halcombe went on; "and it leaves me, as it leaves her, in the
dark. They both came back safe, last night, after they left
you, and they passed the first part of the evening with Mr.
Todd's family, as usual. Just before supper-time, however,
Anne Catherick startled them all by being suddenly seized
with faintness. She had had a similar attack, of a less alarming kind, on the day she arrived at the farm; and Mrs. Todd
had connected it, on that occasion, with something she was
reading at the time in our local newspaper, which lay on the
farm table, and which she had taken up only a minute or two
before."

"Does Mrs. Todd know what particular passage in the
newspaper affected her in that way?" I inquired.

"No," replied Miss Halcombe. "She had looked it over,
and had seen nothing in it to agitate any one. I asked leave,
however, to look it over in my turn; and at the very first page
I opened, I found that the editor had enriched his small stock
of news by drawing upon our family affairs, and had published
my sister's marriage engagement, among his other announce-
ments, copied from the London papers, of Marriages in High
Life. I concluded at once that this was the paragraph which
had so strangely affected Anne Catherick; and I thought I

saw in it, also, the origin of the letter which she sent to our house the next day."

"There can be no doubt in either case. But what did you hear about her second attack of faintness yesterday evening?"

"Nothing. The cause of it is a complete mystery. There was no stranger in the room. The only visitor was our dairy-maid, who, as I told you, is one of Mr. Todd's daughters; and the only conversation was the usual gossip about local affairs. They heard her cry out, and saw her turn deadly pale, without the slightest apparent reason. Mrs. Todd and Mrs. Clements took her up-stairs; and Mrs. Clements remained with her. They were heard talking together until long after the usual bedtime; and, early this morning, Mrs. Clements took Mrs. Todd aside, and amazed her beyond all power of expression, by saying that they must go. The only explanation Mrs. Todd could extract from her guest was, that something had happened, which was not the fault of any one at the farm-house, but which was serious enough to make Anne Catherick resolve to leave Limmeridge immediately. It was quite useless to press Mrs. Clements to be more explicit. She only shook her head, and said that, for Anne's sake, she must beg and pray that no one would question her. All she could repeat, with every appearance of being seriously agitated herself, was that Anne must go, that she must go with her, and that the destination to which they might both betake themselves must be kept a secret from everybody. I spare you the recital of Mrs. Todd's hospitable remonstrances and refusals. It ended in her driving them both to the nearest station, more than three hours since. She tried hard, on the way, to get them to speak more plainly; but without success. And she set them down outside the station-door, so hurt and offended by the unceremonious abruptness of their departure and their unfriendly reluctance to place the least confidence in her, that she drove away in anger, without so much as stopping to bid them good-by. That is exactly what has taken place. Search your own memory, Mr. Hartright, and tell me if anything happened in the burial-ground yesterday evening which can at all account for the extraordinary departure of those two women this morning."

"I should like to account first, Miss Halcombe, for the sudden change in Anne Catherick which alarmed them at the farm-house, hours after she and I had parted, and when time enough had elapsed to quiet any violent agitation that I might have been unfortunate enough to cause. Did you inquire particularly about the gossip which was going on in the room when she turned faint?"

"Yes. But Mrs. Todd's household affairs seem to have divided her attention, that evening, with the talk in the farm-house parlour. She could only tell me that it was 'just the news' — meaning, I suppose, that they all talked as usual about each other."

"The dairymaid's memory may be better than her mother's," I said. "It may be as well for you to speak to the girl, Miss Halcombe, as soon as we get back."

My suggestion was acted on the moment we returned to the house. Miss Halcombe led me round to the servants' offices, and we found the girl in the dairy, with her sleeves tucked up to her shoulders, cleaning a large milk-pan, and singing blithely over her work.

"I have brought this gentleman to see your dairy, Hannah," said Miss Halcombe. "It is one of the sights of the house, and it always does you credit."

The girl blushed and curtseyed, and said, shyly, that she hoped she always did her best to keep things neat and clean.

"We have just come from your father's," Miss Halcombe continued. "You were there yesterday evening, I hear; and you found visitors at the house?"

"Yes, miss."

"One of them was taken faint and ill, I am told? I suppose nothing was said or done to frighten her? You were not talking of anything very terrible were you?"

"Oh, no, miss!" said the girl, laughing. "We were only talking of the news."

"Your sisters told you the news at Todd's Corner, I suppose?"

"Yes, miss."

"And you told them the news at Limmeridge House?"

"Yes, miss. And I'm quite sure nothing was said to frighten the poor thing, for I was talking when she was taken ill. It gave me quite a turn, miss, to see it, never having been taken faint myself."

Before any more questions could be put to her, she was called away to receive a basket of eggs at the dairy door. As she left us, I whispered to Miss Halcombe:

"Ask her if she happened to mention, last night, that visitors were expected at Limmeridge House."

Miss Halcombe showed me, by a look, that she understood, and put the question as soon as the dairymaid returned to us.

"Oh, yes, miss; I mentioned that," said the girl, simply. "The company coming, and the accident to the brindled cow, was all the news I had to take to the farm."

"Did you mention names? Did you tell them that Sir Percival Glyde was expected on Monday?"

"Yes, miss — I told them Sir Percival Glyde was coming. I hope there was no harm in it; I hope I didn't do wrong."

"Oh no, no harm. Come, Mr. Hartright; Hannah will begin to think us in the way, if we interrupt her any longer over her work."

We stopped and looked at one another, the moment we were alone again.

"Is there any doubt in your mind, *now*, Miss Halcombe?"

"Sir Percival Glyde shall remove that doubt, Mr. Hartright — or, Laura Fairlie shall never be his wife."

XV.

As we walked round to the front of the house, a fly from the railway approached us along the drive. Miss Halcombe waited on the door steps until the fly drew up; and then advanced to shake hands with an old gentleman, who got out briskly the moment the steps were let down. Mr. Gilmore had arrived.

I looked at him, when we were introduced to each other, with an interest and a curiosity which I could hardly conceal. This old man was to remain at Limmeridge House after I had left it; he was to hear Sir Percival Glyde's explanation, and was to give Miss Halcombe the assistance of his experience in forming her judgment; he was to wait until the question of the marriage was set at rest; and his hand, if that question were ecided in the affirmative, was to draw the settlement which ound Miss Fairlie irrevocably to her engagement. Even then, when I knew nothing by comparison with what I know now, I looked at the family lawyer with an interest which I had never felt before in the presence of any man breathing who was a total stranger to me.

In external appearance, Mr. Gilmore was the exact opposite of the conventional idea of an old lawyer. His complexion was florid; his white hair was worn rather long and kept carefully brushed; his black coat, waistcoat, and trousers, fitted him with perfect neatness; his white cravat was carefully tied; and his lavender-coloured kid gloves might have adorned the hands of a fashionable clergyman, without fear and without reproach. His manners were pleasantly marked by the formal grace and refinement of the old school of politeness, quickened by the invigorating sharpness and readiness of a man whose business in life obliges him always to keep his faculties in good working order. A sanguine constitution and fair prospects to begin with; a long subsequent career of creditable and comfortable prosperity; a cheerful, diligent, widely-respected old age — such were the general impressions I derived from my introduction to Mr. Gilmore; and it is but fair to him to add, that the knowledge I gained by later and better experience only tended to confirm them.

I left the old gentleman and Miss Halcombe to enter the house together, and to talk of family matters undisturbed by the restraint of a stranger's presence. They crossed the hall on their way to the drawing-room; and I descended the steps again, to wander about the garden alone.

My hours were numbered at Limmeridge House; my departure the next morning was irrevocably settled; my share in the investigation which the anonymous letter had rendered necessary, was at an end. No harm could be done to any one but myself, if I let my heart loose again, for the little time that was left me, from the cold cruelty of restraint which necessity had forced me to inflict upon it, and took my farewell of the scenes which were associated with the brief dream-time of my happiness and my love.

I turned instinctively to the walk beneath my study-window, where I had seen her the evening before with her little dog; and followed the path which her dear feet had trodden so often, till I came to the wicket gate that led into her rose garden. The winter bareness spread drearily over it, now. The flowers that she had taught me to distinguish by their names, the flowers that I had taught her to paint from, were gone; and the tiny white paths that led between the beds, were damp and green already. I went on to the avenue of trees, where we had breathed together the warm fragrance of August evenings; where we had admired together the myriad combinations of shade and sunlight that dappled the ground at our feet. The leaves fell about me from the groaning branches, and the earthy decay in the atmosphere chilled me to the bones. A little farther on, and I was out of the grounds, and following the lane that wound gently upward to the nearest hills. The old felled tree by the wayside, on which we had sat to rest, was sodden with rain; and the tuft of ferns and grasses which I had drawn for her, nestling under the rough stone wall in front of us, had turned to a pool of water, stagnating round an island of draggled weeds. I gained the summit of the hill; and looked at the view which we had so often admired in the happier time.   It was cold and barren — it was no longer the view that I remembered.   The sunshine of her presence was far from me; the charm of her voice no longer murmured in my ear. She had talked to me, on the spot from which I now looked down, of her father, who was her last surviving parent; had told me how fond of each other they had been, and how sadly she missed him still, when she entered certain rooms in the house, and when she took up forgotten occupations and amusements with which he had been associated.   Was the view that I had seen, while listening to those words, the view that I saw now, standing on the hill-top by myself?   I turned, and left it; I wound my way back again, over the moor, and round the sandhills, down to the beach.   There was the white rage of the surf, and the multitudinous glory of the leaping waves — but where was the place on which she had once drawn idle figures with her parasol in the sand; the place where we had sat together, while she talked to me about myself and my home, while she asked me a woman's minutely observant questions about my mother and my sister, and innocently wondered whether I should ever leave my lonely chambers and have a wife and a house of my own?   Wind and wave had long since smoothed out the trace of her which she had left in those marks on the sand.   I looked over the wide monotony of the sea-side prospect, and the place in which we two had idled away the sunny hours, was as lost to me as if I had never known it, as strange to me as if I stood already on a foreign shore.

The empty silence of the beach struck cold to my heart. I returned to the house and the garden, where traces were left to speak of her at every turn.

On the west terrace walk, I met Mr. Gilmore. He was evidently in search of me, for he quickened his pace when we caught sight of each other.   The state of my spirits little fitted me for the society of a stranger.   But the meeting was inevitable; and I resigned myself to make the best of it.

"You are the very person I wanted to see," said the old gentleman.   "I had two words to say to you, my dear sir;

and, if you have no objection, I will avail myself of the present opportunity. To put it plainly, Miss Halcombe and I have been talking over family affairs — affairs which are the cause of my being here — and, in the course of our conversation, she was naturally led to tell me of this unpleasant matter connected with the anonymous letter, and of the share which you have most creditably and properly taken in the proceedings so far. That share, I quite understand, gives you an interest which you might not otherwise have felt, in knowing that the future management of the investigation, which you have begun, will be placed in safe hands. My dear sir, make yourself quite easy on that point — it will be placed in *my* hands."

"You are, in every way, Mr. Gilmore, much fitter to advise and to act in the matter than I am. Is it an indiscretion, on my part, to ask if you have decided yet on a course of proceeding?"

"So far as it is possible to decide, Mr. Hartright, I have decided. I mean to send a copy of the letter, accompanied by a statement of the circumstances, to Sir Percival Glyde's solicitor in London, with whom I have some acquaintance. The letter itself, I shall keep here, to show to Sir Percival as soon as he arrives. The tracing of the two women, I have already provided for, by sending one of Mr. Fairlie's servants — a confidential person — to the station to make inquiries: the man has his money and his directions, and he will follow the women in the event of his finding any clue. This is all that can be done until Sir Percival comes on Monday. I have no doubt myself that every explanation which can be expected from a gentleman and a man of honour, he will readily give. Sir Percival stands very high, sir — an eminent position, a reputation above suspicion — I feel quite easy about results; quite easy, I am rejoiced to assure you. Things of this sort happen constantly in my experience. Anonymous letters — unfortunate woman — sad state of society. I don't deny that there are peculiar complications in this case; but the case itself is, most unhappily, common — common."

"I am afraid, Mr. Gilmore, I have the misfortune to differ from you in the view I take of the case."

"Just so, my dear sir — just so. I am an old man; and I take the practical view. You are a young man; and you take the romantic view. Let us not dispute about our views. I live, professionally, in an atmosphere of disputation, Mr. Hartright; and I am only too glad to escape from it, as I am escaping here. We will wait for events — yes, yes, yes; we will wait for events. Charming place, this. Good shooting? Probably not — none of Mr. Fairlie's land is preserved, I think. Charming place, though; and delightful people. You draw and paint, I hear, Mr. Hartright? Enviable accomplishment. What style?"

We dropped into general conversation — or, rather, Mr. Gilmore talked, and I listened. My attention was far from him, and from the topics on which he discoursed so fluently. The solitary walk of the last two hours had wrought its effect on me — it had set the idea in my mind of hastening my departure from Limmeridge House. Why should I prolong the hard trial of saying farewell by one unnecessary minute? What further service was required of me by any one? There was no useful purpose to be served by my stay in Cumberland; there was no restriction of time in the permission to leave which my employer had granted to me. Why not end it, there and then?

I determined to end it. There were some hours of daylight still left — there was no reason why my journey back to London should not begin on that afternoon. I made the first civil excuse that occurred to me for leaving Mr. Gilmore; and returned at once to the house.

On my way up to my own room, I met Miss Halcombe on the stairs. She saw, by the hurry of my movements and the change in my manner, that I had some new purpose in view; and asked what had happened.

I told her the reasons which induced me to think of hastening my departure, exactly as I have told them here.

"No, no," she said, earnestly and kindly, "leave us like

a friend; break bread with us once more. Stay here and dine; stay here and help us to spend our last evening with you as happily, as like our first evenings, as we can. It is my invitation; Mrs. Vesey's invitation ——" she hesitated a little, and then added, "Laura's invitation as well."

I promised to remain. God knows I had no wish to leave even the shadow of a sorrowful impression with any one of them.

My own room was the best place for me till the dinner bell rang. I waited there till it was time to go down stairs.

I had not spoken to Miss Fairlie — I had not even seen her — all that day. The first meeting with her, when I entered the drawing-room, was a hard trial to her self-control and to mine. She, too, had done her best to make our last evening renew the golden bygone time — the time that could never come again. She had put on the dress which I used to admire more than any other that she possessed — a dark blue silk, trimmed quaintly and prettily with old-fashioned lace; she came forward to meet me with her former readiness; she gave me her hand with the frank, innocént good will of happier days. The cold fingers that trembled round mine; the pale cheeks with a bright red spot burning in the midst of them; the faint smile that struggled to live on her lips and died away from them while I looked at it, told me at what sacrifice of herself her outward composure was maintained. My heart could take her no closer to me, or I should have loved her then as I had never loved her yet.

Mr. Gilmore was a great assistance to us. He was in high good humour, and he led the conversation with unflagging spirit. Miss Halcombe seconded him resolutely; and I did all I could to follow her example. The kind blue eyes whose slightest changes of expression I had learnt to interpret so well, looked at me appealingly when we first sat down to table. Help my sister — the sweet anxious face seemed to say — help my sister, and you will help *me*.

We got through the dinner, to all outward appearance at least, happily enough. When the ladies had risen from table, and when Mr. Gilmore and I were left alone in the dining-room, a new interest presented itself to occupy our attention, and to give me an opportunity of quieting myself by a few minutes of needful and welcome silence. The servant who had been despatched to trace Anne Catherick and Mrs. Clements, returned with his report, and was shown into the dining-room immediately.

"Well," said Mr. Gilmore, "what have you found out?"

"I have found out, sir," answered the man, "that both the women took tickets, at our station here, for Carlisle."

"You went to Carlisle, of course, when you heard that?"

"I did, sir; but I am sorry to say I could find no further trace of them."

"You inquired at the railway?"

"Yes, sir."

"And at the different inns?"

"Yes, sir."

"And you left the statement I wrote for you, at the police station?"

"I did, sir."

"Well, my friend, you have done all you could, and I have done all I could; and there the matter must rest till further notice. We have played our trump cards, Mr. Hart-right," continued the old gentleman, when the servant had withdrawn. "For the present, at least, the women have out-manœuvred us; and our only resource, now, is to wait till Sir Percival Glyde comes here on Monday next. Won't you fill your glass again? Good bottle of port, that — sound, substantial, old wine. I have got better in my own cellar, though."

We returned to the drawing-room — the room in which the happiest evenings of my life had been passed; the room which, after this last night, I was never to see again. Its aspect was altered since the days had shortened and the weather had grown cold. The glass doors on the terrace side were closed, and hidden by thick curtains. Instead of the soft twilight obscurity, in which we used to sit, the bright radiant glow of lamplight now dazzled my eyes. All was changed — in-doors and out, all was changed.

Miss Halcombe and Mr. Gilmore sat down together at the card-table; Mrs. Vesey took her customary chair. There was no restraint on the disposal of *their* evening; and I felt the restraint on the disposal of mine all the more painfully from observing it. I saw Miss Fairlie lingering near the music stand. The time had been when I might have joined her there. I waited irresolutely — I knew neither where to go nor what to do next. She cast one quick glance at me, took a piece of music suddenly from the stand, and came towards me of her own accord.

"Shall I play some of those little melodies of Mozart's, which you used to like so much?" she asked, opening the music nervously, and looking down at it while she spoke.

Before I could thank her, she hastened to the piano. The chair near it, which I had always been accustomed to occupy, stood empty. She struck a few chords — then glanced round at me — then looked back again at her music.

"Won't you take your old place?" she said, speaking very abruptly, and in very low tones.

"I may take it on the last night," I answered.

She did not reply: she kept her attention riveted on the music — music which she knew by memory, which she had played over and over again, in former times, without the book. I only knew that she had heard me, I only knew that she was aware of my being close to her, by seeing the red spot on the cheek that was nearest to me, fade out, and the face grow pale all over.

"I am very sorry you are going," she said, her voice almost sinking to a whisper; her eyes looking more and more intently at the music; her fingers flying over the keys of the piano with a strange feverish energy which I had never noticed in her before.

"I shall remember those kind words, Miss Fairlie, long after to-morrow has come and gone."

The paleness grew whiter on her face, and she turned it farther away from me.

"Don't speak of to-morrow," she said. "Let the music speak to us of to-night, in a happier language than ours."

Her lips trembled — a faint sigh fluttered from them, which she tried vainly to suppress. Her fingers wavered on the piano; she struck a false note; confused herself in trying to set it right; and dropped her hands angrily on her lap. Miss Halcombe and Mr. Gilmore looked up in astonishment from the card-table at which they were playing. Even Mrs. Vesey, dozing in her chair, woke at the sudden cessation of the music, and inquired what had happened.

"You play at whist, Mr. Hartright?" asked Miss Halcombe, with her eyes directed significantly at the place I occupied.

I knew what she meant; I knew she was right; and I rose at once to go to the card-table. As I left the piano, Miss Fairlie turned a page of the music, and touched the keys again with a surer hand.

"I *will* play it," she said, striking the notes almost passionately. "I *will* play it on the last night."

"Come, Mrs. Vesey," said Miss Halcombe; "Mr. Gilmore and I are tired of écarté — come and be Mr. Hartright's partner at whist."

The old lawyer smiled satirically. His had been the winning hand; and he had just turned up a king. He evidently attributed Miss Halcombe's abrupt change in the card-table arrangements to a lady's inability to play the losing game.

The rest of the evening passed without a word or a look from her. She kept her place at the piano; and I kept mine at the card-table. She played unintermittingly — played as if the music was her only refuge from herself. Sometimes, her fingers touched the notes with a lingering fondness, a soft, plaintive, dying tenderness, unutterably beautiful and mournful to hear — sometimes, they faltered and failed her, or hurried over the instrument mechanically as if their task wus a burden to them. But still, change and waver as they might in the expression they imparted to the music, their resolution to play never faltered. She only rose from the piano when we all rose to say good night.

Mrs. Vesey was the nearest to the door, and the first to shake hands with me.

"I shall not see you again, Mr. Hartright," said the old lady. "I am truly sorry you are going away. You have been very kind and attentive; and an old woman, like me, feels kindness and attention. I wish you happy, sir — I wish you a kind good-by."

Mr. Gilmore came next.

"I hope we shall have a future opportunity of bettering our acquaintance, Mr. Hartright. You quite understand about that little matter of business being safe in my hands? Yes, yes, of course. Bless me, how cold it is! Don't let me keep you at the door. Bon voyage, my dear sir — bon voyage, as the French say."

Miss Halcombe followed.

"Half-past seven to-morrow morning," she said; then added, in a whisper, "I have heard and seen more than you think. Your conduct to-night has made me your friend for life."

Miss Fairlie came last. I could not trust myself to look at her, when I took her hand, and when I thought of the next morning.

"My departure must be a very early one," I said. "I shall be gone, Miss Fairlie, before you —"

"No, no," she interposed, hastily; "not before I am out of my room. I shall be down to breakfast with Marian. I am not so ungrateful, not so forgetful of the past three months —"

Her voice failed her; her hand closed gently round mine — then dropped it suddenly. Before I could say, "Good night," she was gone.

The end comes fast to meet me — comes inevitably, as the light of the last morning came at Limmeridge House.

It was barely half-past seven when I went down stairs — but I found them both at the breakfast-table waiting for me. In the chill air, in the dim light, in the gloomy morning silence of the house, we three sat down together, and tried to eat, tried to talk. The struggle to preserve appearances was hopeless and useless; and I rose to end it.

As I held out my hand, as Miss Halcombe, who was nearest to me, took it, Miss Fairlie turned away suddenly, and hurried from the room.

"Better so," said Miss Halcombe, when the door had closed — "better so, for you and for her."

I waited a moment before I could speak — it was hard to lose her, without a parting word, or a parting look. I controlled myself; I tried to take leave of Miss Halcombe in fitting terms; but all the farewell words I would fain have spoken, dwindled to one sentence.

"Have I deserved that you should write to me?" was all I could say.

"You have nobly deserved everything that I can do for you, as long as we both live. Whatever the end is, you shall know it."

"And if I can ever be of help again, at any future time, long after the memory of my presumption and my folly is forgotten —"

I could add no more. My voice faltered, my eyes moistened, in spite of me.

She caught me by both hands — she pressed them with the strong, steady grasp of a man — her dark eyes glittered — her brown complexion flushed deep — the force and energy of her face glowed and grew beautiful with the pure inner light of her generosity and her pity.

"I will trust you — if ever the time comes, I will trust you as *my* friend and *her* friend; as *my* brother and *her* brother." She stopped; drew me nearer to her — the fearless, noble creature — touched my forehead, sisterlike, with her lips; and called me by my Christian name. "God bless you, Walter!" she said. "Wait here alone, and compose yourself

—I had better not stay for both our sakes; I had better see you go from the balcony upstairs."

She left the room. I turned away towards the window, where nothing faced me but the lonely autumn landscape — I turned away to master myself, before I, too, left the room in my turn, and left it for ever.

A minute passed — it could hardly have been more — when I heard the door open again softly; and the rustling of a woman's dress on the carpet, moved towards me. My heart beat violently as I turned round. Miss Fairlie was approaching me from the farther end of the room.

She stopped and hesitated, when our eyes met, and when she saw that we were alone. Then, with that courage which women lose so often in the small emergency, and so seldom in the great, she came on nearer to me, strangely pale and strangely quiet, drawing one hand after her along the table by which she walked, and holding something at her side, in the other, which was hidden by the folds of her dress.

"I only went into the drawing-room," she said, "to look for this. It may remind you of your visit here, and of the friends you leave behind you. You told me I had improved very much when I did it — and I thought you might like —"

She turned her head away, and offered me a little sketch drawn throughout by her own pencil, of the summer-house in which we had first met. The paper trembled in her hand as she held it out to me — trembled in mine, as I took it from her.

I was afraid to say what I felt — I only answered: "It shall never leave me; all my life long it shall be the treasure that I prize most. I am very grateful for it — very grateful to *you*, for not letting me go away without bidding you good-by."

"Oh!" she said, innocently, "how could I let you go, after we have passed so many happy days together!"

"Those days may never return, Miss Fairlie — my way of life and yours are very far apart. But if a time should come,

9*

when the devotion of my whole heart and soul and strength will give you a moment's happiness, or spare you a moment's sorrow, will you try to remember the poor drawing-master who has taught you? Miss Halcombe has promised to trust me — will you promise, too?"

The farewell sadness in the kind-blue eyes shone dimly through her gathering tears.

"I promise it," she said, in broken tones. "Oh don't look at me like that!   I promise it with all my heart."

I ventured a little nearer to her, and held out my hand.

"You have many friends who love you, Miss Fairlie. Your happy future is the dear object of many hopes. May I say, at parting, that it is the dear object of *my* hopes too?"

The tears flowed fast down her cheeks. She rested one trembling hand on the table to steady herself, while she gave me the other. I took it in mine — I held it fast. My head drooped over it, my tears fell on it, my lips pressed it — not in love; oh, not in love, at that last moment, but in the agony and the self-abandonment of despair.

"For God's sake, leave me!" she said faintly.

The confession of her heart's secret burst from her in those pleading words. I had no right to hear them, no right to answer them: they were the words that banished me, in the name of her sacred weakness, from the room. It was all over. I dropped her hand; I said no more. The blinding tears shut her out from my eyes, and I dashed them away to look at her for the last time. One look as she sank into a chair, as her arms fell on the table, as her fair head dropped on them wearily. One farewell look; and the door had closed upon her — the great gulf of separation had opened between us — the image of Laura Fairlie was a memory of the past already.

THE STORY CONTINUED

BY

VINCENT GILMORE,

OF CHANCERY LANE, SOLICITOR.

I.

I write these lines at the request of my friend, Mr. Walter Hartright. They are intended to convey a description of certain events which seriously affected Miss Fairlie's interests, and which took place after the period of Mr. Hartright's departure from Limmeridge House.

There is no need for me to say whether my own opinion does or does not sanction the disclosure of the remarkable family story, of which my narrative forms an important component part. Mr. Hartright has taken that responsibility on himself; and circumstances yet to be related will show that he has amply earned the right to do so, if he chooses to exercise it. The plan he has adopted for presenting the story to others, in the most truthful and most vivid manner, requires that it should be told, at each successive stage in the march of events, by the persons who were directly concerned in those events at the time of their occurrence. My appearance here, as narrator, is the necessary consequence of this arrangement. I was present during the sojourn of Sir Percival Glyde in Cumberland, and was personally concerned in one important result of his short residence under Mr. Fairlie's roof. It is my duty, therefore, to add these new links to the chain of events, and to take up the chain itself at the point where, for the present only, Mr. Hartright has dropped it.

I arrived at Limmeridge House, on Friday the second of November.

My object was to remain at Mr. Fairlie's until the arrival of Sir Percival Glyde. If that event led to the appointment of any given day for Sir Percival's union with Miss Fairlie, I was to take the necessary instructions back with me to London, and to occupy myself in drawing the lady's marriage-settlement.

On the Friday I was not favoured by Mr. Fairlie with an interview. He had been, or had fancied himself to be, an invalid for years past; and he was not well enough to receive me. Miss Halcombe was the first member of the family whom I saw. She met me at the house door; and introduced me to Mr. Hartright, who had been staying at Limmeridge for some time past.

I did not see Miss Fairlie until later in the day, at dinner time. She was not looking well, and I was sorry to observe it. She is a sweet lovable girl, as amiable and attentive to every one about her as her excellent mother used to be — though, personally speaking, she takes after her father. Mrs. Fairlie had dark eyes and hair; and her elder daughter, Miss Halcombe, strongly reminds me of her. Miss Fairlie played to us in the evening — not so well as usual, I thought. We had a rubber at whist; a mere profanation, so far as play was concerned, of that noble game. I had been favourably impressed by Mr. Hartright, on our first introduction to one another; but I soon discovered that he was not free from the social failings incidental to his age. There are three things that none of the young men of the present generation can do. They can't sit over their wine; they can't play at whist; and they can't pay a lady a compliment. Mr. Hartright was no exception to the general rule. Otherwise, even in those early days and on that short acquaintance, he struck me as being a modest and gentlemanlike young man.

So the Friday passed. I say nothing about the more serious matters which engaged my attention on that day — the anonymous letter to Miss Fairlie; the measures I thought it right to adopt when the matter was mentioned to me; and the conviction I entertained that every possible explanation of the circumstances would be readily afforded by Sir Percival Glyde, having all been fully noticed, as I understand, in the narrative which precedes this.

On the Saturday, Mr. Hartright had left before I got down to breakfast. Miss Fairlie kept her room all day; and Miss Halcombe appeared to me to be out of spirits. The house was not what it used to be in the time of Mr. and Mrs. Philip Fairlie. I took a walk by myself in the forenoon: and looked about at some of the places which I first saw when I was staying at Limmeridge to transact family business, more than thirty years since. They were not what they used to be either.

At two o'clock Mr. Fairlie sent to say he was well enough to see me. *He* had not altered, at any rate, since I first knew him. His talk was to the same purpose as usual — all about himself and his ailments, his wonderful coins, and his matchless Rembrandt etchings. The moment I tried to speak of the business that had brought me to his house, he shut his eyes and said I "upset" him. I persisted in upsetting him by returning again and again to the subject. All I could ascertain was that he looked on his niece's marriage as a settled thing, that her father had sanctioned it, that he sanctioned it himself, that it was a desirable marriage, and that he should be personally rejoiced when the worry of it was over. As to the settlement, if I would consult his niece, and afterwards dive as deeply as I pleased into my own knowledge of the family affairs, and get everything ready, and limit his share in the business, as guardian, to saying, Yes, at the right moment — why of course he would meet my views, and everybody else's views, with infinite pleasure. In the mean time, there I saw him, a helpless sufferer, confined to his room. Did I think he looked as if he wanted teasing? No. Then why tease him?

I might, perhaps, have been a little astonished at this extraordinary absence of all self-assertion on Mr. Fairlie's part, in the character of guardian, if my knowledge of the family

affairs had not been sufficient to remind me that he was a
single man, and that he had nothing more than a life-interest
in the Limmeridge property. As matters stood, therefore, I
was neither surprised nor disappointed at the result of the
interview. Mr. Fairlie had simply justified my expectations
— and there was an end of it.

Sunday was a dull day, out of doors and in. A letter
arrived for me from Sir Percival Glyde's solicitor, acknowledging the receipt of my copy of the anonymous letter, and my
accompanying statement of the case. Miss Fairlie joined us
in the afternoon, looking pale and depressed, and altogether
unlike herself. I had some talk with her, and ventured on a
delicate allusion to Sir Percival. She listened, and said nothing. All other subjects she pursued willingly; but this subject she allowed to drop. I began to doubt whether she might
not be repenting of her engagement — just as young ladies
often do, when repentance comes too late.

On Monday Sir Percival Glyde arrived.

I found him to be a most prepossessing man, so far as manners and appearance were concerned. He looked rather older
than I had expected; his head being bald over the forehead,
and his face somewhat marked and worn. But his movements
were as active and his spirits as high as a young man's. His
meeting with Miss Halcombe was delightfully hearty and unaffected; and his reception of me, upon my being presented to
him, was so easy and pleasant that we got on together like old
friends. Miss Fairlie was not with us when he arrived, but she
entered the room about ten minutes afterwards. Sir Percival
rose and paid his compliments with perfect grace. His evident
concern on seeing the change for the worse in the young lady's
looks was expressed with a mixture of tenderness and respect,
with an unassuming delicacy of tone, voice, and manner, which
did equal credit to his good breeding and his good sense. I
was rather surprised, under these circumstances, to see that
Miss Fairlie continued to be constrained and uneasy in his
presence, and that she took the first opportunity of leaving
the room again. Sir Percival neither noticed the restraint in

her reception of him, nor her sudden withdrawal from our society.   He had not obtruded his attentions on her while she was present, and he did not embarrass Miss Halcombe by any allusion to her departure when she was gone.   His tact and taste were never at fault on this or on any other occasion while I was in his company at Limmeridge House.

As soon as Miss Fairlie had left the room, he spared us all embarrassment on the subject of the anonymous letter, by adverting to it of his own accord.   He had stopped in London on his way from Hampshire; had seen his solicitor; had read the documents forwarded by me; and had travelled on to Cumberland, anxious to satisfy our minds by the speediest and the fullest explanation that words could convey.   On hearing him express himself to this effect, I offered him the original letter which I had kept for his inspection. He thanked me, and declined to look at it; saying that he had seen the copy, and that he was quite willing to leave the original in our hands.

The statement itself, on which he immediately entered, was as simple and satisfactory as I had all along anticipated it would be.

Mrs. Catherick, he informed us, had, in past years, laid him under some obligations for faithful services rendered to his family connexions and to himself.   She had been doubly unfortunate in being married to a husband who had deserted her, and in having an only child whose mental faculties had been in a disturbed condition from a very early age. Although her marriage had removed her to a part of Hampshire far distant from the neighbourhood in which Sir Percival's property was situated, he had taken care not to lose sight of her; his friendly feeling towards the poor woman, in consideration of her past services, having been greatly strengthened by his admiration of the patience and courage with which she supported her calamities.   In course of time, the symptoms of mental affliction in her unhappy daughter increased to such a serious extent, as to make it a matter of necessity to place her under proper medical care.   Mrs. Catherick herself recognised this necessity; but she also felt the prejudice common to persons occupying her respectable station, against allowing her child to be admitted, as a pauper, into a public Asylum.   Sir Percival had respected this prejudice, as he respected honest independence of feeling in any rank of life; and had resolved to mark his grateful sense of Mrs. Catherick's early attachment to the interests of himself and his family, by defraying the expense of her daughter's maintenance in a trustworthy private Asylum.   To her mother's regret, and to his own regret, the unfortunate creature had discovered the share which circumstances had induced him to take in placing her under restraint, and had conceived the most intense hatred and distrust of him in consequence.   To that hatred and distrust — which had expressed itself in various ways in the Asylum — the anonymous letter, written after her escape, was plainly attributable.   If Miss Halcombe's or Mr. Gilmore's recollection of the document did not confirm that view, or if they wished for any additional particulars about the Asylum (the address of which he mentioned, as well as the names and addresses of the two doctors on whose certificates the patient was admitted), he was ready to answer any question and to clear up any uncertainty.   He had done his duty to the unhappy young woman, by instructing his solicitor to spare no expense in tracing her, and in restoring her once more to medical care; and he was now only anxious to do his duty towards Miss Fairlie and towards her family, in the same plain, straightforward way.

I was the first to speak in answer to this appeal.   My own course was plain to me.   It is the great beauty of the Law that it can dispute any human statement, made under any circumstances, and reduced to any form. · If I had felt professionally called upon to set up a case against Sir Percival Glyde, on the strength of his own explanation, I could have done so beyond all doubt.   But my duty did not lie in this direction: my function was of the purely judicial kind.   I was to weigh the explanation we had just heard; to allow all due force to the high reputation of the gentleman who offered it; and to decide honestly whether the probabilities, on Sir Percival's own showing, were plainly with him, or plainly against him. My own conviction was that they were plainly with him; and I accordingly declared that his explanation was, to my mind, unquestiouably a satisfactory one.

Miss Halcombe, after looking at me very earnestly, said a few words, on her side, to the same effect — with a certain hesitation of manner, however, which the circumstances did not seem to me to warrant. I am unable to say, positively, whether Sir Percival noticed this or not. My opinion is that he did; seeing that he pointedly resumed the subject, although he might, now, with all propriety, have allowed it to drop.

"If my plain statement of facts had only been addressed to Mr. Gilmore," he said, "I should consider any further reference to this unhappy matter as unnecessary. I may fairly expect Mr. Gilmore, as a gentleman, to believe me on my word; and when he has done me that justice, all discussion of the subject between us has come to an end. But my position with a lady is not the same. I owe to her, what I would concede to no man alive — a *proof* of the truth of my assertion. You cannot ask for that proof, Miss Halcombe; and it is therefore my duty to you, and still more to Miss Fairlie, to offer it. May I beg that you will write at once to the mother of this unfortunate woman — to Mrs. Catherick — to ask for her testimony in support of the explanation which I have just offered to you."

I saw Miss Halcombe change colour, and look a little uneasy. Sir Percival's suggestion, politely as it was expressed, appeared to her, as it appeared to me, to point, very delicately, at the hesitation which her manner had betrayed a moment or two since.

"I hope, Sir Percival, you don't do me the injustice to suppose that I distrust you," she said, quickly.

"Certainly not, Miss Halcombe. I make my proposal purely as an act of attention to *you*. Will you excuse my obstinacy if I still venture to press it?"

He walked to the writing-table, as he spoke; drew a chair to it; and opened the paper case.

"Let me beg you to write the note," he said, "as a favour to *me*. It need not occupy you more than a few minutes. You have only to ask Mrs. Catherick two questions. First, if her daughter was placed in the Asylum with her knowledge and approval. Secondly, if the share I took in the matter was such as to merit the expression of her gratitude towards myself? Mr. Gilmore's mind is at ease on this unpleasant subject; and your mind is at ease — pray set my mind at ease also, by writing the note."

"You oblige me to grant your request, Sir Percival, when I would much rather refuse it." With those words Miss Halcombe rose from her place, and went to the writing-table. Sir Percival thanked her, handed her a pen, and then walked away towards the fireplace. Miss Fairlie's little Italian greyhound was lying on the rug. He held out his hand, and called to the dog good-humouredly.

"Come, Nina," he said; "we remember each other, don't we?"

The little beast, cowardly, and cross-grained as pet-dogs usually are, looked up at him sharply, shrank away from his outstretched hand, whined, shivered, and hid itself under a sofa. It was scarcely possible that he could have been put out by such a trifle as a dog's reception of him — but I observed, nevertheless, that he walked away towards the window very suddenly. Perhaps his temper is irritable at times? If so, I can sympathise with him. My temper is irritable at times, too.

Miss Halcombe was not long in writing the note. When it was done, she rose from the writing-table, and handed the open sheet of paper to Sir Percival. He bowed; took it from her; folded it up immediately, without looking at the contents; sealed it; wrote the address; and handed it back to her in silence. I never saw anything more gracefully and more becomingly done, in my life.

"You insist on my posting this letter, Sir Percival?" said Miss Halcombe.

"I beg you will post it," he answered. "And now that it is written and sealed up, allow me to ask one or two last questions about the unhappy woman to whom it refers. I have read the communication which Mr. Gilmore kindly addressed to my solicitor, describing the circumstances under which the writer of the anonymous letter was identified. But there are certain points to which that statement does not refer. Did Anne Catherick see Miss Fairlie?"

"Certainly not," replied Miss Halcombe.

"Did she see you?"

"No."

"She saw nobody from the house, then, except a certain Mr. Hartright, who accidentally met with her in the church-yard here?"

"Nobody else."

"Mr. Hartright was employed at Limmeridge as a drawing-master, I believe? Is he a member of one of the Water-Colour Societies?"

"I believe he is," answered Miss Halcombe.

He paused for a moment, as if he was thinking over the last answer, and then added:

"Did you find out where Anne Catherick was living, when she was in this neighbourhood?"

"Yes. At a farm on the moor, called Todd's Corner."

"It is a duty we all owe to the poor creature herself to trace her," continued Sir Percival. "She may have said something at Todd's Corner which may help us to find her. I will go there, and make inquiries on the chance. In the mean time, as I cannot prevail on myself to discuss this painful subject with Miss Fairlie, may I beg, Miss Halcombe, that you will kindly undertake to give her the necessary explanation, deferring it of course until you have received the reply to that note."

Miss Halcombe promised to comply with his request. He thanked her — nodded pleasantly — and left us, to go and establish himself in his own room. As he opened the door, the cross-grained greyhound poked out her sharp muzzle from under the sofa, and barked and snapped at him.

"A good morning's work, Miss Halcombe," I said, as soon as we were alone. "Here is an anxious day well ended already."

"Yes," she answered; "no doubt. I am very glad your mind is satisfied."

"*My* mind! Surely, with that note in your hand, your mind is at ease too?"

"Oh, yes — how can it be otherwise? I know the thing could not be," she went on, speaking more to herself than to me; "but I almost wish Walter Hartright had stayed here long enough to be present at the explanation, and to hear the proposal to me to write this note."

I was a little surprised — perhaps a little piqued, also, by these last words.

"Events, it is true, connected Mr. Hartright very remarkably with the affair of the letter," I said; "and I readily admit that he conducted himself, all things considered, with great delicacy and discretion. But I am quite at a loss to understand what useful influence his presence could have exercised in relation to the effect of Sir Percival's statement on your mind or mine."

"It was only a fancy," she said, absently. "There is no need to discuss it, Mr. Gilmore. Your experience ought to be, and is, the best guide I can desire."

I did not altogether like her thrusting the whole responsibility, in this marked manner, on my shoulders. If Mr. Fairlie had done it, I should not have been surprised. But resolute, clear-minded Miss Halcombe, was the very last person in the world whom I should have expected to find shrinking from the expression of an opinion of her own.

"If any doubts still trouble you," I said, "why not mention them to me at once? Tell me plainly, have you any reason to distrust Sir Percival Glyde?"

"None whatever."

"Do you see anything improbable, or contradictory, in his explanation?"

"How can I say I do, after the proof he has offered me of the truth of it? Can there be better testimony in his favour, Mr. Gilmore, than the testimony of the woman's mother?"

"None better. If the answer to your note of inquiry proves to be satisfactory, I, for one, cannot see what more any friend of Sir Percival's can possibly expect from him."

"Then we will post the note," she said, rising to leave the room, "and dismiss all further reference to the subject, until the answer arrives. Don't attach any weight to my hesitation. I can give no better reason for it than that I have been over-anxious about Laura lately; and anxiety, Mr. Gilmore, unsettles the strongest of us."

She left me abruptly; her naturally firm voice faltering as she spoke those last words. A sensitive, vehement, passionate nature — a woman of ten thousand in these trivial, superficial times. I had known her from her earliest years; I had seen her tested, as she grew up, in more than one trying family crisis, and my long experience made me attach an importance to her hesitation under the circumstances here detailed, which I should certainly not have felt in the case of another woman. I could see no cause for any uneasiness or any doubt; but she had made me a little uneasy, and a little doubtful, nevertheless. In my youth, I should have chafed and fretted under the irritation of my own unreasonable state of mind. In my age, I knew better; and went out philosophically to walk it off.

II.

We all met again at dinner-time.

Sir Percival was in such boisterous high spirits that I hardly recognized him as the same man whose quiet tact, refinement, and good sense had impressed me so strongly at the interview of the morning. The only trace of his former self that I could detect, reappeared, every now and then, in his manner towards Miss Fairlie. A look or a word from her, suspended his loudest laugh, checked his gayest flow of talk, and rendered him all attention to her, and to no one else at table, in an instant. Although he never openly tried to draw her into the conversation, he never lost the slightest chance she gave him of letting her drift into it by accident, and of saying the words to her, under those favourable circumstances, which a man with less tact and delicacy would have pointedly addressed to her the moment they occurred to him. Rather to my surprise, Miss Fairlie appeared to be sensible of his attentions, without being moved by them. She was a little confused from time to time, when he looked at her, or spoke to her; but she never warmed towards him. Rank, fortune, good breeding, good looks, the respect of a gentleman, and the devotion of a lover, were all humbly placed at her feet, and, so far as appearances went, were all offered in vain.

On the next day, the Tuesday, Sir Percival went in the morning (taking one of the servants with him as a guide) to Todd's Corner. His inquiries, as I afterwards heard, led to no results. On his return, he had an interview with Mr. Fairlie; and in the afternoon he and Miss Halcombe rode out together. Nothing else happened worthy of record. The evening passed as usual. There was no change in Sir Percival, and no change in Miss Fairlie.

The Wednesday's post brought with it an event — the reply from Mrs. Catherick. I took a copy of the document, which I have preserved, and which I may as well present in this place. It ran as follows: —

"MADAM, — I beg to acknowledge the receipt of your letter, inquiring whether my daughter, Anne, was placed under medical superintendence with my knowledge and approval, and whether the share taken in the matter by Sir Percival Glyde was such as to merit the expression of my gratitude towards that gentleman. Be pleased to accept my answer in the affirmative to both those questions, and believe me to remain, your obedient servant,

"JANE ANNE CATHERICK."

Short, sharp, and to the point: in form, rather a business-like letter for a woman to write; in substance, as plain a confirmation as could be desired of Sir Percival Glyde's statement. This was my opinion, and with certain minor reservations, Miss Halcombe's opinion also. Sir Percival, when the letter was shown to him, did not appear to be struck by the sharp, short tone of it. He told us that Mrs. Catherick was a woman of few words, a clear-headed, straightforward, unimaginative person, who wrote briefly and plainly, just as she spoke.

The next duty to be accomplished, now that the answer had been received, was to acquaint Miss Fairlie with Sir Percival's explanation. Miss Halcombe had undertaken to do this, and had left the room to go to her sister, when she suddenly returned again, and sat down by the easy-chair in which I was reading the newspaper. Sir Percival had gone out a minute before, to look at the stables, and no one was in the room but ourselves.

"I suppose we have really and truly done all we can?" she said, turning and twisting Mrs. Catherick's letter in her hand.

"If we are friends of Sir Percival's, who know him and trust him, we have done all, and more than all, that is necessary," I answered, a little annoyed by this return of her hesitation. "But if we are enemies who suspect him —"

"That alternative is not even to be thought of," she interposed. "We are Sir Percival's friends; and, if generosity and forbearance can add to our regard for him, we ought to be Sir Percival's admirers as well. You know that he saw Mr. Fairlie yesterday, and that he afterwards went out with me?"

"Yes. I saw you riding away together."

"We began the ride by talking about Anne Catherick, and about the singular manner in which Mr. Hartright met with her. But we soon dropped that subject; and Sir Percival spoke next, in the most unselfish terms, of his engagement with Laura. He said he had observed that she was out of spirits, and he was willing, if not informed to the contrary, to attribute to that cause the alteration in her manner towards him during his present visit. If, however, there was any other more serious reason for the change, he would entreat that no constraint might be placed on her inclinations either by Mr. Fairlie or by me. All he asked, in that case, was that she would recall to mind, for the last time, what the circumstances were under which the engagement between them was made, and what his conduct had been from the beginning of the courtship to the present time. If, after due reflection on those two subjects, she seriously desired that he should withdraw his pretensions to the honour of becoming her husband — and if she would tell him so plainly, with her own lips — he would sacrifice himself by leaving her perfectly free to withdraw from the engagement."

"No man could say more than that, Miss Halcombe. As to my experience, few men in his situation would have said as much."

She paused after I had spoken those words, and looked at me with a singular expression of perplexity and distress.

"I accuse nobody and I suspect nothing," she broke out, abruptly. "But I cannot and will not accept the responsibility of persuading Laura to this marriage."

"That is exactly the course which Sir Percival Glyde has himself requested you to take," I replied, in astonishment. "He has begged you not to force her inclinations."

"And he indirectly obliges me to force them, if I give her his message."

"How can that possibly be?"

"Consult your own knowledge of Laura, Mr. Gilmore. If I tell her to reflect on the circumstances of her engagement, I at once appeal to two of the strongest feelings in her nature — to her love for her father's memory, and to her strict regard for truth. You know that she never broke a promise in her life;

you know that she entered on this engagement at the beginning of her father's fatal illness, and that he spoke hopefully and happily of her marriage to Sir Percival Glyde on his death-bed."

I own that I was a little shocked at this view of the case.

"Surely," I said, "you don't mean to infer that when Sir Percival spoke to you yesterday, he speculated on such a result as you have just mentioned?"

Her frank, fearless face answered for her before she spoke.

"Do you think I would remain an instant in the company of any man whom I suspected of such baseness as that?" she asked, angrily.

I liked to feel her hearty indignation flash out on me in that way. We see so much malice and so little indignation in my profession.

"In that case," I said, "excuse me if I tell you, in our legal phrase, that you are travelling out of the record. Whatever the consequences may be, Sir Percival has a right to expect that your sister should carefully consider her engagement from every reasonable point of view before she claims her release from it. If that unlucky letter has prejudiced her against him, go at once, and tell her that he has cleared himself in your eyes and in mine. What objection can she urge against him after that? What excuse can she possibly have for changing her mind about a man whom she had virtually accepted for her husband more than two years ago?"

"In the eyes of law and reason, Mr. Gilmore, no excuse, I dare say. If she still hesitates, and if I still hesitate, you must attribute our strange conduct, if you like, to caprice in both cases, and we must bear the imputation as well as we can."

With those words, she suddenly rose, and left me. When a sensible woman has a serious question put to her, and evades it by a flippant answer, it is a sure sign, in ninety-nine cases out of a hundred, that she has something to conceal. I returned to the perusal of the newspaper, strongly suspecting that Miss Halcombe and Miss Fairlie had a secret between them which they were keeping from Sir Percival and keeping from me. I thought this hard on both of us — especially on Sir Percival.

My doubts — or, to speak more correctly, my convictions — were confirmed by Miss Halcombe's language and manner, when I saw her again, later in the day. She was suspiciously brief and reserved in telling me the result of her interview with her sister. Miss Fairlie, it appeared, had listened quietly while the affair of the letter was placed before her in the right point of view; but when Miss Halcombe next proceeded to say that the object of Sir Percival's visit at Limmeridge was to prevail on her to let a day be fixed for the marriage, she checked all further reference to the subject by begging for time. If Sir Percival would consent to spare her for the present, she would undertake to give him his final answer, before the end of the year. She pleaded for this delay with such anxiety and agitation, that Miss Halcombe had promised to use her influence, if necessary, to obtain it; and there, at Miss Fairlie's earnest entreaty, all further discussion of the marriage question had ended.

The purely temporary arrangement thus proposed might have been convenient enough to the young lady ; but it proved somewhat embarrassing to the writer of these lines. That morning's post had brought a letter from my partner, which obliged me to return to town the next day, by the afternoon train. It was extremely probable that I should find no second opportunity of presenting myself at Limmeridge House during the remainder of the year. In that case, supposing Miss Fairlie ultimately decided on holding to her engagement, my necessary personal communication with her, before I drew her settlement, would become something like a downright impossibility; and we should be obliged to commit to writing questions which ought always to be discussed on both sides by word of mouth. I said nothing about this difficulty, until Sir Percival had been consulted on the subject of the desired delay. He was too gallant a gentleman not to grant the request immediately. When Miss Halcombe informed me of this, I told her that I must absolutely speak to her sister, before I left Limmeridge; and it was, therefore, arranged that I should see Miss Fairlie in her own sitting-room, the next morning. She did not come down to dinner, or join us in the evening. Indisposition was the excuse; and I thought Sir Percival looked, as well he might, a little annoyed when he heard of it.

The next morning as soon as breakfast was over, I went up to Miss Fairlie's sitting-room. The poor girl looked so pale and sad, and came forward to welcome me so readily and prettily, that the resolution to lecture her on her caprice and indecision, which I had been forming all the way up-stairs, failed me on the spot. I led her back to the chair from which she had risen, and placed myself opposite to her. Her cross-grained pet greyhound was in the room, and I fully expected a barking and snapping reception. Strange to say, the whimsical little brute falsified my expectations by jumping into my lap, and poking its sharp muzzle familiarly into my hand the moment I sat down.

"You used often to sit on my knee when you were a child, my dear," I said, "and now your little dog seems determined to succeed you in the vacant throne. Is that pretty drawing your doing?"

I pointed to a little album, which lay on the table by her side, and which she had evidently been looking over when I came in. The page that lay open had a small water-colour landscape very neatly mounted on it. This was the drawing which had suggested my question: an idle question enough — but how could I begin to talk of business to her the moment I opened my lips?

"No," she said, looking away from the drawing rather confusedly; "it is not my doing."

Her fingers had a restless habit, which I remembered in her, as a child, of always playing with the first thing that came to hand, whenever any one was talking to her. On this occasion they wandered to the album, and toyed absently about the margin of the little water-colour drawing.   The expression of melancholy deepened on her face.   She did not look at the drawing, or look at me.   Her eyes moved uneasily from object to object in the room; betraying plainly that she suspected what my purpose was in coming to speak to her.   Seeing that, I thought it best to get to the purpose with as little delay as possible.

"One of the errands, my dear, which brings me here is to bid you good-by," I began.   "I must get back to London to-day; and, before I leave, I want to have a word with you on the subject of your own affairs."

"I am very sorry you are going, Mr. Gilmore," she said, looking at me kindly.   "It is like the happy old times to have you here."

"I hope I may be able to come back, and recall those pleasant memories once more," I continued; "but as there is some uncertainty about the future, I must take my opportunity when I can get it, and speak to you now.   I am your old lawyer and your old friend; and I may remind you, I am sure, without offence, of the possibility of your marrying Sir Percival Glyde."

She took her hand off the little album as suddenly as if it had turned hot and burnt her.   Her fingers twined together nervously in her lap; her eyes looked down again at the floor; and an expression of constraint settled on her face which looked almost like an expression of pain.

"Is it absolutely necessary to speak of my marriage engagement?" she asked, in low tones.

"It is necessary to refer to it," I answered; "but not to dwell on it.   Let us merely say that you may marry, or that you may not marry.   In the first case, I must be prepared, beforehand, to draw your settlement; and I ought not to do that without, as a matter of politeness, first consulting you. This may be my only chance of hearing what your wishes are. Let us, therefore, suppose the case of your marrying, and let me inform you, in as few words as possible, what your position is now, and what you may make it, if you please, in the future."

I explained to her the object of a marriage-settlement; and then told her exactly what her prospects were — in the first place, on her coming of age, and, in the second place, on the decease of her uncle — marking the distinction between the property in which she had a life interest only, and the property which was left at her own control. She listened attentively, with the constrained expression still on her face, and her hands still nervously clasped together in her lap.

"And, now," I said, in conclusion, "tell me if you can think of any condition which, in the case we have supposed, you would wish me to make for you — subject, of course, to your guardian's approval, as you are not yet of age."

She moved uneasily in her chair — then looked in my face, on a sudden, very earnestly.

"If it does happen," she began, faintly; "if I am —"

"If you are married," I added, helping her out.

"Don't let him part me from Marian," she cried, with a sudden outbreak of energy. "Oh, Mr. Gilmore, pray make it law that Marian is to live with me!"

Under other circumstances, I might perhaps have been amused at this essentially feminine interpretation of my question, and of the long explanation which had preceded it. But her looks and tones, when she spoke, were of a kind to make me more than serious — they distressed me. Her words, few as they were, betrayed a desperate clinging to the past which boded ill for the future.

"Your having Marian Halcombe to live with you, can easily be settled by private arrangement," I said. "You hardly understood my question, I think. It referred to your own property — to the disposal of your money. Supposing you were to make a will, when you come of age, who would you like the money to go to?"

"Marian has been mother and sister both to me," said the good, affectionate girl, her pretty blue eyes glistening while she spoke. "May I leave it to Marian, Mr. Gilmore?"

"Certainly, my love," I answered.   "But remember what a large sum it is. Would you like it all to go to Miss Halcombe?"

She hesitated; her colour came and went; and her hand stole back again to the little album.

"Not all of it," she said. "There is some one else, besides Marian —"

She stopped; her colour heightened; and the fingers of the hand that rested upon the album beat gently on the margin of the drawing, as if her memory had set them going mechanically with the remembrance of a favourite tune.

"You mean some other member of the family besides Miss Halcombe?" I suggested, seeing her at a loss to proceed.

The heightening colour spread to her forehead and her neck, and the nervous fingers suddenly clasped themselves fast round the edge of the book.

"There is some one else," she said, not noticing my last words, though she had evidently heard them; "there is some one else who might like a little keep-sake, if — if I might leave it.   There would be no harm, if I should die first —"

She paused again.   The colour that had spread over her cheeks suddenly, as suddenly left them.   The hand on the album resigned its hold, trembled a little, and moved the book away from her.   She looked at me for an instant — then turned her head aside in the chair.   Her handkerchief fell to the floor as she changed her position, and she hurriedly hid her face from me in her hands.

Sad! To remember her, as I did, the liveliest, happiest child that ever laughed the day through; and to see her now, in the flower of her age and her beauty, so broken and so brought down as this!

In the distress that she caused me, I forgot the years that had passed, and the change they had made in our position towards one another.   I moved my chair close to her, and picked up her handkerchief from the carpet, and drew her hands from her face gently.   "Don't cry, my love," I said, and dried the tears that were gathering in her eyes, with my own hand, as if she had been the little Laura Fairlie of ten long years ago.

It was the best way I could have taken to compose her. She laid her head on my shoulder, and smiled faintly through her tears.

"I am very sorry for forgetting myself," she said, artlessly. "I have not been well — I have felt sadly weak and nervous lately; and I often cry without reason when I am alone. I am better now; I can answer you as I ought, Mr. Gilmore, I can indeed."

"No, no, my dear," I replied; "we will consider the subject as done with, for the present. You have said enough to sanction my taking the best possible care of your interests; and we can settle details at another opportunity. Let us have done with business, now, and talk of something else."

I led her at once into speaking on other topics. In ten minutes' time, she was in better spirits; and I rose to take my leave.

"Come here again," she said earnestly. "I will try to be worthier of your kind feeling for me and for my interests if you will only come again."

Still clinging to the past — that past which I represented to her, in my way, as Miss Halcombe did in hers! It troubled me sorely to see her looking back, at the beginning of her career, just as I look back at the end of mine.

"If I do come again, I hope I shall find you better," I said — "better and happier. God bless you, my dear!"

She only answered by putting up her cheek to me to be kissed. Even lawyers have hearts; and mine ached a little as I took leave of her.

The whole interview between us had hardly lasted more than half an hour — she had not breathed a word, in my presence, to explain the mystery of her evident distress and dismay at the prospect of her marriage — and yet she had contrived to win me over to her side of the question, I neither knew how nor why. I had entered the room, feeling that Sir Percival Glyde had fair reason to complain of the manner in which she was treating him. I left it, secretly hoping that matters might end in her taking him at his word and claiming her release. A man of my age and experience ought to have known better than to vacillate in this unreasonable manner. I can make no excuse for myself; I can only tell the truth, and say — so it was.

The hour for my departure was now drawing near. I sent to Mr. Fairlie to say that I would wait on him to take leave if he liked, but that he must excuse my being rather in a hurry. He sent a message back, written in pencil on a slip of paper: "Kind love and best wishes, dear Gilmore. Hurry of any kind is inexpressibly injurious to me. Pray take care of yourself. Good-by."

Just before I left, I saw Miss Halcombe, for a moment, alone.

"Have you said all you wanted to Laura?" she asked.

"Yes," I replied. "She is very weak and nervous — I am glad she has you to take care of her."

Miss Halcombe's sharp eyes studied my face attentively.

"You are altering your opinion about Laura," she said. "You are readier to make allowances for her than you were yesterday."

No sensible man ever engages, unprepared, in a fencing match of words with a woman. I only answered:

"Let me know what happens. I will do nothing till I hear from you."

She still looked hard in my face. "I wish it was all over, and well over, Mr. Gilmore — and so do you." With those words she left me.

Sir Percival most politely insisted on seeing me to the carriage door.

"If you are ever in my neighbourhood," he said, "pray don't forget that I am sincerely anxious to improve our acquaintance. The tried and trusted old friend of this family will be always a welcome visitor in any house of mine."

A really irresistible man — courteous, considerate, delightfully free from pride — a gentleman, every inch of him. As

I drove away to the station, I felt as if I could cheerfully do anything to promote the interests of Sir Percival Glyde — anything in the world, except drawing the marriage-settlement of his wife.

III.

A WEEK passed, after my return to London, without the receipt of any communication from Miss Halcombe.

On the eighth day, a letter in her handwriting was placed among the other letters on my table.

It announced that Sir Percival Glyde had been definitely accepted, and that the marriage was to take place, as he had originally desired, before the end of the year. In all-probability the ceremony would be performed during the last fortnight in December. Miss Fairlie's twenty-first birthday was late in March. She would, therefore, by this arrangement, become Sir Percival's wife about three months before she was of age.

I ought not to have been surprised, I ought not to have been sorry; but I was surprised and sorry, nevertheless. Some little disappointment, caused by the unsatisfactory shortness of Miss Halcombe's letter, mingled itself with these feelings, and contributed its share towards upsetting my serenity for the day. In six lines my correspondent announced the proposed marriage; in three more, she told me that Sir Percival had left Cumberland to return to his house in Hampshire; and in two concluding sentences she informed me, first, that Laura was sadly in want of change and cheerful society; secondly, that she had resolved to try the effect of some such change forthwith, by taking her sister away with her on a visit to certain old friends in Yorkshire. There the letter ended, without a word to explain what the circumstances were which had decided Miss Fairlie to accept Sir Percival Glyde in one short week from the time when I had last seen her.

At a later period, the cause of this sudden determination

was fully explained to me. It is not my business to relate it imperfectly, on hearsay evidence. The circumstances came within the personal experience of Miss Halcombe; and, when her narrative succeeds mine, she will describe them in every particular, exactly as they happened. In the mean time, the plain duty for me to perform — before I, in my turn, lay down my pen and withdraw from the story — is to relate the one remaining event connected with Miss Fairlie's proposed marriage in which I was concerned, namely, the drawing of the settlement.

It is impossible to refer intelligibly to this document, without first entering into certain particulars, in relation to the bride's pecuniary affairs. I will try to make my explanation briefly and plainly, and to keep it free from professional obscurities and technicalities. The matter is of the utmost importance. I warn all readers of these lines that Miss Fairlie's inheritance is a very serious part of Miss Fairlie's story, and that Mr. Gilmore's experience, in this particular, must be their experience also, if they wish to understand the narratives which are yet to come.

Miss Fairlie's expectations, then, were of a twofold kind; comprising her possible inheritance of real property, or land, when her uncle died, and her absolute inheritance of personal property, or money, when she came of age.

Let us take the land first.

In the time of Miss Fairlie's paternal grandfather (whom we will call Mr. Fairlie, the elder) the entailed succession to the Limmeridge estate stood thus:

Mr. Fairlie, the elder, died and left three sons, Philip, Frederick, and Arthur. As eldest son, Philip succeeded to the estate. If he died without leaving a son, the property went to the second brother, Frederick. And if Frederick died also without leaving a son, the property went to the third brother, Arthur.

As events turned out, Mr. Philip Fairlie died leaving an only daughter, the Laura of this story; and the estate, in consequence, went, in course of law, to the second brother,

Frederick, a single man. The third brother, Arthur, had died many years before the decease of Philip, leaving a son and a daughter. The son, at the age of eighteen, was drowned at Oxford. His death left Laura, the daughter of Mr. Philip Fairlie, presumptive heiress to the estate; with every chance of succeeding to it, in the ordinary course of nature, on her uncle Frederick's death, if the said Frederick died without leaving male issue.

Except in the event, then, of Mr. Frederick Fairlie's marrying and leaving an heir (the two very last things in the world that he was likely to do), his niece, Laura, would have the property on his death; possessing, it must be remembered, nothing more than a life-interest in it. If she died single, or died childless, the estate would revert to her cousin Magdalen, the daughter of Mr. Arthur Fairlie. If she married, with a proper settlement — or, in other words, with the settlement I meant to make for her — the income from the estate (a good three thousand a year) would, during her lifetime, be at her own disposal. If she died before her husband, he would naturally expect to be left in the enjoyment of the income, for *his* lifetime. If she had a son, that son would be the heir, to the exclusion of her cousin Magdalen. Thus, Sir Percival's prospects in marrying Miss Fairlie (so far as his wife's expectations from real property were concerned) promised him these two advantages, on Mr. Frederick Fairlie's death: First, the use of three thousand a year (by his wife's permission, while she lived, and, in his own right, on her death, if he survived her); and, secondly, the inheritance of Limmeridge for his son, if he had one.

So much for the landed property, and for the disposal of the income from it, on the occasion of Miss Fairlie's marriage. Thus far, no difficulty or difference of opinion on the lady's settlement was at all likely to arise between Sir Percival's lawyer and myself.

The personal estate, or, in other words, the money to which Miss Fairlie would become entitled on reaching the age of twenty-one years, is the next point to consider.

This part of her inheritance was, in itself, a comfortable little fortune. It was derived under her father's will, and it amounted to the sum of twenty thousand pounds. Besides this, she had a life-interest in ten thousand pounds more; which latter amount was to go on her decease, to her aunt Eleanor, her father's only sister. It will greatly assist in setting the family affairs before the reader in the clearest possible light, if I stop here for a moment, to explain why the aunt had been kept waiting for her legacy until the death of the niece.

Mr. Philip Fairlie had lived on excellent terms with his sister Eleanor, as long as she remained a single woman. But when her marriage took place, somewhat late in life, and when that marriage united her to an Italian gentleman, named Fosco — or, rather, to an Italian nobleman, seeing that he rejoiced in the title of Count — Mr. Fairlie disapproved of her conduct so strongly that he ceased to hold any communication with her, and even went the length of striking her name out of his will. The other members of the family all thought his serious manifestation of resentment at his sister's marriage more or less unreasonable. Count Fosco, though not a rich man, was not a penniless adventurer either. He had a small, but sufficient income of his own; he had lived many years in England; and he held an excellent position in society. These recommendations, however, availed nothing with Mr. Fairlie. In many of his opinions he was an Englishman of the old school; and he hated a foreigner, simply and solely because he was a foreigner. The utmost that he could be prevailed on to do, in after years, mainly at Miss Fairlie's intercession, was to restore his sister's name to its former place in his will, but to keep her waiting for her legacy by giving the income of the money to his daughter for life, and the money itself, if her aunt died before her, to her cousin Magdalen. Considering the relative ages of the two ladies, the aunt's chance, in the ordinary course of nature, of receiving the ten thousand pounds, was thus rendered doubtful in the extreme; and Madame Fosco resented her brother's treatment of her as unjustly as usual in such cases, by refusing to see her niece, and declining to believe that Miss Fairlie's intercession had ever been exerted to restore her name to Mr. Fairlie's will.

Such was the history of the ten thousand pounds. Here again no difficulty could arise with Sir Percival's legal adviser. The income would be at the wife's disposal, and the principal would go to her aunt, or her cousin, on her death.

All preliminary explanations being now cleared out of the way, I came, at last, to the real knot of the case — to the twenty thousand pounds.

This sum was absolutely Miss Fairlie's own, on her completing her twenty-first year; and the whole future disposition of it depended, in the first instance, on the conditions I could obtain for her in her marriage-settlement. The other clauses contained in that document were of a formal kind, and need not be recited here. But the clause relating to the money is too important to be passed over. A few lines will be sufficient to give the necessary abstract of it.

My stipulation in regard to the twenty thousand pounds, was simply this: The whole amount was to be settled so as to give the income to the lady for her life; afterwards to Sir Percival for his life; and the principal to the children of the marriage. In default of issue, the principal was to be disposed of as the lady might by her will direct, for which purpose I reserved to her the right of making a will. The effect of these conditions may be thus summed up. If Lady Glyde died without leaving children, her half-sister, Miss Halcombe, and any other relatives or friends whom she might be anxious to benefit, would, on her husband's death, divide among them such shares of her money as she desired them to have. If, on the other hand, she died, leaving children, then their interest, naturally and necessarily, superseded all other interests whatsoever. This was the clause; and no one who reads it, can fail, I think, to agree with me that it meted out equal justice to all parties.

We shall see how my proposals were met on the husband's side.

At the time when Miss Halcombe's letter reached me, I was even more busily occupied than usual. But I contrived to make leisure for the settlement. I had drawn it, and had sent it for approval to Sir Percival's solicitor, in less than a week from the time when Miss Halcombe had informed me of the proposed marriage.

After a lapse of two days, the document was returned to me, with notes and remarks of the baronet's lawyer. His objections, in general, proved to be of the most trifling and technical kind, until he came to the clause relating to the twenty thousand pounds. Against this, there were double lines drawn in red ink, and the following note was appended to them:

"Not admissible. The *principal* to go to Sir Percival Glyde, in the event of his surviving Lady Glyde, and there being no issue."

That is to say, not one farthing of the twenty thousand pounds was to go to Miss Halcombe, or to any other relative or friend of Lady Glyde's. The whole sum, if she left no children, was to slip into the pockets of her husband.

The answer I wrote to this audacious proposal was as short and sharp as I could make it. "My dear sir. Miss Fairlie's settlement. I maintain the clause to which you object, exactly as it stands. Yours truly." The rejoinder came back in a quarter of an hour. "My dear sir. Miss Fairlie's settlement. I maintain the red ink to which you object, exactly as it stands. Yours truly." In the detestable slang of the day, we were now both "at a dead-lock," and nothing was left for it but to refer to our clients on either side.

As matters stood, my client — Miss Fairlie not having yet completed her twenty-first year — was her guardian, Mr. Frederick Fairlie. I wrote by that day's post and put the case before him exactly as it stood; not only urging every argument I could think of to induce him to maintain the clause as I had drawn it, but stating to him plainly the mercenary motive which was at the bottom of the opposition to my settlement of the twenty thousand pounds. The knowledge of Sir Percival's affairs which I had necessarily gained when the provisions of the deed on *his* side were submitted in due course to my examination, had but too plainly informed me that the debts on his estate were enormous, and that his income, though nominally a large one, was, virtually, for a man in his position, next to nothing. The want of ready money was the practical necessity of Sir Percival's existence; and his lawyer's note on the clause in the settlement was nothing but the frankly selfish expression of it.

Mr. Fairlie's answer reached me by return of post, and proved to be wandering and irrelevant in the extreme. Turned into plain English, it practically expressed itself to this effect: " Would dear Gilmore be so very obliging as not to worry his friend and client about such a trifle as a remote contingency? Was it likely that a young woman of twenty-one would die before a man of forty-five, and die without children? On the other hand, in such a miserable world as this, was it possible to over-estimate the value of peace and quietness? If those two heavenly blessings were offered in exchange for such an earthly trifle as a remote chance of twenty thousand pounds, was it not a fair bargain? Surely, yes. Then why not make it?"

I threw the letter away in disgust. Just as it had fluttered to the ground, there was a knock at my door; and Sir Percival's solicitor, Mr. Merriman, was shown in. There are many varieties of sharp practitioners in this world, but, I think, the hardest of all to deal with are the men who over-reach you under the disguise of inveterate good humour. A fat, well-fed, smiling friendly man of business is of all parties to a bargain the most hopeless to deal with. Mr. Merriman was one of this class.

"And how is good Mr. Gilmore?" he began, all in a glow with the warmth of his own amiability. "Glad to see you, sir, in such excellent health. I was passing your door; and I thought I would look in, in case you might have something to say to me. Do — now pray do let us settle this little difference of ours by word of mouth, if we can! Have you heard from your client yet?"

"Yes. Have you heard from yours?"

"My dear, good sir! I wish I had heard from him to any purpose — I wish, with all my heart, the responsibility was off my shoulders; but he is obstinate, — or, let me rather say, resolute — and he won't take it off. 'Merriman, I leave details to you. Do what you think right for my interests; and consider me as having personally withdrawn from the business until it is all over.' Those were Sir Percival's words a fortnight ago; and all I can get him to do now is to repeat them. I am not a hard man, Mr. Gilmore, as you know. Personally or privately, I do assure you, I should like to sponge out that note of mine at this very moment. But if Sir Percival won't go into the matter, if Sir Percival will blindly leave all his interests in my sole care, what course can I possibly take except the course of asserting them? My hands are bound — don't you see, my dear sir? — my hands are bound."

"You maintain your note on the clause, then, to the letter?" I said.

"Yes — deuce take it! I have no other alternative." He walked to the fireplace, and warmed himself, humming the fag end of a tune in a rich convivial bass voice. "What does your side say?" he went on; "now pray tell me — what does your side say?"

I was ashamed to tell him. I attempted to gain time — nay, I did worse. My legal instincts got the better of me; and I even tried to bargain.

"Twenty thousand pounds is rather a large sum to be given up by the lady's friends at two days' notice," I said.

"Very true," replied Mr. Merriman, looking down thoughtfully at his boots. "Properly put, sir — most properly put!"

"A compromise, recognizing the interests of the lady's family as well as the interests of the husband might not, perhaps, have frightened my client quite so much." I went on. "Come! come! this contingency resolves itself into a matter of bargaining after all. What is the least you will take?"

"The least we will take, "said Mr. Merriman, "is nineteen-thousand-nine-hundred-and-ninety-nine-pounds-nineteen-shillings-and-eleven-pence-three-farthings. Ha! ha! ha! Excuse me, Mr. Gilmore. I must have my little joke."

"Little enough!" I remarked. "The joke is just worth the odd farthing it was made for."

Mr. Merriman was delighted. He laughed over my retort till the room rang again. I was not half so good-humoured, on my side; I came back to business, and closed the interview.

"This is Friday," I said. "Give us till Tuesday next for our final answer."

"By all means," replied Mr. Merriman. "Longer, my dear sir, if you like." He took up his hat to go; and then addressed me again. "By the way," he said, "your clients in Cumberland have not heard anything more of the woman who wrote the anonymous letter, have they?"

"Nothing more," I answered. "Have you found no trace of her?"

"Not yet," said my legal friend. "But we don't despair. Sir Percival has his suspicions that Somebody is keeping her in hiding; and we are having that Somebody watched."

"You mean the old woman who was with her in Cumberland," I said.

"Quite another party, sir," answered Mr. Merriman. "We don't happen to have laid hands on the old woman yet. Our Somebody is a man. We have got him close under our eye here in London; and we strongly suspect he had something to do with helping her in the first instance to escape from the Asylum. Sir Percival wanted to question him, at once; but I said, 'No. Questioning him will only put him on his guard: watch him, and wait.' We shall see what happens. A dangerous woman to be at large, Mr. Gilmore; nobody knows what she may do next. I wish you good morning, sir. On Tuesday

11*

next I shall hope for the pleasure of hearing from you." He smiled amiably and went out.

My mind had been rather absent during the latter part of the conversation with my legal friend. I was so anxious about the matter of the settlement, that I had little attention to give to any other subject; and, the moment I was left alone again, I began to think over what my next proceeding ought to be.

In the case of any other client, I should have acted on my instructions, however personally distasteful to me, and have given up the point about the twenty thousand pounds on the spot. But I could not act with this business-like indifference towards Miss Fairlie. I had an honest feeling of affection and admiration for her; I remembered gratefully that her father had been the kindest patron and friend to me that ever man had; I had felt towards her, while I was drawing the settlement, as I might have felt, if I had not been an old bachelor, towards a daughter of my own; and I was determined to spare no personal sacrifice in her service and where her interests were concerned. Writing a second time to Mr. Fairlie was not to be thought of; it would only be giving him a second opportunity of slipping through my fingers. Seeing him and personally remonstrating with him, might possibly be of more use. The next day was Saturday. I determined to take a return ticket, and jolt my old bones down to Cumberland, on the chance of persuading him to adopt the just, the independent, and the honourable course. It was a poor chance enough, no doubt; but, when I had tried it, my conscience would be at ease. I should then have done all that a man in my position could do to serve the interests of my old friend's only child.

The weather on Saturday was beautiful, a west wind and a bright sun. Having felt latterly a return of that fulness and oppression of the head, against which my doctor warned me so seriously more than two years since, I resolved to take the opportunity of getting a little extra exercise, by sending my bag on before me, and walking to the terminus in Eustonsquare. As I came out into Holborn, a gentleman walking by rapidly, stopped and spoke to me. It was Mr. Walter Hartright.

If he had not been the first to greet me, I should certainly have passed him. He was so changed that I hardly knew him again. His face looked pale and haggard — his manner was hurried and uncertain — and his dress, which I remembered as neat and gentlemanlike when I saw him at Limmeridge, was so slovenly now, that I should really have been ashamed of the appearance of it on one of my own clerks.

"Have you been long back from Cumberland?" he asked. "I heard from Miss Halcombe lately. I am aware that Sir Percival Glyde's explanation has been considered satisfactory. Will the marriage take place soon? Do you happen to know, Mr. Gilmore?"

He spoke so fast, and crowded his questions together so strangely and confusedly that I could hardly follow him. However accidentally intimate he might have been with the family at Limmeridge, I could not see that he had any right to expect information on their private affairs; and I determined to drop him, as easily as might be, on the subject of Miss Fairlie's marriage.

"Time will show, Mr. Hartright," I said — "time will show. I dare say if we look out for the marriage in the papers we shall not be far wrong. Excuse my noticing it — but I am sorry to see you not looking so well as you were when we last met."

A momentary nervous contraction quivered about his lips and eyes, and made me half reproach myself for having answered him in such a significantly guarded manner.

"I had no right to ask about her marriage," he said, bitterly. "I must wait to see it in the newspapers like other people. Yes," he went on, before I could make any apologies, "I have not been well lately. I want a change of scene and occupation. You have a large circle of acquaintance, Mr. Gilmore. If you should hear of any expedition abroad which may be in want of a draughtsman, and if you have no friend of your own who can take advantage of the opportunity, I should feel greatly obliged by your letting me know of it. I can answer for my testimonials being satisfactory; and I don't care where I go, what the climate is, or how long I am away." He looked about him, while he said this, at the throng of strangers passing us by on either side, in a strange, suspicious manner, as if he thought that some of them might be watching us.

"If I hear of anything of the kind I will not fail to mention it," I said; and then added, so as not to keep him altogether at arm's length on the subject of the Fairlies, "I am going down to Limmeridge to-day on business. Miss Halcombe and Miss Fairlie are away just now, on a visit to some friends in Yorkshire."

His eyes brightened, and he seemed about to say something in answer; but the same momentary nervous spasm crossed his face again. He took my hand, pressed it hard, and disappeared among the crowd, without saying another word. Though he was little more than a stranger to me, I waited for a moment, looking after him almost with a feeling of regret. I had gained, in my profession, sufficient experience of young men, to know what the outward signs and tokens were of their beginning to go wrong; and, when I resumed my walk to the railway, I am sorry to say I felt more than doubtful about Mr. Hartright's future.

IV.

Leaving by an early train, I got to Limmeridge in time for dinner. The house was oppressively empty and dull. I had expected that good Mrs. Vesey would have been company for me in the absence of the young ladies; but she was confined to her room by a cold. The servants were so surprised at seeing me that they hurried and bustled absurdly, and made all sorts of annoying mistakes. Even the butler, who was old enough to have known better, brought me a bottle of port that was chilled. The reports of Mr. Fairlie's health were just as usual, and when I sent up a message to announce my arrival, I was told that he would be delighted to see me the next morning, but that the sudden news of my appearance had prostrated him with palpitations for the rest of the evening. The wind howled dismally all night, and strange cracking and groaning noises sounded here, there, and everywhere in the empty house. I slept as wretchedly as possible; and got up, in a mighty bad humour, to breakfast by myself the next morning.

At ten o'clock I was conducted to Mr. Fairlie's apartments. He was in his usual room, his usual chair, and his usual aggravating state of mind and body. When I went in, his valet was standing before him, holding up for inspection a heavy volume of etchings, as long and as broad as my office writing-desk. The miserable foreigner grinned in the most abject manner, and looked ready to drop with fatigue, while his master composedly turned over the etchings, and brought their hidden beauties to light with the help of a magnifying glass.

"You very best of good old friends," said Mr. Fairlie, leaning back lazily before he could look at me, "are you *quite* well? How nice of you to come here and see me in my solitude. Dear Gilmore!"

I had expected that the valet would be dismissed when I appeared; but nothing of the sort happened. There he stood, in front of his master's chair, trembling under the weight of the etchings; and there Mr. Fairly sat, serenely twirling the magnifying glass between his white fingers and thumbs.

"I have come to speak to you on a very important matter," I said; "and you will therefore excuse me, if I suggest that we had better be alone."

The unfortunate valet looked at me gratefully. Mr. Fairlie faintly repeated my last three words, "better be alone," with every appearance of the utmost possible astonishment.

I was in no humour for trifling; and I resolved to make him understand what I meant.

"Oblige me by giving that man permission to withdraw," I said, pointing to the valet.

Mr. Fairlie arched his eyebrows, and pursed up his lips, in sarcastic surprise.

"Man?" he repeated. "You provoking old Gilmore, what can you possibly mean by calling him a man? He's nothing of the sort. He might have been a man half an hour ago, before I wanted my etchings; and he may be a man half an hour hence, when I don't want them any longer. At present he is simply a portfolio stand. Why object, Gilmore, to a portfolio stand?"

"I *do* object. For the third time, Mr. Fairlie, I beg that we may be alone."

My tone and manner left him no alternative but to comply with my request. He looked at the servant, and pointed peevishly to a chair at his side.

"Put down the etchings and go away," he said. "Don't upset me by losing my place? Have you, or have you not, lost my place? Are you sure you have *not?* And have you put my hand-bell quite within my reach? Yes? Then, why the devil don't you go?"

The valet went out. Mr. Fairlie twisted himself round in his chair, polished the magnifying glass with his delicate cambric handkerchief, and indulged himself with a sidelong inspection of the open volume of etchings. It was not easy to keep my temper under these circumstances; but I did keep it.

"I have come here at great personal inconvenience," I said, "to serve the interests of your niece and your family; and I think I have established some slight claim to be favoured with your attention in return."

"Don't bully me!" exclaimed Mr. Fairlie, falling back helplessly in the chair, and closing his eyes. "Please don't bully me. I'm not strong enough."

I was determined not to let him provoke me, for Laura Fairlie's sake.

"My object," I went on, "is to entreat you to reconsider your letter, and not to force me to abandon the just rights of your niece, and of all who belong to her. Let me state the case to you once more, and for the last time."

Mr. Fairlie shook his head and sighed piteously.

"This is heartless of you, Gilmore — very heartless," he said. "Never mind; go on."

I put all the points to him carefully; I set the matter before him in every conceivable light. He lay back in the chair the whole time I was speaking, with his eyes closed. When I had done, he opened them indolently, took his silver smelling-bottle from the table, and sniffed at it with an air of gentle relish.

"Good Gilmore!" he said, between the sniffs, "how very nice this is of you! How you reconcile one to human nature!"

"Give me a plain answer to a plain question, Mr. Fairlie. I tell you again, Sir Percival Glyde has no shadow of a claim to expect more than the income of the money. The money itself, if your niece has no children, ought to be under her control, and to return to her family. If you stand firm, Sir Percival must give way — he must give way, I tell you, or he exposes himself to the base imputation of marrying Miss Fairlie entirely from mercenary motives."

Mr. Fairlie shook the silver smelling-bottle at me playfully.

"You dear old Gilmore; how you do hate rank and family, don't you? How you detest Glyde, because he happens to be a baronet. What a Radical you are — oh, dear me, what a Radical you are!"

A Radical!!!! I could put up with a good deal of provocation, but, after holding the soundest Conservative principles all my life, I could *not* put up with being called a Radical. My blood boiled at it — I started out of my chair — I was speechless with indignation.

"Don't shake the room!" cried Mr. Fairlie — "for Heaven's sake, don't shake the room! Worthiest of all possible Gilmores, I meant no offence. My own views are so extremely liberal that I think I am a Radical myself. Yes. We are a pair of Radicals. Please don't be angry. I can't quarrel — I haven't stamina enough. Shall we drop the subject? Yes. Come and look at these sweet etchings. Do let me teach you to understand the heavenly pearliness of these lines. Do, now, there's a good Gilmore!"

While he was maundering on in this way I was, fortunately for my own self-respect, returning to my senses. When I spoke again I was composed enough to treat his impertinence with the silent contempt that it deserved.

"You are entirely wrong, sir," I said, "in supposing that I speak from any prejudice against Sir Percival Glyde. I may regret that he has so unreservedly resigned himself in this matter to his lawyer's direction as to make any appeal to himself impossible; but I am not prejudiced against him. What I have said would equally apply to any other man in his situation, high or low. The principle I maintain is a recognised principle. If you were to apply at the nearest town here, to the first respectable solicitor you could find, he would tell you, as a stranger, what I tell you, as a friend. He would inform you that it is against all rule to abandon the lady's money entirely to the man she marries. He would decline, on grounds of common legal caution, to give the husband, under any circumstances whatever, an interest of twenty thousand pounds in his wife's death."

"Would he really, Gilmore?" said Mr. Fairlie. "If he said anything half so horrid I do assure you I should tinkle my bell for Louis, and have him sent out of the house immediately."

"You shall not irritate me, Mr. Fairlie — for your niece's sake and for her father's sake, you shall not irritate me. You shall take the whole responsibility of this discreditable settlement on your own shoulders before I leave the room."

"Don't! — now please don't!" said Mr. Fairlie. "Think

how precious your time is, Gilmore; and don't throw it away.
I would dispute with you if I could, but I can't — I haven't
stamina enough. You want to upset me, to upset yourself,
to upset Glyde, and to upset Laura; and — oh, dear me! —
for the sake of the very last thing in the world that is likely to
happen. No, dear friend — for the sake of peace and quietness, positively No!"

"I am to understand, then, that you hold by the determination expressed in your letter?"

"Yes, please. So glad we understand each other at last.
Sit down again — do!"

I walked at once to the door; and Mr. Fairlie resignedly
"tinkled" his hand-bell. Before I left the room I turned round
and addressed him for the last time.

"Whatever happens in the future, sir," I said, "remember
that my plain duty of warning you has been performed. As
the faithful friend and servant of your family, I tell you, at
parting, that no daughter of mine should be married to any
man alive under such a settlement as you are forcing me to
make for Miss Fairlie."

The door opened behind me, and the valet stood waiting
on the threshold.

"Louis," said Mr. Fairlie, "show Mr. Gilmore out, and
then come back and hold up my etchings for me again. Make
them give you a good lunch down stairs — do, Gilmore, make
my idle beasts of servants give you a good lunch."

I was too much disgusted to reply; I turned on my heel,
and left him in silence. There was an up train at two o'clock
in the afternoon; and by that train I returned to London.

On the Tuesday I sent in the altered settlement, which
practically disinherited the very persons whom Miss Fairlie's
own lips had informed me she was most anxious to benefit.
I had no choice. Another lawyer would have drawn up the
deed if I had refused to undertake it.

My task is done. My personal share in the events of the
family story extends no farther than the point which I have

just reached.   Other pens than mine will describe the strange circumstances which are now shortly to follow. Seriously and sorrowfully, I close this brief record.   Seriously and sorrowfully, I repeat here the parting words that I spoke at Limmeridge House: — No daughter of mine should have been married to any man alive under such a settlement as I was compelled to make for Laura Fairlie.

THE STORY CONTINUED

BY

MARIAN HALCOMBE,

IN EXTRACTS FROM HER DIARY.

I.

*   *   *   *   *   * †

Limmeridge House, Nov. 8th.

This morning Mr. Gilmore left us.

His interview with Laura had evidently grieved and surprised him more than he liked to confess. I felt afraid, from his look and manner when we parted, that she might have inadvertently betrayed to him the real secret of her depression and of my anxiety. This doubt grew on me so, after he had gone, that I declined riding out with Sir Percival, and went up to Laura's room instead.

I have been sadly distrustful of myself, in this difficult and lamentable matter, ever since I found out my own ignorance of the strength of Laura's unhappy attachment. I ought to have known that the delicacy and forbearance and sense of honour which drew me to poor Hartright, and made me so sincerely admire and respect him, were just the qualities to appeal most irresistibly to Laura's natural sensitiveness and natural generosity of nature. And yet, until she opened her heart to me of her own accord, I had no suspicion that this new feeling had taken root so deeply. I

---

† The passages omitted, here and elsewhere, in Miss Halcombe's Diary, are only those which bear no reference to Miss Fairlie or to any of the persons with whom she is associated in these pages.

once thought time and care might remove it. I now fear that it will remain with her and alter her for life. The discovery that I have committed such an error in judgment as this, makes me hesitate about everything else. I hesitate about Sir Percival, in the face of the plainest proofs. I hesitate even in speaking to Laura. On this very morning, I doubted, with my hand on the door, whether I should ask her the questions I had come to put, or not.

When I went into her room, I found her walking up and down in great impatience. She looked flushed and excited; and she came forward at once, and spoke to me before I could open my lips.

"I wanted you," she said. "Come and sit down on the sofa with me. Marian! I can bear this no longer — I must and will end it."

There was too much colour in her cheeks, too much energy in her manner, too much firmness in her voice. The little book of Hartright's drawings — the fatal book that she will dream over whenever she is alone — was in one of her hands. I began by gently and firmly taking it from her, and putting it out of sight on a side-table.

"Tell me quietly, my darling, what you wish to do," I said. "Has Mr. Gilmore been advising you?"

She shook her head. "No, not in what I am thinking of now. He was very kind and good to me, Marian, — and I am ashamed to say I distressed him by crying. I am miserably helpless; I can't control myself. For my own sake and for all our sakes, I must have courage enough to end it."

"Do you mean courage enough to claim your release?" I asked.

"No," she said, simply. "Courage, dear, to tell the truth."

She put her arms round my neck, and rested her head quietly on my bosom. On the opposite wall hung the miniature portrait of her father. I bent over her, and saw that she was looking at it while her head lay on my breast.

"I can never claim my release from my engagement," she

went on. "Whatever way it ends, it must end wretchedly for *me*. All I can do, Marian, is not to add the remembrance that I have broken my promise and forgotten my father's dying words, to make that wretchedness worse."

"What is it you propose, then?" I asked.

"To tell Sir Percival Glyde the truth, with my own lips," she answered, "and to let him release me, if he will, not because I ask him, but because he knows all."

"What do you mean, Laura, by 'all?' Sir Percival will know enough (he has told me so himself) if he knows that the engagement is opposed to your own wishes."

"Can I tell him that, when the engagement was made for me by my father, with my own consent? I should have kept my promise; not happily, I am afraid, but still contentedly —" she stopped, turned her face to me, and laid her cheek close against mine — "I should have kept my engagement, Marian, if another love had not grown up in my heart, which was not there when I first promised to be Sir Percival's wife."

"Laura! you will never lower yourself by making a confession to him?"

"I shall lower myself, indeed, if I gain my release by hiding from him what he has a right to know."

"He has not the shadow of a right to know it!"

"Wrong, Marian, wrong! I ought to deceive no one — least of all the man to whom my father gave me, and to whom I gave myself." She put her lips to mine, and kissed me. "My own love," she said, softly, "you are so much too fond of me and so much too proud of me, that you forget, in my case, what you would remember in your own. Better that Sir Percival should doubt my motives and misjudge my conduct if he will, than that I should be first false to him in thought, and then mean enough to serve my own interests by hiding the falsehood."

I held her away from me in astonishment. For the first time in our lives, we had changed places; the resolution was all on her side, the hesitation all on mine. I looked into the pale, quiet, resigned young face; I saw the pure, innocent heart, in the loving eyes that looked back at me — and the poor, worldly cautions and objections that rose to my lips, dwindled and died away in their own emptiness. I hung my head in silence. In her place, the despicably small pride which makes so many women deceitful, would have been my pride, and would have made me deceitful, too.

"Don't be angry with me, Marian," she said, mistaking my silence.

I only answered by drawing her close to me again. I was afraid of crying if I spoke. My tears do not flow so easily as they ought — they come, almost like men's tears, with sobs that seem to tear me in pieces, and that frighten every one about me.

"I have thought of this, love, for many days," she went on, twining and twisting my hair with that childish restlessness in her fingers, which poor Mrs. Vesey still tries so patiently and so vainly to cure her of — "I have thought of it very seriously, and I can be sure of my courage, when my own conscience tells me I am right. Let me speak to him to-morrow — in your presence, Marian. I will say nothing that is wrong, nothing that you or I need be ashamed of — but, oh, it will ease my heart so to end this miserable concealment! Only let me know and feel that I have no deception to answer for on my side; and then, when he has heard what I have to say, let him act towards me as he will."

She sighed, and put her head back in its old position on my bosom. Sad misgivings about what the end would be, weighed upon my mind; but, still distrusting myself, I told her that I would do as she wished. She thanked me, and we passed gradually into talking of other things.

At dinner she joined us again, and was more easy and more herself with Sir Percival, than I have seen her yet. In the evening she went to the piano, choosing new music of the dexterous, tuneless, florid kind. The lovely old melodies of Mozart, which poor Hartright was so fond of, she has never played since he left. The book is no longer in the music-stand,

She took the volume away herself, so that nobody might find it out and ask her to play from it.

I had no opportunity of discovering whether her purpose of the morning had changed or not, until she wished Sir Percival good night — and then her own words informed me that it was unaltered. She said, very quietly, that she wished to speak to him, after breakfast, and that he would find her in her sitting-room with me. He changed colour at those words, and I felt his hand trembling a little when it came to my turn to take it. The event of the next morning would decide his future life; and he evidently knew it.

I went in, as usual, through the door between our two bed-rooms, to bid Laura good-night before she went to sleep. In stooping over her to kiss her, I saw the little book of Hartright's drawings half hidden under her pillow, just in the place where she used to hide her favourite toys when she was a child. I could not find it in my heart to say anything; but I pointed to the book and shook my head. She reached both hands up to my cheeks, and drew my face down to hers till our lips met.

"Leave it there to-night," she whispered; "to-morrow may be cruel, and may make me say good-by to it for ever."

9th. — The first event of the morning was not of a kind to raise my spirits; a letter arrived for me, from poor Walter Hartright. It is the answer to mine, describing the manner in which Sir Percival cleared himself of the suspicions raised by Anne Catherick's letter. He writes shortly and bitterly about Sir Percival's explanations; only saying that he has no right to offer an opinion on the conduct of those who are above him. This is sad; but his occasional references to himself grieve me still more. He says that the effort to return to his old habits and pursuits, grows harder instead of easier to him, every day; and he implores me, if I have any interest, to exert it to get him employment that will necessitate his absence from England, and take him among new scenes and new people. I have been made all the readier to comply with this request, by a passage at the end of his letter, which has almost alarmed me.

After mentioning that he has neither seen nor heard anything of Anne Catherick, he suddenly breaks off, and hints in the most abrupt, mysterious manner, that he has been perpetually watched and followed by strange men ever since he returned to London. He acknowledges that he cannot prove this extraordinary suspicion by fixing on any particular persons; but he declares that the suspicion itself is present to him night and day. This has frightened me, because it looks as if his one fixed idea about Laura was becoming too much for his mind. I will write immediately to some of my mother's influential old friends in London, and press his claims on their notice. Change of scene and change of occupation may really be the salvation of him at this crisis in his life.

Greatly to my relief, Sir Percival sent an apology for not joining us at breakfast. He had taken an early cup of coffee in his own room, and he was still engaged there in writing letters. At eleven o'clock, if that hour was convenient, he would do himself the honour of waiting on Miss Fairlie and Miss Halcombe.

My eyes were on Laura's face while the message was being delivered. I had found her unaccountably quiet and composed on going into her room in the morning; and so she remained all through breakfast. Even when we were sitting together on the sofa in her room, waiting for Sir Percival, she still preserved her self-control.

"Don't be afraid of me, Marian," was all she said: "I may forget myself with an old friend like Mr. Gilmore, or with a dear sister like you; but I will not forget myself with Sir Percival Glyde."

I looked at her, and listened to her in silent surprise. Through all the years of our close intimacy, this passive force in her character had been hidden from me — hidden even from herself, till love found it, and suffering called it forth.

As the clock on the mantelpiece struck eleven, Sir Percival knocked at the door, and came in. There was suppressed anxiety and agitation in every line of his face. The dry, sharp cough, which teases him at most times, seemed to be troubling him more incessantly than ever. He sat down opposite to us at the table; and Laura remained by me. I looked attentively at them both, and he was the palest of the two.

He said a few unimportant words, with a visible effort to preserve his customary ease of manner. But his voice was not to be steadied, and the restless uneasiness in his eyes was not to be concealed. He must have felt this himself; for he stopped in the middle of a sentence, and gave up even the attempt to hide his embarrassment any longer.

There was just one moment of dead silence before Laura addressed him.

"I wish to speak to you, Sir Percival," she said, "on a subject that is very important to us both. My sister is here, because her presence helps me, and gives me confidence. She has not suggested one word of what I am going to say: I speak from my own thoughts, not from hers. I am sure you will be kind enough to understand that, before I go any farther?"

Sir Percival bowed. She had proceeded thus far, with perfect outward tranquillity, and perfect propriety of manner. She looked at him, and he looked at her. They seemed, at the outset at least, resolved to understand one another plainly.

"I have heard from Marian," she went on, "that I have only to claim my release from our engagement, to obtain that release from you. It was forbearing and generous on your part, Sir Percival, to send me such a message. It is only doing you justice to say that I am grateful for the offer; and I hope and believe that it is only doing myself justice to tell you that I decline to accept it."

His attentive face relaxed a little. But I saw one of his feet, softly, quietly, incessantly beating on the carpet under the table; and I felt that he was secretly as anxious as ever.

"I have not forgotten," she said, "that you asked my father's permission before you honoured me with a proposal of marriage. Perhaps, you have not forgotten, either, what I said when I consented to our engagement? I ventured to tell you that my father's influence and advice had mainly decided me to give you my promise. I was guided by my father, because I had always found him the truest of all advisers, the best and fondest of all protectors and friends. I have lost him now; I have only his memory to love; but my faith in that dear dead friend has never been shaken. I believe, at this moment, as truly as I ever believed, that he knew what was best, and that his hopes and wishes ought to be my hopes and wishes too."

Her voice trembled, for the first time. Her restless fingers stole their way into my lap, and held fast by one of my hands. There was another moment of silence; and then Sir Percival spoke.

"May I ask," he said, "if I have ever proved myself unworthy of the trust, which it has been hitherto my greatest honour and greatest happiness to possess?"

"I have found nothing in your conduct to blame," she answered. "You have always treated me with the same delicacy and the same forbearance. You have deserved my trust; and, what is of far more importance in my estimation, you have deserved my father's trust, out of which mine grew. You have given me no excuse, even if I had wanted to find one, for asking to be released from my pledge. What I have said so far, has been spoken with the wish to acknowledge my whole obligation to you. My regard for that obligation, my regard for my father's memory, and my regard for my own promise, all forbid me to set the example, on *my* side, of withdrawing from our present position. The breaking of our engagement must be entirely your wish and your act, Sir Percival — not mine."

The uneasy beating of his foot suddenly stopped; and he leaned forward eagerly across the table.

"My act?" he said. "What reason can there be, on *my* side, for withdrawing?"

1 heard her breath quickening; I felt her hand growing

cold. In spite of what she had said to me, when we were alone, I began to be afraid of her. I was wrong.

"A reason that it is very hard to tell you," she answered. "There is a change in me, Sir Percival — a change which is serious enough to justify you, to yourself and to me, in breaking off our engagement."

His face turned so pale again, that even his lips lost their colour. He raised the arm which lay on the table; turned a little away in his chair; and supported his head on his hand, so that his profile only was presented to us.

"What change?" he asked. The tone in which he put the question jarred on me — there was something painfully suppressed in it.

She sighed heavily, and leaned towards me a little, so as to rest her shoulder against mine. I felt her trembling, and tried to spare her by speaking myself. She stopped me by a warning pressure of her hand, and then addressed Sir Percival once more; but, this time, without looking at him.

"I have heard," she said, "and I believe it, that the fondest and truest of all affections is the affection which a woman ought to bear to her husband. When our engagement began, that affection was mine to give, if I could, and yours to win, if you could. Will you pardon me, and spare me, Sir Percival, if I acknowledge that it is not so any longer?"

A few tears gathered in her eyes, and dropped over her cheeks slowly, as she paused and waited for his answer. He did not utter a word. At the beginning of her reply, he had moved the hand on which his head rested, so that it hid his face. I saw nothing but the upper part of his figure at the table. Not a muscle of him moved. The fingers of the hand which supported his head were dented deep in his hair. They might have expressed hidden anger, or hidden grief — it was hard to say which — there was no significant trembling in them. There was nothing, absolutely nothing to tell the secret of his thoughts at that moment — the moment which was the crisis of his life and the crisis of hers.

I was determined to make him declare himself, for Laura's sake.

"Sir Percival!" I interposed, sharply; "have you nothing to say, when my sister has said so much? More, in my opinion," I added, my unlucky temper getting the better of me, "than any man alive, in your position, has a right to hear from her."

That last rash sentence opened a way for him by which to escape me if he chose; and he instantly took advantage of it.

"Pardon me, Miss Halcombe," he said, still keeping his hand over his face — "pardon me, if I remind you that I have claimed no such right."

The few plain words which would have brought him back to the point from which he had wandered, were just on my lips, when Laura checked me by speaking again.

"I hope I have not made my painful acknowledgment in vain," she continued. "I hope it has secured me your entire confidence in what I have still to say?"

"Pray be assured of it." He made that brief reply, warmly; dropping his hand on the table, while he spoke, and turning towards us again. Whatever outward change had passed over him, was gone now. His face was eager and expectant — it expressed nothing but the most intense anxiety to hear her next words.

"I wish you to understand that I have not spoken from any selfish motive," she said. "If you leave me, Sir Percival, after what you have just heard, you do not leave me to marry another man — you only allow me to remain a single woman for the rest of my life. My fault towards you has begun and ended in my own thoughts. It can never go any farther. No word has passed —" She hesitated, in doubt about the expression she should use next; hesitated, in a momentary confusion which it was very sad and very painful to see. "No word has passed," she patiently and resolutely resumed, "between myself and the person to whom I am now referring for the first and last time in your presence, of my feelings towards him, or of his feeling towards me — no word ever can pass — neither he nor I are likely, in this world, to meet again. I earnestly beg you to spare me from saying any more, and to believe me, on my word, in what I have just told you. It is the truth, Sir Percival—the truth which *I* think my promised husband has a claim to hear, at any sacrifice of my own feelings. I trust to his generosity to pardon me, and to his honour to keep my secret."

"Both those trusts are sacred to me," he said, "and both shall be sacredly kept."

After answering in those terms, he paused, and looked at her, as if he was waiting to hear more.

"I have said all I wish to say," she added, quietly — "I have said more than enough to justify you in withdrawing from your engagement."

"You have said more than enough," he answered, "to make it the dearest object of my life to *keep* the engagement." With those words he rose from his chair, and advanced a few steps towards the place where she was sitting.

She started violently, and a faint cry of surprise escaped her. Every word she had spoken had innocently betrayed her purity and truth to a man who thoroughly understood the priceless value of a pure and true woman. Her own noble conduct had been the hidden enemy, throughout, of all the hopes she had trusted to it. I had dreaded this from the first. I would have prevented it, if she had allowed me the smallest chance of doing so. I even waited and watched, now, when the harm was done, for a word from Sir Percival that would give me the opportunity of putting him in the wrong.

"You have left it to *me*, Miss Fairlie, to resign you," he continued. "I am not heartless enough to resign a woman who has just shown herself to be the noblest of her sex."

He spoke with such warmth and feeling, with such passionate enthusiasm and yet with such perfect delicacy, that she raised her head, flushed up a little, and looked at him with sudden animation and spirit.

"No!" she said, firmly. "The most wretched of her sex, if she must give herself in marriage when she cannot give her love."

"May she not give it in the future," he asked, "if the one object of her husband's life is to deserve it?"

"Never!" she answered. "If you still persist in maintaining our engagement, I may be your true and faithful wife, Sir Percival — your loving wife, if I know my own heart, never!"

She looked so irresistibly beautiful as she said those brave words that no man alive could have steeled his heart against her. I tried hard to feel that Sir Percival was to blame, and to say so; but my womanhood would pity him, in spite of myself.

"I gratefully accept your faith and truth," he said. "The least that *you* can offer is more to me than the utmost that I could hope for from any other woman in the world."

Her left hand still held mine; but her right hand hung listlessly at her side. He raised it gently to his lips — touched it with them, rather than kissed it — bowed to me — and then, with perfect delicacy and discretion, silently quitted the room.

She neither moved, nor said a word, when he was gone — she sat by me, cold and still, with her eyes fixed on the ground. I saw it was hopeless and useless to speak; and I only put my arm round her, and held her to me in silence. We remained together so, for what seemed a long and weary time — so long and so weary, that I grew uneasy and spoke to her softly, in the hope of producing a change.

The sound of my voice seemed to startle her into consciousness. She suddenly drew herself away from me, and rose to her feet.

"I must submit, Marian, as well as I can," she said. "My new life has its hard duties; and one of them begins to-day."

As she spoke, she went to a side-table near the window, on which her sketching materials were placed; gathered them together carefully; and put them in a drawer of her cabinet. She locked the drawer, and brought the key to me.

"I must part from everything that reminds me of him," she

said. "Keep the key wherever you please — I shall never want it again."

Before I could say a word, she had turned away to her book-case, and had taken from it the album that contained Walter Hartright's drawings. She hesitated for a moment, holding the little volume fondly in her hands — then lifted it to her lips and kissed it.

"Oh, Laura! Laura!" I said, not angrily, not reprovingly — with nothing but sorrow in my voice, and nothing but sorrow in my heart.

"It is the last time, Marian," she pleaded. "I am bidding it good-by for ever."

She laid the book on the table, and drew out the comb that fastened her hair. It fell, in its matchless beauty, over her back and shoulders, and dropped round her, far below her waist. She separated one long, thin lock from the rest, cut it off, and pinned it carefully, in the form of a circle, on the first blank page of the album. The moment it was fastened, she closed the volume hurriedly, and placed it in my hands.

"You write to him, and he writes to you," she said. " While I am alive, if he asks after me, always tell him I am well, and never say I am unhappy. Don't distress him, Marian — for *my* sake, don't distress him. If I die first, promise you will give him this little book of his drawings, with my hair in it. There can be no harm, when I am gone, in telling him that I put it there with my own hands. And say — oh, Marian, say for me, then, what I can never say for myself — say I loved him!"

She flung her arms round my neck, and whispered the last words in my ear with a passionate delight in uttering them which it almost broke my heart to hear. All the long restraint she had imposed on herself, gave way in that first last outburst of tenderness. She broke from me with hysterical vehemence, and threw herself on the sofa, in a paroxysm of sobs and tears that shook her from head to foot.

I tried vainly to soothe her and reason with her; she was past being soothed, and past being reasoned with. It was the sad, sudden end for us two, of this memorable day. When the fit had worn itself out, she was too exhausted to speak. She slumbered towards the afternoon; and I put away the book of drawings so that she might not see it when she woke. My face was calm, whatever my heart might be, when she opened her eyes again and looked at me. We said no more to each other about the distressing interview of the morning. Sir Percival's name was not mentioned, Walter Hartright was not alluded to again by either of us for the remainder of the day.

10th. — Finding that she was composed and like herself, this morning, I returned to the painful subject of yesterday, for the sole purpose of imploring her to let me speak to Sir Percival and M. Fairlie, more plainly and strongly than she could speak to either of them herself, about this lamentable marriage. She interposed, gently but firmly, in the middle of my remonstrances.

"I left yesterday to decide," she said; "and yesterday *has* decided. It is too late to go back."

Sir Percival spoke to me this afternoon, about what had passed in Laura's room. He assured me that the unparalleled trust she had placed in him had awakened such an answering . conviction of her innocence and integrity in his mind, that he was guiltless of having felt even a moment's unworthy jealousy, either at the time when he was in her presence, or afterwards when he had withdrawn from it. Deeply as he lamented the unfortunate attachment which had hindered the progress he might otherwise have made in her esteem and regard, he firmly believed that it had remained unacknowledged in the past, and that it would remain, under all changes of circumstance which it was possible to contemplate, unacknowledged in the future. This was his absolute conviction; and the strongest proof he could give of it was the assurance, which he now offered, that he felt no curiosity to know whether the attachment was of recent date or not, or who had been the object of it. His implicit confidence in Miss Fairlie made him satisfied with what she had thought fit to say to him, and he was honestly innocent of the slightest feeling of anxiety to hear more.

He waited, after saying those words, and looked at me. I was so conscious of my unreasonable prejudice against him — so conscious of an unworthy suspicion, that he might be speculating on my impulsively answering the very questions which he had just described himself as resolved not to ask — that I evaded all reference to this part of the subject with something like a feeling of confusion on my own part. At the same time, I was resolved not to lose even the smallest opportunity of trying to plead Laura's cause; and I told him boldly that I regretted his generosity had not carried him one step farther, and induced him to withdraw from the engagement altogether.

Here, again, he disarmed me by not attempting to defend himself. He would merely beg me to remember the difference there was between his allowing Miss Fairlie to give him up, which was a matter of submission only, and his forcing himself to give up Miss Fairlie, which was, in other words, asking him to be the suicide of his own hopes. Her conduct of the day before had so strengthened the unchangeable love and admiration of two long years, that all active contention against those feelings, on his part, was henceforth entirely out of his power. I must think him weak, selfish, unfeeling towards the very woman whom he idolised, and he must bow to my opinion as resignedly as he could; only putting it to me, at the same time, whether her future as a single woman, pining under an unhappily placed attachment which she could never acknowledge, could be said to promise her a much brighter prospect than her future as the wife of a man who worshipped the very ground she walked on? In the last case there was hope from time, however slight it might be — in the first case, on her own showing, there was no hope at all.

I answered him — more because my tongue is a woman's, and must answer, than because I had anything convincing to say. It was only too plain that the course Laura had adopted the day before, had offered him the advantage if he chose to

take it — and that he *had* chosen to take it.   I felt this at the
time, and I feel it just as strongly now, while I write these
lines, in my own room.   The one hope left, is that his motives
really spring, as he says they do, from the irresistible strength
of his attachment to Laura.

Before I close my diary for to-night, I must record that I
wrote to-day, in poor Hartright's interests, to two of my
mother's old friends in London — both men of influence and
position. If they can do anything for him, I am quite sure they
will.   Except Laura, I never was more anxious about any one
than I am now about Walter.   All that had happened since he
left us has only increased my strong regard and sympathy for
him.   I hope I am doing right in trying to help him to employment abroad — I hope, most earnestly and anxiously, that
it will end well.

11th. — Sir Percival had an interview with Mr. Fairlie; and
I was sent for to join them.

I found Mr. Fairlie greatly relieved at the prospect of the
"family worry" (as he was pleased to describe his niece's marriage) being settled at last.   So far, I did not feel called on to
say anything to him about my own opinion; but when he proceeded, in his most aggravatingly languid manner, to suggest
that the time for the marriage had better be settled next, in
accordance with Sir Percival's wishes, I enjoyed the satisfaction of assailing Mr. Fairlie's nerves with as strong a protest
against hurrying Laura's decision as I could put into words.
Sir Percival immediately assured me that he felt the force of
my objection, and begged me to believe that the proposal had
not been made in consequence of any interference on his part.
Mr. Fairlie leaned back in his chair, closed his eyes, said we
both of us did honour to human nature, and then repeated his
suggestion, as coolly as if neither Sir Percival nor I had said
a word in opposition to it.   It ended in my flatly declining to
mention the subject to Laura, unless she first approached it of
her own accord.   I left the room at once after making that
declaration.   Sir Percival looked seriously embarrassed and

distressed. Mr. Fairlie stretched out his lazy legs on his velvet footstool; and said: "Dear Marian! how I envy you your robust nervous system! Don't bang the door!"

On going to Laura's room, I found that she had asked for me, and that Mrs. Vesey had informed her that I was with Mr. Fairlie. She inquired at once what I had been wanted for; and I told her all that had passed, without attempting to conceal the vexation and annoyance that I really felt. Her answer surprised and distressed me inexpressibly; it was the very last reply that I should have expected her to make.

"My uncle is right," she said. "I have caused trouble and anxiety enough to you, and to all about me. Let me cause no more, Marian — let Sir Percival decide."

I remonstrated warmly; but nothing that I could say moved her.

"I am held to my engagement," she replied; "I have broken with my old life. The evil day will not come the less surely because I put it off. No, Marian! once again, my uncle is right. I have caused trouble enough and anxiety enough; and I will cause no more."

She used to be pliability itself; but she was now inflexibly passive in her resignation — I might almost say in her despair. Dearly as I love her, I should have been less pained if she had been violently agitated; it was so shockingly unlike her natural character to see her as cold and insensible as I saw her now.

12th. — Sir Percival put some questions to me, at breakfast, about Laura, which left me no choice but to tell him what she had said.

While we were talking, she herself came down and joined us. She was just as unnaturally composed in Sir Percival's presence as she had been in mine. When breakfast was over, he had an opportunity of saying a few words to her privately, in a recess of one of the windows. They were not more than two or three minutes together; and, on their separating, she left the room with Mrs. Vesey, while Sir Percival came to me.

He said he had entreated her to favour him by maintaining her privilege of fixing the time for the marriage at her own will and pleasure. In reply, she had merely expressed her acknowledgements, and had desired him to mention what his wishes were to Miss Halcombe.

I have no patience to write more. In this instance, as in every other, Sir Percival has carried his point, with the utmost possible credit to himself, in spite of everything that I can say or do. His wishes are now, what they were, of course, when he first came here; and Laura having resigned herself to the one inevitable sacrifice of the marriage, remains as coldly hopeless and enduring as ever. In parting with the little occupations and relics that reminded her of Hartright, she seems to have parted with all her tenderness and all her impressibility. It is only three o'clock in the afternoon while I write these lines, and Sir Percival has left us already, in the happy hurry of a bridegroom, to prepare for the bride's reception at his house in Hampshire. Unless some extraordinary event happens to prevent it, they will be married exactly at the time when he wished to be married — before the end of the year. My very fingers burn as I write it!

13th.— A sleepless night, through uneasiness about Laura. Towards the morning, I came to a resolution to try what change of scene would do to rouse her. She cannot surely remain in her present torpor of insensibility, if I take her away from Limmeridge and surround her with the pleasant faces of old friends? After some consideration, I decided on writing to the Arnolds, in Yorkshire. They are simple, kind-hearted hospitable people; and she has known them from her childhood. When I had put the letter in the post-bag, I told her what I had done. It would have been a relief to me if she had shown the spirit to resist and object. But no — she only said, "I will go anywhere with *you*, Marian. I dare say you are right — I dare say the change will do me good."

14th. — I wrote to Mr. Gilmore, informing him that there

was really a prospect of this miserable marriage taking place, and also mentioning my idea of trying what change of scene would do for Laura. I had no heart to go into particulars. Time enough for them, when we get nearer to the end of the year.

15th. — Three letters for me. The first, from the Arnolds, full of delight at the prospect of seeing Laura and me. The second, from one of the gentlemen to whom I wrote on Walter Hartright's behalf, informing me that he has been fortunate enough to find an opportunity of complying with my request. The third, from Walter himself; thanking me, poor fellow, in the warmest terms, for giving him an opportunity of leaving his home, his country, and his friends. A private expedition to make excavations among the ruined cities of Central America is, it seems, about to sail from Liverpool. The draughtsman who had been already appointed to accompany it, has lost heart, and withdrawn at the eleventh hour; and Walter is to fill his place. He is to be engaged for six months certain, from the time of the landing in Honduras, and for a year afterwards, if the excavations are successful, and if the funds hold out. His letter ends with a promise to write me a farewell line, when they are all on board ship, and when the pilot leaves them. I can only hope and pray earnestly that he and I are both acting in this matter for the best. It seems such a serious step for him to take, that the mere contemplation of it startles me. And yet, in his unhappy position, how can I expect him, or wish him, to remain at home?

16th. — The carriage is at the door. Laura and I set out on our visit to the Arnolds to-day.

*   *   *   *   *

Polesdean Lodge, Yorkshire.

23rd.— A week in these new scenes and among these kind-hearted people has done her some good, though not so much as I had hoped. I have resolved to prolong our stay for another week at least. It is useless to go back to Limmeridge, till there is an absolute necessity for our return.

24th. — Sad news by this morning's post. The expedition to Central America sailed on the twenty-first. We have parted with a true man; whe have lost a faithful friend. Walter Hartright has left England.

25th. — Sad news yesterday; ominous news to-day. Sir Percival Glyde has written to Mr. Fairlie; and Mr. Fairlie has written to Laura and me, to recall us to Limmeridge immediately.

What can this mean? Has the day for the marriage been fixed in our absence?

II.

Limmeridge House.

NOVEMBER 27th. — My forebodings are realized. The marriage is fixed for the twenty-second of December.

The day after we left for Polesdean Lodge, Sir Percival wrote, it seems, to Mr. Fairlie, to say that the necessary repairs and alterations in his house in Hampshire would occupy a much longer time in completion than he had originally anticipated. The proper estimates were to be submitted to him as soon as possible; and it would greatly facilitate his entering into definite arrangements with the workpeople, if he could be informed of the exact period at which the wedding ceremony might be expected to take place. He could then make all his calculations in reference to time, besides writing the necessary apologies to friends who had been engaged to visit him that winter, and who could not, of course, be received when the house was in the hands of the workmen.

To this letter Mr. Fairlie had replied by requesting Sir Percival himself to suggest a day for the marriage, subject to Miss Fairlie's approval, which her guardian willingly undertook to do his best to obtain. Sir Percival wrote back by the next post, and proposed (in accordance with his own views and wishes, from the first) the latter part of December — perhaps the twenty-second, or twenty-fourth, or any other day that the lady and her guardian might prefer. The lady not being at hand to speak for herself, her guardian had decided in her absence, on the earliest day mentioned — the twenty-second of December — and had written to recall us to Limmeridge in consequence.

After explaining these particulars to me at a private interview yesterday, Mr. Fairlie suggested, in his most amiable manner, that I should open the necessary negociations to-day. Feeling that resistance was useless, unless I could first obtain Laura's authority to make it, I consented to speak to her, but declared, at the same time, that I would on no consideration undertake to gain her consent to Sir Percival's wishes. Mr. Fairlie complimented me on my "excellent conscience," much as he would have complimented me, if we had been out walking, on my "excellent constitution," and seemed perfectly satisfied, so far, with having simply shifted one more family responsibility from his own shoulders to mine.

This morning, I spoke to Laura as I had promised. The composure — I may almost say, the insensibility — which she has so strangely and so resolutely maintained ever since Sir Percival left us, was not proof against the shock of the news I had to tell her. She turned pale, and trembled violently.

"Not so soon!" she pleaded. "Oh, Marian, not so soon!"

The slightest hint she could give was enough for me. I rose to leave the room, and fight her battle for her at once with Mr. Fairlie.

Just as my hand was on the door, she caught fast hold of my dress, and stopped me.

"Let me go!" I said. "My tongue burns to tell your uncle that he and Sir Percival are not to have it all their own way."

She sighed bitterly, and still held my dress.

"No!" she said, faintly. "Too late, Marian — too late!"

"Not a minute too late," I retorted. "The question of

time is *our* question — and trust me, Laura, to take a woman's full advantage of it."

I unclasped her hand from my gown while I spoke; but she slipped both her arms round my waist at the same moment, and held me more effectually than ever.

"It will only involve us in more trouble and more confusion," she said. "It will set you and my uncle at variance, and bring Sir Percival here again with fresh causes of complaint ——"

"So much the better!" I cried out, passionately. "Who cares for his causes of complaint? Are you to break your heart to set his mind at ease? No man under heaven deserves these sacrifices from us women. Men! They are the enemies of our innocence and our peace — they drag us away from our parents' love and our sisters' friendship — they take us body and soul to themselves, and fasten our helpless lives to theirs as they chain up a dog to his kennel. And what does the best of them give us in return? Let me go, Laura — I'm mad when I think of it!"

The tears — miserable, weak, women's tears of vexation and rage — started to my eyes. She smiled sadly; and put her handkerchief over my face, to hide for me the betrayal of my own weakness — the weakness of all others which she knew that I most despised.

"Oh, Marian!" she said. "*You* crying! Think what you would say to me; if the places were changed, and if those tears were mine. All your love and courage and devotion will not alter what *must* happen, sooner or later. Let my uncle have his way. Let us have no more troubles and heart-burnings that any sacrifice of mine can prevent. Say you will live with me, Marian, when I am married — and say no more."

But I did say more. I forced back the contemptible tears that were no relief to *me*, and that only distressed *her*; and reasoned and pleaded as calmly as I could. It was of no avail. She made me twice repeat the promise to live with her when she was married, and then suddenly asked a question which turned my sorrow and my sympathy for her into a new direction.

"While we were at Polesdean," she said, "you had a letter, Marian ——"

Her altered tone; the abrupt manner in which she looked away from me, and hid her face on my shoulder; the hesitation which silenced her before she had completed her question all told me, but too plainly, to whom the half-expressed inquiry pointed.

"I thought, Laura, that you and I were never to refer to him again," I said, gently.

"You had a letter from him?" she persisted.

"Yes," I replied, "if you must know it."

"Do you mean to write to him again?"

I hesitated. I had been afraid to tell her of his absence from England, or of the manner in which my exertions to serve his new hopes and projects had connected me with his departure. What answer could I make? He was gone where no letters could reach him for months, perhaps for years, to come.

"Suppose I do mean to write to him again," I said, at last. "What then, Laura?"

Her cheek grew burning hot against my neck; and her arms trembled and tightened round me.

"Don't tell him about *the twenty-second*," she whispered. "Promise, Marian — pray promise you will not even mention my name to him when you write next."

I gave the promise. No words can say how sorrowfully 1 gave it. She instantly took her arm from my waist, walked away to the window, and stood looking out, with her back to me. After a moment she spoke once more, but without turning round, without allowing me to catch the smallest glimpse of her face.

"Are you going to my uncle's room?" she asked. "Will you say that I consent to whatever arrangement he may think best? Never mind leaving me, Marian. I shall be better alone for a little while."

I went out. If, as soon as I got into the passage, I could have transported Mr. Fairlie and Sir Percival Glyde to the uttermost ends of the earth, by lifting one of my fingers, that finger would have been raised without an instant's hesitation. For once my unhappy temper now stood my friend. I should have broken down altogether and burst into a violent fit of crying, if my tears had not been all burnt up in the heat of my anger. As it was, I dashed into Mr. Fairlie's room — called to him as harshly as possible, "Laura consents to the twenty-second" — and dashed out again without waiting for a word of answer. I banged the door after me; and I hope I shattered Mr. Fairlie's nervous system for the rest of the day.

28th. — This morning, I read poor Hartright's farewell letter over again; a doubt having crossed my mind since yesterday, whether I am acting wisely in concealing the fact of his departure from Laura.

On reflection, I still think I am right. The allusions in his letter to the preparations made for the expedition to Central America, all show that the leaders of it know it to be dangerous. If the discovery of this makes *me* uneasy, what would it make *her?* It is bad enough to feel that his departure has deprived us of the friend of all others to whose devotion we could trust, in the hour of need, if ever that hour comes and finds us helpless. But it is far worse to know that he has gone from us to face the perils of a bad climate, a wild country, and a disturbed population. Surely it would be a cruel candour to tell Laura this, without a pressing and a positive necessity for it?

I almost doubt whether I ought not to go a step farther, and burn the letter at once, for fear of its one day falling into wrong hands. It not only refers to Laura in terms which ought to remain a secret for ever between the writer and me: but it reiterates his suspicion — so obstinate, so unaccountable, and so alarming — that he has been secretly watched since he left Limmeridge. He declares that he saw the faces of the two strange men, who followed him about the streets of London, watching him among the crowd which gathered at Liverpool to see the expedition embark; and he positively asserts that he heard the name of Anne Catherick pronounced behind him, as he got into the boat. His own words are, "These events have a meaning, these events must lead to a result. The mystery of Anne Catherick is *not* cleared up yet. She may never cross my path again; but if ever she crosses yours, make better use of the opportunity, Miss Halcombe, than I made of it. I speak on strong conviction; I entreat you to remember what I say." These are his own expressions. There is no danger of my forgetting them — my memory is only too ready to dwell on any words of Hartright's that refer to Anne Catherick. But there is danger in my keeping the letter. The merest accident might place it at the mercy of strangers. I may fall ill; I may die — better to burn it at once, and have one anxiety the less.

It is burnt! The ashes of his farewell letter — the last he may ever write to me — lie in a few black fragments on the hearth. Is this the sad end to all that sad story? Oh, not the end — surely, surely not the end already!

29 th. — The preparations for the marriage have begun. The dressmaker has come to receive her orders. Laura is perfectly impassive, perfectly careless about the question of all others in which a woman's personal interests are most closely bound up. She has left it all to the dressmaker and to me. If poor Hartright had been the baronet, and the husband of her father's choice, how differently she would have behaved! How anxious and capricious she would have been; and what a hard task the best of dressmakers would have found it to please her!

30 th. — We hear every day from Sir Percival. The last news is, that the alterations in his house will occupy from four to six months, before they can be properly completed. If painters, paper-hangers, and upholsterers could make happiness as well as splendour, I should be interested about their proceedings in Laura's future home. As it is, the only part of Sir Percival's last letter which does not leave me as it found me, perfectly indifferent to all his plans and projects, is the part which refers to the wedding tour. He proposes, as Laura

is delicate, and as the winter threatens to be unusually severe, to take her to Rome, and to remain in Italy until the early part of next summer. If this plan should not be approved, he is equally ready, although he has no establishment of his own in town, to spend the season in London, in the most suitable furnished house that can be obtained for the purpose.

Putting myself and my own feelings entirely out of the question (which it is my duty to do, and which I have done), I, for one, have no doubt of the propriety of adopting the first of these proposals. In either case, a separation between Laura and me is inevitable. It will be a longer separation, in the event of their going abroad, than it would be in the event of their remaining in London — but we must set against this disadvantage, the benefit to Laura on the other side, of passing the winter in a mild climate; and, more than that, the immense assistance in raising her spirits, and reconciling her to her new existence, which the mere wonder and excitement of travelling for the first time in her life in the most interesting country in the world, must surely afford. She is not of a disposition to find resources in the conventional gaieties and excitements of London. They would only make the first oppression of this lamentable marriage fall the heavier on her. I dread the beginning of her new life more than words can tell; but I see some hope for her if she travels — none if she remains at home.

It is strange to look back at this latest entry in my journal, and to find that I am writing of the marriage and the parting with Laura, as people write of a settled thing. It seems so cold and so unfeeling to be looking at the future already in this cruelly composed way. But what other way is possible, now that the time is drawing so near? Before another month is over our heads, she will be *his* Laura instead of mine! *His* Laura! I am as little able to realize the idea which those two words convey — my mind feels almost as dulled and stunned by it, as if writing of her marriage were like writing of her death.

December 1st. — A sad, sad day; a day that I have no heart to describe at any length. After weakly putting it off, last night, I was obliged to speak to her this morning of Sir Percival's proposal about the wedding tour.

In the full conviction that I should be with her, wherever she went, the poor child — for a child she is still in many things — was almost happy at the prospect of seeing the wonders of Florence and Rome and Naples. It nearly broke my heart to dispel her delusion, and to bring her face to face with the hard truth. I was obliged to tell her that no man tolerates a rival — not even a woman rival — in his wife's affections, when he first marries, whatever he may do afterwards. I was obliged to warn her, that my chance of living with her permanently under her own roof, depended entirely on my not arousing Sir Percival's jealousy and distrust by standing between them at the beginning of their marriage, in the position of the chosen depository of his wife's closest secrets. Drop by drop, I poured the profaning bitterness of this world's wisdom into that pure heart and that innocent mind, while every higher and better feeling within me recoiled from my miserable task. It is over now. She has learnt her hard, her inevitable lesson. The simple illusions of her girlhood are gone; and my hand has stripped them off. Better mine than his — that is all my consolation — better mine than his.

So the first proposal is the proposal accepted. They are to go to Italy; and I am to arrange, with Sir Percival's permission, for meeting them and staying with them, when they return to England. In other words, I am to ask a personal favour, for the first time in my life, and to ask it of the man of all others to whom I least desire to owe a serious obligation of any kind. Well! I think I could do even more than that, for Laura's sake.

2nd. — On looking back, I find myself always referring to Sir Percival in disparaging terms. In the turn affairs have now taken, I must and will root out my prejudice against him.

I cannot think how it first got into my mind. It certainly never existed in former times.

Is it Laura's reluctance to become his wife that has set me against him? Have Hartright's perfectly intelligible prejudices infected me without my suspecting their influence? Does that letter of Anne Catherick's still leave a lurking distrust in my mind, in spite of Sir Percival's explanation, and of the proof in my possession of the truth of it? I cannot account for the state of my own feelings: the one thing I am certain of is, that it is my duty — doubly my duty, now — not to wrong Sir Percival by unjustly distrusting him. If it has got to be a habit with me always to write of him in the same unfavourable manner, I must and will break myself of this unworthy tendency, even though the effort should force me to close the pages of my journal till the marriage is over! I am seriously dissatisfied with myself — I will write no more to-day.

*   *   *   *   *

December 16th. — A whole fortnight has passed; and I have not once opened these pages. I have been long enough away from my journal, to come back to it, with a healthier and better mind, I hope, so far as Sir Percival is concerned.

There is not much to record of the past two weeks. The dresses are almost all finished; and the new travelling trunks have been sent here from London. Poor dear Laura hardly leaves me for a moment, all day; and, last night, when neither of us could sleep, she came and crept into my bed to talk to me there. "I shall lose you so soon, Marian," she said; "I must make the most of you while I can."

They are to be married at Limmeridge Church; and, thank Heaven, not one of the neighbours is to be invited to the ceremony. The only visitor will be our old friend, Mr. Arnold, who is to come from Polesdean, to give Laura away; her uncle being far too delicate to trust himself outside the door in such inclement weather as we now have. If I were not determined, from this day forth, to see nothing but the bright side of our prospects, the melancholy absence of any male relative of Laura's, at the most important moment of her life, would make me very gloomy and very distrustful of the future. But I have done with gloom and distrust — that is to say, I have done with writing about either the one or the other in this journal.

Sir Percival is to arrive to-morrow. He offered, in case we wished to treat him on terms of rigid etiquette, to write and ask our clergyman to grant him the hospitality of the rectory, during the short period of his sojourn at Limmeridge, before the marriage. Under the circumstances, neither Mr. Fairlie nor I thought it at all necessary for us to trouble ourselves about attending to trifling forms and ceremonies. In our wild moorland country, and in this great lonely house, we may well claim to be beyond the reach of the trivial conventionalities which hamper people in other places. I wrote to Sir Percival to thank him for his polite offer, and to beg that he would occupy his old rooms, just as usual, at Limmeridge House.

17th. — He arrived to-day, looking, as I thought, a little worn and anxious, but still talking and laughing like a man in the best possible spirits. He brought with him some really beautiful presents, in jewelry, which Laura received with her best grace, and, outwardly at least, with perfect self-possession. The only sign I can detect of the struggle it must cost her to preserve appearances at this trying time, expresses itself in a sudden unwillingness, on her part, ever to be left alone. Instead of retreating to her own room, as usual, she seems to dread going there. When I went up-stairs to-day, after lunch, to put on my bonnet for a walk, she volunteered to join me; and, again, before dinner, she threw the door open between our two rooms, so that we might talk to each other while we were dressing. "Keep me always doing something," she said; "keep me always in company with somebody. Don't let me think — that is all I ask now, Marian — don't let me think."

This sad change in her, only increases her attractions for

Sir Percival. He interprets it, I can see, to his own advantage. There is a feverish flush in her cheeks, a feverish brightness in her eyes, which he welcomes as the return of her beauty and the recovery of her spirits. She talked to-day at dinner with a gaiety and carelessness so false, so shockingly out of her character, that I secretly longed to silence her and take her away. Sir Percival's delight and surprise appeared to be beyond all expression. The anxiety which I had noticed on his face when he arrived, totally disappeared from it; and he looked even to my eyes, a good ten years younger than he really is.

There can be no doubt — though some strange perversity prevents me from seeing it myself — there can be no doubt that Laura's future husband is a very handsome man. Regular features form a personal advantage to begin with — and he has them. Bright brown eyes, either in man or woman, are a great attraction — and he has them. Even baldness, when it is only baldness over the forehead (as in his case), is rather becoming, than not, in a man, for it heightens the head and adds to the intelligence of the face. Grace and ease of movement; untiring animation of manner; ready, pliant, conversational powers — all these are unquestionable merits, and all these he certainly possesses. Surely, Mr. Gilmore, ignorant as he is of Laura's secret, was not to blame for feeling surprised that she should repent of her marriage engagement? Any one else in his place, would have shared our good old friend's opinion. If I were asked, at this moment, to say plainly what defects I have discovered in Sir Percival, I could only point out two. One, his incessant restlessness and excitability — which may be caused, naturally enough, by unusual energy of character. The other, his short, sharp, illtempered manner of speaking to the servants — which may be only a bad habit, after all. No: I cannot dispute it, and I will not dispute it — Sir Percival is a very handsome and a very agreeable man. There! I have written it down, at last, and I am glad it's over.

18th. — Feeling weary and depressed, this morning, I left Laura with Mrs. Vesey, and went out alone for one of my brisk mid-day walks, which I have discontinued too much of late. I took the dry airy road, over the moor, that leads to Todd's Corner. After having been out half an hour, I was excessively surprised to see Sir Percival approaching me from the direction of the farm. He was walking rapidly, swinging his stick; his head erect as usual, and his shooting jacket flying open in the wind. When we met, he did not wait for me to ask any questions — he told me, at once, that he had been to the farm to inquire if Mr. or Mrs. Todd had received any tidings since his last visit to Limmeridge, of Anne Catherick.

"You found, of course, that they had heard nothing?" I said.

"Nothing whatever," he replied. "I begin to be seriously afraid that we have lost her. Do you happen to know," he continued, looking me in the face very attentively, "if the artist — Mr. Hartright — is in a position to give us any further information?"

"He has neither heard of her, nor seen her, since he left Cumberland," I answered.

"Very sad," said Sir Percival, speaking like a man who was disappointed, and yet, oddly enough, looking, at the same time, like a man who was relieved. "It is impossible to say what misfortunes may not have happened to the miserable creature. I am inexpressibly annoyed at the failure of all my efforts to restore her to the care and protection which she so urgently needs."

This time he really looked annoyed. I said a few sympathising words; and we then talked of other subjects, on our way back to the house. Surely, my chance meeting with him on the moor has disclosed another favourable trait in his character? Surely, it was singularly considerate and un-selfish of him to think of Anne Catherick on the eve of·his marriage, and to go all the way to Todd's Corner to make inquiries about her, when he might have passed the time so much more agreeably in Laura's society? Considering that he can only have acted from motives of pure charity, his conduct, under the circumstances, shows unusual good feeling, and deserves extraordinary praise. Well! I give him extraordinary praise — and there's an end of it.

19th. — More discoveries in the inexhaustible mine of Sir Percival's virtues.

To-day, I approached the subject of my proposed sojourn under his wife's roof, when he brings her back to England. I had hardly dropped my first hint in this direction, before he caught me warmly by the hand, and said I had made the very offer to him, which he had been, on his side, most anxious to make to me. I was the companion of all others whom he most sincerely longed to secure for his wife; and he begged me to believe that I had conferred a lasting favour on him by making the proposal to live with Laura after her marriage, exactly as I had always lived with her before it.

When I thanked him, in her name and in mine, for his considerate kindness to both of us, we passed next to the subject of his wedding tour, and began to talk of the English society in Rome to which Laura was to be introduced. He ran over the names of several friends whom he expected to meet abroad this winter. They were all English, as well as I can remember, with one exception. The one exception was Count Fosco.

The mention of the Count's name, and the discovery that he and his wife are likely to meet the bride and bridegroom on the continent, puts Laura's marriage, for the first time, in a distinctly favourable light. It is likely to be the means of healing a family feud. Hitherto Madame Fosco has chosen to forget her obligations as Laura's aunt, out of sheer spite against the late Mr. Fairlie for his conduct in the affair of the legacy. Now, however, she can persist in this course of conduct no longer. Sir Percival and Count Fosco are old and fast friends, and their wives will have no choice but to meet on civil terms. Madame Fosco, in her maiden days, was one of the most impertinent women I ever met with — capricious, exacting, and vain to the last degree of absurdity. If her husband has succeeded in bringing her to her senses, he deserves the gratitude of every member of the family — and he may have mine to begin with.

I am becoming anxious to know the Count. He is the most intimate friend of Laura's husband; and, in that capacity, he excites my strongest interest. Neither Laura nor I have ever seen him. All I know of him is that his accidental presence, years ago, on the steps of the Trinità del Monte at Rome, assisted Sir Percival's escape from robbery and assassination, at the critical moment when he was wounded in the hand, and might, the next instant, have been wounded in the heart. I remember also that, at the time of the late Mr. Fairlie's absurd objections to his sister's marriage, the Count wrote him a very temperate and sensible letter on the subject, which, I am ashamed to say, remained unanswered. This is all I know of Sir Percival's friend. I wonder if he will ever come to England? I wonder if I shall like him?

My pen is running away into mere speculation. Let me return to sober matter of fact. It is certain that Sir Percival's reception of my venturesome proposal to live with his wife, was more than kind, it was almost affectionate. I am sure Laura's husband will have no reason to complain of me, if I can only go on as I have begun. I have already declared him to be handsome, agreeable, full of good feeling towards the unfortunate, and full of affectionate kindness towards me. Really, I hardly know myself again, in my new character of Sir Percival's warmest friend.

20th. — I hate Sir Percival! I flatly deny his good looks. I consider him to be eminently ill-tempered and disagreeable, and totally wanting in kindness and good feeling. Last night, the cards for the married couple were sent home. Laura opened the packet, and saw her future name in print, for the first time.　Sir Percival looked over her shoulder familiarly at the new card which had already transformed Miss Fairlie into Lady Glyde — smiled with the most odious self-complacency — and whispered something in her ear.　I don't know what it was — Laura has refused to tell me — but I saw her face turn to such a deadly whiteness that I thought she would have fainted.　He took no notice of the change: he seemed to be barbarously unconscious that he had said anything to pain her.　All my old feelings of hostility towards him revived on the instant; and all the hours that have passed, since, have done nothing to dissipate them.　I am more unreasonable and more unjust than ever.　In three words — how glibly my pen writes them! — in three words, I hate him.

21st. — Have the anxieties of this anxious time shaken me a little, at last?　I have been writing, for the last few days, in a tone of levity which, Heaven knows, is far enough from my heart, and which it has rather shocked me to discover on looking back at the entries in my journal.

Perhaps I may have caught the feverish excitement of Laura's spirits, for the last week.　If so the fit has already passed away from me, and has left me in a very strange state of mind.　A persistent idea has been forcing itself on my attention, ever since last night, that something will yet happen to prevent the marriage.　What has produced this singular fancy?　Is it the indirect result of my apprehensions for Laura's future?　Or has it been unconsciously suggested to me by the increasing restlessness and irritability which I have certainly observed in Sir Percival's manner, as the wedding-day draws nearer and nearer?　Impossible to say. I know that I have the idea — surely the wildest idea, under the circumstances, that ever entered a woman's head? — but try as I may, I cannot trace it back to its source.

This last day has been all confusion and wretchedness.

How can I write about it? — and yet, I must write. Anything is better than brooding over my own gloomy thoughts.

Kind Mrs. Vesey, whom we have all too much overlooked and forgotten of late, innocently caused us a sad morning to begin with. She has been, for months past, secretly making a warm Shetland shawl for her dear pupil — a most beautiful and surprising piece of work to be done by a woman at her age and with her habits. The gift was presented this morning; and poor warm-hearted Laura completely broke down when the shawl was put proudly on her shoulders by the loving old friend and guardian of her motherless childhood. I was hardly allowed time to quiet them both, or even to dry my own eyes, when I was sent for by Mr. Fairlie, to be favoured by a long recital of his arrangements for the preservation of his own tranquillity on the wedding-day.

"Dear Laura" was to receive his present — a shabby ring, with her affectionate uncle's hair for an ornament, instead of a precious stone, and with a heartless French inscription, inside, about congenial sentiments and eternal friendship — "dear Laura" was to receive this tender tribute from my hands immediately, so that she might have plenty of time to recover from the agitation produced by the gift, before she appeared in Mr. Fairlie's presence. "Dear Laura" was to pay him a little visit that evening, and to be kind enough not to make a scene. "Dear Laura" was to pay him another little visit in her wedding dress, the next morning, and to be kind enough, again, not to make a scene. "Dear Laura" was too look in once more, for the third time, before going away, but without harrowing his feelings by saying *when* she was going away, and without tears — "in the name of pity, in the name of everything, dear Marian, that is most affectionate and most domestic and most delightfully and charmingly self-composed, *without tears!*" I was so exasperated by this miserable selfish trifling, at such a time, that I should certainly have shocked Mr. Fairlie by some of the hardest and rudest truths he has ever heard in his life, if the arrival of Mr.

Arnold from Polesdean had not called me away to new duties down stairs.

The rest of the day is indescribable. I believe no one in the house really knew how it passed. The confusion of small events, all huddled together one on the other, bewildered every one. There were dresses sent home, that had been forgotten; there were trunks to be packed and unpacked and packed again; there were presents from friends far and near, friends high and low. We were all needlessly hurried; all nervously expectant of the morrow. Sir Percival, especially, was too restless, now, to remain five minutes together in the same place. That short, sharp cough of his troubled him more than ever. He was in and out of the house all day long: and he seemed to grow so inquisitive, on a sudden, that he questioned the very strangers who came on small errands to the house. Add to all this, the one perpetual thought, in Laura's mind and mine, that we were to part the next day, and the haunting dread, unexpressed by either of us, and yet ever present to both, that this deplorable marriage might prove to be one fatal error of her life and the one hopeless sorrow of mine. For the first time in all the years of our close and happy intercourse we almost avoided looking each other in the face; and we refrained, by common consent, from speaking together in private, through the whole evening. I can dwell on it no longer. Whatever future sorrows may be in store for me, I shall always look back on this twenty-first of December as the most comfortless and most miserable day of my life.

I am writing these lines in the solitude of my own room, long after midnight; having just come back from a stolen look at Laura in her pretty little white bed — the bed she has occupied since the days of her girlhood.

There she lay, unconscious that I was looking at her — quiet, more quiet than I had dared to hope, but not sleeping. The glimmer of the night-light showed me that her eyes were only partially closed: the traces of tears glistened between her eyelids. My little keepsake — only a brooch — lay on the table at her bedside, with her prayer-book, and the miniature portrait of her father which she takes with her wherever she goes. I waited a moment, looking at her from behind her pillow, as she lay beneath me, with one arm and hand resting white on the white coverlid, so still, so quietly breathing, that the frill on her night-dress never moved — I waited, looking at her, as I have seen her thousands of times, as I shall never see her again — and then stole back to my room. My own love! with all your wealth, and all your beauty, how friendless you are! The one man who would give his heart's life to serve you, is far away, tossing, this stormy night, on the awful sea. Who else is left to you? No father, no brother — no living creature but the helpless, useless woman who writes these sad lines, and watches by you for the morning, in sorrow that she cannot compose, in doubt that she cannot conquer. Oh, what a trust is to be placed in that man's hands to-morrow! If ever he forgets it; if ever he injures a hair of her head! —

THE TWENTY-SECOND OF DECEMBER. *Seven o'clock.* A wild unsettled morning. She has just risen — better and calmer, now that the time has come, than she was yesterday.

Ten o'clock. She is dressed. We have kissed each other; we have promised each other not to lose courage. I am away for a moment in my own room. In the whirl and confusion of my thoughts, I can detect that strange fancy of some hindrance happening to stop the marriage, still hanging about my mind. Is it hanging about *his* mind, too? I see him from the window, moving hither and thither uneasily among the carriages at the door. — How can I write such folly! The marriage is a certainty. In less than half an hour we start for the church.

Eleven o'clock. It is all over. They are married.

Three o'clock.   They are gone!   I am blind with crying –
I can write no more —

✻   ✻   ✻   ✻   ✻

III.

✻   ✻   ✻   ✻   ✻

Blackwater Park, Hampshire.

JUNE 27, 1850. — Six months to look back on — six long,
lonely months, since Laura and I last saw each other!

How many days have I still to wait? Only one! To-morrow, the twenty-eighth, the travellers return to England. I can
hardly realize my own happiness; I can hardly believe that
the next four-and-twenty hours will complete the last day of
separation between Laura and me.

She and her husband have been in Italy all the winter, and
afterwards in the Tyrol. They come back, accompanied by
Count Fosco and his wife, who propose to settle somewhere in
the neighbourhood of London, and who have engaged to stay
at Blackwater Park for the summer months before deciding
on a place of residence. So long as Laura returns, no matter
who returns with her. Sir Percival may fill the house from
floor to ceiling, if he likes, on condition that his wife and I in-
habit it together.

Meanwhile, here I am, established at Blackwater Park;
"the ancient and interesting seat" (as the county history
obligingly informs me) "of Sir Percival Glyde, Bart." — and
the future abiding-place (as I may now venture to add, on my
account) of plain Marian Halcombe, spinster, now settled in a
snug little sitting-room, with a cup of tea by her side, and all
her earthly possessions ranged round her in three boxes and a
bag.

I left Limmeridge yesterday; having received Laura's
delightful letter from Paris, the day before. I had been previously uncertain whether I was to meet them in London, or in
Hampshire; but this last letter informed me, that Sir Percival

proposed to land at Southampton, and to travel straight on to his country-house. He has spent so much money abroad, that he has none left to defray the expenses of living in London, for the remainder of the season; and he is economically resolved to pass the summer and autumn quietly at Blackwater. Laura has had more than enough of excitement and change of scene; and is pleased at the prospect of country tranquillity and retirement which her husband's prudence provides for her. As for me, I am ready to be happy anywhere in her society. We are all, therefore, well contented in our various ways, to begin with.

Last night, I slept in London, and was delayed there so long, to-day, by various calls and commissions that I did not reach Blackwater, this evening, till after dusk.

Judging by my vague impressions of the place, thus far, it is the exact opposite of Limmeridge.

The house is situated on a dead flat, and seems to be shut in — almost suffocated, to my north-country notions, by trees. I have seen nobody, but the man-servant who opened the door to me, and the housekeeper, a very civil person who showed me the way to my own room, and got me my tea. I have a nice little boudoir and bedroom, at the end of a long passage on the first floor. The servants and some of the spare rooms are on the second floor; and all the living rooms are on the ground floor. I have not seen one of them yet, and I know nothing about the house, except that one wing of it is said to be five hundred years old, that it had a moat round it once, and that it gets its name of Blackwater from a lake in the park.

Eleven o'clock has just struck, in a ghostly and solemn manner, from a turret over the centre of the house, which I saw when I came in. A large dog has been woke, apparently by the sound of the bell, and is howling and yawning drearily, somewhere round a corner. I hear echoing footsteps in the passages below, and the iron thumping of bolts and bars at the house door. The servants are evidently going to bed. Shall I follow their example?

No: I am not half sleepy enough. Sleepy, did I say? I feel as if I should never close my eyes again. The bare anticipation of seeing that dear face and hearing that well-known voice to-morrow, keeps me in a perpetual fever of excitement. If I only had the privileges of a man, I would order out Sir Percival's best horse instantly, and tear away on a night-gallop, eastward, to meet the rising sun — a long, hard, heavy, ceaseless gallop of hours and hours, like the famous highwayman's ride to York. Being, however, nothing but a woman, condemned to patience, propriety, and petticoats, for life, I must respect the housekeeper's opinions, and try to compose myself in some feeble and feminine way.

Reading is out of the question — I can't fix my attention on books. Let me try if I can write myself into sleepiness and fatigue My journal has been very much neglected of late. What can I recall — standing, as I now do, on the threshold of a new life — of persons and events, of chances and changes, during the past six months — the long, weary, empty interval since Laura's wedding-day?

Walter Hartright is uppermost in my memory; and he passes first in the shadowy procession of my absent friends. I received a few lines from him, after the landing of the expedition in Honduras, written more cheerfully and hopefully than he has written yet. A month or six weeks later, I saw an extract from an American newspaper, describing the departure of the adventurers on their inland journey. They were last seen entering a wild primeval forest, each man with his rifle on his shoulder and his baggage at his back. Since that time, civilization has lost all trace of them. Not a line more have I received from Walter; not a fragment of news from the expedition has appeared in any of the public journals.

The same dense, disheartening obscurity hangs over the fate and fortunes of Anne Catherick, and her companion, Mrs. Clements. Nothing whatever has been heard of either of them. Whether they are in the country or out of it, whether they are living or dead, no one knows. Even Sir Percival's solicitor has lost all hope, and has ordered the useless search after the fugitives to be finally given up.

Our good old friend Mr. Gilmore has met with a sad check in his active professional career. Early in the spring, we were alarmed by hearing that he had been found insensible at his desk, and that the seizure was pronounced to be an apoplectic fit. He had been long complaining of fulness and oppression in the head; and his doctor had warned him of the consequences that would follow his persistency in continuing to work, early and late, as if he was still a young man. The result now is that he has been positively ordered to keep out of his office for a year to come, at least, and to seek repose of body and relief of mind by altogether changing his usual mode of life. The business is left, accordingly, to be carried on by his partner; and he is, himself, at this moment, away in Germany, visiting some relations who are settled there in mercantile pursuits. Thus, another true friend, and trustworthy adviser, is lost to us — lost, I earnestly hope and trust, for a time only.

Poor Mrs. Vesey travelled with me, as far as London. It was impossible to abandon her to solitude at Limmeridge, after Laura and I had both left the house; and we have arranged that she is to live with an unmarried younger sister of hers, who keeps a school at Clapham. She is to come here this autumn to visit her pupil — I might almost say her adopted child. I saw the good old lady safe to her destination; and left her in the care of her relative, quietly happy at the prospect of seeing Laura again, in a few months' time.

As for Mr. Fairlie, I believe I am guilty of no injustice if I describe him as being unutterably relieved by having the house clear of us women. The idea of his missing his niece is simply preposterous — he used to let months pass in the old times, without attempting to see her — and, in my case and Mrs. Vesey's, I take leave to consider his telling us both that he was half heart-broken at our departure, to be equivalent to a confession that he was secretly rejoiced to get rid of us. His last caprice has led him to keep two photographers incessantly employed on producing sun-pictures of all the treasures and curiosities in his possession. One complete copy of the collection of the photographs is to be presented to the Mechanics' Institution of Carlisle, mounted on the finest cardboard, with ostentatious red-letter inscriptious underneath. "Madonna and Child by Raphael. In the possession of Frederick Fairlie, Esquire." "Copper coin of the period of Tiglath Pileser. In the possession of Frederick Fairlie, Esquire." "Unique Rembrandt etching. Known all over Europe, as *The Smudge*, from a priuter's blot in the corner which exists in no other copy. Valued at three hundred guineas. In the possession of Frederic Fairlie, Esq." Dozens of photographs of this sort, and all inscribed in this manner, were completed before I left Cumberland; and hundreds more remain to be done. With this new interest to occupy him, Mr. Fairlie will be a happy man for months and months to come; and the two unfortunate photographers will share the social martyrdom which he has hitherto inflicted on his valet alone.

So much for the persons and events which hold the foremost place in my memory. What, next, of the oue person who holds the foremost place in my heart? Laura has been present to my thoughts all the while 1 have been writing these lines. What can I recall of her, during the past six mouths, before I close my journal for the night?

I have only her letters to guide me; and, on the most important of all the questions which our correspondence can discuss, every one of those letters leaves me in the dark.

Does he treat her kindly? Is she happier now than she was when I parted with her on the wedding-day? All my letters have contained these two inquiries, put more or less directly, now in one form, and now in another; and all, on that point only, have remained without reply, or have been answered as if my questions merely related to the state of her health. She informs me, over and over again, that she is perfectly well; that travelling agrees with her; that she is getting through the winter, for the first time in her life, without catching cold — but not a word can I find anywhere which tells me plainly that she is reconciled to her marriage, and that she can now look back to the twenty-second of December without any bitter feelings of repentance and regret. The name of her husband is only mentioned in her letters, as she might mention the name of a friend who was travelling with them, and who had undertaken to make all the arrangements for the journey. "Sir Percival" has settled that we leave on such a day; "Sir Percival" has decided that we travel by such a road. Sometimes she writes, "Percival" only, but very seldom — in nine cases out of ten, she gives him his title.

I cannot find that his habits and opinions have changed and coloured hers in any single particular. The usual moral transformation which is insensibly wrought in a young, fresh, sensitive woman by her marriage, seems never to have taken place in Laura. She writes of her own thoughts and impressions, amid all the wonders she has seen, exactly as she might have written to some one else, if I had been travelling with her instead of her husband. I see no betrayal anywhere, of sympathy of any kind existing between them. Even when she wanders from the subject of her travels, and occupies herself with the prospects that await her in England, her speculations are busied with her future as my sister, and persistently neglect to notice her future as Sir Percival's wife. In all this, there is no under-tone of complaint, to warn me that she is absolutely unhappy in her married life. The impression I have derived from our correspondence does not, thank God, lead me to any such distressing conclusion as that. I only see a sad torpor, an unchangeable indifference, when I turn my mind from her in the old character of a sister, and look at her, through the medium of her letters, in the new character of a wife. In other words, it is always Laura Fairlie who has been writing to me for the last six months, and never Lady Glyde.

The strange silence which she maintains on the subject of her husband's character and conduct, she preserves with almost equal resolution in the few references which her later letters contain to the name of her husband's bosom friend, Count Fosco.

For some unexplained reason, the Count and his wife appear to have changed their plans abruptly, at the end of last autumn, and to have gone to Vienna, instead of going to Rome, at which latter place Sir Percival had expected to find them when he left England. They only quitted Vienna in the spring, and travelled as far as the Tyrol to meet the bride and bridegroom on their homeward journey. Laura writes readily enough about the meeting with Madame Fosco, and assures me that she has found her aunt so much changed for the better — so much quieter and so much more sensible as a wife than she was as a single woman — that I shall hardly know her again when I see her here. But, on the subject of Count Fosco (who interests me infinitely more than his wife), Laura is provokingly circumspect and silent. She only says that he puzzles her, and that she will not tell me what her impression of him is, until I have seen him, and formed my own opinion first.

This, to my mind, looks ill for the Count. Laura has preserved, far more perfectly than most people do in later life, the child's subtle faculty of knowing a friend by instinct; and, if I am right in assuming that her first impression of Count Fosco has not been favourable, I, for one, am in some danger of doubting and distrusting that illustrious foreigner before I have so much as set eyes on him. But, patience, patience; this uncertainty, and many uncertainties more, cannot last much longer. To-morrow will see all my doubts in a fair way of being cleared up, sooner or later.

Twelve o'clock has struck; and I have just come back to close these pages, after looking out at my open window.

It is a still, sultry, moonless night. The stars are dull and few. The trees that shut out the view on all sides, look dimly black and solid in the distance, like a great wall of rock. I hear the croaking of frogs, faint and far off; and the echoes of the great clock hum in the airless calm, long after the strokes have ceased. I wonder how Blackwater Park will look in the daytime? I don't altogether like it by night.

28th. — A day of investigations and discoveries — a more interesting day, for many reasons, than I had ventured to anticipate.

I began my sight-seeing, of course, with the house.

The main body of the building is of the time of that highly overrated woman, Queen Elizabeth. On the ground floor, there are two hugely long galleries, with low ceilings, lying parallel with each other, and rendered additionally dark and dismal by hideous family portraits — every one of which I should like to burn. The rooms on the floor above the two galleries, are kept in tolerable repair, but are very seldom used. The civil housekeeper, who acted as my guide, offered to show me over them; but considerately added that she feared I should find them rather out of order. My respect for the integrity of my own petticoats and stockings, infinitely exceeds my respect for all the Elizabethan bedrooms in the kingdom; so I positively declined exploring the upper regions of dust and dirt at the risk of soiling my nice clean clothes. The housekeeper said, "I am quite of your opinion, miss;" and appeared to think me the most sensible woman she had met with for a long time past.

So much, then, for the main building. Two wings are added, at either end of it. The half-ruined wing on the left (as you approach the house) was once a place of residence standing by itself, and was built in the fourteenth century. One of Sir Percival's maternal ancestors — I don't remember, and don't care, which — tacked on the main building, at right angles to it, in the aforesaid Queen Elizabeth's time. The housekeeper told me that the architecture of "the old wing," both outside and inside, was considered remarkably fine by good judges. On further investigation, I discovered that good judges could only exercise their abilities on Sir Percival's piece of antiquity by previously dismissing from their minds all fear of damp, darkness, and rats. Under these circumstances, I unhesitatingly acknowledged myself to be no judge at all; and suggested that we should treat "the old wing" precisely as we had previously treated the Elizabethan bedrooms.   Once more, the housekeeper said, "I am quite of your opinion, miss;" and once more she looked at me, with undisguised admiration of my extraordinary common sense.

We went, next, to the wing on the right, which was built, by way of completing the wonderful architectural jumble at Blackwater Park, in the time of George the Second.

This is the habitable part of the house, which has been repaired and redecorated, inside, on Laura's account.   My two rooms, and all the good bedrooms besides, are on the first floor; and the basement contains a drawing-room, a dining-room, a morning-room, a library, and a pretty little boudoir for Laura — all very nicely ornamented in the bright modern way, and all very elegantly furnished with the delightful modern luxuries.   None of the rooms are anything like so large and airy as our rooms at Limmeridge; but they all look pleasant to live in.   I was terribly afraid, from what I had heard of Blackwater Park, of fatiguing antique chairs, and dismal stained glass, and musty, frouzy hangings, and all the barbarous lumber which people born without a sense of comfort accumulate about them, in defiance of the consideration due to the convenience of their friends.   It is an inexpressible relief to find that the nineteenth century has invaded this strange future home of mine, and has swept the dirty "good old times" out of the way of our daily life.

I dawdled away the morning — part of the time in the rooms down stairs; and part, out of doors, in the great square which is formed by the three sides of the house, and by the lofty iron railings and gates which protect it in front.   A large circular fishpond, with stone sides, and an allegorical leaden monster in the middle, occupies the centre of the square.   The pond itself is full of gold and silver fish, and is encircled by a broad belt of the softest turf I ever walked on.   I loitered here, on the shady side, pleasantly enough, till luncheon time; and, after that, took my broad straw hat, and wandered out alone, in the warm lovely sunlight, to explore the grounds.

Daylight confirmed the impression which I had felt the night before, of there being too many trees at Blackwater.

The house is stifled by them. They are, for the most part, young, and planted far too thickly. I suspect there must have been a ruinous cutting down of timber, all over the estate, before Sir Percival's time , and an angry anxiety , on the part of the next possessor, to fill up all the gaps as thickly and rapidly as possible. After looking about me, in front of the house, I observed a flower-garden on my left hand, and walked towards it, to see what I could discover in that direction.

On a nearer view , the garden proved to be small and poor and ill-kept. I left it behind me, opened a little gate in a ring fence, and found myself in a plantation of fir-trees.

A pretty, winding path, artificially made, led me on among the trees; and my north-country experience soon informed me that I was approaching sandy heathy ground. After a walk of more than half a mile, I should think, among the firs, the path took a sharp turn; the trees abruptly ceased to appear on either side of me; and I found myself standing suddenly on the margin of a vast open space, and looking down at the Blackwater lake from which the house takes its name.

The ground, shelving away below me, was all sand, with a few little heathy hillocks to break the monotony of it in certain places. The lake itself had evidently once flowed to the spot on which I stood, and had been gradually wasted and dried up to less than a third of its former size. I saw its still, stagnant waters, a quarter of a mile away from me in the hollow, separated into pools and ponds, by twining reeds and rushes, and little knolls of earth. On the farther bank from me, the trees rose thickly again, and shut out the view, and cast their black shadows on the sluggish, shallow water. As I walked down to the lake, I saw that the ground on its farther side was damp and marshy, overgrown with rank grass and dismal willows. The water, which was clear enough on the open sandy side, where the sun shone, looked black and poisonous opposite to me, where it lay deeper under the shade of the spongy banks, and the rank overhanging thickets and tangled trees. The frogs were croaking, and the rats were slipping in and out of the shadowy water, like live shadows themselves, as I got nearer to the marshy side of the lake. I saw here, lying half in and half out of the water, the rotten wreck of an old overturned boat, with a sickly spot of sunlight glimmering through a gap in the trees on its dry surface, and a snake basking in the midst of the spot, fantastically coiled, and treacherously still. Far and near, the view suggested the same dreary impressions of solitude and decay; and the glorious brightness of the summer sky overhead, seemed only to deepen and harden the gloom and barrenness of the wilderness on which it shone. I turned and retraced my steps to the high, heathy ground; directing them a little aside from my former path towards a shabby old wooden shed, which stood on the outer skirt of the fir plantation, and which had hitherto been too unimportant to share my notice with the wide, wild prospect of the lake.

On approaching the shed, I found that it had once been a boat-house, and that an attempt had apparently been made to convert it afterwards into a sort of rude arbour, by placing inside it a firwood seat, a few stools, and a table. I entered the place, and sat down for a little while, to rest and get my breath again.

I had not been in the boat-house more than a minute, when it struck me that the sound of my own quick breathing was very strangely echoed by something beneath me. I listened intently for a moment, and heard a low, thick, sobbing breath that seemed to come from the ground under the seat which I was occupying. My nerves are not easily shaken by trifles; but, on this occasion, I started to my feet in a fright — called out — received no answer — summoned back my recreant courage — and looked under the seat.

There, crouched up in the farthest corner, lay the forlorn cause of my terror, in the shape of a poor little dog — a black and white spaniel. The creature moaned feebly when I looked at it and called to it, but never stirred. I moved away the seat and looked closer. The poor little dog's eyes were glasing fast, and there were spots of blood on its glossy white side.

The misery of a weak, helpless, dumb creature is surely one of the saddest of all the mournful sights which this world can show. I lifted the poor dog in my arms as gently as I could, and contrived a sort of make-shift hammock for him to lie in, by gathering up the front of my dress all round him. In this way, I took the creature, as painlessly as possible, and as fast as possible, back to the house.

Finding no one in the hall, I went up at once to my own sitting-room, made a bed for the dog with one of my old shawls, and rang the bell. The largest and fattest of all possible housemaids answered it, in a state of cheerful stupidity which would have provoked the patience of a saint. The girl's fat, shapeless face actually stretched into a broad grin, at the sight of the wounded creature on the floor.

"What do you see there to laugh at?" I asked, as angrily as if she had been a servant of my own. "Do you know whose dog it is?"

"No, miss, that I certainly don't." She stopped, and looked down at the spaniel's injured side — brightened suddenly with the irradiation of a new idea — and, pointing to the wound with a chuckle of satisfaction, said, "That's Baxter's doings, that is."

I was so exasperated that I could have boxed her ears. "Baxter?" I said. "Who is the brute you call Baxter?"

The girl grinned again, more cheerfully than ever. "Bless you, miss! Baxter's the keeper; and when he finds strange dogs hunting about, he takes and shoots 'em. It's keeper's dooty, miss. I think that dog will die. Here's where he's been shot, aint it? That's Baxter's doings, that is. Baxter's doings, miss, and Baxter's dooty."

I was almost wicked enough to wish that Baxter had shot the housemaid instead of the dog. Seeing that it was quite useless to expect this densely impenetrable personage to give me any help in relieving the suffering creature at our feet, I told her to request the housekeeper's attendance, with my compliments. She went out exactly as she had come in, grinning from ear to ear.   As the door closed on her, she said to herself, softly, "It's Baxter's doings and Baxter's dooty — that's what it is."

The housekeeper, a person of some education and intelligence, thoughtfully brought up-stairs with her some milk and some warm water.   The instant she saw the dog on the floor, she started and changed colour.

"Why, Lord bless me," cried the housekeeper, "that must be Mrs. Catherick's dog!"

"Whose?"   I asked, in the utmost astonishment.

"Mrs. Catherick's.   You seem to know Mrs. Catherick, Miss Halcombe?"

"Not personally.   But I have heard of her.   Does she live here?   Has she had any news of her daughter?"

"No, Miss Halcombe.   She came here to ask for news."

"When?"

"Only yesterday.   She said some one had reported that a stranger answering to the description of her daughter had been seen in our neighbourhood.   No such report has reached us here; and no such report was known in the village, when I sent to make inquiries there on Mrs. Catherick's account.   She certainly brought this poor little dog with her when she came, and I saw it trot out after her when she went away.   I suppose the creature strayed into the plantations, and got shot. Where did you find it, Miss Halcombe?"

"In the old shed that looks out on the lake."

"Ah, yes, that is the plantation side, and the poor thing dragged itself, I suppose, to the nearest shelter, as dogs will, to die.   If you can moisten its lips with the milk, Miss Halcombe, I will wash the clotted hair from the wound.   I am very much afraid it is too late to do any good.   However, we can but try."

Mrs. Catherick!   The name still rang in my ears, as if the housekeeper had only that moment surprised me by uttering it.   While we were attending to the dog, the words of Walter Hartright's caution to me returned to my memory.   "If ever

Anne Catherick crosses your path, make better use of the opportunity, Miss Halcombe, than I made of it." The finding of the wounded spaniel had led me already to the discovery of Mrs. Catherick's visit to Blackwater Park; and that event might lead, in its turn, to something more. I determined to make the most of the chance which was now offered to me, and to gain as much information as I could.

"Did you say that Mrs. Catherick lived anywhere in this neighbourhood?" I asked.

"Oh, dear, no," said the housekeeper. "She lives at Welmingham; quite at the other end of the county—five-and-twenty miles off at least."

"I suppose you have known Mrs. Catherick for some years?"

"On the contrary, Miss Halcombe; I never saw her before she came here, yesterday. I had heard of her, of course, because I had heard of Sir Percival's kindness in putting her daughter under medical care. Mrs. Catherick is rather a strange person in her manners, but extremely respectable-looking. She seemed sorely put out, when she found that there was no foundation — none, at least, that any of *us* could discover — for the report of her daughter having been seen in this neighbourhood."

"I am rather interested about Mrs. Catherick," I went on, continuing the conversation as long as possible. "I wish I had arrived here soon enough to see her yesterday. Did she stay for any length of time?"

"Yes," said the housekeeper, "she stayed for some time. And I think she would have remained longer, if I had not been called away to speak to a strange gentleman — a gentleman who came to ask when Sir Percival was expected back. Mrs. Catherick got up and left at once, when she heard the maid tell me what the visitor's errand was. She said to me, at parting, that there was no need to tell Sir Percival of her coming here. I thought that rather an odd remark to make, especially to a person in my responsible situation."

I thought it an odd remark, too. Sir Percival had certainly led me to believe, at Limmeridge, that the most perfect confidence existed between himself and Mrs. Catherick. If that was the case, why should she be anxious to have her visit at Blackwater Park kept a secret from him?

"Probably," I said, seeing that the housekeeper expected me to give my opinion on Mrs. Catherick's parting words; "probably, she thought the announcement of her visit might vex Sir Percival to no purpose, by reminding him that her lost daughter was not found yet. Did she talk much on that subject?"

"Very little," replied the housekeeper. "She talked principally of Sir Percival, and asked a great many questions about where he had been travelling, and what sort of lady his new wife was. She seemed to be more soured and put out than distressed, by failing to find any traces of her daughter in these parts. 'I give her up,' were the last words she said that I can remember; 'I give her up, ma'am, for lost.' And from that, she passed at once to her questions about Lady Glyde; wanting to know if she was a handsome, amiable lady, comely and healthy and young — Ah, dear! I thought how it would end. Look, Miss Halcombe! the poor thing is out of its misery at last!"

The dog was dead. It had given a faint, sobbing cry, it had suffered an instant's convulsion of the limbs, just as those last words, "comely and healthy and young," dropped from the housekeeper's lips. The change had happened with startling suddenness — in one moment the creature lay lifeless under our hands.

Eight o'clock. I have just returned from dining down stairs, in solitary state. The sunset is burning redly on the wilderness of trees that I see from my window; and I am poring over my journal again, to calm my impatience for the return of the travellers. They ought to have arrived, by my calculations, before this. How still and lonely the house is in the drowsy evening quiet! Oh, me! how many minutes more before I hear the carriage wheels and run down stairs to find myself in Laura's arms?

The poor little dog! I wish my first day at Blackwater Park had not been associated with death — though it is only the death of a stray animal.

Welmingham — I see, on looking back through these private pages of mine, that Welmingham is the name of the place where Mrs. Catherick lives. Her note is still in my possession, the note in answer to that letter about her unhappy daughter which Sir Percival obliged me to write. One of these days, when I can find a safe opportunity, I will take the note with me by way of introduction, and try what I can make of Mrs. Catherick at a personal interview. I don't understand her wishing to conceal her visit to this place from Sir Percival's knowledge; and I don't feel half so sure, as the housekeeper seems to do, that her daughter Anne is not in the neighbourhood, after all. What would Walter Hartright have said in this emergency? Poor, dear Hartright! I am beginning to feel the want of his honest advice and his willing help, already.

Surely, I heard something. Was it a bustle of footsteps below stairs? Yes! I hear the horses' feet; I hear the rolling wheels —

IV.

July 1st. — The confusion of their arrival has had time to subside. Two days have elapsed since the return of the travellers; and that interval has sufficed to put the new machinery of our lives at Blackwater Park in fair working order. I may now return to my journal, with some little chance of being able to continue the entries in it as collectedly as usual.

I think I must begin by putting down an odd remark, which has suggested itself to me since Laura came back.

When two members of a family, or two intimate friends, are separated, and one goes abroad and one remains at home, the return of the relative or friend who has been travelling, always seems to place the relative or friend who has been staying at home at a painful disadvantage, when the two first meet. The sudden encounter of the new thoughts and new habits eagerly gained in the one case, with the old thoughts and old habits passively preserved in the other, seems, at first, to part the sympathies of the most loving relatives and the fondest friends, and to set a sudden strangeness, unexpected by both and uncontrollable by both, between them on either side. After the first happiness of my meeting with Laura was over, after we had sat down together, hand in hand, to recover breath enough and calmness enough to talk, I felt this strangeness instantly, and I could see that she felt it too. It has partially worn away, now that we have fallen back into most of our old habits; and it will probably disappear before long. But it has certainly had an influence over the first impressions that I have formed of her, now that we are living together again — for which reason only I have thought fit to mention it here.

She has found me unaltered; but I have found her changed.

Changed in person, and, in one respect, changed in character. I cannot absolutely say that she is less beautiful than she used to be: I can only say that she is less beautiful to *me*.

Others, who do not look at her with my eyes and my recollections, would probably think her improved. There is more colour, and more decision and roundness of outline in her face than there used to be; and her figure seems more firmly set, and more sure and easy in all its movements than it was in her maiden days. But I miss something when I look at her — something that once belonged to the happy, innocent life of Laura Fairlie, and that I cannot find in Lady Glyde. There was, in the old times, a freshness, a softness, an ever-varying and yet ever-remaining tenderness of beauty in her face, the charm of which is not possible to express in words — or, as poor Hartright used often to say, in painting, either. This is gone. I thought I saw the faint reflexion of it, for a moment, when she turned pale under the agitation of our sudden meeting, on the evening of her return; but it has never reappeared since. None of her letters had prepared me for a personal change in her. On the contrary, they had led me to expect that her marriage had left her, in appearance at least, quite unaltered. Perhaps, I read her letters wrongly, in the past, and am now reading her face wrongly, in the present? No matter! Whether her beauty has gained, or whether it has lost, in the last six months, the separation, either way, has made her own dear self more precious to me than ever — and that is one good result of her marriage, at any rate!

The second change, the change that I have observed in her character, has not surprised me, because I was prepared for it, in this case, by the tone of her letters. Now that she is at home again, I find her just as unwilling to enter into any details on the subject of her married life, as I had previously found her, all through the time of our separation, when we could only communicate with each other by writing. At the first approach I made to the forbidden topic, she put her hand on my lips, with a look and gesture which touchingly, almost painfully, recalled to my memory the days of her girlhood and the happy bygone time when there were no secrets between us.

"Whenever you and I are together, Marian," she said, "we shall both be happier and easier with one another, if we accept my married life for what it is, and say and think as little about it as possible. I would tell you everything, darling, about myself," she went on, nervously buckling and unbuckling the ribbon round my waist, "if my confidences could only end there. But they could not — they would lead me into confidences about my husband, too; and, now I am married, I think I had better avoid them, for his sake, and for your sake, and for mine. I don't say that they would distress you, or distress me — I wouldn't have you think that for the world. But — I want to be so happy, now I have got you back again; and I want you to be so happy too —" She broke off abruptly, and looked round the room, my own sitting-room, in which we were talking. "Ah!" she cried, clapping her hands with a bright smile of recognition, "another old friend found already! Your bookcase, Marian — your dear-little-shabby-old-satin-wood bookcase — how glad I am you brought it with you from Limmeridge! And the horrid, heavy, man's umbrella, that you always would walk out with when it rained! And, first and foremost of all, your own dear, dark, clever, gipsy-face, looking at me just as usual! It is so like home again to be here. How can we make it more like home still? I will put my father's portrait in your room instead of in mine — and I will keep all my little treasures from Limmeridge here — and we will pass hours and hours every day with these four friendly walls round us. Oh, Marian!" she said, suddenly seating herself on a footstool at my knees, and looking up earnestly in my face, "promise you will never marry, and leave me. It is selfish to say so, but you are so much better off as a single woman — unless — unless you are very fond of your husband — but you won't be very fond of anybody but me, will you?" She stopped again; crossed my hands on my lap; and laid her face on them. "Have you been writing many letters, and receiving many letters, lately?" she asked, in low, suddenly-altered tones. I understood what the question meant; but I thought it my duty not to encourage her by meeting her half way. "Have you heard from him?" she went on, coaxing me to forgive the more direct appeal on which she now ventured, by kissing my hands, upon which her face still rested. "Is he well and happy, and getting on in his profession? Has he recovered himself — and forgotten *me?*"

She should not have asked those questions. She should have remembered her own resolution, on the morning when Sir Percival held her to her marriage engagement, and when she resigned the book of Hartright's drawings into my hands for ever. But, ah me! where is the faultless human creature who can persevere in a good resolution, without sometimes failing and falling back? Where is the woman who has ever really torn from her heart the image that has been once fixed in it by a true love? Books tell us that such unearthly creatures have existed — but what does our own experience say in answer to books?

l made no attempt to remonstrate with her: perhaps, because I sincerely appreciated the fearless candour which let me see, what other women in her position might have had reasons for concealing even from their dearest friends — perhaps, because I felt, in my own heart and conscience, that, in her place I should have asked the same questions and had the same thoughts. All I could honestly do was to reply that I had not written to him or heard from him lately, and then to turn the conversation to less dangerous topics.

There had been much to sadden me in our interview — my first confidential interview with her since her return. The change which her marriage has produced in our relations towards each other, by placing a forbidden subject between us, for the first time in our lives; the melancholy conviction of the dearth of all warmth of feeling, of all close sympathy, between her husband and herself, which her own unwilling words now force on my mind; the distressing discovery that the influence of that ill-fated attachment still remains (no matter how innocently, how harmlessly) rooted as deeply as ever in her heart — all these are disclosures to sadden any woman who loves her as dearly, and feels for her as acutely, as I do.

There is only one consolation to set against them — a consolation that ought to comfort me, and that does comfort me. All the graces and gentlenesses of her character; all the frank affection of her nature; all the sweet, simple, womanly charms which used to make her the darling and delight of every one who approached her, have come back to me with herself. Of my other impressions I am sometimes a little inclined to doubt. Of this last, best, happiest of all impressions, I grow more and more certain, every hour in the day.

Let me turn, now, from her to her travelling companions. Her husband must engage my attention first. What have I observed in Sir Percival, since his return, to improve my opinion of him?

I can hardly say. Small vexations and annoyances seem to have beset him since he came back: and no man, under those circumstances, is ever presented at his best. He looks, as I think, thinner than he was when he left England. His wearisome cough and his comfortless restlessness have certainly increased. His manner — at least, his manner towards me — is much more abrupt than it used to be. He greeted me, on the evening of his return, with little or nothing of the ceremony and civility of former times — no polite speeches of welcome — no appearance of extraordinary gratification at seeing me — nothing but a short shake of the hand, and a sharp "How-d'ye-do, Miss Halcombe — glad to see you again." He seemed to accept me as one of the necessary fixtures of Blackwater Park; to be satisfied at finding me established in my proper place; and then to pass me over altogether.

Most men show something of their dispositions in their own houses, which they have concealed elsewhere; and Sir Percival has already displayed a mania for order and regularity, which is quite a new revelation of him, so far as my previous knowledge of his character is concerned. If I take a book from the library and leave it on the table, he follows me, and puts it back again. If I rise from a chair, and let it remain where I have been sitting, he carefully restores it to its proper place against the wall. He picks up stray flower-blossoms from the carpet, and mutters to himself as discontentedly as if they were hot cinders burning holes in it; and he storms at the servants, if there is a crease in the tablecloth, or a knife missing from its place at the dinner-table, as fiercely as if they had personally insulted him.

I have already referred to the small annoyances which appear to have troubled him since his return. Much of the alteration for the worse which I have noticed in him, may be due to these. I try to persuade myself that it is so, because I am anxious not to be disheartened already about the future. It is certainly trying to any man's temper to be met by a vexation the moment he sets foot in his own house again, after a long absence; and this annoying circumstance did really happen to Sir Percival in my presence.

On the evening of their arrival, the housekeeper followed

me into the hall to receive her master and mistress and their guests. The instant he saw her, Sir Percival asked if any one had called lately. The housekeeper mentioned to him, in reply, what she had previously mentioned to me, the visit of the strange gentleman to make inquiries about the time of her master's return. He asked immediately for the gentleman's name. No name had been left. The gentleman's business? No business had been mentioned. What was the gentleman like? The house-keeper tried to describe him; but failed to distinguish the nameless visitor by any personal peculiarity which her master could recognize. Sir Percival frowned, stamped angrily on the floor, and walked on into the house, taking no notice of anybody. Why he should have been so discomposed by a trifle I cannot say — but he was seriously discomposed, beyond all doubt.

Upon the whole, it will be best, perhaps, if I abstain from forming a decisive opinion of his manners, language, and conduct in his own house, until time has enabled him to shake off the anxieties, whatever they may be, which now evidently trouble his mind in secret. I will turn over to a new page; and my pen shall let Laura's husband alone for the present.

The two guests — the Count and Countess Fosco — come next in my catalogue. I will dispose of the Countess first, so as to have done with the woman as soon as possible.

Laura was certainly not chargeable with any exaggeration, in writing me word that I should hardly recognise her aunt again, when we met. Never before have I beheld such a change produced in a woman by her marriage as has been produced in Madame Fosco.

As Eleanor Fairlie (aged seven-and-thirty), she was always talking pretentious nonsense, and always worrying the unfortunate men with every small exaction which a vain and foolish woman can impose on long-suffering male humanity. As Madame Fosco (aged three-and-forty), she sits for hours together without saying a word, frozen up in the strangest manner in herself. The hideously ridiculous lovelocks which used to hang on either side of her face, are now replaced by

stiff little rows of very short curls, of the sort that one sees in
old-fashioned wigs. A plain, matronly cap covers her head,
and makes her look, for the first time in her life, since I remember her, like a decent woman. Nobody (putting her husband out of the question, of course) now sees in her, what
everybody once saw — I mean the structure of the female
skeleton, in the upper regions of the collar-bones and the
shoulder-blades. Clad in quiet black or gray gowns, made
high round the throat — dresses that she would have laughed
at, or screamed at, as the whim of the moment inclined her, in
her maiden days — she sits speechless in corners; her dry
white hands (so dry that the pores of her skin look chalky) incessantly engaged, either in monotonous embroidery work, or
in rolling up endless little cigarettes for the Count's own particular smoking. On the few occasions when her cold blue
eyes are off her work, they are generally turned on her husband, with the look of mute submissive inquiry which we are
all familiar with in the eyes of a faithful dog. The only
approach to an inward thaw which I have yet detected under
her outer covering of icy constraint, has betrayed itself, once
or twice, in the form of a suppressed tigerish jealousy of any
woman in the house (the maids included) to whom the Count
speaks, or on whom he looks, with anything approaching to
special interest or attention. Except in this one particular,
she is always, morning, noon, and night, in-doors and out, fair
weather or foul, as cold as a statue, and as impenetrable as the
stone out of which it is cut. For the common purposes of
society the extraordinary change thus produced in her, is,
beyond all doubt, a change for the better, seeing that it has
transformed her into a civil, unobtrusive woman, who is never
in the way. How far she is really reformed or deteriorated in
her secret self, is another question. I have once or twice seen
sudden changes of expression on her pinched lips, and heard
sudden inflexions of tone in her calm voice, which have led me
to suspect that her present state of suppression may have
sealed up something dangerous in her nature, which used to
evaporate harmlessly in the freedom of her former life. It is

quite possible that I may be altogether wrong in this idea. My own impression, however, is, that I am right. Time will show.

And the magician who has wrought this wonderful transformation — the foreign husband who has tamed this once wayward Englishwoman till her own relations hardly know her again — the Count himself? What of the Count?

This, in two words: He looks like a man who could tame anything. If he had married a tigress, instead of a woman, he would have tamed the tigress. If he had married *me*, I should have made his cigarettes as his wife does — I should have held my tongue when he looked at me, as she holds hers.

I am almost afraid to confess it, even to these secret pages. The man has interested me, has attracted me, has forced me to like him. In two short days, he has made his way straight into my favourable estimation — and how he has worked the miracle, is more than I can tell.

It absolutely startles me, now he is in my mind, to find how plainly I see him! — how much more plainly than I see Sir Percival, or Mr. Fairlie, or Walter Hartright, or any other absent person of whom I think, with the one exception of Laura herself! I can hear his voice, as if he was speaking at this moment. I know what his conversation was yesterday, as well as if I was hearing it now. How am I to describe him? There are peculiarities in his personal appearance, his habits, and his amusements which I should blame in the boldest terms, or ridicule in the most merciless manner, if I had seen them in another man. What is it that makes me unable to blame them, or to ridicule them in *him!*

For example, he is immensely fat. Before this time, I have always especially disliked corpulent humanity. I have always maintained that the popular notion of connecting excessive grossness of size and excessive good-humour as inseparable allies, was equivalent to declaring, either that no people but amiable people ever get fat, or that the accidental addition of so many pounds of flesh has a directly favourable influence over the disposition of the person on whose body they accumulate. I have invariably combated both these absurd assertions by quoting examples of fat people who were as mean, vicious, and cruel, as the leanest and the worst of their neighbours. I have asked whether Henry the Eighth was an amiable character? whether Pope Alexander the Sixth was a good man? Whether Mr. Murderer and Mrs. Murderess Manning were not both unusually stout people? Whether hired nurses, proverbially as cruel a set of women as are to be found in all England, were not, for the most part, also as fat a set of women as are to be found in all England? — and so on, through dozens of other examples, modern and ancient, native and foreign, high and low. Holding these strong opinions on the subject with might and main, as I do at this moment, here, nevertheless, is Count Fosco, as fat as Henry the Eighth himself, established in my favour, at one day's notice, without let or hindrance from his own odious corpulence. Marvellous indeed!

Is it his face that has recommended him?

It may be his face. He is a most remarkable likeness, on a large scale, of the Great Napoleon. His features have Napoleon's magnificent regularity: his expression recalls the grandly calm, immovable power of the Great Soldier's face. This striking resemblance certainly impressed me, to begin with; but there is something in him besides the resemblance, which has impressed me more. I think the influence I am now trying to find, is in his eyes. They are the most unfathomable gray eyes I ever saw: and they have at times a cold, clear, beautiful, irresistible glitter in them, which forces me to look at him, and yet causes me sensations, when I do look, which I would rather not feel. Other parts of his face and head have their strange peculiarities. His complexion, for instance, has a singular sallow-fairness, so much at variance with the dark-brown colour of his hair, that I suspect the hair of being a wig; and his face, closely shaven all over, is smoother and freer from all marks and wrinkles than mine, though (according to Sir Percival's account of him) he is close on sixty years of age. But these are not the prominent personal characteristics which distinguish him, to my mind, from all the other men I have ever seen. The marked peculiarity which singles him out from the rank and file of humanity, lies entirely, so far as I can tell at present, in the extraordinary expression and extraordinary power of his eyes.

His manner, and his command of our language, may also have assisted him, in some degree, to establish himself in my good opinion. He has that quiet deference, that look of pleased, attentive interest, in listening to a woman, and that secret gentleness in his voice, in speaking to a woman, which, say what we may, we can none of us resist. Here, too, his unusual command of the English language necessarily helps him. I had often heard of the extraordinary aptitude which many Italians show in mastering our strong, hard Northern speech; but, until I saw Count Fosco, I had never supposed it possible that any foreigner could have spoken English as he speaks it. There are times when it is almost impossible to detect, by his accent, that he is not a countryman of our own; and, as for fluency, there are very few born Englishmen who can talk with as few stoppages and repetitions as the Count. He may construct his sentences, more or less, in the foreign way; but I have never yet heard him use a wrong expression, or hesitate for a moment in his choice of a word.

All the smallest characteristics of this strange man have something strikingly original and perplexingly contradictory in them. Fat as he is, and old as he is, his movements are astonishingly light and easy. He is as noiseless in a room as any of us women; and, more than that, with all his look of unmistakable mental firmness and power, he is as nervously sensitive as the weakest of us. He starts at chance noises as inveterately as Laura herself. He winced and shuddered yesterday, when Sir Percival beat one of the spaniels, so that I felt ashamed of my own want of tenderness and sensibility, by comparison with the Count.

The relation of this last incident reminds me of one of his

most curious peculiarities, which I have not yet mentioned — his extraordinary fondness for pet animals.

Some of these he has left on the Continent, but he has brought with him to this house a cockatoo, two canary-birds, and a whole family of white mice. He attends to all the necessities of these strange favourites himself, and he has taught the creatures to be surprisingly fond of him, and familiar with him. The cockatoo, a most vicious and treacherous bird towards every one else, absolutely seems to love him. When he lets it out of its cage, it hops on to his knee, and claws its way up his great big body, and rubs its top-knot against his sallow double chin in the most caressing manner imaginable. He has only to set the doors of the canaries' cages open, and to call them; and the pretty little cleverly trained creatures perch fearlessly on his hand, mount his fat outstretched fingers one by one, when he tells them to "go upstairs," and sing together as if they would burst their throats with delight, when they get to the top finger. His white mice live in a little pagoda of gaily-painted wirework, designed and made by himself. They are almost as tame as the canaries, and they are perpetually let out, like the canaries. They crawl all over him, popping in and out of his waistcoat, and sitting in couples, white as snow, on his capacious shoulders. He seems to be even fonder of his mice than of his other pets, smiles at them, and kisses them, and calls them by all sorts of endearing names. If it be possible to suppose an Englishman with any taste for such childish interests and amusements as these, that Englishman would certainly feel rather ashamed of them, and would be anxious to apologise for them, in the company of grown-up people. But the Count, apparently, sees nothing ridiculous in the amazing contrast between his colossal self and his frail little pets. He would blandly kiss his white mice, and twitter to his canary-birds amid an assembly of English fox-hunters, and would only pity them as barbarians when they were all laughing their loudest at him.

It seems hardly credible, while I am writing it down, but it is certainly true, that this same man, who has all the fondness of an old maid for his cockatoo, and all the small dexterities of an organ-boy in managing his white mice, can talk, when anything happens to rouse him, with a daring independence of thought, a knowledge of books in every language, and an experience of society in half the capitals of Europe, which would make him the prominent personage of any assembly in the civilized world. This trainer of canary-birds, this architect of a pagoda for white mice, is (as Sir Percival himself has told me) one of the first experimental chemists living, and has discovered, among other wonderful inventions, a means of petrifying the body after death, so as to preserve it, as hard as marble, to the end of time. This fat, indolent, elderly man, whose nerves are so finely strung that he starts at chance noises, and winces when he sees a house-spaniel get a whipping, went into the stableyard on the morning after his arrival, and put his hand on the head of a chained bloodhound — a beast so savage that the very groom who feeds him keeps out of his reach. His wife and I were present, and I shall not soon forget the scene that followed, short as it was.

"Mind that dog, sir," said the groom; "he flies at everybody!" "He does that, my friend," replied the Count, quietly, "because everybody is afraid of him. Let us see if he flies at *me*." And he laid his plump, yellow-white fingers, on which the canary-birds had been perching ten minutes before, upon the formidable brute's head; and looked him straight in the eyes. "You big dogs are all cowards," he said, addressing the animal contemptuously, with his face and the dog's within an inch of each other. "You would kill a poor cat, you infernal coward. You would fly at a starving beggar, you infernal coward. Anything that you can surprise unawares — anything that is afraid of your big body, and your wicked white teeth, and your slobbering, bloodthirsty mouth, is the thing you like to fly at. You could throttle me at this moment, you mean, miserable bully; and you daren't so much as look me in the face, because I'm not afraid of you. Will you think better of it, and try your teeth in my fat neck? Bah!

not you!" He turned away, laughing at the astonishment of the men in the yard; and the dog crept back meekly to his kennel. "Ah! my nice waistcoat!" he said, pathetically. "I am sorry I came here. Some of that brute's slobber has got on my pretty clean waistcoat." Those words express another of his incomprehensible oddities. He is as fond of fine clothes as the veriest fool in existence; and has appeared in four magnificent waistcoats, already — all of light garish colours, and all immensely large even for him — in the two days of his residence at Blackwater Park.

His tact and cleverness in small things are quite as noticeable as the singular inconsistencies in his character, and the childish triviality of his ordinary tastes and pursuits.

I can see already that he means to live on excellent terms with all of us, during the period of his sojourn in this place. He has evidently discovered that Laura secretly dislikes him (she confessed as much to me, when I pressed her on the subject) — but he has also found out that she is extravagantly fond of flowers. Whenever she wants a nosegay, he has got one to give her, gathered and arranged by himself; and, greatly to my amusement, he is always cunningly provided with a duplicate, composed of exactly the same flowers, grouped in exactly the same way, to appease his icily jealous wife, before she can so much as think herself aggrieved. His management of the Countess (in public) is a sight to see. He bows to her; he habitually addresses her as "my angel;" he carries his canaries to pay her little visits on his fingers, and to sing to her; he kisses her hand, when she gives him his cigarettes; he presents her with sugar-plums, in return, which he puts into her mouth playfully, from a box in his pocket. The rod of iron with which he rules her never appears in company — it is a private rod, and is always kept upstairs.

His method of recommending himself to *me*, is entirely different. He flatters my vanity, by talking to me as seriously and sensibly as if I was a man. Yes! I can find him out when

I am away from him; I know he flatters my vanity, when I think of him up here, in my own room — and yet, when I go down stairs, and get into his company again, he will blind me again, and I shall be flattered again, just as if I had never found him out at all! He can manage me, as he manages his wife and Laura, as he managed the bloodhound in the stable-yard, as he manages Sir Percival himself, every hour in the day. "My good Percival! how I like your rough English humour!" — "My good Percival! how I enjoy your solid English sense!" He puts the rudest remarks Sir Percival can make on his effeminate tastes and amusements, quietly away from him in that manner — always calling the baronet by his Christian name; smiling at him with the calmest superiority; patting him on the shoulder; and bearing with him benignantly, as a good-humoured father bears with a wayward son.

The interest which I really cannot help feeling in this strangely original man, has led me to question Sir Percival about his past life.

Sir Percival either knows little, or will tell me little, about it. He and the Count first met many years ago, at Rome, under the dangerous circumstances to which I have alluded elsewhere. Since that time, they have been perpetually together in London, in Paris, and in Vienna — but never in Italy again; the Count having, oddly enough, not crossed the frontiers of his native country for years past. Perhaps, he has been made the victim of some political persecution? At all events, he seems to be patriotically anxious not to lose sight of any of his own countrymen who may happen to be in England. On the evening of his arrival, he asked how far we were from the nearest town, and whether we knew of any Italian gentlemen who might happen to be settled there. He is certainly in correspondence with people on the Continent, for his letters have all sorts of odd stamps on them; and I saw one for him, this morning, waiting in his place at the breakfast-table, with a huge official-looking seal on it. Perhaps he is in correspondence with his government? And yet, that is hardly to be reconciled, either, with my other idea that he may be a political exile.

How much I seem to have written about Count Fosco! And what does it all amount to? — as poor, dear Mr. Gilmore would ask, in his impenetrable business-like way. I can only repeat that I do assuredly feel, even on this short acquaintance, a strange, half-willing, half-unwilling liking for the Count. He seems to have established over me the same sort of ascendency which he has evidently gained over Sir Percival. Free, and even rude, as he may occasionally be in his manner towards his fat friend, Sir Percival is nevertheless afraid, as I can plainly see, of giving any serious offence to the Count. I wonder whether I am afraid, too? I certainly never saw a man, in all my experience, whom I should be so sorry to have for an enemy. Is this because I like him, or because I am afraid of him? *Chi sa?* — as Count Fosco might say in his own language. Who knows?

JULY 2ND. — Something to chronicle, to-day, besides my own idea and impressions. A visitor has arrived — quite unknown to Laura and to me; and, apparently, quite unexpected by Sir Percival.

We were all at lunch, in the room with the new French windows that open into the verandah; and the Count (who devours pastry as I have never yet seen it devoured by any human beings but girls at boarding-schools) had just amused us by asking gravely for his fourth tart — when the servant entered, to announce the visitor.

"Mr. Merriman has just come, Sir Percival, and wishes to see you immediately."

Sir Percival started, and looked at the man, with an expression of angry alarm.

"Mr. Merriman?" he repeated as if he thought his own ears must have deceived him.

"Yes, Sir Percival: Mr. Merriman, from London."

"Where is he?"

"In the library, Sir Percival."

He left the table the instant the last answer was given; and hurried out of the room without saying a word to any of us.

"Who is Mr. Merriman?" asked Laura, appealing to me.

"I have not the least idea," was all I could say in reply.

The Count had finished his fourth tart, and had gone to a side-table to look after his vicious cockatoo. He turned round to us, with the bird perched on his shoulder.

"Mr. Merriman is Sir Percival's solicitor," he said quietly.

Sir Percival's solicitor. It was a perfectly straight-forward answer to Laura's question; and yet, under the circumstances, it was not satisfactory. If Mr. Merriman had been specially sent for by his client, there would have been nothing very wonderful in his leaving town to obey the summons. But when a lawyer travels from London to Hampshire, without being sent for, and when his arrival at a gentleman's house seriously startles the gentleman himself, it may be safely taken for granted that the legal visitor is the bearer of some very important and very unexpected news — news which may be either very good or very bad, but which cannot, in either case, be of the common every-day kind.

Laura and I sat silent at the table, for a quarter of an hour or more, wondering uneasily what had happened, and waiting for the chance of Sir Percival's speedy return. There were no signs of his return; and we rose to leave the room.

The Count, attentive as usual, advanced from the corner in which he had been feeding his cockatoo, with the bird still perched on his shoulder, and opened the door for us. Laura and Madame Fosco went out first. Just as I was on the point of following them, he made a sign with his hand, and spoke to me, before I passed him, in the oddest manner.

"Yes," he said; quietly answering the unexpressed idea at that moment in my mind, as if I had plainly confided it to him in so many words — "yes, Miss Halcombe; something *has* happened."

I was on the point of answering, "I never said so." But the vicious cockatoo ruffled his clipped wings, and gave a screech that set all my nerves on edge in an instant, and made me only too glad to get out of the room.

I joined Laura at the foot of the stairs. The thought in her mind was the same as the thought in mine, which Count Fosco had surprised — and, when she spoke, her words were almost the echo of his. She, too, said to me, secretly, that she was afraid something had happened.

V.

July 2ND. — I have a few lines more to add to this day's entry before I go to bed to-night.

About two hours after Sir Percival rose from the luncheon-table to receive his solicitor, Mr. Merriman, in the library, I left my room, alone, to take a walk in the plantations. Just as I was at the end of the landing, the library door opened, and the two gentlemen came out. Thinking it best not to disturb them by appearing on the stairs, I resolved to defer going down till they had crossed the hall. Although they spoke to each other in guarded tones, their words were pronounced with sufficient distinctness of utterance to reach my ears.

"Make your mind easy, Sir Percival," I heard the lawyer say. "It all rests with Lady Glyde."

I had turned to go back to my own room, for a minute or two; but the sound of Laura's name, on the lips of a stranger, stopped me instantly. I dare say it was very wrong and very discreditable to listen — but where is the woman, in the whole range of our sex, who can regulate her actions by the abstract principles of honour, when those principles point one way, and when her affections, and the interests which grow out of them, point the other?

I listened; and, under similar circumstances, I would listen again — yes! with my ear at the keyhole, if I could not possibly manage it in any other way.

"You quite understand, Sir Percival?" the lawyer went on. "Lady Glyde is to sign her name in the presence of a witness — or of two witnesses, if you wish to be particularly careful — and is then to put her finger on the seal, and say, 'I deliver this as my act and deed.' If that is done in a week's time, the arrangement will be perfectly successful, and the anxiety will be all over. If not ——"

"What do you mean by 'if not?'" asked Sir Percival, angrily. "If the thing *must* be done, it *shall* be done. I promise you that, Merriman."

"Just so, Sir Percival — just so; but there are two alternatives in all transactions; and we lawyers like to look both of them in the face boldly. If through any extraordinary circumstance the arrangement should *not* be made, I think I may be able to get the parties to accept bills at three months. But how the money is to be raised when the bills fall due ——"

"Damn the bills! The money is only to be got in one way; and in that way, I tell you again, it *shall* be got. Take a glass of wine, Merriman, before you go."

"Much obliged, Sir Percival; I have not a moment to lose if I am to catch the up-train. You will let me know as soon as the arrangement is complete? and you will not forget the caution I recommended ——"

"Of course I won't. There's the dog-cart at the door for you. My groom will get you to the station in no time. Benjamin, drive like mad! Jump in. If Mr. Merriman misses the train, you lose your place. Hold fast, Merriman, and if you are upset, trust to the devil to save his own." With that parting benediction, the baronet turned about, and walked back to the library.

I had not heard much; but the little that had reached my ears was enough to make me feel uneasy. The "something" that "had happened," was but too plainly a serious money-embarrassment; and Sir Percival's relief from it depended upon Laura. The prospect of seeing her involved in her husband's secret difficulties filled me with dismay, exaggerated, no doubt, by my ignorance of business and my settled distrust of Sir Percival. Instead of going out, as I proposed, I went back immediately to Laura's room to tell her what I had heard.

She received my bad news so composedly as to surprise me. She evidently knows more of her husband's character and her husband's embarrassments than I have suspected up to this time.

"I feared as much," she said, "when I heard of that strange gentleman who called, and declined to leave his name."

"Who do you think the gentleman was, then?" 1 asked.

"Some person who has heavy claims on Sir Percival," she answered; "and who has been the cause of Mr. Merriman's visit here to-day."

"Do you know anything about those claims?"

"No; I know no particulars."

"You will sign nothing, Laura, without first looking at it?"

"Certainly not, Marian. Whatever I can harmlessly and honestly do to help him I will do — for the sake of making your life and mine, love, as easy and as happy as possible. But I will do nothing, ignorantly, which we might, one day, have reason to feel ashamed of. Let us say no more about it, now. You have got your hat on — suppose we go and dream away the afternoon in the grounds?'

On leaving the house we directed our steps to the nearest shade.

As we passed an open space among the trees in front of the house, there was Count Fosco, slowly walking backwards and forwards on the grass, sunning himself in the full blaze of the hot July afternoon. He had a broad straw hat on, with a violet coloured ribbon round it. A blue blouse, with profuse white fancy-work over the bosom, covered his prodigious body, and was girt about the place where his waist might once have been, with a broad scarlet leather belt. Nankeen trousers, displaying more white fancy-work over the ankles, and purple morocco slippers, adorned his lower extremities. He was singing Figaro's famous song in the Barber of Seville, with that crisply fluent vocalization which is never heard from any other than an Italian throat; accompanying himself on the concertina, which he played with ecstatic throwings-up of his arms, and graceful twistings and turnings of his head, like a fat St. Cecilia masquerading in male attire. "Figaro quà! Figaro là! Figaro sù! Figaro giù!" sang the Count, jauntily tossing up the concertina at arm's length, and bowing to us, on one side of the instrument, with the airy grace and elegance of Figaro himself at twenty years of age.

"Take my word for it, Laura, that man knows something of Sir Percival's embarrassments," I said, as we returned the Count's salutation from a safe distance.

"What makes you think that?" she asked.

"How should he have known, otherwise, that Mr. Merriman was Sir Percival's solicitor?" I rejoined. "Besides, when I followed you out of the luncheon-room, he told me, without a single word of inquiry on my part, that something had happened. Depend upon it, he knows more than we do."

"Don't ask him any questions, if he does. Don't take him into our confidence!"

"You seem to dislike him, Laura, in a very determined manner. What has he said or done to justify you?"

"Nothing, Marian. On the contrary, he was all kindness and attention on our journey home, and he several times checked Sir Percival's outbreaks of temper, in the most considerate manner towards *me*. Perhaps, I dislike him because he has so much more power over my husband than I have. Perhaps it hurts my pride to be under any obligations to his interference. All I know is, that I *do* dislike him."

The rest of the day and evening passed quietly enough. The Count and I played at chess. For the first two games he politely allowed me to conquer him; and then, when he saw that I had found him out, begged my pardon, and, at the third game, checkmated me in ten minutes. Sir Percival never once referred, all through the evening, to the lawyer's visit. But either that event, or something else, had produced a singular alteration for the better in him. He was as polite and agreeable to all of us, as he used to be in the days of his probation at Limmeridge; and he was so amazingly attentive and kind to his wife, that even icy Madame Fosco was roused into looking at him with a grave surprise. What does this mean? I think I can guess; I am afraid Laura can guess; and I am sure Count Fosco knows. I caught Sir Percival looking at him for approval more than once in the course of the evening.

JULY 3RD. — A day of events. I most fervently hope I may not have to add, a day of disasters as well.

Sir Percival was as silent at breakfast as he had been the evening before, on the subject of the mysterious "arrangement" (as the lawyer called it), which is hanging over our heads. An hour afterwards, however, he suddenly entered the morning-room, where his wife and I were waiting, with our hats on, for Madame Fosco to join us; and inquired for the Count.

"We expect to see him here directly," I said.

"The fact is," Sir Percival went on, walking nervously about the room, "I want Fosco and his wife in the library, for a mere business formality; and I want you there, Laura, for a minute, too." He stopped, and appeared to notice, for the first time, that we were in our walking costume. "Have you just come in?" he asked, "or were you just going out?"

"We were all thinking of going to the lake this morning," said Laura. "But if you have any other arrangement to propose —"

"No, no," he answered, hastily. "My arrangement can wait. After lunch will do as well for it, as after breakfast. All going to the lake, eh? A good idea. Let's have an idle morning; I'll be one of the party."

There was no mistaking his manner, even if it had been possible to mistake the uncharacteristic readiness which his words expressed, to submit his own plans and projects to the convenience of others. He was evidently relieved at finding any excuse for delaying the business formality in the library, to which his own words had referred. My heart sank within me, as I drew the inevitable inference.

The Count and his wife joined us, at that moment. The lady had her husband's embroidered tobacco-pouch, and her store of paper in her hand, for the manufacture of the eternal cigarettes. The gentleman, dressed, as usual, in his blouse and straw hat, carried the gay little pagoda-cage, with his darling white mice in it, and smiled on them, and on us, with a bland amiability which it was impossible to resist.

"With your kind permission," said the Count, "I will take my small family, here — my poor-little-harmless-pretty-Mouseys, out for an airing along with us. There are dogs about the house, and shall I leave my forlorn white children at the mercies of the dogs? Ah, never!"

He chirruped paternally at his small white children through the bars of the pagoda; and we all left the house for the lake.

In the plantation, Sir Percival strayed away from us. It seems to be part of his restless disposition always to separate himself from his companions on these occasions, and always to occupy himself, when he is alone, in cutting new walking-sticks for his own use. The mere act of cutting and lopping, at hazard, appears to please him. He has filled the house with walking-sticks of his own making, not one of which he ever takes up for a second time. When they have been once used, his interest in them is all exhausted, and he thinks of nothing but going on, and making more.

At the old boat-house, he joined us again. I will put down

the conversation that ensued, when we were all settled in our places, exactly as it passed. It is an important conversation, so far as I am concerned, for it has seriously disposed me to distrust the influence which Count Fosco has exercised over my thoughts and feelings, and to resist it, for the future, as resolutely as I can.

The boat-house was large enough to hold us all; but Sir Percival remained outside, trimming the last new stick with his pocket-axe. We three women found plenty of room on the large seat. Laura took her work, and Madame Fosco began her cigarettes. I, as usual, had nothing to do. My hands always were, and always will be, as awkward as a man's. The Count good-humouredly took a stool, many sizes too small for him, and balanced himself on it with his back against the side of the shed, which creaked and groaned under his weight. He put the pagoda-cage on his lap, and let out the mice to crawl over him as usual. They are pretty, innocent-looking little creatures; but the sight of them creeping about a man's body is, for some reason, not pleasant to me. It excites a strange, responsive creeping in my own nerves; and suggests hideous ideas of men dying in prison, with the crawling creatures of the dungeon preying on them undisturbed.

The morning was windy and cloudy; and the rapid alternations of shadow and sunlight over the waste of the lake, made the view look doubly wild, weird, and gloomy.

"Some people call that picturesque," said Sir Percival, pointing over the wide prospect with his half-finished walking-stick. "I call it a blot on a gentleman's property. In my great-grandfather's time, the lake flowed to this place. Look at it now! It is not four feet deep anywhere, and it is all puddles and pools. I wish I could afford to drain it, and plant it all over. My bailiff (a superstitious idiot) says he is quite sure the lake has a curse on it, like the Dead Sea. What do you think, Fosco? It looks just the place for a murder, doesn't it?"

"My good Percival!" remonstrated the Count. "What

is your solid English sense thinking of? The water is too shallow to hide the body; and there is sand everywhere to print off the murderer's footsteps. It is, upon the whole, the very worst place for a murder that I ever set my eyes on."

"Humbug!" said Sir Percival, cutting away fiercely at his stick. "You know what I mean. The dreary scenery — the lonely situation. If you choose to understand me, you can — if you don't choose, I am not going to trouble myself to explain my meaning."

"And why not," asked the Count, "when your meaning can be explained by anybody in two words? If a fool was going to commit a murder, your lake is the first place he would choose for it. If a wise man was going to commit a murder, your lake is the last place he would choose for it. Is that your meaning? If it is, there is your explanation for you, ready made. Take it, Percival, with your good Fosco's blessing." .

Laura looked at the Count, with her dislike for him appearing a little too plainly in her face. He was so busy with his mice that he did not notice her.

"I am sorry to hear the lake-view connected with anything so horrible as the idea of murder," she said. "And if Count Fosco must divide murderers into classes, I think he has been very unfortunate in his choice of expressions. To describe them as fools only, seems like treating them with an indulgence to which they have no claim. And to describe them as wise men, sounds to me like a downright contradiction in terms. I have always heard that truly wise men are truly good men, and have a horror of crime."

"My dear lady," said the Count, "those are admirable sentiments; and I have seen them stated at the tops of copy-books." He lifted one of the white mice in the palm of his hand, and spoke to it in his whimsical way. "My pretty little smooth white rascal," he said, "here is a moral lesson for you. A truly wise Mouse is a truly good Mouse. Mention that, if you please, to your companions, and never gnaw at the bars of your cage again as long as you live."

"It is easy to turn everything into ridicule," said Laura, resolutely; "but you will not find it quite so easy, Count Fosco, to give me an instance of a wise man who has been a great criminal."

The Count shrugged his huge shoulders, and smiled on Laura in the friendliest manner.

"Most true!" he said. "The fool's crime is the crime that is found out; and the wise man's crime is the crime that is *not* found out. If I could give you an instance, it would not be the instance of a wise man. Dear Lady Glyde, your sound English common sense has been too much for me. It is checkmate for *me* this time, Miss Halcombe — ha?"

"Stand to your guns, Laura," sneered Sir Percival, who had been listening in his place at the door. "Tell him, next, that crimes cause their own detection. There's another bit of copy-book morality for you, Fosco. Crimes cause their own detection. What infernal humbug!"

"I believe it to be true," said Laura, quietly.

Sir Percival burst out laughing; so violently, so outrageously, that he quite startled us all — the Count more than any of us.

"I believe it, too," I said, coming to Laura's rescue.

Sir Percival, who had been unaccountably amused at his wife's remark, was, just as unaccountably, irritated by mine. He struck the new stick savagely on the sand, and walked away from us.

"Poor dear Percival!" cried Count Fosco, looking after him gaily; "he is the victim of English spleen. But, my dear Miss Halcombe, my dear Lady Glyde, do you really believe that crimes cause their own detection? And you, my angel," he continued, turning to his wife, who had not uttered a word yet, "do you think so too?"

"I wait to be instructed," replied the Countess, in tones of freezing reproof, intended for Laura and me, "before I venture on giving my opinion in the presence of well-informed men."

"Do you, indeed?" I said. "I remember the time,

Countess, when you advocated the Rights of Women — and freedom of female opinion was one of them."

"What is your view of the subject, Count?" asked Madame Fosco, calmly proceeding with her cigarettes, and not taking the least notice of me.

The Count stroked one of his white mice reflectively with his chubby little finger before he answered.

"It is truly wonderful," he said, "how easily Society can console itself for the worst of its short-comings with a little bit of clap-trap. The machinery it has set up for the detection of crime is miserably ineffective — and yet only invent a moral epigram, saying that it works well, and you blind everybody to its blunders, from that moment. Crimes cause their own detection, do they? And murder will out (another moral epigram), will it? Ask Coroners who sit at inquests in large towns if that is true, Lady Glyde. Ask secretaries of life-assurance companies, if that is true, Miss Halcombe. Read your own public journals. In the few cases that get into the newspapers, are there not instances of slain bodies found, and no murderers ever discovered? Multiply the cases that are reported by the cases that are *not* reported, and the bodies that are found by the bodies that are *not* found; and what conclusion do you come to? This. That there are foolish criminals who are discovered, and wise criminals who escape. The hiding of a crime, or the detection of a crime, what is it? A trial of skill between the police on one side, and the individual on the other. When the criminal is a brutal, ignorant fool, the police, in nine cases out of ten, win. When the criminal is a resolute, educated, highly-intelligent man, the police, in nine cases out of ten, lose. If the police win, you generally hear all about it. If the police lose, you generally hear nothing. And on this tottering foundation you build up your comfortable moral maxim that Crime causes its own detection! Yes — all the crime *you* know of. And, what of the rest?"

"Devilish true, and very well put," cried a voice at the entrance of the boat-house. Sir Percival had recovered his equanimity, and had come back while we were listening to the Count.

"Some of it may be true," I said; "and all of it may be very well put.   But I don't see why Count Fosco should celebrate the victory of the criminal over society with so much exultation, or why you, Sir Percival, should applaud him so loudly for doing it."

"Do you hear that, Fosco?" asked Sir Percival.   "Take my advice, and make your peace with your audience.   Tell them Virtue's a fine thing — they like that, I can promise you."

The Count laughed inwardly and silently; and two of the white mice in his waistcoat, alarmed by the internal convulsion going on beneath them, darted out in a violent hurry, and scrambled into their cage again.

"The ladies, my good Percival, shall tell *me* about virtue," he said.   "They are better authorities than I am; for they know what virtue is, and I don't."

"You hear him?" said Sir Percival.   "Isn't it awful?"

"It is true," said the Count, quietly.   "I am a citizen of the world, and I have met, in my time, with so many different sorts of virtue, that I am puzzled, in my old age, to say which is the right sort and which is the wrong.   Here, in England, there is one virtue.   And there, in China, there is another virtue.   And John Englishman says my virtue is the genuine virtue.   And John Chinaman says my virtue is the genuine virtue.   And I say Yes to one, or No to the other, and am just as much bewildered about it in the case of John with the top-boots as I am in the case of John with the pigtail.   Ah, nice little Mousey! come, kiss me.   What is your own private notion of a virtuous man, my pret-pret-pretty?   A man who keeps you warm, and gives you plenty to eat.   And a good notion, too, for it is intelligible, at the least."

"Stay a minute, Count," I interposed.   "Accepting your illustration, surely we have one unquestionable virtue in England, which is wanting in China.   The Chinese authorities kill thousands of innocent people, on the most frivolous pretexts. We, in England, are free from all guilt of that kind — we commit no such dreadful crime — we abhor reckless bloodshed, with all our hearts."

"Quite right, Marian," said Laura. "Well thought of, and well expressed."

"Pray allow the Count to proceed," said Madame Fosco, with stern civility. "You will find, young ladies, that *he* never speaks without having excellent reasons for all that he says."

"Thank you, my angel," replied the Count. "Have a bonbon?" He took out of his pocket a pretty little inlaid box, and placed it open on the table. "Chocolat à la Vanille," cried the impenetrable man, cheerfully rattling the sweet-meats in the box, and bowing all round. "Offered by Fosco as an act of homage to the charming society."

"Be good enough to go on, Count," said his wife, with a spiteful reference to myself. "Oblige me by answering Miss Halcombe."

"Miss Halcombe is unanswerable," replied the polite Italian — "that is to say, so far as she goes. Yes! I agree with her. John Bull does abhor the crimes of John Chinaman. He is the quickest old gentleman at finding out the faults that are his neighbours', and the slowest old gentleman at finding out the faults that are his own, who exists on the face of creation. Is he so very much better in his way, than the people whom he condemns in their way? English society, Miss Halcombe, is as often the accomplice, as it is the enemy of crime. Yes! yes! Crime is in this country what crime is in other countries — a good friend to a man and to those about him as often as it is an enemy. A great rascal provides for his wife and family. The worse he is, the more he makes them the objects for your sympathy. He often provides, also, for himself. A profligate spendthrift who is always borrowing money, will get more from his friends than the rigidly honest man who only borrows of them once, under pressure of the direst want. In the one case, the friends will not be at all surprised, and they will give. In the other case, they will be very much surprised, and they will hesitate. Is the prison that Mr. Scoundrel lives in, at the end of his career, a more uncomfortable place than the

workhouse that Mr. Honesty lives in, at the end of *his* career?
When John-Howard-Philanthropist wants to relieve misery,
he goes to find it in prisons, where crime is wretched — not
in huts and hovels, where virtue is wretched too. Who is the
English poet who has won the most universal sympathy — who
makes the easiest of all subjects for pathetic writing and pathetic painting? That nice young person who began life with
a forgery, and ended it by a suicide — your dear, romantic,
interesting Chatterton. Which gets on best, do you think, of
two poor starving dressmakers — the woman who resists temptation, and is honest, or the woman who falls under temptation, and steals? You all know that the stealing is the making of that second woman's fortune — it advertises her from
length to breadth of goodhumoured, charitable England —
and she is relieved, as the breaker of a commandment, when
she would have been left to starve, as the keeper of it. Come
here, my jolly little Mouse! Hey! presto! pass! I transform
you, for the time being, into a respectable lady. Stop there,
in the palm of my great big hand, my dear, and listen. You
marry the poor man whom you love, Mouse; and one half
your friends pity, and the other half blame you. And, now,
on the contrary, you sell yourself for gold to a man you don't
care for; and all your friends rejoice over you; and a minister
of public worship sanctions the base horror of the vilest of all
human bargains; and smiles and smirks afterwards at your
table, if you are polite enough to ask him to breakfast. Hey!
presto! pass! Be a mouse again, and squeak. If you continue to be a lady much longer, I shall have you telling me
that Society abhors crime — and then, Mouse, I shall doubt
if your own eyes and ears are really of any use to you. Ah!
I am a bad man, Lady Glyde, am I not? I say what other
people only think; and when all the rest of the world is in a
conspiracy to accept the mask for the true face, mine is the
rash hand that tears off the plump pasteboard, and shows the
bare bones beneath. I will get up on my big elephant's legs,
before I do myself any more harm in your amiable estimations
— I will get up, and take a little airy walk of my own. Dear

ladies, as your excellent Sheridan said, I go — and leave my
character behind me."

He got up; put the cage on the table; and paused, for a
moment, to count the mice in it. "One, two, three, four——
Ha!" he cried, with a look of horror, "where, in the name of
Heaven, is the fifth — the youngest, the whitest, the most
amiable of all — my Benjamin of mice!"

Neither Laura nor I were in any favourable disposition to
be amused. The Count's glib cynicism had revealed a new
aspect of his nature from which we both recoiled. But it was
impossible to resist the comical distress of so very large a man
at the loss of so very small a mouse. We laughed, in spite of
ourselves; and when Madame Fosco rose to set the example of
leaving the boat-house empty, so that her husband might
search it to its remotest corners, we rose also to follow her out.

Before we had taken three steps, the Count's quick eye
discovered the lost mouse under the seat that we had been occupying. He pulled aside the bench; took the little animal
up in his hand: and then suddenly stopped, on his knees, looking intently at a particular place on the ground just beneath
him.

When he rose to his feet again, his hand shook so that he
could hardly put the mouse back in the cage, and his face was
of a faint livid yellow hue all over.

"Percival!" he said, in a whisper. "Percival! come here."

Sir Percival had paid no attention to any of us, for the last
ten minutes. He had been entirely absorbed in writing figures
on the sand, and then rubbing them out again, with the point
of his stick.

"What's the matter, now?" he asked, lounging carelessly
into the boat-house.

"Do you see nothing, there?" said the Count, catching
him nervously by the collar with one hand, and pointing with
the other to the place near which he had found the mouse.

"I see plenty of dry sand," answered Sir Percival; "and
a spot of dirt in the middle of it."

"Not dirt," whispered the Count, fastening the other hand suddenly on Sir Percival's collar, and shaking it in his agitation. "Blood."

Laura was near enough to hear the last word, softly as he whispered it. She turned to me with a look of terror.

"Nonsense, my dear," I said. "There is no need to be alarmed. It is only the blood of a poor little stray dog."

Everybody was astonished, and everybody's eyes were fixed on me inquiringly.

"How do you know that?" asked Sir Percival, speaking first.

"I found the dog here, dying, on the day when you all returned from abroad," I replied. "The poor creature had strayed into the plantation, and had been shot by your keeper."

"Whose dog was it?" inquired Sir Percival. "Not one of mine."

"Did you try to save the poor thing?" asked Laura, earnestly. "Surely you tried to save it, Marian?"

"Yes," I said; "the housekeeper and I both did our best—but the dog was mortally wounded, and he died under our hands."

"Whose dog was it?" persisted Sir Percival, repeating his question a little irritably. "One of mine?"

"No; not one of yours."

"Whose then? Did the housekeeper know?"

The housekeeper's report of Mrs. Catherick's desire to conceal her visit to Blackwater Park from Sir Percival's knowledge, recurred to my memory the moment he put that last question; and I half doubted the discretion of answering it. But, in my anxiety to quiet the general alarm, I had thoughtlessly advanced too far to draw back, except at the risk of exciting suspicions, which might only make matters worse. There was nothing for it but to answer at once, without reference to results.

"Yes," I said. "The housekeeper knew. She told me it was Mrs. Catherick's dog."

Sir Percival had hitherto remained at the inner end of the boat-house with Count Fosco, while I spoke to him from the door. But the instant Mrs. Catherick's name passed my lips, he pushed by the Count roughly, and placed himself face to face with me, under the open daylight.

"How came the housekeeper to know it was Mrs. Catherick's dog?" he asked, fixing his eyes on mine with a frowning interest and attention, which half angered, half startled me.

"She knew it," I said, quietly, "because Mrs. Catherick brought the dog with her."

"Brought it with her? Where did she bring it with her?"

"To this house."

"What the devil did Mrs. Catherick want at this house?"

The manner in which he put the question was even more offensive than the language in which he expressed it. I marked my sense of his want of common politeness, by silently turning away from him.

Just as I moved, the Count's persuasive hand was laid on his shoulder, and the Count's mellifluous voice interposed to quiet him.

"My dear Percival! — gently — gently."

Sir Percival looked round in his angriest manner. The Count only smiled, and repeated the soothing application.

"Gently, my good friend — gently!"

Sir Percival hesitated — followed me a few steps — and, to my great surprise, offered me an apology.

"I beg your pardon, Miss Halcombe," he said. "I have been out of order lately; and I am afraid I am a little irritable. But I should like to know what Mrs. Catherick could possibly want here. When did she come? Was the housekeeper the only person who saw her?"

"The only person," I answered, "so far as I know."

The Count interposed again.

"In that case, why not question the housekeeper?" he said. "Why not go, Percival, to the fountain-head of information at once?"

"Quite right!" said Sir Percival. "Of course the housekeeper is the first person to question. Excessively stupid of me not to see it myself." With those words, he instantly left us to return to the house.

The motive of the Count's interference, which had puzzled me at first, betrayed itself when Sir Percival's back was turned. He had a host of questions to put to me about Mrs. Catherick, and the cause of her visit to Blackwater Park, which he could scarcely have asked in his friend's presence. I made my answers as short as I civilly could — for I had already determined to check the least approach to any exchanging of confidences between Count Fosco and myself. Laura, however, unconsciously helped him to extract all my information, by making inquiries herself, which left me no alternative but to reply to her, or to appear in the very unenviable and very false character of a depositary of Sir Percival's secrets. The end of it was, that, in about ten minutes' time, the Count knew as much as I know of Mrs. Catherick, and of the events which have so strangely connected us with her daughter, Anne, from the time when Hartright met with her, to this day.

The effect of my information on him was, in one respect, curious enough.

Intimately as he knows Sir Percival, and closely as he appears to be associated with Sir Percival's private affairs in general, he is certainly as far as I am from knowing anything of the true story of Anne Catherick. The unsolved mystery in connexion with this unhappy woman is now rendered doubly suspicious, in my eyes, by the absolute conviction which I feel, that the clue to it has been hidden by Sir Percival from the most intimate friend he has in the world. It was impossible to mistake the eager curiosity of the Count's look and manner while he drank in greedily every word that fell from my lips. There are many kinds of curiosity, I know — but there is no misinterpreting the curiosity of blank surprise: if I ever saw it in my life, I saw it in the Count's face.

While the questions and answers were going on, we had all

been strolling quietly back, through the plantation. As soon as we reached the house, the first object that we saw in front of it was Sir Percival's dog-cart, with the horse put to and the groom waiting by it in his stable-jacket. If these unexpected appearances were to be trusted, the examination of the housekeeper had produced important results already.

"A fine horse, my friend," said the Count, addressing the groom with the most engaging familiarity of manner "You are going to drive out?"

"*I* am not going, sir," replied the man, looking at his stable-jacket, and evidently wondering whether the foreign gentleman took it for his livery. "My master drives himself."

"Aha!" said the Count, "does he indeed? I wonder he gives himself the trouble when he has got you to drive for him. Is he going to fatigue that nice, shining, pretty horse by taking him very far, to-day?"

"I don't know, sir," answered the man. "The horse is a mare, if you please, sir. She's the highest-couraged thing we've got in the stables. Her name's Brown Molly, sir; and she'll go till she drops. Sir Percival usually takes Isaac of York for the short distances."

"And your shining courageous Brown Molly for the long?"

"Yes, sir."

"Logical inference, Miss Halcombe," continued the Count, wheeling round briskly, and addressing me : "Sir Percival is going a long distance to-day."

I made no reply. I had my own inferences to draw, from what I knew through the housekeeper and from what I saw before me; and I did not choose to share them with Count Fosco.

When Sir Percival was in Cumberland (I thought to myself), he walked away a long distance, on Anne's account, to question the family at Todd's Corner. Now he is in Hampshire, is he going to drive away a long distance, on

Anne's account again, to question Mrs. Catherick at Welmingham?

We all entered the house. As we crossed the hall, Sir Percival came out from the library to meet us. He looked hurried and pale and anxious — but, for all that, he was in his most polite mood, when he spoke to us.

"I am sorry to say, I am obliged to leave you," he began — "a long drive — a matter — that I can't very well put off. I shall be back in good time to-morrow — but, before I go, I should like that little business-formality, which I spoke of this morning, to be settled. Laura, will you come into the library? It won't take a minute—a mere formality. Countess, may I trouble you also? I want you and the Countess, Fosco, to be witnesses to a signature — nothing more. Come in at once, and get it over."

He held the library door open until they had passed in, followed them, and shut it softly.

I remained, for a moment afterwards, standing alone in the hall, with my heart beating fast, and my mind misgiving me sadly. Then, I went on to the staircase, and ascended slowly to my own room.

VI.

JULY 3RD. — Just as my hand was on the door of my room, I heard Sir Percival's voice calling to me from below.

"I must beg you to come down stairs again," he said. "It is Fosco's fault, Miss Halcombe, not mine. He has started some nonsensical objection to his wife being one of the witnesses, and has obliged me to ask you to join us in the library."

I entered the room immediately with Sir Percival. Laura was waiting by the writing-table, twisting and turning her garden hat uneasily in her hands. Madame Fosco sat near her, in an arm-chair, imperturbably admiring her husband, who stood by himself at the other end of the library, picking off the dead leaves from the flowers in the window.

The moment I appeared, the Count advanced to meet me, and to offer his explanations.

"A thousand pardons, Miss Halcombe," he said. "You know the character which is given to my countrymen by the English? We Italians are all wily and suspicious by nature, in the estimation of the good John Bull. Set me down, if you please, as being no better than the rest of my race. I am a wily Italian and a suspicious Italian. You have thought so yourself, dear lady, have you not? Well! it is part of my wiliness and part of my suspicion to object to Madame Fosco being a witness to Lady Glyde's signature, when I am also a witness myself."

"There is not the shadow of a reason for his objection," interposed Sir Percival. "I have explained to him that the law of England allows Madame Fosco to witness a signature as well as her husband."

"I admit it," resumed the Count. "The law of England says, Yes — but the conscience of Fosco says, No." He spread out his fat fingers on the bosom of his blouse, and bowed solemnly, as if he wished to introduce his conscience to us all, in the character of an illustrious addition to the society. "What this document which Lady Glyde is about to sign, may be," he continued, "I neither know nor desire to know. I only say this: circumstances may happen in the future which may oblige Percival, or his representatives, to appeal to the two witnesses; in which case it is certainly desirable that those witnesses should represent two opinions which are perfectly independent the one of the other. This cannot be if my wife signs as well as myself, because we have but one opinion between us, and that opinion is mine. I will not have it cast in my teeth, at some future day, that Madame Fosco acted under my coercion, and was, in plain fact, no witness at all. I speak in Percival's interest when I propose that my name shall appear (as the nearest friend of the husband), and your name, Miss Halcombe (as the nearest friend of the wife). I am a Jesuit, if you please to think so — a splitter of straws — a man of trifles and crotchets and scruples — but you will humour me, I hope, in merciful consideration for my suspicious Italian character, and my uneasy Italian conscience." He bowed again, stepped back a few paces, and withdrew his conscience from our society as politely as he had introduced it.

The Count's scruples might have been honourable and reasonable enough, but there was something in his manner of expressing them which increased my unwillingness to be concerned in the business of the signature. No consideration of less importance than my consideration for Laura, would have induced me to consent to be a witness at all. One look, however, at her anxious face, decided me to risk anything rather than desert her.

"I will readily remain in the room," I said. "And if I find no reason for starting any small scruples, on my side, you may rely on me as a witness."

Sir Percival looked at me sharply, as if he was about to say something. But, at the same moment, Madame Fosco attracted his attention by rising from her chair. She had caught her husband's eye, and had evidently received her orders to leave the room.

"You needn't go," said Sir Percival.

Madame Fosco looked for her orders again, got them again, said she would prefer leaving us to our business, and resolutely walked out. The Count lit a cigarette, went back to the flowers in the window, and puffed little jets of smoke at the leaves, in a state of the deepest anxiety about killing the insects.

Meanwhile, Sir Percival unlocked a cupboard beneath one of the bookcases, and produced from it a piece of parchment folded, longwise, many times over. He placed it on the table, opened the last fold only, and kept his hand on the rest. The last fold displayed a strip of blank parchment with little wafers stuck on it at certain places. Every line of the writing was hidden in the part which he still held folded up under his hand. Laura and I looked at each other. Her face was pale — but it showed no indecision and no fear.

Sir Percival dipped a pen in ink, and handed it to his wife.

"Sign your name, there," he said, pointing to the place. "You and Fosco are to sign afterwards, Miss Halcombe, opposite those two wafers. Come here, Fosco! witnessing a signature is not to be done by mooning out of window and smoking into the flowers."

The Count threw away his cigarette, and joined us at the table, with his hands carelessly thrust into the scarlet belt of his blouse, and his eyes steadily fixed on Sir Percival's face. Laura, who was on the other side of her husband, with the pen in her hand, looked at him, too. He stood between them, holding the folded parchment down firmly on the table, and glancing across at me, as I sat opposite to him, with such a sinister mixture of suspicion and embarrassment in his face, that he looked more like a prisoner at the bar than a gentleman in his own house.

"Sign there," he repeated, turning suddenly on Laura, and pointing once more to the place on the parchment.

"What is it I am to sign?" she asked, quietly.

"I have no time to explain," he answered. "The dog-cart is at the door; and I must go directly. Besides, if I had time, you wouldn't understand. It is a purely formal document — full of legal technicalities, and all that sort of thing. Come! come! sign your name, and let us have done as soon as possible."

"I ought surely to know what I am signing, Sir Percival, before I write my name?"

"Nonsense! What have women to do with business? I tell you again, you can't understand it."

"At any rate, let me try to understand it. Whenever Mr. Gilmore had any business for me to do, he always explained it, first; and I always understood him."

"I dare say he did. He was your servant, and was obliged to explain. I am your husband, and am *not* obliged.

How much longer do you mean to keep me here? I tell you again, there is no time for reading anything: the dog-cart is waiting at the door. Once for all, will you sign, or will you not?"

She still had the pen in her hand; but she made no approach to signing her name with it.

"If my signature pledges me to anything," she said, "surely, I have some claim to know what that pledge is?"

He lifted up the parchment, and struck it angrily on the table.

"Speak out!" he said. "You were always famous for telling the truth. Never mind Miss Halcombe; never mind Fosco — say, in plain terms, you distrust me."

The Count took one of his hands out of his belt, and laid it on Sir Percival's shoulder. Sir Percival shook it off irritably. The Count put it on again with unruffled composure.

"Control your unfortunate temper, Percival," he said. "Lady Glyde is right."

"Right!" cried Sir Percival. "A wife right in distrusting her husband!"

"It is unjust and cruel to accuse me of distrusting you," said Laura. "Ask Marian if I am not justified in wanting to know what this writing requires of me, before I sign it?"

"I won't have any appeals made to Miss Halcombe," retorted Sir Percival. "Miss Halcombe has nothing to do with the matter."

I had not spoken hitherto, and I would much rather not have spoken now. But the expression of distress in Laura's face when she turned it towards me, and the insolent injustice of her husband's conduct, left me no other alternative than to give my opinion, for her sake, as soon as I was asked for it.

"Excuse me, Sir Percival," I said — "but, as one of the witnesses to the signature, I venture to think that I *have* something to do with the matter. Laura's objection seems to me to be a perfectly fair one; and, speaking for myself only, I cannot assume the responsibility of witnessing her signature, unless she first understands what the writing is which you wish her to sign."

"A cool declaration, upon my soul!" cried Sir Percival. "The next time you invite yourself to a man's house, Miss Halcombe, I recommend you not to repay his hospitality by taking his wife's side against him in a matter that doesn't concern you."

I started to my feet as suddenly as if he had struck me. If I had been a man, I would have knocked him down on the threshold of his own door, and have left his house, never, on any earthly consideration, to enter it again. But I was only a woman — and I loved his wife so dearly!

Thank God, that faithful love helped me, and I sat down again, without saying a word. *She* knew what I had suffered and what I had suppressed. She ran round to me, with the tears streaming from her eyes. "Oh, Marian!" she whispered softly. "If my mother had been alive, she could have done no more for me!"

"Come back and sign!" cried Sir Percival, from the other side of the table.

"Shall I?" she asked in my ear; "I will, if you tell me."

"No," I answered. "The right and the truth are with you — sign nothing, unless you have read it first."

"Come back and sign!" he reiterated, in his loudest and angriest tones.

The Count, who had watched Laura and me with a close and silent attention, interposed for the second time.

"Percival!" he said. "*I* remember that I am in the presence of ladies. Be good enough, if you please, to remember it, too."

Sir Percival turned on him, speechless with passion. The Count's firm hand slowly tightened its grasp on his shoulder, and the Count's steady voice, quietly repeated, "Be good enough, if you please, to remember it, too."

They both looked at each other: Sir Percival slowly drew his shoulder from under the Count's hand; slowly turned his face away from the Count's eyes; doggedly looked down for a little while at the parchment on the table; and then spoke, with the sullen submission of a tamed animal, rather than the becoming resignation of a convinced man.

"I don't want to offend anybody," he said, "but my wife's obstinacy is enough to try the patience of a saint. I have told her this is merely a formal document — and what more can she want? You may say what you please; but it is no part of a woman's duty to set her husband at defiance. Once more, Lady Glyde, and for the last time, will you sign or will you not?"

Laura returned to his side of the table, and took up the pen again.

"I will sign with pleasure," she said, "if you will only treat me as a responsible being. I care little what sacrifice is required of me, if it will affect no one else, and lead to no ill results —"

"Who talked of a sacrifice being required of you?" he broke in, with a half-suppressed return of his former violence.

"I only meant," she resumed, "that I would refuse no concession which I could honourably make. If I have a scruple about signing my name to an engagement of which I know nothing, why should you visit it on me so severely? It is rather hard, I think, to treat Count Fosco's scruples so much more indulgently than you have treated mine."

This unfortunate, yet most natural, reference to the Count's extraordinary power over her husband, indirect as it was, set Sir Percival's smouldering temper on fire again in an instant.

"Scruples!" he repeated. "*Your* scruples! It is rather late in the day for you to be scrupulous. I should have thought you had got over all weakness of that sort, when you made a virtue of necessity by marrying *me*."

The instant he spoke those words, Laura threw down the pen — looked at him with an expression in her eyes, which throughout all my experience of her, I had never seen in them before — and turned her back on him in dead silence.

This strong expression of the most open and the most bitter contempt, was so entirely unlike herself, so utterly out of her character, that it silenced us all. There was something hidden, beyond a doubt, under the mere surface-brutality of the words which her husband had just addressed to her. There was some lurking insult beneath them, of which I was wholly ignorant, but which had left the mark of its profanation so plainly on her face that even a stranger might have seen it.

The Count, who was no stranger, saw it as distinctly as I did. When I left my chair to join Laura, I heard him whisper under his breath to Sir Percival: "You idiot!"

Laura walked before me to the door as I advanced; and, at the same time, her husband spoke to her once more.

"You positively refuse, then, to give me your signature?" he said, in the altered tone of a man who was conscious that he had let his own licence of language seriously injure him.

"After what you have just said to me," she replied, firmly, "I refuse my signature until I have read every line in that parchment from the first word to the last. Come away, Marian, we have remained here long enough."

"One moment!" interposed the Count, before Sir Percival could speak again — "one moment, Lady Glyde, I implore you!"

Laura would have left the room without noticing him; but I stopped her.

"Don't make an enemy of the Count!" I whispered. "Whatever you do, don't make an enemy of the Count!"

She yielded to me. I closed the door again; and we stood near it, waiting. Sir Percival sat down at the table, with his elbow on the folded parchment, and his head resting on his clenched fist. The Count stood between us — master of the dreadful position in which we were placed, as he was master of everything else.

"Lady Glyde," he said, with a gentleness which seemed to address itself to our forlorn situation instead of to ourselves, "pray pardon me, if I venture to offer one suggestion; and pray believe that I speak out of my profound respect and my friendly regard for the mistress of this house." He turned sharply towards Sir Percival. "Is it absolutely necessary," he asked, "that this thing here, under your elbow, should be signed to-day?"

"It is necessary to my plans and wishes," returned the other, sulkily. "But that consideration, as you may have noticed, has no influence with Lady Glyde."

"Answer my plain question, plainly. Can the business of the signature be put off till to-morrow — Yes or No?"

"Yes — if you will have it so."

"Then, what are you wasting your time for, here? Let the signature wait till to-morrow — let it wait till you come back."

Sir Percival looked up with a frown and an oath.

"You are taking a tone with me that I don't like," he said. "A tone I won't bear from any man."

"I am advising you for your good," returned the Count, with a smile of quiet contempt. "Give yourself time; give Lady Glyde time. Have you forgotten that your dog-cart is waiting at the door? My tone surprises you — ha? I dare say it does — it is the tone of a man who can keep his temper. How many doses of good advice have I given you in my time? More than you can count. Have I ever been wrong? I defy you to quote me an instance of it. Go! take your drive. The matter of the signature can wait till to-morrow. Let it wait — and renew it when you come back."

Sir Percival hesitated, and looked at his watch. His anxiety about the secret journey which he was to take that day, revived by the Count's words, was now evidently disputing possession of his mind with his anxiety to obtain Laura's signature. He considered for a little while; and then got up from his chair.

"It is easy to argue me down," he said, "when I have no time to answer you. I will take your advice, Fosco — not because I want it, or believe in it, but because I can't stop here any longer." He paused, and looked round darkly at his wife. "If you don't give me your signature when I come back to-morrow —!" The rest was lost in the noise of his opening the book-case cupboard again, and locking up the parchment once more. He took his hat and gloves off the table, and made for the door. Laura and I drew back to let him pass. "Remember to-morrow!" he said to his wife; and went out.

We waited to give him time to cross the hall, and drive away. The Count approached us while we were standing near the door.

"You have just seen Percival at his worst, Miss Halcombe," he said. "As his old friend, I am sorry for him and ashamed of him. As his old friend, I promise you that he shall not break out to-morrow in the same disgraceful manner in which he has broken out to-day."

Laura had taken my arm while he was speaking, and she pressed it significantly when he had done. It would have been a hard trial to any woman to stand by and see the office of apologist for her husband's misconduct quietly assumed by his male friend in her own house — and it was a trial to *her*. I thanked the Count civilly, and led her out. Yes! I thanked him: for I felt already, with a sense of inexpressible helplessness and humiliation, that it was either his interest or his caprice to make sure of my continuing to reside at Blackwater Park; and I knew, after Sir Percival's conduct to me, that without the support of the Count's influence, I could not hope to remain there. His influence, the influence of all others that I dreaded most, was actually the one tie which now held me to Laura in the hour of her utmost need!

We heard the wheels of the dog-cart crashing on the

gravel of the drive, as we came into the hall. Sir Percival had started on his journey.

"Where is he going to, Marian?" Laura whispered. "Every fresh thing he does, seems to terrify me about the future. Have you any suspicions?"

After what she had undergone that morning, I was unwilling to tell her my suspicions.

"How should I know his secrets," I said, evasively.

"I wonder if the housekeeper knows?" she persisted.

"Certainly not," I replied. "She must be quite as ignorant as we are."

Laura shook her head doubtfully.

"Did you not hear from the housekeeper that there was a report of Anne Catherick having been seen in this neighbourhood? Don't you think he may have gone away to look for her?"

"I would rather compose myself, Laura, by not thinking about it, at all; and, after what has happened, you had better follow my example. Come into my room, and rest and quiet yourself a little."

We sat down together close to the window, and let the fragrant summer air breathe over our faces.

"I am ashamed to look at you, Marian," she said, "after what you submitted to down stairs, for my sake. Oh, my own love, I am almost heart-broken, when I think of it! But I will try to make it up to you — I will indeed!"

"Hush! hush!" I replied; "don't talk so. What is the trifling mortification of my pride compared to the dreadful sacrifice of your happiness?"

"You heard what he said to me?" she went on, quickly and vehemently. "You heard the words — but you don't know what they meant — you don't know why I threw down the pen and turned my back on him." She rose in sudden agitation, and walked about the room. "I have kept many things from your knowledge, Marian, for fear of distressing you, and making you unhappy at the outset of our new lives. You don't know how he has used me. And yet, you ought to

know, for you saw how he used me to-day. You heard him
sneer at my presuming to be scrupulous; you heard him say
I had made a virtue of necessity in marrying him." She sat
down again; her face flushed deeply, and her hands twisted
and twined together in her lap. "I can't tell you about it
now," she said; "I shall burst out crying if I tell you now —
later, Marian, when I am more sure of myself. My poor head
aches, darling — aches, aches, aches. Where is your smelling-bottle? Let me talk to you about yourself. I wish I had
given him my signature, for your sake. Shall I give it to him,
to-morrow? I would rather compromise myself than compromise you. After your taking my part against him, he will lay
all the blame on you, if I refuse again. What shall we do?
Oh, for a friend to help us and advise us! — a friend we could
really trust!"

She sighed bitterly. I saw in her face that she was thinking of Hartright — saw it the more plainly because her last
words set me thinking of him, too. In six months only from
her marriage, we wanted the faithful service he had offered
to us in his farewell words. How little I once thought that we
should ever want it at all!

"We must do what we can to help ourselves," I said. "Let
us try to talk it over calmly, Laura — let us do all in our power
to decide for the best."

Putting what she knew of her husband's embarrassments,
and what I had heard of his conversation with the lawyer,
together, we arrived necessarily at the conclusion that the
parchment in the library had been drawn up for the purpose
of borrowing money, and that Laura's signature was absolutely necessary to fit it for the attainment of Sir Percival's
object.

The second question, concerning the nature of the legal
contract by which the money was to be obtained, and the
degree of personal responsibility to which Laura might subject herself if she signed it in the dark, involved considerations
which lay far beyond any knowledge and experience that
either of us possessed. My own convictions led me to believe

that the hidden contents of the parchment concealed a transaction of the meanest and the most fraudulent kind.

I had not formed this conclusion in consequence of Sir Percival's refusal to show the writing, or to explain it; for that refusal might well have proceeded from his obstinate disposition and his domineering temper alone. My sole motive for distrusting his honesty, sprang from the change which I had observed in his language and his manners at Blackwater Park, a change which convinced me that he had been acting a part throughout the whole period of his probation at Limmeridge House. His elaborate delicacy; his ceremonious politeness, which harmonized so agreeably with Mr. Gilmore's old-fashioned notions; his modesty with Laura, his candour with me, his moderation with Mr. Fairlie — all these were the artifices of a mean, cunning, and brutal man, who had dropped his disguise when his practised duplicity had gained its end, and had openly shown himself in the library, on that very day. I say nothing of the grief which this discovery caused me on Laura's account, for it is not to be expressed by any words of mine. I only refer to it at all, because it decided me to oppose her signing the parchment, whatever the consequences might be, unless she was first made acquainted with the contents.

Under these circumstances, the one chance for us when to-morrow came, was to be provided with an objection to giving the signature, which might rest on sufficiently firm commercial or legal grounds to shake Sir Percival's resolution, and to make him suspect that we two women understood the laws and obligations of business as well as himself.

After some pondering, I determined to write to the only honest man within reach whom we could trust to help us discreetly, in our forlorn situation. That man was Mr. Gilmore's partner — Mr. Kyrle — who conducted the business, now that our old friend had been obliged to withdraw from it, and to leave London on account of his health. I explained to Laura that I had Mr. Gilmore's own authority for placing implicit confidence in his partner's integrity, discretion, and accurate knowledge of all her affairs; and, with her full approval, I sat down at once to write the letter.

I began by stating our position to Mr. Kyrle exactly as it was; and then asked for his advice in return, expressed in plain, downright terms which we could comprehend without any danger of misinterpretations and mistakes. My letter was as short as I could possibly make it, and was, I hope, unencumbered by needless apologies and needless details.

Just as I was about to put the address on the envelope, an obstacle was discovered by Laura, which in the effort and pre-occupation of writing, had escaped my mind altogether.

"How are we to get the answer in time?" she asked. "Your letter will not be delivered in London before to-morrow morning; and the post will not bring the reply here till the morning after."

The only way of overcoming this difficulty was to have the answer brought to us from the lawyer's office by a special messenger. I wrote a postscript to that effect, begging that the messenger might be despatched with the reply by the eleven o'clock morning train, which would bring him to our station at twenty minutes past one, and so enable him to reach Blackwater Park by two o'clock at the latest. He was to be directed to ask for me, to answer no questions addressed to him by any one else, and to deliver his letter into no hands but mine.

"In case Sir Percival should come back to-morrow before two o'clock," I said to Laura, "the wisest plan for you to adopt is to be out in the grounds, all the morning, with your book or your work, and not to appear at the house till the messenger has had time to arrive with the letter. I will wait here for him, all the morning, to guard against any misadventures or mistakes. By following this arrangement I hope and believe we shall avoid being taken by surprise. Let us go down to the drawing-room now. We may excite suspicion if we remain shut up together too long."

"Suspicion?" she repeated. "Whose suspicion can we excite, now that Sir Percival has left the house? Do you mean Count Fosco?"

"Perhaps I do, Laura."

"You are beginning to dislike him as much as I do, Marian."

"No; not to dislike him. Dislike is always, more or less, associated with contempt — I can see nothing in the Count to despise."

"You are not afraid of him, are you?"

"Perhaps I am — a little."

"Afraid of him, after his interference in our favour to-day!"

"Yes. I am more afraid of his interference than I am of Sir Percival's violence. Remember what I said to you in the library. Whatever you do, Laura, don't make an enemy of the Count!"

We went down stairs. Laura entered the drawing-room; while I proceeded across the hall, with my letter in my hand, to put it into the post-bag, which hung against the wall opposite to me.

The house door was open; and, as I crossed past it, I saw Count Fosco and his wife standing talking together on the steps outside, with their faces turned towards me.

The Countess came into the hall, rather hastily, and asked if I had leisure enough for five minutes' private conversation. Feeling a little surprised by such an appeal from such a person, I put my letter into the bag, and replied that I was quite at her disposal. She took my arm with unaccustomed friendliness and familiarity; and instead of leading me into an empty room, drew me out with her to the belt of turf which surrounded the large fish-pond.

As we passed the Count on the steps, he bowed and smiled, and then went at once into the house; pushing the hall-door to after him, but not actually closing it.

The Countess walked me gently round the fish-pond. I expected to be made the depositary of some extraordinary confidence; and I was astonished to find that Madame Fosco's communication for my private ear was nothing more than a polite assurance of her sympathy for me, after what had happened in the library. Her husband had told her of all that had passed, and of the insolent manner in which Sir Percival had spoken to me. This information had so shocked and distressed her, on my account and on Laura's, that she had made up her mind, if anything of the sort happened again, to mark her sense of Sir Percival's outrageous conduct by leaving the house. The Count had approved of her idea, and she now hoped that I approved of it, too.

I thought this a very strange proceeding on the part of such a remarkably reserved woman as Madame Fosco — especially after the interchange of sharp speeches which had passed between us during the conversation in the boat-house, on that very morning. However, it was my plain duty to meet a polite and friendly advance, on the part of one of my elders, with a polite and friendly reply. I answered the Countess, accordingly, in her own tone; and then, thinking we had said all that was necessary on either side, made an attempt to get back to the house.

But Madame Fosco seemed resolved not to part with me, and, to my unspeakable amazement, resolved also to talk. Hitherto, the most silent of women, she now persecuted me with fluent conventionalities on the subject of married life, on the subject of Sir Percival and Laura, on the subject of her own happiness, on the subject of the late Mr. Fairlie's conduct to her in the matter of her legacy, and on half a dozen other subjects besides, until she had detained me, walking round and round the fish-pond for more than half an hour, and had quite wearied me out. Whether she discovered this, or not, I cannot say, but she stopped as abruptly as she had begun — looked towards the house door — resumed her icy manner in a moment — and dropped my arm of her own accord, before I could think of an excuse for accomplishing my own release from her.

As I pushed open the door, and entered the hall, I found myself suddenly face to face with the Count again. He was just putting a letter into the post-bag.

After he had dropped it in, and had closed the bag, he

asked me where I had left Madame Fosco. I told him; and he went out at the hall door, immediately, to join his wife. His manner, when he spoke to me, was so unusually quiet and subdued that I turned and looked after him, wondering if he were ill or out of spirits.

Why my next proceeding was to go straight up to the post-bag, and take out my own letter, and look at it again, with a vague distrust on me; and why the looking at it for the second time instantly suggested the idea to my mind of sealing the envelope for its greater security — are mysteries which are either too deep or too shallow for me to fathom. Women, as everybody knows, constantly act on impulses which they cannot explain even to themselves; and I can only suppose that one of those impulses was the hidden cause of my unaccountable conduct on this occasion.

Whatever influence animated me, I found cause to congratulate myself on having obeyed it, as soon as I prepared to seal the letter in my own room. I had originally closed the envelope, in the usual way, by moistening the adhesive point and pressing it on the paper beneath; and, when I now tried it with my finger, after a lapse of full three-quarters of an hour, the envelope opened on the instant, without sticking or tearing. Perhaps I had fastened it insufficiently? Perhaps there might have been some defect in the adhesive gum?

Or, perhaps — No! it is quite revolting enough to feel that third conjecture stirring in my mind. I would rather not see it confronting me, in plain black and white.

I almost dread to-morrow — so much depends on my discretion and self-control. There are two precautions at all events, which I am sure not to forget. I must be careful to keep up friendly appearances with the Count; and must be well on my guard, when the messenger from the office comes here with the answer to my letter.

VII

JULY 3RD. — When the dinner hour brought us together again, Count Fosco was in his usual excellent spirits. He exerted himself to interest and amuse us, as if he was determined to efface from our memories all recollection of what had passed in the library that afternoon. Lively descriptions of his adventures in travelling; amusing anecdotes of remarkable people whom he had met with abroad; quaint comparisons between the social customs of various nations, illustrated by examples drawn from men and women indiscriminately all over Europe; humorous confessions of the innocent follies of his own early life, when he ruled the fashions of a second-rate Italian town, and wrote preposterous romances, on the French model, for a second-rate Italian newspaper — all flowed in succession so easily and so gaily from his lips, and all addressed our various curiosities and various interests so directly and so delicately, that Laura and I listened to him with as much attention, and, inconsistent as it may seem, with as much admiration also, as Madame Fosco herself. Women can resist a man's love, a man's fame, a man's personal appearance, and a man's money; but they cannot resist a man's tongue, when he knows how to talk to them.

After dinner, while the favourable impression which he had produced on us was still vivid in our minds, the Count modestly withdrew to read in the library.

Laura proposed a stroll in the grounds to enjoy the close of the long evening. It was necessary, in common politeness, to ask Madame Fosco to join us; but, this time, she had apparently received her orders beforehand, and she begged we would kindly excuse her. "The Count will probably want a fresh supply of cigarettes," she remarked, by way of apology; "and nobody can make them to his satisfaction, but myself." Her cold blue eyes almost warmed as she spoke the words — she looked actually proud of being the officiating medium through which her lord and master composed himself with tobacco-smoke!

Laura and I went out together alone.

It was a misty, heavy evening. There was a sense of blight in the air; the flowers were drooping in the garden, and the ground was parched and dewless. The western heaven, as we saw it over the quiet trees, was of a pale yellow hue, and the sun was setting faintly in a haze. Coming rain seemed near: it would fall probably with the fall of night.

"Which way shall we go?" I asked.

"Towards the lake, Marian, if you like," she answered.

"You seem unaccountably fond, Laura, of that dismal lake."

"No; not of the lake, but of the scenery about it. The sand and heath, and the fir-trees, are the only objects I can discover, in all this large place, to remind me of Limmeridge. But we will walk in some other direction, if you prefer it."

"I have no favourite walks at Blackwater Park, my love. One is the same as another to me. Let us go to the lake — we may find it cooler in the open space than we find it here."

We walked through the shadowy plantation in silence. The heaviness in the evening air oppressed us both; and, when we reached the boat-house, we were glad to sit down and rest, inside.

A white fog hung low over the lake. The dense brown line of the trees on the opposite bank, appeared above it, like a dwarf forest floating in the sky. The sandy ground, shelving downward from where we sat, was lost mysteriously in the outward layers of the fog. The silence was horrible. No rustling of the leaves — no bird's note in the wood — no cry of waterfowl from the pools of the hidden lake. Even the croaking of the frogs had ceased to-night.

"It is very desolate and gloomy," said Laura. "But we can be more alone here than anywhere else."

She spoke quietly, and looked at the wilderness of sand and mist with steady, thoughtful eyes. I could see that her mind was too much occupied to feel the dreary impressions from without, which had fastened themselves already on mine.

"I promised, Marian, to tell you the truth about my married life, instead of leaving you any longer to guess it for yourself," she began. "That secret is the first I have ever had from you, love, and I am determined it shall be the last. I was silent, as you know, for your sake — and perhaps a little for my own sake as well. It is very hard for a woman to confess that the man to whom she has given her whole life, is the man of all others who cares least for the gift. If you were married yourself, Marian — and especially if you were happily married — you would feel for me as no single woman *can* feel, however kind and true she may be."

What answer could I make? I could only take her hand, and look at her with my whole heart, as well as my eyes would let me.

"How often," she went on, "I have heard you laughing over what you used to call your 'poverty!' how often you have made me mock-speeches of congratulation on my wealth! Oh, Marian, never laugh again. Thank God for your poverty — it has made you your own mistress, and has saved you from the lot that has fallen on *me*."

A sad beginning on the lips of a young wife! — sad in its quiet, plain-spoken truth. The few days we had all passed together at Blackwater Park, had been many enough to show me — to show any one — what her husband had married her for.

"You shall not be distressed," she said, "by hearing how soon my disappointments and my trials began — or, even by knowing what they were. It is bad enough to have them on *my* memory. If I tell you how he received the first, and last, attempt at remonstrance that I ever made, you will know how he has always treated me, as well as if I had described it in so many words. It was one day at Rome, when we had ridden out together to the tomb of Cecilia Metella. The sky was calm and lovely — and the grand old ruin looked beautiful — and the remembrance that a husband's love had raised it in the old time to a wife's memory, made me feel more tenderly and more anxiously towards *my* husband than I had ever felt yet. 'Would you build such a tomb for *me*, Percival?' I asked him. 'You said you loved me dearly, before we were married; and yet, since that time —' I could get no farther. Marian! he was not even looking at me! I pulled down my veil, thinking it best not to let him see that the tears were in my eyes. I fancied he had not paid any attention to me; but he had. He said, 'Come away,' and laughed to himself, as he helped me on to my horse. He mounted his own horse; and laughed again as we rode away. 'If I do build you a tomb,' he said, 'it will be done with your own money. I wonder whether Cecilia Metella had a fortune, and paid for hers.' I made no reply — how could I, when I was crying behind my veil? 'Ah, you light-complexioned women are all sulky,' he said. 'What do you want? compliments and soft speeches? Well! I'm in a good humour this morning. Consider the compliments paid, and the speeches said.' Men little know, when they say hard things to us, how well we remember them, and how much harm they do us. It would have been better for me if I had gone on crying; but his contempt dried up my tears, and hardened my heart. From that time, Marian, I never checked myself again in thinking of Walter Hartright. I let the memory of those happy days, when we were so fond of each other in secret, come back, and comfort me. What else had I to look to for consolation? If we had been together, you would have helped me to better things. I know it was wrong, darling — but tell me if I was wrong, without any excuse."

I was obliged to turn my face from her. "Don't ask me!" I said. "Have I suffered as you have suffered? What right have I to decide?"

"I used to think of him," she pursued, dropping her voice, and moving closer to me — "I used to think of him, when Percival left me alone at night, to go among the Opera people. I used to fancy what I might have been, if it had pleased God to bless me with poverty, and if I had been his wife. I used to see myself in my neat cheap gown, sitting at home and waiting for him, while he was earning our bread — sitting at home and working for him, and loving him all the better because I *had* to work for him — seeing him come in tired, and taking off his hat and coat for him — and, Marian, pleasing him with little dishes at dinner that I had learnt to make for his sake. — Oh! I hope he is never lonely enough and sad enough to think of me, and see me, as I have thought of *him* and seen *him!*"

As she said those melancholy words, all the lost tenderness returned to her voice, and all the lost beauty trembled back into her face. Her eyes rested as lovingly on the blighted, solitary, ill-omened view before us, as if they saw the friendly hills of Cumberland in the dim and threatening sky.

"Don't speak of Walter any more," I said, as soon as I could control myself. "Oh, Laura, spare us both the wretchedness of talking of him, now!"

She roused herself, and looked at me tenderly.

"I would rather be silent about him for ever," she answered, "than cause you a moment's pain."

"It is in your interests," I pleaded; "it is for your sake that I speak. If your husband heard you —"

"It would not surprise him, if he did hear me."

She made that strange reply with a weary calmness and coldness. The change in her manner, when she gave the answer, startled me almost as much as the answer itself.

"Not surprise him!" I repeated. "Laura! remember what you are saying — you frighten me!"

"It is true," she said — "it is what I wanted to tell you to-day, when we were talking in your room. My only secret when I opened my heart to him at Limmeridge, was a harmless secret, Marian — you said so yourself. The name was all I kept from him — and he has discovered it."

I heard her; but I could say nothing. Her last words had killed the little hope that still lived in me.

"It happened at Rome," she went on, as wearily calm and cold as ever. "We were at a little party, given to the English by some friends of Sir Percival's — Mr. and Mrs. Markland. Mrs. Markland had the reputation of sketching very beautifully; and some of the guests prevailed on her to show us her drawings. We all admired them, — but something I said attracted her attention particularly to me. 'Surely you draw yourself?' she asked. 'I used to draw a little once,' I answered, 'but I have given it up.' 'If you have once drawn,' she said, 'you may take to it again one of these days; and, if you do, I wish you would let me recommend you a master.' I said nothing — you know why, Marian — and tried to change the conversation. But Mrs. Markland persisted. 'I have had all sorts of teachers,' she went on; 'but the best of all, the most intelligent and the most attentive was a Mr. Hartright. If you ever take up your drawing again, do try him as a master. He is a young man — modest and gentlemanlike — I am sure you will like him.' Think of those words being spoken to me publicly, in the presence of strangers — strangers who had been invited to meet the bride and bridegroom! I did all I could to control myself — I said nothing, and looked down close at the drawings. When I ventured to raise my head again, my eyes and my husband's eyes met; and I knew, by his look, that my face had betrayed me. 'We will see about Mr. Hartright,' he said, looking at me all the time, 'when we get back to England. I agree with you, Mrs. Markland — I think Lady Glyde is sure to like him.' He laid an emphasis on the last words which made my cheeks burn, and set my heart beating as if it would stifle me. Nothing more was said — we came away early. He was silent in the carriage, driving back to the hotel. He helped me out, and followed me up-stairs as usual. But the moment we were in the drawing-room, he locked the door, pushed me down into a chair, and stood over me with his hands on my shoulders. 'Ever since that morning when you made your audacious confession to me at Limmeridge,' he said, 'I have wanted to find out the man; and I found him in your face, to-night. Your drawing-master was the man; and his name is Hartright. You shall repent it, and he shall repent it, to the last hour of your lives. Now go to bed, and dream of him, if you like — with the marks of my horsewhip on his shoulder.' Whenever he is angry with me now, he refers to what I acknowledged to him in your presence, with a sneer or a threat. I have no power to prevent him from

putting his own horrible construction on the confidence I placed
in him. I have no influence to make him believe me, or to
keep him silent. You looked surprised, to-day, when you heard
him tell me that I had made a virtue of necessity in marrying
him. You will not be surprised again, when you hear him
repeat it, the next time he is out of temper — Oh, Marian!
don't! don't! you hurt me!"

I had caught her in my arms; and the sting and torment
of my remorse had closed them round her like a vice. Yes! my
remorse. The white despair of Walter's face, when my cruel
words struck him to the heart in the summer-house at Limmeridge, rose before me in mute, unendurable reproach. My
hand had pointed the way which led the man my sister loved,
step by step, far from his country and his friends. Between
those two young hearts I had stood, to sunder them for ever,
the one from the other — and his life and her life lay wasted
before me, alike, in witness of the deed. I had done this; and
done it for Sir Percival Glyde.

For Sir Percival Glyde.

I heard her speaking, and I knew by the tone of her voice
that she was comforting me — *I*, who deserved nothing but the
reproach of her silence! How long it was before I mastered
the absorbing misery of my own thoughts, I cannot tell. I was
first conscious that she was kissing me; and then my eyes
seemed to wake on a sudden to their sense of outward things,
and I knew that I was looking mechanically straight before
me at the prospect of the lake.

"It is late," I heard her whisper. "It will be dark in the
plantation." She shook my arm, and repeated, "Marian! it
will be dark in the plantation."

"Give me a minute longer," I said — "a minute, to get
better in."

I was afraid to trust myself to look at her yet; and I kept
my eyes fixed on the view.

It *was* late. The dense brown line of trees in the sky had
faded in the gathering darkness, to the faint resemblance of a

long wreath of smoke. The mist over the lake below had stealthily enlarged, and advanced on us. The silence was as breathless as ever — but the horror of it had gone, and the solemn mystery of its stillness was all that remained.

"We are far from the house," she whispered. "Let us go back."

She stopped suddenly, and turned her face from me towards the entrance of the boat-house.

"Marian!" she said, trembling violently. "Do you see nothing? Look!"

"Where?"

"Down there, below us."

She pointed. My eyes followed her hand; and I saw it, too.

A living figure was moving over the waste of heath in the distance. It crossed our range of view from the boat-house, and passed darkly along the outer edge of the mist. It stopped far off, in front of us — waited — and passed on; moving slowly, with the white cloud of mist behind it and above it — slowly, slowly, till it glided by the edge of the boat-house, and we saw it no more.

We were both unnerved by what had passed between us that evening. Some minutes elapsed before Laura would venture into the plantation, and before I could make up my mind to lead her back to the house.

"Was it a man, or a woman?" she asked, in a whisper, as we moved, at last, into the dark dampness of the outer air.

"I am not certain."

"Which do you think?"

"It looked like a woman."

"I was afraid it was a man in a long cloak."

"It may be a man. In this dim light it is not possible to be certain."

"Wait, Marian! I'm frightened — I don't see the path. Suppose the figure should follow us?"

"Not at all likely, Laura. There is really nothing to be alarmed about. The shores of the lake are not far from the village, and they are free to any one to walk on, by day or night. It is only wonderful we have seen no living creature there before."

We were now in the plantation. It was very dark — so dark, that we found some difficulty in keeping the path. I gave Laura my arm, and we walked as fast as we could on our way back.

Before we were half way through, she stopped, and forced me to stop with her. She was listening.

"Hush," she whispered. "I hear something behind us."

"Dead leaves," I said to cheer her, "or a twig blown off the trees."

"It is summer time, Marian; and there is not a breath of wind. Listen!"

I heard the sound, too — a sound like a light footstep following us.

"No matter who it is, or what it is," I said; "let us walk on. In another minute, if there is anything to alarm us, we shall be near enough to the house to be heard."

We went on quickly — so quickly, that Laura was breathless by the time we were nearly through the plantation, and within sight of the lighted windows.

I waited a moment, to give her breathing-time. Just as we were about to proceed, she stopped me again, and signed to me with her hand to listen once more. We both heard distinctly a long, heavy sigh, behind us, in the black depths of the trees.

"Who's there?" I called out.

There was no answer.

"Who's there?" I repeated.

An instant of silence followed; and then we heard the light fall of the footsteps again, fainter and fainter — sinking away into the darkness — sinking, sinking, sinking — till they were lost in the silence.

We hurried out from the trees to the open lawn beyond; crossed it rapidly; and without another word passing between us, reached the house.

In the light of the hall-lamp, Laura looked at me, with white cheeks and startled eyes.

"I am half dead with fear," she said. "Who could it have been?"

"We will try to guess to-morrow," I replied. "In the mean time, say nothing to any one of what we have heard and seen."

"Why not?"

"Because silence is safe — and we have need of safety in this house."

I sent Laura up stairs immediately — waited a minute to take off my hat, and put my hair smooth — and then went at once to make my first investigations in the library, on pretence of searching for a book.

There sat the Count, filling out the largest easy-chair in the house; smoking and reading calmly, with his feet on an ottoman, his cravat across his knees, and his shirt collar wide open. And there sat Madame Fosco, like a quiet child, on a stool by his side, making cigarettes. Neither husband nor wife could, by any possibility, have been out late that evening, and have just got back to the house in a hurry. I felt that my object in visiting the library was answered the moment I set eyes on them.

Count Fosco rose in polite confusion, and tied his cravat on when I entered the room.

"Pray don't let me disturb you," I said. "I have only come here to get a book."

"All unfortunate men of my size suffer from the heat," said the Count, refreshing himself gravely with a large green fan. "I wish I could change places with my excellent wife. She is as cool, at this moment, as a fish in the pond outside."

The Countess allowed herself to thaw under the influence of her husband's quaint comparison. "I am never warm, Miss Halcombe," she remarked, with the modest air of a woman who was confessing to one of her own merits.

"Have you and Lady Glyde been out this evening?"

asked the Count, while I was taking a book from the shelves, to preserve appearances.

"Yes; we went out to get a little air."

"May I ask in what direction?"

"In the direction of the lake — as far as the boat-house."

"Aha? As far as the boat-house?"

Under other circumstances, I might have resented his curiosity. But, to-night I hailed it as another proof that neither he nor his wife were connected with the mysterious appearance at the lake.

"No more adventures, I suppose, this evening?" he went on. "No more discoveries, like your discovery of the wounded dog?"

He fixed his unfathomable gray eyes on me, with that cold, clear, irresistible glitter in them, which always forces me to look at him, and always makes me uneasy, while I do look. An unutterable suspicion that his mind is prying into mine, overcomes me at these times; and it overcame me now.

"No," I said, shortly; "no adventures—no discoveries."

I tried to look away from him, and leave the room. Strange as it seems, I hardly think I should have succeeded in the attempt, if Madame Fosco had not helped me by causing him to move and look away first.

"Count, you are keeping Miss Halcombe standing," she said.

The moment he turned round to get me a chair, I seized my opportunity — thanked him — made my excuses — and slipped out.

An hour later, when Laura's maid happened to be in her mistress's room, I took occasion to refer to the closeness of the night, with a view to ascertaining next how the servants had been passing their time.

"Have you been suffering much from the heat, down stairs?" I asked.

"No, miss," said the girl; "we have not felt it to speak of."

"You have been out in the woods, then, I suppose?"

"Some of us thought of going, miss. But cook said she should take her chair into the cool court-yard, outside the kitchen door; and, on second thoughts, all the rest of us took our chairs out there, too."

The housekeeper was now the only person who remained to be accounted for.

"Is Mrs. Michelson gone to bed yet?" I inquired.

"I should think not, miss," said the girl, smiling. "Mrs. Michelson is more likely to be getting up, just now, than going to bed."

"Why? What do you mean? Has Mrs. Michelson been taking to her bed in the daytime?"

"No, miss; not exactly, but the next thing to it. She's been asleep all the evening, on the sofa in her own room."

Putting together what I observed for myself in the library and what I have just heard from Laura's maid, one conclusion seems inevitable. The figure we saw at the lake, was not the figure of Madame Fosco, of her husband, or of any of the servants. The footsteps we heard behind were not the footsteps of any one belonging to the house.

Who could it have been?

It seems useless to inquire. I cannot even decide whether the figure was a man's or a woman's. I can only say that I think it was a woman's.

VIII.

July 4th. — The misery of self-reproach which I suffered yesterday evening, on hearing what Laura told me in the boat-house, returned in the loneliness of the night, and kept me waking and wretched for hours.

I lighted my candle at last, and searched through my old journals to see what my share in the fatal error of her marriage had really been, and what I might have once done to save her from it. The result soothed me a little — for it showed that, however blindly and ignorantly I acted, I acted for the best.

Crying generally does me harm; but it was not so last night—
I think it relieved me. I rose this morning with a settled resolution and a quiet mind. Nothing Sir Percival can say or do
shall ever irritate me again, or make me forget, for one moment, that I am staying here, in defiance of mortifications, in-
sults, and threats, for Laura's service and for Laura's sake.

The speculations in which we might have indulged, this
morning, on the subject of the figure at the lake and the footsteps in the plantation, have been all suspended by a trifling
accident which has caused Laura great regret. She has lost·
the little brooch I gave her for a keepsake, on the day before
her marriage. As she wore it when we went out yesterday
evening, we can only suppose that it must have dropped from
her dress, either in the boat-house, or on our way back. The
servants have been sent to search, and have returned un-
successful. And now Laura herself has gone to look for it.
Whether she finds it, or not, the loss will help to excuse her
absence from the house, if Sir Percival returns before the
letter from Mr. Gilmore's partner is placed in my hands.

One o'clock has just struck. I am considering whether I
had better wait here for the arrival of the messenger from
London, or slip away quietly, and watch for him outside the
lodge gate.

My suspicion of everybody and everything in this house
inclines me to think that the second plan may be the best.
The Count is safe in the breakfast-room. I heard him, through
the door, as I ran up-stairs, ten minutes since, exercising
his canary-birds at their tricks: — "Come out on my little
finger, my pret-pret-pretties! Come out, and hop up-stairs!
One, two, three — and up! Three, two, one — and down!
One, two, three — twit-twit-twit-tweet!" The birds burst
into their usual ecstasy of singing, and the Count chirruped
and whistled at them in return, as if he was a bird himself.
My room door is open, and I can hear the shrill singing and
whistling at this very moment. If I am really to slip out,
without being observed — now is my time.

Four o'clock. The three hours that have passed since I made my last entry, have turned the whole march of events at Blackwater Park in a new direction. Whether for good or for evil, I cannot and dare not decide.

Let me get back first to the place at which I left off — or I shall lose myself in the confusion of my own thoughts.

I went out, as I had proposed, to meet the messenger with my letter from London, at the lodge gate. On the stairs I saw no one. In the hall I heard the Count still exercising his birds. But on crossing the quadrangle outside, I passed Madame Fosco, walking by herself in her favourite circle, round and round the great fish-pond. I at once slackened my pace, so as to avoid all appearance of being in a hurry; and even went the length, for caution's sake, of inquiring if she thought of going out before lunch. She smiled at me in the friendliest manner — said she preferred remaining near the house — nodded pleasantly — and re-entered the hall. I looked back, and saw that she had closed the door before I had opened the wicket by the side of the carriage gates.

In less than a quarter of an hour, I reached the lodge.

The lane outside took a sudden turn to the left, ran on straight for a hundred yards or so, and then took another sharp turn to the right to join the high road. Between these two turns, hidden from the lodge on one side and from the way to the station on the other, I waited, walking backwards and forwards. High hedges were on either side of me; and for twenty minutes by my watch, I neither saw nor heard anything. At the end of that time, the sound of a carriage caught my ear; and I was met, as I advanced towards the second turning, by a fly from the railway. I made a sign to the driver to stop. As he obeyed me, a respectable-looking man put his head out of the window to see what was the matter.

"I beg your pardon," I said; "but am I right in supposing that you are going to Blackwater Park?"

"Yes, ma'am."

"With a letter for any one?"

"With a letter for Miss Halcombe, ma'am."

"You may give me the letter. I am Miss Halcombe."

The man touched his hat, got out of the fly immediately, and gave me the letter.

I opened it at once, and read these lines. I copy them here, thinking it best to destroy the original for caution's sake.

"DEAR MADAM. — Your letter received this morning, has caused me very great anxiety. I will reply to it as briefly and plainly as possible.

"My careful consideration of the statement made by yourself, and my knowledge of Lady Glyde's position, as defined in the settlement, lead me, I regret to say, to the conclusion that a loan of the trust money to Sir Percival (or, in other words, a loan of some portion of the twenty thousand pounds of Lady Glyde's fortune), is in contemplation, and that she is made a party to the deed, in order to secure her approval of a flagrant breach of trust, and to have her signature produced against her, if she should complain hereafter. It is impossible, on any other supposition, to account, situated as she is, for her execution to a deed of any kind being wanted at all.

"In the event of Lady Glyde's signing such a document as I am compelled to suppose the deed in question to be, her trustees would be at liberty to advance money to Sir Percival out of her twenty thousand pounds. If the amount so lent should not be paid back, and if Lady Glyde should have children, their fortune will then be diminished by the sum, large or small, so advanced. In plainer terms still, the transaction, for anything that Lady Glyde knows to the contrary, may be a fraud upon her unborn children.

"Under these serious circumstances, I would recommend Lady Glyde to assign as a reason for withholding her signature, that she wishes the deed to be first submitted to myself, as her family solicitor (in the absence of my partner, Mr. Gilmore). No reasonable objection can be made to taking this course — for if the transaction is an honourable one, there will necessarily be no difficulty in my giving my approval.

"Sincerely assuring you of my readiness to afford any
additional help or advice that may be wanted, I beg to remain,
Madam, your faithful servant,

"WILLIAM KYRLE."

I read this kind and sensible letter very thankfully. It
supplied Laura with a reason for objecting to the signature
which was unanswerable, and which we could both of us understand. The messenger waited near me while I was reading,
to receive his directions when I had done.

"Will you be good enough to say that I understand the
letter, and that I am very much obliged?" I said. "There is
no other reply necessary at present."

Exactly at the moment when I was speaking those words,
holding the letter open in my hand, Count Fosco turned the
corner of the lane from the high road, and stood before me as
if he had sprung up out of the earth.

The suddenness of his appearance, in the very last place
under heaven in which I should have expected to see him, took
me completely by surprise. The messenger wished me good
morning, and got into the fly again. I could not say a word
to him — I was not even able to return his bow. The conviction that I was discovered — and by that man, of all others —
absolutely petrified me.

"Are you going back to the house, Miss Halcombe?" he
inquired, without showing the least surprise on his side, and
without even looking after the fly, which drove off while he
was speaking to me.

I collected myself sufficiently to make a sign in the affirmative.

"I am going back, too," he said. "Pray allow me the
pleasure of accompanying you. Will you take my arm? You
look surprised at seeing me!"

I took his arm. The first of my scattered senses that came
back, was the sense that warned me to sacrifice anything
rather than make an enemy of him.

"You look surprised at seeing me!" he repeated, in his quietly pertinacious way.

"I thought, Count, I heard you with your birds in the breakfast-room," I answered, as quietly and firmly as I could.

"Surely. But my little feathered children, dear lady, are only too like other children. They have their days of perversity; and this morning was one of them. My wife came in, as I was putting them back in their cage, and said she had left you going out alone for a walk. You told her so, did you not?"

"Certainly."

"Well, Miss Halcombe, the pleasure of accompanying you was too great a temptation for me to resist. At my age there is no harm in confessing so much as that, is there? I seized my hat, and set off to offer myself as your escort. Even so fat an old man as Fosco is surely better than no escort at all? I took the wrong path — I came back, in despair — and here I am arrived (may I say it?) at the height of my wishes."

He talked on, in this complimentary strain, with a fluency which left me no exertion to make beyond the effort of maintaining my composure. He never referred in the most distant manner to what he had seen in the lane, or to the letter which I still had in my hand. This ominous discretion helped to convince me that he must have surprised, by the most dishonourable means, the secret of my application in Laura's interests, to the lawyer; and that, having now assured himself of the private manner in which I had received the answer, he had discovered enough to suit his purposes, and was only bent on trying to quiet the suspicions which he knew he must have aroused in my mind. I was wise enough, under these circumstances, not to attempt to deceive him by plausible explanations — and woman enough, notwithstanding my dread of him, to feel as if my hand was tainted by resting on his arm.

On the drive in front of the house we met the dog-cart being taken round to the stables. Sir Percival had just returned. He came out to meet us at the house-door. Whatever other

results his journey might have had, it had not ended in softening his savage temper.

"Oh! here are two of you come back," he said, with a
lowering face. "What is the meaning of the house being
deserted in this way? Where is Lady Glyde?"

I told him of the loss of the brooch, and said that Laura
had gone into the plantation to look for it.

"Brooch or no brooch," he growled, sulkily, "I recommend
her not to forget her appointment in the library, this afternoon. I shall expect to see her in half an hour."

I took my hand from the Count's arm, and slowly ascended
the steps. He honoured me with one of his magnificent bows;
and then addressed himself gaily to the scowling master of the
house.

"Tell me, Percival," he said, "have you had a pleasant
drive? And has your pretty shining Brown Molly come back
at all tired?"

"Brown Molly be hanged — and the drive, too! I want my
lunch."

"And I want five minutes' talk with you, Percival, first,"
returned the Count. "Five minutes' talk, my friend, here on
the grass."

"What about?"

"About business that very much concerns you."

I lingered long enough, in passing through the hall-door,
to hear this question and answer, and to see Sir Percival thrust
his hands into his pockets, in sullen hesitation.

"If you want to badger me with any more of your infernal
scruples," he said, "I, for one, won't hear them. I want my
lunch!"

"Come out here, and speak to me," repeated the Count,
still perfectly uninfluenced by the rudest speech that his friend
could make to him.

Sir Percival descended the steps. The Count took him by
the arm, and walked him away gently. The "business," I was
sure, referred to the question of the signature. They were
speaking of Laura and of me, beyond a doubt. I felt heart-

sick and faint with anxiety. It might be of the last importance to both of us to know what they were saying to each other at that moment—and not one word of it could, by any possibility, reach my ears.

I walked about the house, from room to room, with the lawyer's letter in my bosom (I was afraid, by this time, even to trust it under lock and key), till the oppression of my suspense half maddened me. There were no signs of Laura's return; and I thought of going out to look for her. But my strength was so exhausted by the trials and anxieties of the morning, that the heat of the day quite overpowered me; and, after an attempt to get to the door, I was obliged to return to the drawing-room, and lie down on the nearest sofa to recover.

I was just composing myself, when the door opened softly, and the Count looked in.

"A thousand pardons, Miss Halcombe," he said; "I only venture to disturb you because I am the bearer of good news. Percival — who is capricious in everything, as you know — has seen fit to alter his mind, at the last moment; and the business of the signature is put off for the present. A great relief to all of us, Miss Halcombe, as I see with pleasure in your face. Pray present my best respects and felicitations, when you mention this pleasant change of circumstances to Lady Glyde."

He left me before I had recovered my astonishment. There could be no doubt that this extraordinary alteration of purpose in the matter of the signature, was due to his influence; and that his discovery of my application to London yesterday, and of my having received an answer to it to-day, had offered him the means of interfering with certain success.

I felt these impressions; but my mind seemed to share the exhaustion of my body, and I was in no condition to dwell on them, with any useful reference to the doubtful present, or the threatening future. I tried a second time to run out, and find Laura; but my head was giddy, and my knees trembled under me. There was no choice but to give it up again, and return to the sofa, sorely against my will.

The quiet in the house, and the low murmuring hum of summer insects outside the open window, soothed me. My eyes closed of themselves; and I passed gradually into a strange condition, which was not waking — for I knew nothing of what was going on about me; and not sleeping — for I was conscious of my own repose. In this state, my fevered mind broke loose from me, while my weary body was at rest; and, in a trance, or day-dream of my fancy — I know not what to call it — I saw Walter Hartright. I had not thought of him, since I rose that morning; Laura had not said one word to me either directly or indirectly referring to him — and yet, I saw him now, as plainly as if the past time had returned, and we were both together again at Limmeridge House.

He appeared to me as one among many other men, none of whose faces I could plainly discern. They were all lying on the steps of an immense ruined temple. Colossal tropical trees — with rank creepers twining endlessly about their trunks, and hideous stone idols glimmering and grinning at intervals behind leaves and stalks and branches — surrounded the temple, and shut out the sky, and threw a dismal shadow over the forlorn band of men on the steps. White exhalations twisted and curled up stealthily from the ground; approached the men in wreaths, like smoke; touched them; and stretched them out dead, one by one, in the places where they lay. An agony of pity and fear for Walter loosened my tongue, and I implored him to escape. "Come back! come back!" I said. "Remember your promise to *her* and to *me*. Come back to us, before the Pestilence reaches you, and lays you dead like the rest!"

He looked at me, with an unearthly quiet in his face. "Wait," he said. "I shall come back. The night, when I met the lost Woman on the highway, was the night which set my life apart to be the instrument of a Design that is yet unseen. Here, lost in the wilderness, or there, welcomed back in the land of my birth, I am still walking on the dark road which leads me, and you, and the sister of your love and mine, to the unknown Retribution and the inevitable End. Wait and look. The Pestilence which touches the rest, will pass *me*."

I saw him again. He was still in the forest; and the numbers of his lost companions had dwindled to very few. The temple was gone, and the idols were gone — and, in their place, the figures of dark, dwarfish men lurked murderously among the trees, with bows in their hands, and arrows fitted to the string. Once more, I feared for Walter, and cried out to warn him. Once more, he turned to me, with the immovable quiet in his face. "Another step," he said, "on the dark road. Wait and look. The arrows that strike the rest, will spare *me*."

I saw him for the third time, in a wrecked ship, stranded on a wild, sandy shore. The overloaded boats were making away from him for the land, and he alone was left, to sink with the ship. I cried to him to hail the hindmost boat, and to make a last effort for his life. The quiet face looked at me in return, and the unmoved voice gave me back the changeless reply. "Another step on the journey. Wait and look. The Sea which drowns the rest, will spare *me*."

I saw him for the last time. He was kneeling by a tomb of white marble; and the shadow of a veiled woman rose out of the grave beneath, and waited by his side. The unearthly quiet of his face had changed to an unearthly sorrow. But the terrible certainty of his words remained the same. "Darker and darker," he said; "farther and farther yet. Death takes the good, the beautiful, and the young — and spares *me*. The Pestilence that wastes, the Arrow that strikes, the Sea that drowns, the Grave that closes over Love and Hope, are steps of my journey, and take me nearer and nearer to the End."

My heart sank under a dread beyond words, under a grief beyond tears. The darkness closed round the pilgrim at the marble tomb; closed round the veiled woman from the grave; closed round the dreamer who looked on them. I saw and heard no more.

I was aroused by a hand laid on my shoulder. It was Laura's.

She had dropped on her knees by the side of the sofa. Her face was flushed and agitated; and her eyes met mine in a wild bewildered manner. I started the instant I saw her.

"What has happened?" I asked. "What has frightened you?"

She looked round at he half-open door — put her lips close to my ear — and answered in a whisper:

"Marian! — the figure at the lake — the footsteps last night — I've just seen her! I've just spoken to her!"

"Who, for Heaven's sake?"

"Anne Catherick."

I was so startled by the disturbance in Laura's face and manner, and so dismayed by the first waking impressions of my dream, that I was not fit to bear the revelation which burst upon me, when that name passed her lips. I could only stand rooted to the floor, looking at her in breathless silence.

She was too much absorbed by what had happened to notice the effect which her reply had produced on me. "I have seen Anne Catherick! I have spoken to Anne Catherick!" she repeated, as if I had not heard her. "Oh, Marian, I have such things to tell you! Come away — we may be interrupted here — come at once into my room."

With those eager words, she caught me by the hand, and led me through the library, to the end room on the ground floor, which had been fitted up for her own especial use. No third person, except her maid, could have any excuse for surprising us here. She pushed me in before her, locked the door, and drew the chintz curtains that hung over the inside.

The strange, stunned feeling which had taken possession of me still remained. But a growing conviction that the complications which had long threatened to gather about her, and to gather about me, had suddenly closed fast round us both, was now beginning to penetrate my mind. I could not express it in words — I could hardly even realise it dimly in my own thoughts. "Anne Catherick!" I whispered to myself, with useless, helpless reiteration — "Anne Catherick!"

Laura drew me to the nearest seat, an ottoman in the middle of the room. "Look!" she said; "look here!" — and pointed to the bosom of her dress.

I saw, for the first time, that the lost brooch was pinned in its place again. There was something real in the sight of it, something real in the touching of it afterwards, which seemed to steady the whirl and confusion in my thoughts, and to help me to compose myself.

"Where did you find your brooch?" The first words I could say to her were the words which put that trivial question at that important moment.

"*She* found it, Marian."

"Where?"

"On the floor of the boat-house. Oh, how shall I begin — how shall I tell you about it! She talked to me so strangely — she looked so fearfully ill — she left me so suddenly —!"

Her voice rose as the tumult of her recollections pressed upon her mind. The inveterate distrust which weighs, night and day, on my spirits in this house, instantly roused me to warn her — just as the sight of the brooch had roused me to question her, the moment before.

"Speak low," I said. "The window is open, and the garden path runs beneath it. Begin at the beginning, Laura. Tell me, word for word, what passed between that woman and you."

"Shall I close the window first?"

"No; only speak low: only remember that Anne Catherick is a dangerous subject under your husband's roof. Where did you first see her?"

"At the boat-house, Marian. I went out, as you know, to find my brooch; and I walked along the path through the plantation, looking down on the ground carefully at every step. In that way I got on, after a long time, to the boat-house; and, as soon as I was inside it, I went on my knees to hunt over the floor. I was still searching, with my back to the doorway, when I heard a soft, strange voice, behind me, say, 'Miss Fairlie.'"

"Miss Fairlie!"

"Yes — my old name — the dear, familiar name that I thought I had parted from for ever. I started up — not frightened, the voice was too kind and gentle to frighten anybody — but very much surprised. There, looking at me from the doorway, stood a woman, whose face I never remembered to have seen before —"

"How was she dressed?"

"She had a neat, pretty white gown on, and over it a poor worn thin dark shawl. Her bonnet was of brown straw, as poor and worn as the shawl. I was struck by the difference between her gown and the rest of her dress, and she saw that I noticed it. 'Don't look at my bonnet and shawl,' she said, speaking in a quick, breathless, sudden way; 'if I mustn't wear white, I don't care what I wear. Look at my gown, as much as you please; I'm not ashamed of that.' Very strange, was it not? Before I could say anything to soothe her, she held out one of her hands, and I saw my brooch in it. I was so pleased and so grateful, that I went quite close to her to say what I really felt. 'Are you thankful enough to do me one little kindness?' she asked. 'Yes, indeed,' I answered; 'any kindness in my power I shall be glad to show you.' 'Then let me pin your brooch on for you, now I have found it.' Her request was so unexpected, Marian, and she made it with such extraordinary eagerness, that I drew back a step or two, not well knowing what to do. 'Ah!' she said, 'your mother would have let me pin on the brooch.' There was something in her voice and her look, as well as in her mentioning my mother in that reproachful manner, which made me ashamed of my distrust. I took her hand with the brooch in it, and put it up gently on the bosom of my dress. 'You knew my mother?' I said. 'Was it very long ago? have I ever seen you before?' Her hands were busy fastening the brooch: she stopped and pressed them against my breast. 'You don't remember a fine spring day at Limmeridge,' she said, 'and your mother walking down the path that led to the school, with a little girl on each side of her? I have had nothing else to think of since; and *I* remember it. You were one of the little girls, and I was the other. Pretty, clever Miss Fairlie, and poor dazed Anne Catherick were nearer to each other, then, than they are now!' —"

"Did you remember her, Laura, when she told you her name?"

"Yes — I remembered your asking me about Anne Catherick at Limmeridge, and your saying that she had once been considered like me."

"What reminded you of that, Laura?"

"*She* reminded me. While I was looking at her, while she was very close to me, it came over my mind suddenly that we were like each other! Her face was pale and thin and weary — but the sight of it startled me, as if it had been the sight of my own face in the glass after a long illness. The discovery — I don't know why — gave me such a shock, that I was perfectly incapable of speaking to her, for the moment."

"Did she seem hurt by your silence?"

"I am afraid she was hurt by it. 'You have not got your mother's face,' she said, 'or your mother's heart. Your mother's face was dark; and your mother's heart, Miss Fairlie, was the heart of an angel.' 'I am sure I feel kindly towards you,' I said, 'though I may not be able to express it as I ought. Why do you call me Miss Fairlie ——?' 'Because I love the name of Fairlie and hate the name of Glyde,' she broke out violently. I had seen nothing like madness in her before this; but I fancied I saw it now in her eyes. 'I only thought you might not know I was married,' I said, remembering the wild letter she wrote to me at Limmeridge, and trying to quiet her. She sighed bitterly, and turned away from me. 'Not know you were married!' she repeated. 'I am here *because* you are married. I am here to make atonement to you, before I meet your mother in the world beyond the grave.' She drew farther and farther away from me, till she was out of the boat-house — and, then, she watched and listened for a little while. When she turned round to speak again, instead of coming back, she stopped where she was, looking in at me, with a hand on each side of the entrance. 'Did you see me at the lake last night?' she said. 'Did you hear me following you in the wood? I have been waiting for days together to speak to you alone — I have left the only friend I have in the world, anxious and frightened about me — I have risked being shut up again in the madhouse — and all for your sake, Miss Fairlie, all for your sake.' Her words alarmed me, Marian; and yet, there was something in the way she spoke, that made me pity her with all my heart. I am sure my pity must have been sincere, for it made me bold enough to ask the poor creature to come in, and sit down in the boat-house, by my side."

"Did she do so?"

"No. She shook her head, and told me she must stop where she was, to watch and listen, and see that no third person surprised us. And from first to last, there she waited at the entrance, with a hand on each side of it; sometimes bending in suddenly to speak to me; sometimes drawing back suddenly to look about her. 'I was here yesterday,' she said, 'before it came dark; and I heard you, and the lady with you, talking together. I heard you tell her about your husband. I heard you say you had no influence to make him believe you, and no influence to keep him silent. Ah! I knew what those words meant; my conscience told me while I was listening. Why did I ever let you marry him! Oh, my fear — my mad, miserable, wicked fear! —" She covered up her face in her poor worn shawl, and moaned and murmured to herself behind it. I began to be afraid she might break out into some terrible despair which neither she nor I could master. 'Try to quiet yourself,' I said: 'try to tell me how you might have prevented my marriage.' She took the shawl from her face, and looked at me vacantly. 'I ought to have had heart enough to stop at Limmeridge,' she answered. 'I ought never to have let the news of his coming there frighten me away. I ought to have warned you and saved you before it was too late. Why did I only have courage enough to write you that letter? Why did I only do harm, when I wanted and meant to do good? Oh, my fear — my mad, miserable, wicked fear!" She repeated those words again, and hid her face again in the end of her poor worn shawl. It was dreadful to see her, and dreadful to hear her."

"Surely, Laura, you asked what the fear was which she dwelt on so earnestly?"

"Yes; I asked that."

"And what did she say?"

"She asked me, in return, if *I* should not be afraid of a man who had shut me up in a madhouse, and who would shut me up again, if he could? I said, 'Are you afraid still? Surely you would not be here, if you were afraid now?' 'No,' she said, 'I am not afraid now.' I asked why not. She suddenly bent forward into the boat-house, and said, 'Can't you guess why?' I shook my head. 'Look at me,' she went on. I told her I was grieved to see that she looked very sorrowful and very ill. She smiled, for the first time. 'Ill?' she repeated; 'I'm dying. You know why I'm not afraid of him now. Do you think I shall meet your mother in heaven? Will she forgive me, if I do?' I was so shocked and so startled, that I could make no reply. 'I have been thinking of it,' she went on, 'all the time I have been in hiding from your husband, all the time I lay ill. My thoughts have driven me here — I want to make atonement — I want to undo all I can of the harm I once did.' I begged her as earnestly as I could to tell me what she meant. She still looked at me with fixed, vacant eyes. '*Shall* I undo the harm?' she said to herself, doubtfully. 'You have friends to take your part. If *you* know his Secret, he will be afraid of you; he won't dare use you as he used me. He must treat you mercifully for his own sake, if he is afraid of you and your friends. And if he treats you mercifully, and if I can say it was my doing —' I listened eagerly for more; but she stopped at those words."

"You tried to make her go on?"

"I tried; but she only drew herself away from me again, and leaned her face and arms against the side of the boat-house. 'Oh!' I heard her say, with a dreadful, distracted tenderness in her voice, 'oh! if I could only be buried with your mother! If I could only wake at her side, when the angel's trumpet sounds, and the graves give up their dead at the resurrection!' — Marian! I trembled from head to foot — it was horrible to hear her. 'But there is no hope of that,' she said, moving a little, so as to look at me again; 'no hope for a poor stranger like me. *I* shall not rest under the marble cross that I washed with my own hands, and made so white and pure for her sake. Oh no! oh no! God's mercy, not man's, will take me to her, where the wicked cease from troubling and the weary are at rest.' She spoke those words quietly and sorrowfully, with a heavy, hopeless sigh; and then waited a little. Her face was confused and troubled; she seemed to be thinking, or trying to think. 'What was it I said just now?' she asked, after a while. 'When your mother is in my mind, everything else goes out of it. What was I saying? what was I saying?' I reminded the poor creature, as kindly and delicately as I could. 'Ah, yes, yes,' she said, still in a vacant, perplexed manner. 'You are helpless with your wicked husband. Yes. And I must do what I have come to do here — I must make it up to you for having been afraid to speak out at a better time.' 'What *is* it you have to tell me?' I asked. 'The Secret that your cruel husband is afraid of,' she answered. 'I once threatened him with the Secret, and frightened him. You shall threaten him with the Secret, and frighten him, too. Her face darkened; and a hard, angry stare fixed itself in her eyes. She began waving her hand at me in a vacant, unmeaning manner. 'My mother knows the Secret,' she said. 'My mother has wasted under the Secret half her lifetime. One day, when I was grown up, she said something to *me*. And, the next day, your husband —'"

"Yes! yes! Go on. What did she tell you about your husband?"

"She stopped again, Marian, at that point —"

"And said no more?"

"And listened eagerly. 'Hush!' she whispered, still waving her hand at me. 'Hush!' She moved aside out of the doorway, moved slowly and stealthily, step by step, till I lost her past the edge of the boat-house."

"Surely, you followed her?"

"Yes; my anxiety made me bold enough to rise and follow her. Just as I reached the entrance, she appeared again, suddenly, round the side of the boat-house. 'The secret,' I whispered to her — 'wait and tell me the secret!" She caught hold of my arm, and looked at me, with wild, frightened eyes. 'Not now,' she said; 'we are not alone — we are watched. Come here to-morrow, at this time — by yourself — mind — by yourself.' She pushed me roughly into the boat-house again; and I saw her no more."

"Oh, Laura, Laura, another chance lost! If I had only been near you, she should not have escaped us. On which side did you lose sight of her?"

"On the left side, where the ground sinks and the wood is thickest."

"Did you run out again? did you call after her?"

"How could I? I was too terrified to move or speak."

"But when you *did* move — when you came out —?"

"I ran back here, to tell you what had happened."

"Did you see any one, or hear any one in the plantation?"

"No — it seemed to be all still and quiet, when I passed through it."

I waited for a moment to consider. Was this third person, supposed to have been secretly present at the interview, a reality, or the creature of Anne Catherick's excited fancy? It was impossible to determine. The one thing certain was, that we had failed again on the very brink of discovery — failed utterly and irretrievably, unless Anne Catherick kept her appointment at the boat-house, for the next day.

"Are you quite sure you have told me everything that passed. Every word that was said?" I inquired.

"I think so," she answered. "My powers of memory, Marian, are not like yours. But I was so strongly impressed, so deeply interested, that nothing of any importance can possibly have escaped me."

"My dear Laura, the merest trifles are of importance where Anne Catherick is concerned. Think again. Did no chance reference escape her as to the place in which she is living at the present time?"

"None that I can remember."

"Did she not mention a companion and friend — a woman named Mrs. Clements?"

"Oh, yes! yes! I forgot that. She told me Mrs. Clements wanted sadly to go with her to the lake, and take care of her, and begged and prayed that she would not venture into this neighbourhood alone."

"Was that all she said about Mrs. Clements?"

"Yes, that was all."

"She told you nothing about the place in which she took refuge after leaving Todd's Corner?"

"Nothing — I am quite sure."

"Nor where she has lived since? Nor what her illness had been?"

"No, Marian; not a word. Tell me, pray tell me, what you think about it. I don't know what to think, or what to do next."

"You must do this, my love: You must carefully keep the appointment at the boat-house, to-morrow. It is impossible to say what interests may not depend on your seeing that woman again. You shall not be left to yourself a second time. I will follow you, at a safe distance. Nobody shall see me; but I will keep within hearing of your voice, if anything happens. Anne Catherick has escaped Walter Hartright, and has escaped *you*. Whatever happens, she shall not escape *me*."

Laura's eyes read mine attentively.

"You believe," she said, "in this secret that my husband is afraid of? Suppose, Marian, it should only exist, after all, in Anne Catherick's fancy? Suppose she only wanted to see me and to speak to me, for the sake of old remembrances? Her manner was so strange, I almost doubted her. Would you trust her in other things?"

"I trust nothing, Laura, but my own observation of your husband's conduct. I judge Anne Catherick's words by his actions — and I believe there *is* a secret."

I said no more, and got up to leave the room. Thoughts were troubling me, which I might have told her if we had spoken together longer, and which it might have been dangerous for her to know. The influence of the terrible dream from which she had awakened me, hung darkly and heavily over every fresh impression which the progress of her narrative produced on my mind. I felt the ominous Future, coming close; chilling me, with an unutterable awe: forcing on me the conviction of an unseen Design in the long series of complications which had now fastened round us. I thought of Hartright — as I saw him, in the body, when he said fare-well; as I saw him, in the spirit, in my dream — and I, too, began to doubt now whether we were not advancing, blind-fold, to an appointed and an inevitable End.

Leaving Laura to go up-stairs alone, I went out to look about me in the walks near the house. The circumstances under which Anne Catherick had parted from her, had made me secretly anxious to know how Count Fosco was passing the afternoon; and had rendered me secretly distrustful of the results of that solitary journey from which Sir Percival had returned but a few hours since.

After looking for them in every direction, and discovering nothing, I returned to the house, and entered the different rooms on the ground floor, one after another. They were all

20*

empty. I came out again into the hall, and went up-stairs to return to Laura. Madame Fosco opened her door, as I passed it in my way along the passage; and I stopped to see if she could inform me of the whereabouts of her husband and Sir Percival. Yes; she had seen them both from her window more than an hour since. The Count had looked up, with his customary kindness, and had mentioned, with his habitual attention to her in the smallest trifles, that he and his friend were going out together for a long walk.

For a long walk! They had never yet been in each other's company with that object in my experience of them. Sir Percival cared for no exercise but riding: and the Count (except when he was polite enough to be my escort) cared for no exercise at all.

When I joined Laura again, I found that she had called to mind, in my absence, the impending question of the signature to the deed, which, in the interest of discussing her interview with Anne Catherick, we had hitherto overlooked. Her first words when I saw her, expressed her surprise at the absence of the expected summons to attend Sir Percival in the library.

"You may make your mind easy on that subject," I said. "For the present, at least, neither your resolution nor mine will be exposed to any further trial. Sir Percival has altered his plans: the business of the signature is put off."

"Put off?" Laura repeated, amazedly. "Who told you so?"

"My authority is Count Fosco. I believe it is to his interference that we are indebted for your husband's sudden change of purpose."

"It seems impossible, Marian. If the object of my signing was, as we suppose, to obtain money for Sir Percival that he urgently wanted, how can the matter be put off?"

"I think, Laura, we have the means at hand of setting that doubt at rest. Have you forgotten the conversation that I heard between Sir Percival and the lawyer, as they were crossing the hall?"

"No; but I don't remember —"

"I do. There were two alternatives proposed. One, was to obtain your signature to the parchment. The other, was to gain time by giving bills at three months. The last resource is evidently the resource now adopted — and we may fairly hope to be relieved from our share in Sir Percival's embarrassments for some time to come."

"Oh, Marian, it sounds too good to be true!"

"Does it, my love? You complimented me on my ready memory not long since — but you seem to doubt it now. I will get my journal, and you shall see if I am right or wrong."

I went away and got the book at once.

On looking back to the entry referring to the lawyer's visit, we found that my recollection of the two alternatives presented was accurately correct. It was almost as great a relief to my mind as to Laura's, to find that my memory had served me, on this occasion, as faithfully as usual. In the perilous uncertainty of our present situation, it is hard to say what future interests may not depend upon the regularity of the entries in my journal, and upon the reliability of my recollection at the time when I make them.

Laura's face and manner suggested to me that this last consideration had occurred to her as well as to myself. Any way, it is only a trifling matter; and I am almost ashamed to put it down here in writing — it seems to set the forlornness of our situation in such a miserably vivid light. We must have little indeed to depend on, when the discovery that my memory can still be trusted to serve us, is hailed as if it was the discovery of a new friend!

The first bell for dinner separated us. Just as it had done ringing, Sir Percival and the Count returned from their walk. We heard the master of the house storming at the servants for being five minutes late; and the master's guest interposing, as usual, in the interests of propriety, patience, and peace.

*　　　*　　　*　　　*　　　*

The evening has come and gone. No extraordinary event has happened. But I have noticed certain peculiarities in the conduct of Sir Percival and the Count, which have sent me to my bed, feeling very anxious and uneasy about Anne Catherick, and about the results which to-morrow may produce.

I know enough by this time, to be sure that the aspect of Sir Percival which is the most false, and which, therefore, means the worst, is his polite aspect. That long walk with his friend had ended in improving his manners, especially towards his wife. To Laura's secret surprise and to my secret alarm, he called her by her Christian name, asked if she had heard lately from her uncle, inquired when Mrs. Vesey was to receive her invitation to Blackwater, and showed her so many other little attentions, that he almost recalled the days of his hateful courtship of Limmeridge House. This was a bad sign, to begin with; and I thought it more ominous still, that he should pretend, after dinner, to fall asleep in the drawing-room, and that his eyes should cunningly follow Laura and me, when he thought we neither of us suspected him. I have never had any doubt that his sudden journey by himself took him to Welmingham to question Mrs. Catherick — but the experience of to-night has made me fear that the expedition was not undertaken in vain, and that he has got the information which he unquestionably left us to collect. If I knew where Anne Catherick was to be found, I would be up to-morrow with sunrise, and warn her.

While the aspect under which Sir Percival presented himself, to-night, was unhappily but too familiar to me, the aspect under which the Count appeared, was, on the other hand, entirely new in my experience of him. He permitted me, this evening, to make his acquaintance, for the first time, in the character of a Man of Sentiment — of sentiment, as I believe, really felt, not assumed for the occasion.

For instance, he was quiet and subdued; his eyes and his voice expressed a restrained sensibility. He wore (as if there was some hidden connexion between his showiest finery and his deepest feeling) the most magnificent waistcoat he has yet appeared in — it was made of pale sea-green silk, and delicately trimmed with fine silver braid. His voice sank into the tenderest inflections, his smile expressed a thoughtful, fatherly admiration, whenever he spoke to Laura or to me. He pressed his wife's hand under the table, when she thanked him for trifling little attentions at dinner. He took wine with her. "Your health and happiness, my angel!" he said, with fond glistening eyes. He ate little or nothing; and sighed, and said "Good Percival!" when his friend laughed at him. After dinner, he took Laura by the hand, and asked her if she would be "so sweet as to play to him." She complied, through sheer astonishment. He sat by the piano, with his watch-chain resting in folds, like a golden serpent, on the sea-green protuberance of his waistcoat. His immense head lay languidly on one side; and he gently beat time with two of his yellow-white fingers. He highly approved of the music, and tenderly admired Laura's manner of playing — not as poor Hartright used to praise it, with an innocent enjoyment of the sweet sounds, but with a clear, cultivated, practical knowledge of the merits of the composition, in the first place, and of the merits of the player's touch, in the second. As the evening closed in, he begged that the lovely dying light might not be profaned, just yet, by the appearance of the lamps. He came, with his horribly silent tread, to the distant window at which I was standing, to be out of his way and to avoid the very sight of him — he came to ask me to support his protest against the lamps. If any one of them could only have burnt him up, at that moment, I would have gone down to the kitchen, and fetched it myself.

"Surely you like this modest, trembling English twilight?" he said, softly. "Ah! I love it. I feel my inborn admiration of all that is noble and great and good, purified by the breath of Heaven, on an evening like this. Nature has such imperishable charms, such inextinguishable tendernesses for me! — I am an old, fat man: talk which would become your lips, Miss Halcombe, sounds like a derision and a mockery on mine. It is hard to be laughed at in my moments of sentiment, as if my soul was like myself, old and over-grown. Observe, dear lady, what a light is dying on the trees! Does it penetrate your heart, as it penetrates mine?"

He paused — looked at me — and repeated the famous lines of Dante on the Evening-time, with a melody and tenderness which added a charm of their own to the matchless beauty of the poetry itself.

"Bah!" he cried suddenly, as the last cadence of those noble Italian words died away on his lips; "I make an old fool of myself, and only weary you all! Let us shut up the window in our bosoms and get back to the matter-of-fact world. Percival! I sanction the admission of the lamps. Lady Glyde — Miss Halcombe — Eleanor, my good wife — which of you will indulge me with a game at dominoes?"

He addressed us all; but he looked especially at Laura.

She had learnt to feel my dread of offending him, and she accepted his proposal. It was more than I could have done, at that moment. I could not have sat down at the same table with him, for any consideration. His eyes seemed to reach my inmost soul through the thickening obscurity of the twilight. His voice trembled along every nerve in my body, and turned me hot and cold alternately. The mystery and terror of my dream, which had haunted me, at intervals, all through the evening, now oppressed my mind with an unendurable foreboding and an unutterable awe. I saw the white tomb again, and the veiled woman rising out of it, by Hartright's side. The thought of Laura welled up like a spring in the depths of my heart, and filled it with waters of bitterness, never, never known to it before. I caught her by the hand, as she passed me on her way to the table, and kissed her as if that night was to part us for ever. While they were all gazing at me in astonishment, I ran out through the low window which was open before me to the ground — ran out to hide from them in the darkness; to hide even from myself.

We separated, that evening, later than usual. Towards midnight, the summer silence was broken by the shuddering of a low, melancholy wind among the trees. We all felt the sudden chill in the atmosphere; but the Count was the first to notice the stealthy rising of the wind. He stopped while he was lighting my candle for me, and held up his hand warningly:

"Listen!" he said. "There will be a change to-morrow."

IX.

JULY 5TH. — The events of yesterday warned me to be ready, sooner or later, to meet the worst. To-day is not yet at an end; and the worst has come.

Judging by the closest calculation of time that Laura and I could make, we arrived at the conclusion that Anne Catherick must have appeared at the boat-house at half-past two o'clock, on the afternoon of yesterday. I accordingly arranged that Laura should just show herself at the luncheon table, to-day, and should then slip out at the first opportunity; leaving me behind to preserve appearances, and to follow her as soon as I could safely do so. This mode of proceeding, if no obstacles occurred to thwart us, would enable her to be at the boat-house before half-past two; and (when I left the table, in my turn) would take me to a safe position in the plantation, before three.

The change in the weather, which last night's wind warned us to expect, came with the morning. It was raining heavily, when I got up; and it continued to rain until twelve o'clock — when the clouds dispersed, the blue sky appeared, and the sun shone again with the bright promise of a fine afternoon.

My anxiety to know how Sir Percival and the Count would occupy the early part of the day, was by no means set at rest, so far as Sir Percival was concerned, by his leaving us immediately after breakfast, and going out by himself, in spite of the rain. He neither told us where he was going, nor when we might expect him back. We saw him pass the breakfast-room window, hastily, with his high boots and his water-proof coat on — and that was all.

The Count passed the morning quietly, indoors; some part of it, in the library; some part, in the drawing-room, playing odds and ends of music on the piano, and humming to himself. Judging by appearances, the sentimental side of his character was persistently inclined to betray itself still. He was silent and sensitive, and ready to sigh and languish ponderously (as only fat men *can* sigh and languish), on the smallest provocation.

Luncheon-time came; and Sir Percival did not return. The Count took his friend's place at the table — plaintively devoured the greater part of a fruit tart, submerged under a whole jugful of cream — and explained the full merit of the achievement to us, as soon as he had done. "A taste for sweets," he said in his softest tones and his tenderest manner, "is the innocent taste of women and children. I love to share it with them — it is another bond, dear ladies, between you and me."

Laura left the table in ten minutes' time. I was sorely tempted to accompany her. But if we had both gone out together, we must have excited suspicion; and, worse still, if we allowed Anne Catherick to see Laura accompanied by a second person who was a stranger to her, we should in all probability forfeit her confidence from that moment, never to regain it again.

I waited, therefore, as patiently as I could, until the servant came in to clear the table. When I quitted the room, there were no signs, in the house or out of it, of Sir Percival's return. I left the Count with a piece of sugar between his lips, and the vicious cockatoo scrambling up his waistcoat to get at it; while Madame Fosco, sitting opposite to her husband, watched the proceedings of his bird and himself, as attentively as if she had never seen anything of the sort before in her life. On my way to the plantation I kept carefully beyond the range of view from the luncheon-room window. Nobody saw me and nobody followed me. It was then a quarter to three o'clock by my watch.

Once among the trees, I walked rapidly, until I had advanced more than half way through the plantation. At that point, I slackened my pace, and proceeded cautiously — but I saw no one, and heard no voices. By little and little, I came within view of the back of the boat-house — stopped and listened — then went on, till I was close behind it, and must have heard any persons who had been talking inside. Still the silence was unbroken: still, far and near, no sign of a living creature appeared anywhere.

After skirting round by the back of the building, first on one side, and then on the other, and making no discoveries, I ventured in front of it, and fairly looked in. The place was empty.

I called, "Laura!" — at first, softly — then louder and louder. No one answered, and no one appeared. For all that I could see and hear, the only human creature in the neighbourhood of the lake and the plantation, was myself.

My heart began to beat violently; but I kept my resolution, and searched, first the boat-house, and then the ground in front of it, for any signs which might show me whether Laura had really reached the place or not. No mark of her presence appeared inside the building; but I found traces of her outside it, in footsteps on the sand.

I detected the footsteps of two persons — large footsteps, like a man's, and small footsteps, which, by putting my own feet into them and testing their size in that manner, I felt certain were Laura's. The ground was confusedly marked in this way, just before the boat-house. Close against one side of it, under shelter of the projecting roof, I discovered a little hole in the sand — a hole artificially made, beyond a doubt. I just noticed it, and then turned away immediately to trace the footsteps as far as I could, and to follow the direction in which they might lead me.

They led me, starting from the left-hand side of the boat-house, along the edge of the trees, a distance, I should think, of between two and three hundred yards — and then, the sandy ground showed no further trace of them. Feeling that the persons whose course I was tracking, must necessarily have entered the plantation at this point, I entered it, too. At first, I could find no path — but I discovered one, afterwards, just faintly traced among the trees, and followed it. It took me, for some distance, in the direction of the village, until I stopped at a point where another foot-track crossed it. The brambles grew thickly on either side of this second path. I stood, looking down it, uncertain which way to take next; and, while I looked, I saw on one thorny branch, some fragments of fringe from a woman's shawl. A closer examination of the fringe satisfied me that it had been torn from a shawl of Laura's; and I instantly followed the second path. It brought me out, at last, to my great relief, at the back of the house. I say to my great relief, because I inferred that Laura must, for some unknown reason, have returned before me by this roundabout way. I went in by the courtyard and the offices. The first person whom I met in crossing the servants' hall, was Mrs. Michelson, the housekeeper.

"Do you know," I asked, "whether Lady Glyde has come in from her walk or not?"

"My lady came in, a little while ago, with Sir Percival," answered the housekeeper. "I am afraid, Miss Halcombe, something very distressing has happened."

My heart sank within me. "You don't mean an accident!" I said, faintly.

"No, no — thank God, no accident. But my lady ran upstairs to her own room in tears; and Sir Percival has ordered me to give Fanny warning to leave in an hour's time."

Fanny was Laura's maid; a good, affectionate girl who had been with her for years — the only person in the house, whose fidelity and devotion we could both depend upon.

"Where is Fanny?" I inquired.

"In my room, Miss Halcombe. The young woman is quite overcome: and I told her to sit down, and try to recover herself."

I went to Mrs. Michelson's room, and found Fanny in a corner, with her box by her side, crying bitterly.

She could give me no explanation whatever of her sudden

dismissal. Sir Percival had ordered that she should have a month's wages, in place of a month's warning, and go. No reason had been assigned; no objection had been made to her conduct. She had been forbidden to appeal to her mistress, forbidden even to see her for a moment to say good-by. She was to go without explanations or farewells — and to go at once.

After soothing the poor girl by a few friendly words, I asked where she proposed to sleep that night. She replied that she thought of going to the little inn in the village, the landlady of which was a respectable woman, known to the servants at Blackwater Park. The next morning, by leaving early, she might get back to her friends in Cumberland, without stopping in London, where she was a total stranger.

I felt directly that Fanny's departure offered us a safe means of communication with London and with Limmeridge House, of which it might be very important to avail ourselves. Accordingly, I told her that she might expect to hear from her mistress or from me in the course of the evening, and that she might depend on our both doing all that lay in our power to help her, under the trial of leaving us for the present. Those words said, I shook hands with her, and went up-stairs.

The door which led to Laura's room, was the door of an ante-chamber, opening on to the passage. When I tried it, it was bolted on the inside.

I knocked, and the door was opened by the same heavy, overgrown housemaid, whose lumpish insensibility had tried my patience so severely, on the day when I found the wounded dog. I had, since that time, discovered that her name was Margaret Porcher, and that she was the most awkward, slatternly, and obstinate servant in the house.

On opening the door, she instantly stepped out to the threshold, and stood grinning at me in stolid silence.

"Why do you stand there?" I said. "Don't you see that I want to come in?"

"Ah, but you mustn't come in," was the answer, with another and a broader grin still.

"How dare you talk to me in that way? Stand back instantly!"

She stretched out a great red hand and arm on each side of her, so as to bar the doorway, and slowly nodded her addle head at me.

"Master's orders," she said; and nodded again.

I had need of all my self-control to warn me against contesting the matter with *her*, and to remind me that the next words I had to say must be addressed to her master. I turned my back on her, and instantly went down stairs to find him. My resolution to keep my temper under all the irritations that Sir Percival could offer, was, by this time, as completely forgotten — I say so to my shame — as if I had never made it. It did me good — after all I had suffered and suppressed in that house — it actually did me good to feel how angry I was.

The drawing-room and the breakfast-room were both empty. I went on to the library; and there I found Sir Percival, the Count, and Madame Fosco. They were all three standing up, close together, and Sir Percival had a little slip of paper in his hand. As I opened the door, I heard the Count say to him, "No — a thousand times over, no."

I walked straight up to him, and looked him full in the face.

"Am I to understand, Sir Percival, that your wife's room is a prison, and that your housemaid is the gaoler who keeps it?" I asked.

"Yes; that *is* what you are to understand," he answered. "Take care my gaoler hasn't got double duty to do — take care your room is not a prison, too."

"Take *you* care how you treat your wife, and how you threaten *me*," I broke out, in the heat of my anger. "There are laws in England to protect women from cruelty and outrage. If you hurt a hair of Laura's head, if you dare to interfere with my freedom, come what come may, to those laws I will appeal."

Instead of answering me, he turned round to the Count.

"What did I tell you?" he asked. "What do you say now?"

"What I said before," replied the Count — "No."

Even in the vehemence of my anger, I felt his calm, cold, gray eyes on my face. They turned away from me, as soon as he had spoken, and looked significantly at his wife. Madame Fosco immediately moved close to my side, and, in that position, addressed Sir Percival before either of us could speak again.

"Favour me with your attention, for one moment," she said, in her clear icily-suppressed tones. "I have to thank you, Sir Percival, for your hospitality; and to decline taking advantage of it any longer. I remain in no house in which ladies are treated as your wife and Miss Halcombe have been treated here to-day!"

Sir Percival drew back a step, and stared at her in dead silence. The declaration he had just heard — a declaration which he well knew, as I well knew, Madame Fosco would not have ventured to make without her husband's permission — seemed to petrify him with surprise. The Count stood by, and looked at his wife with the most enthusiastic admiration.

"She is sublime!" he said to himself. He approached her, while he spoke, and drew her hand through his arm. "I am at your service, Eleanor," he went on, with a quiet dignity that I had never noticed in him before. "And at Miss Halcombe's service, if she will honour me by accepting all the assistance I can offer her."

"Damn it! what do you mean?" cried Sir Percival, as the Count quietly moved away, with his wife, to the door.

"At other times I mean what I say; but, at this time, I mean what my wife says," replied the impenetrable Italian. "We have changed places, Percival, for once; and Madame Fosco's opinion is — mine."

Sir Percival crumpled up the paper in his hand; and, pushing past the Count, with another oath, stood between him and the door.

"Have your own way," he said, with baffled rage in his low, half-whispering tones. "Have your own way — and see what comes of it." With those words, he left the room.

Madame Fosco glanced inquiringly at her husband. "He has gone away very suddenly," she said. "What does it mean?"

"It means that you and I together have brought the worst-tempered man in all England to his senses," answered the Count. "It means, Miss Halcombe, that Lady Glyde is relieved from a gross indignity, and you from the repetition of an unpardonable insult. Suffer me to express my admiration of your conduct and your courage at a very trying moment."

"Sincere admiration," suggested Madame Fosco.

"Sincere admiration," echoed the Count.

I had no longer the strength of my first angry resistance to outrage and injury to support me. My heart-sick anxiety to see Laura; my sense of my own helpless ignorance of what had happened at the boat-house, pressed on me with an intolerable weight. I tried to keep up appearances, by speaking to the Count and his wife in the tone which they had chosen to adopt in speaking to me. But the words failed on my lips — my breath came short and thick — my eyes looked longingly, in silence, at the door. The Count, understanding my anxiety, opened it, went out, and pulled it to after him. At the same time Sir Percival's heavy step descended the stairs. I heard them whispering together, outside, while Madame Fosco was assuring me in her calmest and most conventional manner, that she rejoiced, for all our sakes, that Sir Percival's conduct had not obliged her husband and herself to leave Blackwater Park. Before she had done speaking, the whispering ceased, the door opened, and the Count looked in.

"Miss Halcombe," he said, "I am happy to inform you that Lady Glyde is mistress again in her own house. I thought it might be more agreeable to you to hear of this change for the better from *me*, than from Sir Percival — and I have, therefore, expressly returned to mention it."

"Admirable delicacy!" said Madame Fosco, paying back her husband's tribute of admiration, with the Count's own coin, in the Count's own manner. He smiled and bowed as if he had received a formal compliment from a polite stranger, and drew back to let me pass out first.

Sir Percival was standing in the hall. As I hurried to the stairs I heard him call impatiently to the Count, to come out of the library.

"What are you waiting there for?" he said; "I want to speak to you."

"And I want to think a little by myself," replied the other. "Wait till later, Percival — wait till later."

Neither he nor his friend said any more. I gained the top of the stairs, and ran along the passage. In my haste and my agitation, I left the door of the antechamber open — but I closed the door of the bedroom the moment I was inside it.

Laura was sitting alone at the far end of the room; her arms resting wearily on a table, and her face hidden in her hands. She started up, with a cry of delight, when she saw me.

"How did you get here?" she asked. "Who gave you leave? Not Sir Percival?"

In my overpowering anxiety to hear what she had to tell me, I could not answer her — I could only put questions, on my side. Laura's eagerness to know what had passed down stairs proved, however, too strong to be resisted. She persistently repeated her inquiries.

"The Count, of course," I answered, impatiently. "Whose influence in the house —?"

She stopped me, with a gesture of disgust.

"Don't speak of him," she cried. "The Count is the vilest creature breathing! The Count is a miserable Spy —!"

Before we could either of us say another word, we were alarmed by a soft knocking at the door of the bedroom.

I had not yet sat down; and I went first to see who it was. When I opened the door, Madame Fosco confronted me, with my handkerchief in her hand.

"You dropped this down stairs, Miss Halcombe," she said; "and I thought I could bring it to you, as I was passing by to my own room."

Her face, naturally pale, had turned to such a ghastly whiteness, that I started at the sight of it. Her hands, so sure and steady at all other times, trembled violently; and her eyes looked wolfishly past me through the open door, and fixed on Laura.

She had been listening before she knocked! I saw it in her white face; I saw it in her trembling hands; I saw it in her look at Laura.

After waiting an instant, she turned from me in silence, and slowly walked away.

I closed the door again, "Oh, Laura! Laura! We shall both rue the day when you called the Count a Spy!"

"You would have called him so yourself, Marian, if you had known what I know. Anne Catherick was right. There *was* a third person watching us in the plantation, yesterday; and that third person —"

"Are you sure it was the Count?"

"I am absolutely certain. He was Sir Percival's spy — he was Sir Percival's informer — he set Sir Percival watching and waiting, all the morning through, for Anne Catherick and for me."

"Is Anne found? Did you see her at the lake?"

"No. She has saved herself by keeping away from the place. When I got to the boat-house, no one was there."

"Yes? yes?"

"I went in, and sat waiting for a few minutes. But my restlessness made me get up again, to walk about a little. As I passed out, I saw some marks on the sand, close under the front of the boat-house. I stooped down to examine them, and discovered a word written in large letters, on the sand. The word was — LOOK."

"And you scraped away the sand, and dug a hollow place in it?"

"How do you know that, Marian?"

"I saw the hollow place myself, when I followed you to the boat-house. Go on — go on!"

"Yes; I scraped away the sand on the surface; and in a

little while, I came to a strip of paper hidden beneath, which had writing on it. The writing was signed with Anne Catherick's initials."

"Where is it?"

"Sir Percival has taken it from me."

"Can you remember what the writing was? Do you think you can repeat it to me?"

"In substance I can, Marian. It was very short. You would have remembered it, word for word."

"Try to tell me what the substance was, before we go any further."

She complied. I write the lines down here, exactly as she repeated them to me. They ran thus:

"I was seen with you, yesterday, by a tall stout old man, and had to run to save myself. He was not quick enough on his feet to follow me, and he lost me among the trees. I dare not risk coming back here to-day, at the same time. I write this, and hide it in the sand, at six in the morning, to tell you so. When we speak next of your wicked husband's Secret we must speak safely or not at all. Try to have patience. I promise you shall see me again; and that soon. — A. C."

The reference to the "tall stout old man" (the terms of which Laura was certain that she had repeated to me correctly), left no doubt as to who the intruder had been. I called to mind that I had told Sir Percival, in the Count's presence, the day before, that Laura had gone to the boat-house to look for her brooch. In all probability he had followed her there, in his officious way, to relieve her mind about the matter of the signature, immediately after he had mentioned the change in Sir Percival's plans to me in the drawing-room. In this case he could only have got to the neighbourhood of the boat-house, at the very moment when Anne Catherick discovered him. The suspiciously hurried manner in which she parted from Laura, had no doubt prompted his useless attempt to follow her. Of the conversation which had previously taken place between them, he could have heard nothing. The distance between the house and the lake, and the time at which he left me in the drawing-room, as compared with the time at which Laura and Anne Catherick had been speaking together, proved that fact to us, at any rate, beyond a doubt.

Having arrived at something like a conclusion, so far, my next great interest was to know what discoveries Sir Percival had made, after Count Fosco had given him his information.

"How came you to lose possession of the letter?" I asked. "What did you do with it, when you found it in the sand?"

"After reading it once through," she replied, "I took it into the boat-house with me, to sit down, and look it over a second time. While I was reading, a shadow fell across the paper. I looked up; and saw Sir Percival standing in the doorway watching me."

"Did you try to hide the letter?"

"I tried — but he stopped me. 'You needn't trouble to hide that,' he said. 'I happen to have read it.' I could only look at him, helplessly — I could say nothing. 'You understand?" he went on; 'I have read it. I dug it up out of the sand two hours since, and buried it again, and wrote the word above it again, and left it ready to your hands. You can't lie yourself out of the scrape now. You saw Anne Catherick in secret yesterday; and you have got her letter in your hand at this moment. I have not caught *her* yet; but I have caught *you*. Give me the letter.' He stepped close up to me — I was alone with him, Marian — what could I do? — I gave him the letter."

"What did he say when you gave it to him?"

"At first, he said nothing. He took me by the arm, and led me out of the boat-house, and looked about him, on all sides, as if he was afraid of our being seen or heard. Then, he clasped his hand fast round my arm, and whispered to me, — 'What did Anne Catherick say to you yesterday? — I insist on hearing every word, from first to last.'"

"Did you tell him?"

"I was alone with him, Marian — his cruel hand was bruising my arm — what could I do?"

"Is the mark on your arm still? Let me see it?"

"Why do you want to see it?"

"I want to see it, Laura, because our endurance must end, and our resistance must begin, to-day. That mark is a weapon to strike him with. Let me see it now — I may have to swear to it, at some future time."

"O, Marian, don't look so! don't talk so! It doesn't hurt me, now!"

"Let me see it!"

She showed me the marks. I was past grieving over them, past crying over them, past shuddering over them. They say we are either better than men, or worse. If the temptation that has fallen in some women's way, and made them worse, had fallen in mine, at that moment —— Thank God! my face betrayed nothing that his wife could read. The gentle, innocent, affectionate creature thought I was frightened for her and sorry for her — and thought no more.

"Don't think too seriously of it, Marian," she said, simply, as she pulled her sleeve down again. "It doesn't hurt me, now."

"I will try to think quietly of it, my love, for your sake. — Well! well! And you told him all that Anne Catherick had said to you — all that you told me?"

"Yes; all. He insisted on it — I was alone with him — I could conceal nothing."

"Did he say anything when you had done?"

"He looked at me, and laughed to himself, in a mocking, bitter way. 'I mean to have the rest out of you,' he said; 'do you hear? — the rest.' I declared to him solemnly that I had told him everything I knew. 'Not you!' he answered: 'you know more than you choose to tell. Won't you tell it? You shall! I'll wring it out of you at home, if I can't wring it out of you, here.' He led me away by a strange path through the plantation — a path where there was no hope of our meeting you — and he spoke no more, till we came within sight of the house. Then he stopped again, and said, 'Will you take a second chance, if I give it to you? Will you think better of it, and tell me the rest?' I could only repeat the same words I had spoken before. He cursed my obstinacy, and went on, and took me with him to the house. 'You can't deceive me,' he said; 'you know more than you choose to tell. I'll have your secret out of you; and I'll have it out of that sister of yours, as well. There shall be no more plotting and whispering between you. Neither you nor she shall see each other again till you have confessed the truth. I'll have you watched morning, noon, and night, till you confess the truth.' He was deaf to everything I could say. He took me straight upstairs into my own room. Fanny was sitting there, doing some work for me; and he instantly ordered her out. 'I'll take good care *you're* not mixed up in the conspiracy,' he said. 'You shall leave this house to-day. If your mistress wants a maid, she shall have one of my choosing.' He pushed me into the room, and locked the door on me — he set that senseless woman to watch me outside — Marian! he looked and spoke like a madman. You may hardly understand it — he did indeed."

"I do understand it, Laura. He *is* mad — mad with the terrors of a guilty conscience. Every word you have said makes me positively certain that when Anne Catherick left you yesterday, you were on the eve of discovering a secret, which might have been your vile husband's ruin — and he thinks you *have* discovered it. Nothing you can say or do, will quiet that guilty distrust, and convince his false nature of your truth. I don't say this, my love, to alarm you. I say it to open your eyes to your position, and to convince you of the urgent necessity of letting me act, as I best can, for your protection, while the chance is our own. Count Fosco's interference has secured me access to you to-day; but he may withdraw that interference to-morrow. Sir Percival has already dismissed Fanny, because she is a quick-witted girl, and devotedly attached to you; and has chosen a woman to take her place, who cares nothing for your interests, and whose dull intelligence lowers her to the level of the watchdog in the yard. It is impossible to say what violent measures he may take next, unless we make the most of our opportunities while we have them."

"What can we do, Marian? Oh, if we could only leave this house, never to see it again!"

"Listen to me, my love — and try to think that you are not quite helpless so long as I am here with you."

"I will think so — I do think so. Don't altogether forget poor Fanny, in thinking of me. She wants help and comfort, too."

"I will not forget her. I saw her before I came up here; and I have arranged to communicate with her to-night. Letters are not safe in the post-bag at Blackwater Park — and I shall have two to write to-day, in your interests, which must pass through no hands but Fanny's."

"What letters?"

"I mean to write first, Laura, to Mr. Gilmore's partner, who has offered to help us in any fresh emergency. Little as I know of the law, I am certain that it can protect a woman from such treatment as that ruffian has inflicted on you to-day. I will go into no details about Anne Catherick, because I have no certain information to give. But the lawyer shall know of those bruises on your arm, and of the violence offered to you in this room — he shall, before I rest to-night!"

"But, think of the exposure, Marian!"

"I am calculating on the exposure. Sir Percival has more to dread from it than you have. The prospect of an exposure may bring him to terms, when nothing else will."

I rose as I spoke; but Laura entreated me not to leave her.

"You will drive him to desperation," she said, "and increase our dangers tenfold."

I felt the truth — the disheartening truth — of those words. But I could not bring myself plainly to acknowledge it to her. In our dreadful position, there was no help and no hope for us, but in risking the worst. I said so, in guarded terms. She sighed bitterly — but did not contest the matter. She only asked about the second letter that I had proposed writing. To whom was it to be addressed?

"To Mr. Fairlie," I said. "Your uncle is your nearest male relative, and the head of the family. He must and shall interfere."

Laura shook her head sorrowfully.

'Yes, yes," I went on; "your uncle is a weak, selfish, worldly man, I know. But he is not Sir Percival Glyde; and he has no such friend about him as Count Fosco. I expect nothing from his kindness, or his tenderness of feeling towards you, or towards me. But he will do anything to pamper his own indolence, and to secure his own quiet. Let me only persuade him that his interference, at this moment, will save him inevitable trouble, and wretchedness, and responsibility hereafter, and he will bestir himself for his own sake. I know how to deal with him, Laura — I have had some practice."

"If you could only prevail on him to let me go back to Limmeridge for a little while, and stay there quietly with you, Marian, I could be almost as happy again as I was before I was married!"

Those words set me thinking in a new direction. Would it be possible to place Sir Percival between the two alternatives of either exposing himself to the scandal of legal interference on his wife's behalf, or of allowing her to be quietly separated from him for a time, under pretext of a visit to her uncle's house? And could he, in that case, be reckoned on as likely to accept the last resource? It was doubtful — more than doubtful. And yet, hopeless as the experiment seemed, surely it was worth trying? I resolved to try it, in sheer despair of knowing what better to do.

"Your uncle shall know the wish you have just expressed," I said; "and I will ask the lawyer's advice on the subject, as well. Good may come of it — and will come of it, I hope."

Saying that, I rose again; and again Laura tried to make me resume my seat.

"Don't leave me," she said, uneasily. "My desk is on that table. You can write here."

It tried me to the quick to refuse her, even in her own interests. But we had been too long shut up alone together already. Our chance of seeing each other again might entirely depend on our not exciting any fresh suspicions. It was full time to show myself, quietly and unconcernedly, among the wretches who were, at that very moment, perhaps, thinking of us and talking of us down stairs. I explained the miserable necessity to Laura; and prevailed on her to recognise it, as I did.

"I will come back again, love, in an hour or less," I said. "The worst is over for to-day. Keep yourself quiet, and fear nothing."

"Is the key in the door, Marian? Can I lock it on the inside?"

"Yes; here is the key. Lock the door; and open it to nobody, until I come up-stairs again."

I kissed her, and left her. It was a relief to me, as I walked away, to hear the key turned in the lock, and to know that the door was at her own command.

X

JULY 5TH. — I had only got as far as the top of the stairs, when the locking of Laura's door suggested to me the precaution of also locking my own door, and keeping the key safely about me while I was out of the room. My journal was already secured, with other papers, in the table-drawer, but my writing materials were left out. These included a seal, bearing the common device of two doves drinking out of the same cup; and some sheets of blotting paper, which had the impression on them of the closing lines of my writing in these pages, traced during the past night. Distorted by the suspicion which had now become a part of myself, even such trifles as these looked too dangerous to be trusted without a guard — even the locked table-drawer seemed to be not sufficiently protected, in my absence, until the means of access to it had been carefully secured as well.

I found no appearance of any one having entered the room while I had been talking with Laura. My writing materials (which I had given the servant instructions never to meddle with) were scattered over the table much as usual. The only circumstance in connection with them that at all struck me was, that the seal lay tidily in the tray with the pencils and the wax. It was not in my careless habits (I am sorry to say) to put it there; neither did I remember putting it there. But, as I could not call to mind, on the other hand, where else I had thrown it down, and as I was also doubtful whether I might not, for once, have laid it mechanically in the right place, I abstained from adding to the perplexity with which the day's events had filled my mind, by troubling it afresh about a trifle. I locked the door; put the key in my pocket; and went down stairs.

Madame Fosco was alone in the hall, looking at the weather-glass.

"Still falling," she said. "I am afraid we must expect more rain."

Her face was composed again to its customary expression and its customary colour. But the hand with which she pointed to the dial of the weather-glass still trembled.

Could she have told her husband already, that she had overheard Laura reviling him, in my company, as a "Spy?" My strong suspicion that she must have told him; my irresistible dread (all the more overpowering from its very vagueness) of the consequences which might follow; my fixed conviction, derived from various little self-betrayals which women notice in each other, that Madame Fosco, in spite of her well-assumed external civility, had not forgiven her niece for innocently standing between her and the legacy of ten thousand pounds — all rushed upon my mind together; all impelled me to speak, in the vain hope of using my own influence and my own powers of persuasion for the atonement of Laura's offence.

"May I trust to your kindness to excuse me, Madame

Fosco, if I venture to speak to you on an exceedingly painful subject?"

She crossed her hands in front of her, and bowed her head solemnly, without uttering a word, and without taking her eyes off mine for a moment.

"When you were so good as to bring me back my hand-kerchief," I went on, "I am very, very much afraid you must have accidentally heard Laura say something which I am unwilling to repeat, and which I will not attempt to defend. I will only venture to hope that you have not thought it of sufficient importance to be mentioned to the Count?"

"I think it of no importance whatever," said Madame Fosco, sharply and suddenly. "But," she added, resuming her icy manner in a moment, "I have no secrets from my husband, even in trifles. When he noticed, just now, that I looked distressed, it was my painful duty to tell him why I was distressed; and I frankly acknowledge to you, Miss Hal-combe, that I *have* told him."

I was prepared to hear it, and yet she turned me cold all over when she said those words.

"Let me earnestly entreat you, Madame Fosco — let me earnestly entreat the Count — to make some allowances for the sad position in which my sister is placed. She spoke while she was smarting under the insult and injustice inflicted on her by her husband — and she was not herself when she said those rash words. May I hope that they will be considerately and generously forgiven?"

"Most assuredly," said the Count's quiet voice, behind me. He had stolen on us, with his noiseless tread, and his book in his hand, from the library.

"When Lady Glyde said those hasty words," he went on, "she did me an injustice, which I lament — and forgive. Let us never return to the subject, Miss Halcombe; let us all com-fortably combine to forget it, from this moment."

"You are very kind," I said; "you relieve me inexpres-sibly ——"

I tried to continue — but his eyes were on me; his deadly

smile, that hides everything, was set, hard and unwavering, on his broad, smooth face. My distrust of his unfathomable falseness, my sense of my own degradation in stooping to conciliate his wife and himself, so disturbed and confused me, that the next word failed on my lips, and I stood there in silence.

"I beg you on my knees to say no more, Miss Halcombe — I am truly shocked that you should have thought it necessary to say so much." With that polite speech, he took my hand — oh, how I despise myself! oh, how little comfort there is, even in knowing that I submitted to it for Laura's sake! — he took my hand, and put it to his poisonous lips. Never did I know all my horror of him till then. That innocent familiarity turned my blood, as if it had been the vilest insult that a man could offer me. Yet I hid my disgust from him — I tried to smile — I, who once mercilessly despised deceit in other women, was as false as the worst of them, as false as the Judas whose lips had touched my hand.

I could not have maintained my degrading self-control — it is all that redeems me in my own estimation to know that I could not — if he had still continued to keep his eyes on my face. His wife's tigerish jealousy came to my rescue, and forced his attention away from me, the moment he possessed himself of my hand. Her cold blue eyes caught light; her dull white cheeks flushed into bright colour; she looked years younger than her age, in an instant.

"Count!" she said. "Your foreign forms of politeness are not understood by Englishwomen."

"Pardon me, my angel! The best and dearest Englishwoman in the world understands them." With those words, he dropped my hand, and quietly raised his wife's hand to his lips, in place of it.

I ran back up the stairs, to take refuge in my own room. If there had been time to think, my thoughts, when I was alone again, would have caused me bitter suffering. But there was no time to think. Happily for the preservation of

my calmness and my courage, there was time for nothing but
action.

The letters to the lawyer and to Mr. Fairlie, were still to
be written; and I sat down at once, without a moment's hesitation, to devote myself to them.

There was no multitude of resources to perplex me — there
was absolutely no one to depend on, in the first instance, but
myself. Sir Percival had neither friends nor relatives in the
neighbourhood whose intercession I could attempt to employ.
He was on the coldest terms — in some cases, on the worst
terms — with the families of his own rank and station who
lived near him. We two women had neither father, nor
brother, to come to the house, and take our parts. There
was no choice, but to write those two doubtful letters — or to
put Laura in the wrong and myself in the wrong, and to make
all peaceable negotiation in the future impossible, by secretly
escaping from Blackwater Park. Nothing but the most im-
minent personal peril could justify our taking that second
course. The letters must be tried first; and I wrote them.

I said nothing to the lawyer about Anne Catherick; because (as I had already hinted to Laura) that topic was connected with a mystery which we could not yet explain, and
which it would therefore be useless to write about to a professional man. I left my correspondent to attribute Sir Percival's disgraceful conduct, if he pleased, to fresh disputes
about money matters; and simply consulted him on the possibility of taking legal proceedings for Laura's protection, in
the event of her husband's refusal to allow her to leave Blackwater Park for a time and return with me to Limmeridge. I
referred him to Mr. Fairlie for the details of this last arrangement — I assured him that I wrote with Laura's authority
— and I ended by entreating him to act in her name, to the
utmost extent of his power, and with the least possible loss of
time.

The letter to Mr. Fairlie occupied me next. I appealed to
him on the terms which I had mentioned to Laura as the most
likely to make him bestir himself; I enclosed a copy of my

letter to the lawyer, to show him how serious the case was; and I represented our removal to Limmeridge as the only compromise which would prevent the danger and distress of Laura's present position from inevitably affecting her uncle as well as herself, at no very distant time.

When I had done, and had sealed and directed the two envelopes, I went back with the letters to Laura's room, to show her that they were written.

"Has anybody disturbed you?" I asked, when she opened the door to me.

"Nobody has knocked," she replied. "But I heard some one in the outer room."

"Was it a man or a woman?"

"A woman. I heard the rustling of her gown."

"A rustling like silk?"

"Yes; like silk."

Madame Fosco had evidently been watching outside. The mischief she might do by herself, was little to be feared. But the mischief she might do, as a willing instrument in her husband's hands, was too formidable to be overlooked.

"What became of the rustling of the gown when you no longer heard it in the ante-room?" I inquired. "Did you hear it go past your wall, along the passage?"

"Yes. I kept still, and listened; and just heard it."

"Which way did it go?"

"Towards your room."

I considered again. The sound had not caught my ears. But I was then deeply absorbed in my letters; and I write with a heavy hand, and a quill pen, scraping and scratching noisily over the paper. It was more likely that Madame Fosco would hear the scraping of my pen than that I should hear the rustling of her dress. Another reason (if I had wanted one) for not trusting my letters to the post-bag in the hall.

Laura saw me thinking. "More difficulties!" she said, wearily; "more difficulties and more dangers!"

"No dangers," I replied. "Some little difficulty, perhaps.

I am thinking of the safest way of putting my two letters into Fanny's hands."

"You have really written them, then? Oh, Marian, run no risks — pray, pray run no risks!"

"No, no — no fear. Let me see — what o'clock is it now?"

It was a quarter to six. There would be time for me to get to the village inn, and to come back again, before dinner. If I waited till the evening, I might find no second opportunity of safely leaving the house.

"Keep the key turned in the lock, Laura," I said, "and don't be afraid about me. If you hear any inquiries made, call through the door, and say that I am gone out for a walk."

"When shall you be back?"

"Before dinner, without fail. Courage, my love. By this time to-morrow, you will have a clear headed, trustworthy man acting for your good. Mr. Gilmore's partner is our next best friend to Mr. Gilmore himself."

A moment's reflection, as soon as 1 was alone, convinced me that I had better not appear in my walking-dress, until I had first discovered what was going on in the lower part of the house. I had not ascertained yet whether Sir Percival was in doors or out.

The singing of the canaries in the library, and the smell of tobacco-smoke that came through the door, which was not closed, told me at once where the Count was. I looked over my shoulder, as I passed the doorway; and saw, to my surprise, that he was exhibiting the docility of the birds, in his most engagingly polite manner, to the housekeeper. He must have specially invited her to see them — for she would never have thought of going into the library of her own accord. The man's slightest actions had a purpose of some kind at the bottom of every one of them. What could be his purpose here?

It was no time then to inquire into his motives. I looked about for Madame Fosco next; and found her following her favourite circle, round and round the fish-pond.

I was a little doubtful how she would meet me, after the outbreak of jealousy, of which I had been the cause so short time since.   But her husband had tamed her in the interval; and she now spoke to me with the same civility as usual.   My only object in addressing myself to her was to ascertain if she knew what had become of Sir Percival.   I contrived to refer to him indirectly; and, after a little fencing on either side, she at last mentioned that he had gone out.

"Which of the horses has he taken?"   I asked, carelessly.

"None of them," she replied.   "He went away, two hours since, on foot.   As I understood it, his object was to make fresh inquiries about the woman named Anne Catherick.   He appears to be unreasonably anxious about tracing her.   Do you happen to know if she is dangerously mad, Miss Halcombe?"

"I do not, Countess."

"Are you going in?"

"Yes, I think so.   I suppose it will soon be time to dress for dinner."

We entered the house together.   Madame Fosco strolled into the library, and closed the door.   I went at once to fetch my hat and shawl.   Every moment was of importance, if I was to get to Fanny at the inn and be back before dinner.

When I crossed the hall again, no one was there; and the singing of the birds in the library had ceased.   I could not stop to make any fresh investigations.   I could only assure myself that the way was clear, and then leave the house, with the two letters safe in my pocket.

On my way to the village, I prepared myself for the possibility of meeting Sir Percival.   As long as I had him to deal with alone, I felt certain of not losing my presence of mind. Any woman who is sure of her own wits, is a match, at any time, for a man who is not sure of his own temper.   I had no such fear of Sir Percival as I had of the Count.   Instead of fluttering, it had composed me, to hear of the errand on which he had gone out.   While the tracing of Anne Catherick was the great anxiety that occupied him, Laura and I might hope for some cessation of any active persecution at his hands. For our sakes now, as well as for Anne's, I hoped and prayed fervently that she might still escape him.

I walked on as briskly as the heat would let me, till I reached the cross-road which led to the village; looking back, from time to time, to make sure that I was not followed by any one.

Nothing was behind me, all the way, but an empty country waggon. The noise made by the lumbering wheels annoyed me; and when I found that the waggon took the road to the village, as well as myself, I stopped to let it go by, and pass out of hearing. As I looked towards it, more attentively than before, I thought I detected, at intervals, the feet of a man walking close behind it; the carter being in front, by the side of his horses. The part of the cross-road which I had just passed over was so narrow, that the waggon coming after me brushed the trees and thickets on either side; and I had to wait until it went by, before I could test the correctness of my impression. Apparently, that impression was wrong, for when the waggon had passed me, the road behind it was quite clear.

I reached the inn without meeting Sir Percival, and without noticing anything more; and was glad to find that the landlady had received Fanny with all possible kindness. The girl had a little parlour to sit in, away from the noise of the tap-room, and a clean bed-chamber at the top of the house. She began crying again, at the sight of me; and said, poor soul, truly enough, that it was dreadful to feel herself turned out into the world, as if she had committed some unpardonable fault, when no blame could be laid at her door by anybody — not even by her master who had sent her away.

"Try to make the best of it, Fanny," I said. "Your mistress and I will stand your friends, and will take care that your character shall not suffer. Now, listen to me. I have very little time to spare, and I am going to put a great trust in your hands. I wish you to take care of these two letters.

The one with the stamp on it you are to put into the post, when you reach London, to-morrow. The other, directed to Mr. Fairlie, you are to deliver to him yourself, as soon as you get home. Keep both the letters about you, and give them up to no one. They are of the last importance to your mistress's interests."

Fanny put the letters into the bosom of her dress. "There they shall stop, miss," she said, "till I have done what you tell me."

"Mind you are at the station in good time to-morrow morning," I continued. "And, when you see the housekeeper at Limmeridge, give her my compliments, and say that you are in my service, until Lady Glyde is able to take you back. We may meet again sooner than you think. So keep a good heart, and don't miss the seven o'clock train."

"Thank you, miss — thank you kindly. It gives one courage to hear your voice again. Please to offer my duty to my lady; and say I left all the things as tidy as I could in the time. Oh, dear! dear! who will dress her for dinner to-day? It really breaks my heart, miss, to think of it."

When I got back to the house, I had only a quarter of an hour to spare, to put myself in order for dinner, and to say two words to Laura before I went down stairs.

"The letters are in Fanny's hands," I whispered to her, at the door. "Do you mean to join us at dinner?"

"Oh, no, no — not for the world!"

"Has anything happened? Has any one disturbed you?"

"Yes — just now — Sir Percival —"

"Did he come in?"

"No: he frightened me by a thump on the door, outside. I said, 'Who's there?' 'You know,' he answered. 'Will you alter your mind, and tell me the rest? You shall! Sooner or later, I'll wring it out of you. You know where Anne Catherick is, at this moment!' 'Indeed, indeed,' I said, 'I don't.' 'You do!' he called back. 'I'll crush your obstinacy — mind that! — I'll wring it out of you!' He went away, with those words — went away, Marian, hardly five minutes ago."

He had not found Anne. We were safe for that night — he had not found her yet.

"You are going down stairs, Marian? Come up again in the evening."

"Yes, yes. Don't be uneasy, if I am a little late — I must be careful not to give offence by leaving them too soon."

The dinner-bell rang; and I hastened away.

Sir Percival took Madame Fosco into the dining-room; and the Count gave me his arm. He was hot and flushed, and was not dressed with his customary care and completeness. Had he, too, been out before dinner, and been late in getting back? or was he only suffering from the heat a little more scverely than usual?

However this might be, he was unquestionably troubled by some secret annoyance or anxiety, which, with all his powers of deception, he was not able entirely to conceal. Through the whole of dinner, he was almost as silent as Sir Percival himself; and he, every now and then, looked at his wife with an expression of furtive uneasiness, which was quite new in my experience of him. The one social obligation which he scemed to be self-possessed enough to perform as carefully as ever, was the obligation of being persistently civil and attentive to me. What vile object he has in view, I cannot still discover; but, be the design what it may, invariable politeness towards myself, invariable humility towards Laura, and invariable suppression (at any cost) of Sir Percival's clumsy violence, have been the means he has resolutely and impenetrably used to get to his end, ever since he set foot in this house. I suspected it, when he first interfered in our favour, on the day when the deed was produced in the library, and I feel certain of it, now.

When Madame Fosco and I rose to leave the table, the Count rose also to accompany us back to the drawing-room.

"What are you going away for?" asked Sir Percival — "I mean *you*, Fosco."

"I am going away, because I have had dinner enough, and wine enough," answered the Count. "Be so kind, Percival, as to make allowances for my foreign habit of going out with the ladies, as well as coming in with them."

"Nonsense! Another glass of claret won't hurt you. Sit down again like an Englishman. I want half an hour's quiet talk with you over our wine."

"A quiet talk, Percival, with all my heart, but not now, and not over the wine. Later in the evening if you please — later in the evening."

"Civil!" said Sir Percival, savagely. "Civil behaviour, upon my soul, to a man in his own house!"

I had more than once seen him look at the Count uneasily during dinner-time, and had observed that the Count carefully abstained from looking at him in return. This circumstance, coupled with the host's anxiety for a little quiet talk over the wine and the guest's obstinate resolution not to sit down again at the table, revived in my memory the request which Sir Percival had vainly addressed to his friend, earlier in the day, to come out of the library and speak to him. The Count had deferred granting that private interview, when it was first asked for in the afternoon, and had again deferred granting it, when it was a second time asked for at the dinner-table. Whatever the coming subject of discussion between them might be, it was clearly an important subject in Sir Percival's estimation — and perhaps (judging from his evident reluctance to approach it), a dangerous subject as well, in the estimation of the Count.

These considerations occurred to me while we were passing from the dining-room to the drawing-room. Sir Percival's angry commentary on his friend's desertion of him had not produced the slightest effect. The Count obstinately accompanied us to the tea-table — waited a minute or two in the room — then went out into the hall and returned with the post-bag in his hands. It was then eight o'clock — the hour at which the letters were always despatched from Blackwater Park.

"Have you any letter for the post, Miss Halcombe?" he asked, approaching me, with the bag.

I saw Madame Fosco, who was making the tea, pause, with the sugar-tongs in her hand, to listen for my answer.

"No, Count, thank you. No letters to-day."

He gave the bag to the servant, who was then in the room; sat down at the piano; and played the air of the lively Neapolitan street-song, "La mia Carolina," twice over. His wife who was usually the most deliberate of women in all her movements, made the tea as quickly as I could have made it myself — finished her own cup in two minutes — and quietly glided out of the room.

I rose to follow her example — partly because I suspected her of attempting some treachery up-stairs with Laura; partly, because I was resolved not to remain alone in the same room with her husband.

Before I could get to the door, the Count stopped me, by a request for a cup of tea. I gave him the cup of tea; and tried a second time to get away. He stopped me again — this time, by going back to the piano, and suddenly appealing to me on a musical question in which he declared that the honour of his country was concerned.

I vainly pleaded my own total ignorance of music, and total want of taste in that direction. He only appealed to me again with a vehemence which set all further protest on my part at defiance. "The English and the Germans (he indignantly declared) were always reviling the Italians for their inability to cultivate the higher kinds of music. We were perpetually talking of our Oratorios; and they were perpetually talking of their Symphonies. Did we forget and did they forget his immortal friend and countryman, Rossini? What was 'Moses in Egypt,' but a sublime oratorio, which was acted on the stage, instead of being coldly sung in a concert-room? What was the overture to Guillaume Tell, but a symphony under another name? Had I heard Moses in

Egypt? Would I listen to this, and this, and this, and say if anything more sublimely sacred and grand had ever been composed by mortal man?" — And, without waiting for a word of assent or dissent on my part, looking me hard in the face all the time, he began thundering on the piano, and singing to it with loud and lofty enthusiasm; only interrupting himself, at intervals, to announce to me fiercely the titles of the different pieces of music: "Chorus of Egyptians, in the Plague of Darkness, Miss Halcombe!" — "Recitativo of Moses, with the tables of the Law." — "Prayer of Israelites, at the passage of the Red Sea. Aha! Aha! Is that sacred? is that sublime?" The piano trembled under his powerful hands; and the teacups on the table rattled, as his big bass voice thundered out the notes, and his heavy foot beat time on the floor.

There was something horrible — something fierce and devilish, in the outburst of his delight at his own singing and playing, and in the triumph with which he watched its effect upon me, as I shrank nearer and nearer to the door. I was released, at last, not by my own efforts, but by Sir Percival's interposition. He opened the dining-room door, and called out angrily to know what "that infernal noise" meant. The Count instantly got up from the piano. "Ah! if Percival is coming," he said, "harmony and melody are both at an end. The Muse of Music, Miss Halcombe, deserts us in dismay; and I, the fat old minstrel, exhale the rest of my enthusiasm in the open air!" He stalked out into the verandah, put his hands in his pockets, and resumed the "recitativo of Moses," sotto voce, in the garden.

I heard Sir Percival call after him, from the dining-room window. But he took no notice: he seemed determined not to hear. That long-deferred quiet talk between them was still to be put off, was still to wait for the Count's absolute will and pleasure.

He had detained me in the drawing-room nearly half an hour from the time when his wife left us. Where had she been, and what had she been doing in that interval?

I went up-stairs to ascertain, but I made no discoveries; and when I questioned Laura, I found that she had not heard anything. Nobody had disturbed her — no faint rustling of the silk dress had been audible, either in the ante-room or in the passage.

It was then twenty minutes to nine. After going to my room to get my journal, I returned, and sat with Laura; sometimes writing, sometimes stopping to talk with her. Nobody came near us, and nothing happened. We remained together till ten o'clock. I then rose; said my last cheering words; and wished her good night. She locked her door again, after we had arranged that I should come in and see her the first thing in the morning.

I had a few sentences more to add to my diary, before going to bed myself; and, as I went down again to the drawing-room, after leaving Laura, for the last time that weary day, I resolved merely to show myself there, to make my excuses, and then to retire an hour earlier than usual, for the night.

Sir Percival, and the Count and his wife, were sitting together. Sir Percival was yawning in an easy-chair; the Count was reading; Madame Fosco was fanning herself. Strange to say, *her* face was flushed, now. She, who never suffered from the heat was most undoubtedly suffering from it to-night.

"I am afraid, Countess, you are not quite so well as usual?" I said.

"The very remark I was about to make to *you*," she replied. "You are looking pale, my dear."

My dear! It was the first time she had ever addressed me with that familiarity! There was an insolent smile, too, on her face, when she said the words.

"I am suffering from one of my bad headaches," I answered, coldly.

"Ah, indeed? Want of exercise, I suppose? A walk before dinner would have been just the thing for you." She referred to the "walk" with a strange emphasis. Had she seen me go out? No matter if she had. The letters were safe now, in Fanny's hands.

"Come, and have a smoke, Fosco," said Sir Percival, rising, with another uneasy look at his friend.

"With pleasure, Percival, when the ladies have gone to bed," replied the Count.

"Excuse me, Countess, if I set you the example of retiring," I said. "The only remedy for such a headache as mine is going to bed."

I took my leave. There was the same insolent smile on the woman's face when I shook hands with her. Sir Percival paid no attention to me. He was looking impatiently at Madame Fosco, who showed no signs of leaving the room with me. The Count smiled to himself behind his book. There was yet another delay to that quiet talk with Sir Percival — and the Countess was the impediment, this time.

XI.

July 5th. — Once safely shut into my own room, I opened these pages, and prepared to go on with that part of the day's record which was still left to write.

For ten minutes or more, I sat idle, with the pen in my hand, thinking over the events of the last twelve hours. When I at last addressed myself to my task, I found a difficulty in proceeding with it which I had never experienced before. In spite of my efforts to fix my thoughts on the matter in hand, they wandered away, with the strangest persistency, in the one direction of Sir Percival and the Count; and all the interest which I tried to concentrate on my journal, centred, instead, on that private interview between them, which had been put off all through the day, and which was now to take place in the silence and solitude of the night.

In this perverse state of my mind, the recollection of what had passed since the morning would not come back to me; and there was no resource but to close my journal and to get away from it for a little while.

I opened the door which led from my bedroom into my sitting-room, and, having passed through, pulled it to again, to prevent any accident, in case of draught, with the candle left on the dressing-table. My sitting-room window was wide open; and I leaned out, listlessly, to look at the night.

It was dark and quiet. Neither moon nor stars were visible. There was a smell like rain in the still, heavy air; and I put my hand out of window. No. The rain was only threatening; it had not come yet.

I remained leaning on the window-sill for nearly a quarter of an hour, looking out absently into the black darkness, and hearing nothing, except, now and then, the voices of the servants, or the distant sound of a closing door, in the lower part of the house.

Just as I was turning away wearily from the window, to go back to the bedroom, and make a second attempt to complete the unfinished entry in my journal, I smelt the odour of tobacco-smoke, stealing towards me on the heavy night air. The next moment I saw a tiny red spark advancing from the farther end of the house in the pitch darkness. I heard no footsteps, and I could see nothing but the spark. It travelled along in the night; passed the window at which I was standing; and stopped opposite my bedroom window, inside which I had left the light burning on the dressing-table.

The spark remained stationary, for a moment, then moved back again in the direction from which it had advanced. As I followed its progress, I saw a second red spark, larger than the first, approaching from the distance. The two met together in the darkness. Remembering who smoked cigarettes, and who smoked cigars, I inferred, immediately, that the Count had come out first to look and listen, under my window, and that Sir Percival had afterwards joined him. They must both have been walking on the lawn — or I should certainly have heard Sir Percival's heavy footfall, though the Count's soft step might have escaped me, even on the gravel walk.

I waited quietly at the window, certain that they could neither of them see me, in the darkness of the room.

"What's the matter?" I heard Sir Percival say, in a low voice. "Why don't you come in and sit down?"

"I want to see the light out of that window," replied the Count, softly.

"What harm does the light do?"

"It shows she is not in bed yet. She is sharp enough to suspect something, and bold enough to come down stairs and listen, if she can get the chance. Patience — Percival — patience."

"Humbug! You're always talking of patience."

"I shall talk of something else presently. My good friend, you are on the edge of your domestic precipice; and if I let you give the women one other chance, on my sacred word of honour, they will push you over it!"

"What the devil do you mean?"

We will come to our explanations, Percival, when the light is out of that window, and when I have had one little look at the rooms on each side of the library, and a peep at the staircase as well."

They slowly moved away; and the rest of the conversation between them (which had been conducted, throughout, in the same low tones) ceased to be audible. It was no matter. I had heard enough to determine me on justifying the Count's opinion of my sharpness and my courage. Before the red sparks were out of sight in the darkness, I had made up my mind that there should be a listener when those two men sat down to their talk — and that the listener, in spite of all the Count's precautions to the contrary, should be myself. I wanted but one motive to sanction the act to my own conscience, and to give me courage enough for performing it; and that motive I had. Laura's honour, Laura's happiness — Laura's life itself — might depend on my quick ears, and my faithful memory, to-night.

I had heard the Count say that he meant to examine the rooms on each side of the library, and the staircase as well, before he entered on any explanations with Sir Percival. This expression of his intentions was necessarily sufficient to inform me that the library was the room in which he proposed that the conversation should take place. The one moment of time which was long enough to bring me to that conclusion, was also the moment which showed me a means of baffling his precautions — or, in other words, of hearing what he and Sir Percival said to each other, without the risk of descending at all into the lower regions of the house.

In speaking of the rooms on the ground floor, I have mentioned incidentally the verandah outside them, on which they all opened by means of French windows, extending from the cornice to the floor. The top of this verandah was flat; the rain-water being carried off from it, by pipes, into tanks which helped to supply the house. On the narrow leaden roof, which ran along past the bedrooms, and which was rather less, I should think, than three feet below the sills of the windows, a row of flower-pots was ranged, with wide intervals between each pot; the whole being protected from falling, in high winds, by an ornamental iron railing along the edge of the roof.

The plan which had now occurred to me was to get out, at my sitting-room window, on to this roof; to creep along noiselessly, till I reached that part of it which was immediately over the library-window; and to crouch down between the flower-pots, with my ear against the outer railing. If Sir Percival and the Count sat and smoked to-night, as I had seen them sitting and smoking many nights before, with their chairs close at the open window, and their feet stretched on the zinc garden seats which were placed under the verandah, every word they said to each other above a whisper (and no long conversation, as we all know by experience, can be carried on *in* a whisper) must inevitably reach my ears. If, on the other hand, they chose, to-night, to sit far back inside the room, then, the chances were, that I should hear little or nothing; and, in that case, I must run the far more serious risk of trying to outwit them down stairs.

Strongly as I was fortified in my resolution by the desperate nature of our situation, I hoped most fervently that I might escape this last emergency. My courage was only a woman's courage, after all; and it was very near to failing me, when I thought of trusting myself on the ground floor, at the dead of night, within reach of Sir Percival and the Count.

I went softly back to my bedroom, to try the safer experiment of the verandah roof, first.

A complete change in my dress was imperatively necessary, for many reasons. I took off my silk gown to begin with, because the slightest noise from it, on that still night, might have betrayed me. I next removed the white and cumbersome parts of my underclothing, and replaced them by a petticoat of dark flannel. Over this, I put my black travelling cloak, and pulled the hood on to my head. In my ordinary evening costume, I took up the room of three men at least. In my present dress, when it was held close about me, no man could have passed through the narrowest spaces more easily than I. The little breadth left on the roof of the verandah, between the flower-pots on one side, and the wall and the windows of the house on the other, made this a serious consideration. If I knocked anything down, if I made the least noise, who could say what the consequences might be ?

I only waited to put the matches near the candle, before I extinguished it, and groped my way back into the sitting-room. I locked that door, as I had locked my bedroom door — then quietly got out of the window, and cautiously set my feet on the leaden roof of the verandah.

My two rooms were at the inner extremity of the new wing of the house in which we all lived; and I had five windows to pass, before I could reach the position it was necessary to take up immediately over the library. The first window belonged to a spare room, which was empty. The second and third windows belonged to Laura's room. The fourth window belonged to Sir Percival's room. The fifth, belonged to the Countess's room. The others, by which it was not necessary for me to pass, were the windows of the Count's dressing-room, of the bath-room, and of the second empty spare room.

No sound reached my ears — the black blinding darkness of the night was all round me when I first stood on the verandah, except at that part of it which Madame Fosco's window overlooked. There, at the very place above the library, to which my course was directed — there, I saw a gleam of light! The Countess was not yet in bed.

It was too late to draw back; it was no time to wait. I determined to go on at all hazards, and trust for security to my own caution and to the darkness of the night. "For Laura's sake!" I thought to myself, as I took the first step forward on the roof, with one hand holding my cloak close round me, and the other groping against the wall of the house. It was better to brush close by the wall, than to risk striking my feet against the flower-pots within a few inches of me, on the other side.

I passed the dark window of the spare room, trying the leaden roof, at each step, with my foot, before I risked resting my weight on it. I passed the dark windows of Laura's room ("God bless her and keep her to-night!"). I passed the dark window of Sir Percival's room. Then, I waited a moment, knelt down, with my hands to support me; and so crept to my position, under the protection of the low wall between the bottom of the lighted window and the verandah roof.

When I ventured to look up at the window itself, I found that the top of it only was open, and that the blind inside was drawn down. While I was looking, I saw the shadow of Madame Fosco pass across the white field of the blind — then pass slowly back again. Thus far, she could not have heard me — or the shadow would surely have stopped at the blind, even if she had wanted courage enough to open the window, and look out?

I placed myself sideways against the railing of the verandah; first ascertaining, by touching them, the position of the flower-pots on either side of me.   There was room enough for me to sit between them, and no more.   The sweet-scented leaves of the flower on my left hand, just brushed my cheek as I lightly rested my head against the railing.

The first sounds that reached me from below were caused by the opening or closing (most probably the latter) of three doors in succession — the doors, no doubt, leading into the hall, and into the rooms on each side of the library, which the Count had pledged himself to examine.   The first object that I saw was the red spark again travelling out into the night, from under the verandah; moving away towards my window; waiting a moment; and then returning to the place from which it had set out.

"The devil take your restlessness!   When do you mean to sit down?" growled Sir Percival's voice beneath me.

"Ouf! how hot it is!" said the Count, sighing and puffing wearily.

His exclamation was followed by the scraping of the garden chairs on the tiled pavement under the verandah — the welcome sound which told me they were going to sit close at the window as usual.   So far, the chance was mine.   The clock in the turret struck the quarter to twelve as they settled themselves in their chairs.   I heard Madame Fosco through the open window, yawning; and saw her shadow pass once more across the white field of the blind.

Meanwhile, Sir Percival and the Count began talking together below; now and then dropping their voices a little lower than usual, but never sinking them to a whisper.   The strangeness and peril of my situation, the dread, which I could not master, of Madame Fosco's lighted window, made it difficult, almost impossible for me, at first, to keep my presence of mind, and to fix my attention solely on the conversation beneath. For some minutes, I could only succeed in gathering the general substance of it.   I understood the Count to say that the one window alight was his wife's; that the ground floor of the house was quite clear; and that they might now speak to each other, without fear of accidents.   Sir Percival merely answered by upbraiding his friend with having unjustifiably slighted his wishes and neglected his interests, all through the day. The Count, thereupon, defended himself by declaring that he had been beset by certain troubles and anxieties which had absorbed all his attention, and that the only safe time to come to an explanation, was a time when they could feel certain of being neither interrupted nor overheard. "We are at a serious crisis in our affairs, Percival," he said; "and if we are to decide on the future at all, we must decide secretly to-night."

That sentence of the Count's was the first which my attention was ready enough to master, exactly as it was spoken. From this point, with certain breaks and interruptions, my whole interest fixed breathlessly on the conversation; and I followed it word for word.

"Crisis?" repeated Sir Percival. "It's a worse crisis than you think for, I can tell you!"

"So I should suppose, from your behaviour for the last day or two," returned the other, coolly. "But, wait a little. Before we advance to what I do *not* know, let us be quite certain of what I *do* know. Let us first see if I am right about the time that is past, before I make any proposal to you for the time that is to come."

"Stop till I get the brandy and water. Have some yourself."

"Thank you, Percival. The cold water with pleasure, a spoon, and the basin of sugar. Eau sucrée, my friend — nothing more."

"Sugar and water, for a man of your age! — There! mix your sickly mess. You foreigners are all alike."

"Now listen, Percival. I will put our position plainly before you, as I understand it; and you shall say if I am right or wrong. You and I both came back to this house from the Continent, with our affairs very seriously embarrassed —"

"Cut it short! I wanted some thousands, and you some hundreds — and, without the money, we were both in a fair way to go to the dogs together. There's the situation. Make what you can of it. Go on."

"Well, Percival, in your own solid English words, you wanted some thousands and I wanted some hundreds; and the only way of getting them was for you to raise the money for your own necessity (with a small margin, beyond, for my poor little hundreds), by the help of your wife. What did I tell you about your wife on our way to England? and what did I tell you again, when we had come here, and when I had seen for myself the sort of woman Miss Halcombe was?"

"How should I know? You talked nineteen to the dozen, I suppose, just as usual."

"I said this: Human ingenuity, my friend, has hitherto only discovered two ways in which a man can manage a woman. One way is to knock her down — a method largely adopted by the brutal lower orders of the people, but utterly abhorrent to the refined and educated classes above them. The other way (much longer, much more difficult, but, in the end, not less certain) is never to accept a provocation at a woman's hands. It holds with animals, it holds with children, and it holds with women, who are nothing but children grown up. Quiet resolution is the one quality the animals, the children, and the women all fail in. If they can once shake this superior quality in their master, they get the better of *him*. If they can never succeed in disturbing it, he gets the better of *them*. I said to you, Remember that plain truth, when you want your wife to help you to the money. I said, Remember it doubly and trebly, in the presence of your wife's sister, Miss Halcombe. Have you remembered it? Not once, in all the complications that have twisted themselves about us in this house. Every provocation that your wife, and her sister, could offer to you, you instantly accepted from them. Your mad temper lost the signature to the deed, lost the ready money, set Miss Halcombe writing to the lawyer, for the first time —"

"First time? Has she written again?"

"Yes; she has written again to-day."

A chair fell on the pavement of the verandah — with a crash, as if it had been kicked down.

It was well for me that the Count's revelation roused Sir Percival's anger, as it did. On hearing that I had been once more discovered, I started so that the railing against which I leaned, cracked again. Had he followed me to the inn? Did he infer that I must have given my letters to Fanny, when I told him I had none for the post-bag? Even if it was so, how could he have examined the letters, when they had gone straight from my hand to the bosom of the girl's dress?

"Thank your lucky star," I heard the Count say next, "that you have me in the house, to undo the harm, as fast as you do it. Thank your lucky star that I said, No, when you were mad enough to talk of turning the key to-day on Miss Halcombe, as you turned it, in your mischievous folly, on your wife. Where are your eyes? Can you look at Miss Halcombe, and not see that she has the foresight and the resolution of a man? With that woman for my friend, I would snap these fingers of mine at the world. With that woman for my enemy, I, with all my brains and experience — I, Fosco, cunning as the devil himself, as you have told me a hundred times — I walk, in your English phrase, upon egg-shells! And this grand creature — I drink her health in my sugar and water — this grand creature, who stands in the strength of her love and her courage, firm as a rock between us two, and that poor flimsy pretty blonde wife of yours — this magnificent woman, whom I admire with all my soul, though I oppose her in your interests and in mine, you drive to extremities, as if she was no sharper and no bolder than the rest of her sex. Percival! Percival! you deserve to fail, and you *have* failed."

There was a pause. I write the villain's words about myself, because I mean to remember them, because I hope yet for the day when I may speak out, once for all in his presence, and cast them back, one by one, in his teeth.

Sir Percival was the first to break the silence again.

"Yes, yes; bully and bluster as much as you like," he said, sulkily; "the difficulty about the money is not the only difficulty. You would be for taking strong measures with the women, yourself — if you knew as much as I do."

"We will come to that second difficulty, all in good time," rejoined the Count. "You may confuse yourself, Percival, as much as you please, but you shall not confuse me. Let the question of the money be settled first. Have I convinced your obstinacy? have I shown you that your temper will not let you help yourself? — Or must I go back, and (as you put it in your dear straightforward English) bully and bluster a little more?"

"Pooh! It's easy enough to grumble at *me*. Say what is to be done — that's a little harder."

"Is it? Bah! This is what is to be done: You give up all direction in the business from to-night; you leave it, for the future, in my hands only. I am talking to a Practical British man — ha? Well, Practical, will that do for you?"

"What do you propose, if I leave it all to you?"

"Answer me first. Is it to be in my hands or not?"

"Say it is in your hands — what then?"

"A few questions, Percival, to begin with. I must wait a little, yet, to let circumstances guide me; and I must know, in every possible way, what those circumstances are likely to be. There is no time to lose. I have told you already that Miss Halcombe has written to the lawyer to-day, for the second time."

"How did you find it out? What did she say?"

"If I told you, Percival, we should only come back at the end to where we are now. Enough that I have found it out — and the finding has caused that trouble and anxiety which made me so inaccessible to you all through to-day. Now, to refresh my memory about your affairs — it is some time since I talked them over with you. The money has been raised, in the absence of your wife's signature, by means of bills at three months — raised at a cost that makes my poverty-stricken foreign hair stand on end to think of it! When the bills are due, is there really and truly no earthly way of paying them but by the help of your wife?"

"None."

"What! You have no money at the bankers!"

"A few hundreds, when I want as many thousands."

"Have you no other security to borrow upon?"

"Not a shred."

"What have you actually got with your wife, at the present moment?"

"Nothing, but the interest of her tweny thousand pounds— barely enough to pay our daily expenses."

"What do you expect from your wife?"

"Three thousand a year, when her uncle dies."

"A fine fortune, Percival. What sort of a man is this uncle? Old?"

"No — neither old nor young."

"A good-tempered, freely-living man? Married? No — I think my wife told me, not married."

"Of course not. If he was married, and had a son, Lady Glyde would not be next heir to the property. I'll tell you what he is. He's a maudlin, twaddling, selfish fool, and bores everybody who comes near him about the state of his health."

"Men of that sort, Percival, live long, and marry malevolently when you least expect it. I don't give you much, my friend, for your chance of the three thousand a year. Is there nothing more that comes to you from your wife?"

"Nothing."

"Absolutely nothing?"

"Absolutely nothing — except in case of her death."

"Aha! in the case of her death."

There was another pause. The Count moved from the verandah to the gravel walk outside. I knew that he had moved, by his voice. "The rain has come at last," I heard him say. It *had* come. The state of my cloak showed that it had been falling thickly for some little time.

The Count went back under the verandah — I heard the chair creak beneath his weight as he sat down in it again.

"Well, Percival," he said; "and, in the case of Lady Glyde's death, what do you get then?"

"If she leaves no children —"

"Which she is likely to do?"

"Which she is not in the least likely to do —"

"Yes?"

"Why, then I get her twenty thousand pounds."

"Paid down?"

"Paid down."

They were silent once more. As their voices ceased, Madame Fosco's shadow darkened the blind again. Instead of passing this time, it remained, for a moment, quite still. I saw her fingers steal round the corner of the blind, and draw it on one side. The dim white outline of her face, looking out straight over me, appeared behind the window. I kept quite still, shrouded from head to foot in my black cloak. The rain, which was fast wetting me, dripped over the glass, blurred it, and prevented her from seeing anything. "More rain!" I heard her say to herself. She dropped the blind — and I breathed again freely.

The talk went on below me; the Count resuming it, this time.

"Percival! do you care about your wife?"

"Fosco! that's rather a downright question."

"I am a downright man; and I repeat it."

"Why the devil do you look at me in that way?"

"You won't answer me? Well, then; let us say your wife dies before the summer is out ——"

"Drop it, Fosco!"

"Let us say your wife dies ——"

"Drop it, I tell you!"

"In that case, you would gain twenty thousand pounds; and you would lose ——"

"I should lose the chance of three thousand a year."

"The *remote* chance, Percival — the remote chance only. And you want money, at once. In your position, the gain is certain — the loss doubtful."

"Speak for yourself as well as for me. Some of the money I want has been borrowed for *you*. And if you come to gain, *my* wife's death would be ten thousand pounds in *your* wife's pocket. Sharp as you are, you seem to have conveniently forgotten Madame Fosco's legacy. Don't look at me in that way! I won't have it! What with your looks and your questions, upon my soul, you make my flesh creep!"

"Your flesh? Does flesh mean conscience in English? I speak of your wife's death, as I speak of a possibility. Why not? The respectable lawyers who scribble-scrabble your deeds and your wills, look the deaths of living people in the face. Do lawyers make your flesh creep? Why should I? It is my business to-night, to clear up your position beyond the possibility of mistake — and I have now done it. Here is your position. If your wife lives, you pay those bills with her signature to the parchment. If your wife dies, you pay them with her death."

As he spoke, the light in Madame Fosco's room was extinguished; and the whole second floor of the house was now sunk in darkness.

"Talk! talk!" grumbled Sir Percival. "One would think, to hear you, that my wife's signature to the deed was got already."

"You have left the matter in my hands," retorted the Count; "and I have more than two months before me to turn round in. Say no more about it, if you please, for the present. When the bills are due, you will see for yourself if my 'talk! talk!' is worth something, or if it is not. And now, Percival, having done with the money-matters, for to-night, I can place my attention at your disposal, if you wish to consult me on that second difficulty which has mixed itself up with our little embarrassments, and which has so altered you for the worse, that I hardly know you again. Speak, my friend — and pardon me if I shock your fiery national tastes by mixing myself a second glass of sugar-and-water."

"It's very well to say speak," replied Sir Percival, in a

far more quiet and more polite tone than he had yet adopted; "but it's not so easy to know how to begin."

"Shall I help you?" suggested the Count. "Shall I give this private difficulty of yours a name? What, if I call it — Anne Catherick?"

"Look here, Fosco, you and I have known each other for a long time; and, if you have helped me out of one or two scrapes before this, I have done the best I could to help you in return, as far as money would go. We have made as many friendly sacrifices, on both sides, as men could; but we have had our secrets from each other, of course — haven't we?"

"You have had a secret from *me*, Percival. There is a skeleton in your cupboard here at Blackwater Park, that has peeped out, in these last few days, at other people besides yourself."

"Well, suppose it has. If it doesn't concern you, you needn't be curious about it, need you?"

"Do I look curious about it?"

"Yes, you do."

"So! so! my face speaks the truth, then? What an immense foundation of good there must be in the nature of a man who arrives at my age, and whose face has not yet lost the habit of speaking the truth! — Come, Glyde! let us be candid one with the other. This secret of yours has sought *me:* I have not sought *it*. Let us say I am curious — do you ask me, as your old friend, to respect your secret, and to leave it, once for all, in your own keeping?"

"Yes — that's just what I do ask."

"Then my curiosity is at an end. It dies in me, from this moment."

"Do you really mean that?"

"What makes you doubt me?"

"I have had some experience, Fosco, of your round about ways; and I am not so sure that you won't worm it out of me after all."

The chair below suddenly creaked again — I felt the

trellis-work pillar under me shake from top to bottom. The Count had started to his feet and had struck it with his hand, in indignation.

"Percival! Percival!" he cried, passionately, "do you know me no better than that? Has all your experience shown you nothing of my character yet? I am a man of the antique type! I am capable of the most exalted acts of virtue — when I have the chance of performing them. It has been the misfortune of my life that I have had few chances. My conception of friendship is sublime! Is it my fault that your skeleton has peeped out at me? Why do I confess my curiosity? You poor superficial Englishman, it is to magnify my own self-control. I could draw your secret out of you, if I liked, as I draw this finger out of the palm of my hand — you know I could! But you have appealed to my friendship; and the duties of friendship are sacred to me. See! I trample my base curiosity under my feet. My exalted sentiments lift me above it. Recognise them, Percival! imitate them, Percival! Shake hands — I forgive you."

His voice faltered over the last words — faltered, as if he was actually shedding tears!

Sir Percival confusedly attempted to excuse himself. But the Count was too magnanimous to listen to him.

"No!" he said. "When my friend has wounded me, I can pardon him without apologies. Tell me, in plain words, do you want my help?"

"Yes, badly enough."

"And you can ask for it without compromising yourself?"

"I can try, at any rate."

"Try, then."

"Well, this is how it stands: — I told you, to-day, that I had done my best to find Anne Catherick, and failed."

"Yes; you did."

"Fosco! I'm a lost man, if I *don't* find her."

"Ha! Is it so serious as that?"

A little stream of light travelled out under the verandah, and fell over the gravel-walk. The Count had taken the lamp from the inner part of the room, to see his friend clearly by the light of it.

"Yes!" he said. "*Your face* speaks the truth this time. Serious, indeed — as serious as the money matters themselves."

"More serious. As true as I sit here, more serious!"

The light disappeared again, and the talk went on.

"I showed you the letter to my wife that Anne Catherick hid in the sand," Sir Percival continued. "There's no boasting in that letter, Fosco — she *does* know the Secret."

"Say as little as possible, Percival, in my presence, of the Secret. Does she know it from you?"

"No; from her mother."

"Two women in possession of your private mind — bad, bad, bad, my friend! One question here, before we go any farther. The motive of your shutting up the daughter in the asylum, is now plain enough to me — but the manner of her escape is not quite so clear. Do you suspect the people in charge of her of closing their eyes purposely, at the instance of some enemy, who could afford to make it worth their while?"

"No; she was the best-behaved patient they had — and, like fools, they trusted her. She's just mad enough to be shut up, and just sane enough to ruin me when she's at large — if you understand that?"

"I do understand it. Now, Percival, come at once to the point; and then I shall know what to do. Where is the danger of your position at the present moment?"

"Anne Catherick is in this neighbourhood, and in communication with Lady Glyde — there's the danger, plain enough. Who can read the letter she hid in the sand, and not see that my wife is in possession of the secret, deny it as she may?"

"One moment, Percival. If Lady Glyde does know the secret, she must know also that it is a compromising secret for *you*. As your wife, surely it is her interest to keep it?"

"Is it? I'm coming to that. It might be her interest

if she cared two straws about me.   But I happen to be an en-
cumbrance in the way of another man.   She was in love with
him, before she married me — she's in love with him now
— an infernal vagabond of a drawing-master, named
Hartright."

"My dear friend! what is there extraordinary in that?
They are all in love with some other man.   Who gets the first
of a woman's heart? In all my experience I have never yet
met with the man who was Number One.   Number Two, sometimes.   Number Three, Four, Five, often.   Number One,
never!   He exists, of course — but, I have not met with
him."

"Wait! I haven't done yet.   Who do you think helped
Anne Catherick to get the start, when the people from the
madhouse were after her?   Hartright.   Who do you think
saw her again in Cumberland? Hartright.   Both times, he
spoke to her alone. Stop! don't interrupt me.   The scoundrel's
as sweet on my wife, as she is on him.   He knows the secret, and
she knows the secret.   Once let them both get together again,
and it's her interest and his interest to turn their information
against me."

"Gently, Percival — gently! Are you insensible to the
virtue of Lady Glyde?"

"That for the virtue of Lady Glyde! I believe in nothing
about her but her money.   Don't you see how the case stands?
She might be harmless enough by herself; but if she and that
vagabond Hartright ——"

"Yes, yes, I see.   Where is Mr. Hartright?"

"Out of the country.   If he means to keep a whole skin on
his bones, I recommend him not to come back in a hurry."

"Are you sure he is out of the country?"

"Certain.   I had him watched from the time he left Cumberland to the time he sailed.   Oh, I've been careful, I can
tell you!   Anne Catherick lived with some people at a farm-
house near Limmeridge.   I went there, myself, after she had
given me the slip, and made sure that they knew nothing.   I
gave her mother a form of letter to write to Miss Halcombe,

exonerating me from any bad motive in putting her under restraint.   I've spent, I'm afraid to say how much, in trying to trace her.   And, in spite of it all, she turns up here, and escapes me on my own property! How do I know who else may speak to her? That prying scoundrel, Hartright, may come back without my knowing it, and may make use of her to-morrow ——"

"Not he, Percival! While I am on the spot, and while that woman is in the neighbourhood, I will answer for our laying hands on her, before Mr. Hartright — even if he does come back.   I see! yes, yes, I see! The finding of Anne Catherick is the first necessity: make your mind easy about the rest. Your wife is here, under your thumb; Miss Halcombe is inseparable from her, and is, therefore, under your thumb also; and Mr. Hartright is out of the country.   This invisible Anne of yours, is all we have to think of for the present.   You have made your inquiries?"

"Yes.   I have been to her mother; I have ransacked the village — and all to no purpose."

"Is her mother to be depended on?"

"Yes."

"She has told your secret once."

"She won't tell it again."

"Why not?   Are her own interests concerned in keeping it, as well as yours?"

"Yes — deeply concerned."

"I am glad to hear it, Percival, for your sake.   Don't be discouraged, my friend.   Our money matters, as I told you, leave me plenty of time to turn round in; and *I* may search for Anne Catherick to-morrow to better purpose than you.   One last question, before we go to bed."

"What is it?"

"It is this.   When I went to the boat-house to tell Lady Glyde that the little difficulty of her signature was put off, accident took me there in time to see a strange woman parting in a very suspicious manner from your wife.   But accident did not bring me near enough to see this same woman's face plainly. I must know how to recognise our invisible Anne. What is she like?"

"Like? Come! I'll tell you in two words. She's a sickly likeness of my wife."

The chair creaked, and the pillar shook once more. The Count was on his feet again — this time in astonishment.

"What!!!" he exclaimed, eagerly.

"Fancy my wife, after a bad illness, with a touch of something wrong in her head — and there is Anne Catherick for you," answered Sir Percival.

"Are they related to each other?"

"Not a bit of it."

"And yet, so like?"

"Yes, so like. What are you laughing about?"

There was no answer, and no sound of any kind. The Count was laughing in his smooth, silent internal way.

"What are you laughing about?" reiterated Sir Percival.

"Perhaps, at my own fancies, my good friend. Allow me my Italian humour — do I not come of the illustrious nation which invented the exhibition of Punch? Well, well, well, I shall know Anne Catherick when I see her — and so enough for to-night. Make your mind easy, Percival. Sleep, my son, the sleep of the just; and see what I will do for you, when daylight comes to help us both. I have my projects and my plans, here in my big head. You shall pay those bills and find Anne Catherick — my sacred word of honour on it, but you shall! Am I a friend to be treasured in the best corner of your heart, or am I not? Am I worth those loans of money which you so delicately reminded me of a little while since? Whatever you do, never wound me in my sentiments any more. Recognise them, Percival! imitate them, Percival! I forgive you again; I shake hands again. Good night!"

Not another word was spoken. I heard the Count close the library door. I heard Sir Percival barring up the window-shutters. It had been raining, raining all the time. I was cramped by my position, and chilled to the bones. When I first tried to move, the effort was so painful to me, that I was obliged to desist. I tried a second time, and succeeded in rising to my knees on the wet roof.

As I crept to the wall, and raised myself against it, I looked back, and saw the window of the Count's dressing-room gleam into light. My sinking courage flickered up in me again, and kept my eyes fixed on his window, as I stole my way back, step by step, past the wall of the house.

The clock struck the quarter after one, when I laid my hands on the window-sill of my own room. I had seen nothing and heard nothing which could lead me to suppose that my retreat had been discovered.

XII.

* * * * *

JULY 6TH. — Eight o'clock. The sun is shining in a clear sky. I have not been near my bed — I have not once closed my weary, wakeful eyes. From the same window at which I looked out into the darkness of last night, I look out, now, at the bright stillness of the morning.

I count the hours that have passed since I escaped to the shelter of this room, by my own sensations — and those hours seem like weeks.

How short a time, and yet how long to *me* — since I sank down in the darkness, here, on the floor, drenched to the skin, cramped in every limb, cold to the bones, a useless, helpless, panic-stricken creature.

I hardly know when I roused myself. I hardly know when I groped my way back to the bedroom, and lighted the candle, and searched (with a strange ignorance, at first, of where to look for them) for dry clothes to warm me. The doing of these things is in my mind, but not the time when they were done.

Can I even remember when the chilled, cramped feeling left me, and the throbbing heat came in its place?

Surely it was before the sun rose? Yes; I heard the clock strike three. I remember the time by the sudden brightness and clearness, the feverish strain and excitement of all my faculties which came with it. I remember my resolution to control myself, to wait patiently hour after hour, till the chance offered of removing Laura from this horrible place, without the danger of immediate discovery and pursuit. I remember the persuasion settling itself in my mind that the words those two men had said to each other, would furnish us, not only with our justification for leaving the house, but with our weapons of defence against them as well. I recal the impulse that awakened in me to preserve those words in writing, exactly as they were spoken, while the time was my own, and while my memory vividly retained them. All this I remember plainly: there is no confusion in my head yet. The coming in here, from the bedroom, with my pen and ink and paper, before sunrise — the sitting down at the widely opened window to get all the air I could to cool me — the ceaseless writing, faster and faster, hotter and hotter, driving on, more and more wakefully, all through the dreadful interval before the house was astir again — how clearly I recal it, from the beginning by candlelight, to the end on the page before this, in the sunshine of the new day!

Why do I sit here still? Why do I weary my hot eyes and my burning head by writing more? Why not lie down and rest myself, and try to quench the fever that consumes me, in sleep?

I dare not attempt it. A fear beyond all other fears has got possession of me. I am afraid of this heat that parches my skin. I am afraid of the creeping and throbbing that I feel in my head. If I lie down now, how do I know that I may have the sense and the strength to rise again?

Oh, the rain, the rain — the cruel rain that chilled me last night!

*　　　*　　　*　　　*　　　*

Nine o'clock. Was it nine struck, or eight? Nine, surely? I am shivering again — shivering, from head to foot, in the summer air. Have I been sitting here asleep? I don't know what I have been doing.

Oh, my God! am I going to be ill?

Ill, at such a time as this!

My head — I am sadly afraid of my head. I can write, but the lines all run together. I see the words. Laura — I can write Laura, and see I write it. Eight or nine — which was it?

So cold, so cold — oh, that rain last night! — and the strokes of the clock, the strokes I can't count, keep striking in my head —

*   *   *   *   *

NOTE.

[At this place the entry in the Diary ceases to be legible. The two or three lines which follow, contain fragments of words only, mingled with blots and scratches of the pen. The last marks on the paper bear some resemblance to the first two letters (L and A) of the name of Lady Glyde.

On the next page of the Diary, another entry appears. It is in a man's handwriting, large, bold, and firmly regular; and the date is "July the 7th." It contains these lines:]

[POSTSCRIPT BY A SINCERE FRIEND.]

The illness of our excellent Miss Halcombe has afforded me the opportunity of enjoying an unexpected intellectual pleasure.

I refer to the perusal (which I have just completed) of this interesting Diary.

There are many hundred pages here. I can lay my hand on my heart, and declare that every page has charmed, refreshed, delighted me.

To a man of my sentiments, it is unspeakably gratifying to be able to say this.

Admirable woman!

I allude to Miss Halcombe.

Stupendous effort!

I refer to the Diary.

Yes! these pages are amazing. The tact which I find here, the discretion, the rare courage, the wonderful power of memory, the accurate observation of character, the easy grace of style, the charming outbursts of womanly feeling, have all

inexpressibly increased my admiration of this sublime creature, of this magnificent Marian. The presentation of my
own character is masterly in the extreme. I certify, with my
whole heart, to the fidelity of the portrait. I feel how vivid an
impression I must have produced to have been painted in such
strong, such rich, such massive colours as these. I lament
afresh the cruel necessity which sets our interests at variance,
and opposes us to each other. Under happier circumstances
how worthy I should have been of Miss Halcombe — how
worthy Miss Halcombe would have been of me.

The sentiments which animate my heart assure me that the
lines I have just written express a Profound Truth.

Those sentiments exalt me above all merely personal considerations. I bear witness, in the most disinterested manner,
to the excellence of the stratagem by which this unparalleled
woman surprised the private interview between Percival and
myself. Also to the marvellous accuracy of her report of the
whole conversation from its beginning to its end.

Those sentiments have induced me to offer to the unim-
pressionable doctor who attends on her, my vast knowledge of
chemistry, and my luminous experience of the more subtle resources which medical and magnetic science have placed at
the disposal of mankind. He has hitherto declined to avail
himself of my assistance. Miserable man!

Finally, those sentiments dictate the lines — grateful,
sympathetic, paternal lines — which appear in this place. I
close the book. My strict sense of propriety restores it (by
the hands of my wife) to its place on the writer's table. Events
are hurrying me away. Circumstances are guiding me to
serious issues. Vast perspectives of success unrol themselves
before my eyes. I accomplish my destiny with a calmness
which is terrible to myself. Nothing but the homage of my
admiration is my own. I deposit it, with respectful tenderness, at the feet of Miss Halcombe.

I breathe my wishes for her recovery.

I condole with her on the inevitable failure of every plan

that she has formed for her sister's benefit. At the same time, I entreat her to believe that the information which I have derived from her diary will in no respect help me to contribute to that failure. It simply confirms the plan of conduct which I had previously arranged. I have to thank these pages for awakening the finest sensibilities in my nature — nothing more.

To a person of similar sensibility, this simple assertion will explain and excuse everything.

Miss Halcombe is a person of similar sensibility.

In that persuasion, I sign myself,

FOSCO.

END OF VOL. I.